The Mystic Marriage

A Novel of Alpennia

Heather Rose Jones

Bella
BOOKS

2015

Bella Books, Inc.
P.O. Box 10543
Tallahassee, FL 32302

Printed in the United States of America on acid-free paper.

First Bella Books Edition 2015

Editor: Katherine V. Forrest
Cover Designer: Kiaro Creative

ISBN: 978-1-59493-441-4

Other Books by Heather Rose Jones

Daughter of Mystery

Author's Note on Pronunciation

For interested readers, there are three basic rules for Alpennian pronunciation. Names are stressed on the first syllable. The letter "z" is pronounced "ts" as in German. The combination "ch" is pronounced "k." Non-Alpennian names follow the rules for their language of origin. So, for example, Antuniet Chazillen's surname is pronounced "katz-ill-en" (hence Gustav's joke about calling her Kätzlein "kitten") while Jeanne de Cherdillac's surname follows French rules and is pronouned "share-dill-ack."

About the Author

Heather Rose Jones is the author of the "Skin Singer" stories in the *Sword and Sorceress* anthology series, as well as non-fiction publications on topics ranging from biotech to historic costumes to naming practices.

Visitors to her social media will find the Lesbian Historic Motif Project she began to change the unexamined assumptions about the place and nature of lesbian-like characters in historic fact, literature, art and imaginations. She has a PhD from U.C. Berkeley in Linguistics, specializing in the semantics of Medieval Welsh prepositions, and works as an industrial discrepancy investigator for a major Bay Area pharmaceutical company.

Dedication

This one is for Lauri,
because sometimes even odd ducks
find their flock.

Acknowledgements

I am very grateful to all my test readers and subject matter experts: Chris L., Ginger T., Irina R., Laurie C. (for gemstone comments), Lauri W. (my alpha-reader), Melanie S. (who volunteered to do detailed proofreading in addition to general comments), Sara U. (my boots on the ground in Heidelberg), Sharon K., Ursula W.

CHAPTER ONE

Antuniet

Heidelberg (July, 1821)

Antuniet looked up from the ruined crucible on the workbench and swore softly. Dawn had come and gone while the delicate mixture cooled from a glowing slurry to a glassy, charred lump. Another failure. She checked the astronomical alignment on her zodiacal watch—rather, her mentor Vitali's watch that he'd lent her in Prague. She felt guilty every time she looked at it. It was twelve hours since the firing began and the watch showed Virgo just rising. The instrument was still accurate; the process had begun according to the instructions. Altmann should have been here to tend to the furnace, but she was too honest to lay the blame on her absent assistant. The cause was impurities in the materials; it had to be. In Prague she'd had reliable sources for the best, but here in Heidelberg it was buyer beware. She'd need to start refining her own ingredients and that would add weeks to every step of the process.

She looked out at the gray sky and tried to judge the time—Vitali's watch was no use for ordinary hours. She slipped it back in the pocket of her skirts, stilling the twinge of guilt. Someday she must return it to him. Someday when she dared return to Prague. The loan of it hadn't been meant to last this long. Had the bells rung the hour yet? She couldn't remember. No, there they were, echoing over the distant market calls and the clopping of the cart horses crossing the Old Bridge. Still another hour before there would be students expecting her. And since it was the tutoring that paid for the equipment and supplies, it was sleep that must wait. Antuniet closed her eyes just for a moment. The weariness swept through her and she felt herself sway dangerously. What would it be like to let it all go? To leave her past entirely in the hands of the dead? To change her name from Chazillen and never return to Rotenek? But then what would be left to live for? Everything else had been cut away by the executioner's sword.

The memory of her brother Estefen's betrayal could still leave her shaking with rage. Not his treason against the prince, but his betrayal of the family. His stupid, selfish, greedy, shortsighted... She slammed her fist against the tabletop to pull her mind back from that dark path. One thing remained: the oath she'd sworn after the night of his execution. Estefen would not be the Chazillens' final legacy. She would find a way to restore their honor in spite of everything.

At first, the alchemical Great Work had been no more than a distraction from what she'd lost. A turn of fate had transformed it into her first true hope of redemption. No, she would start again because to let go of the work would be to let go of all reason to live.

She banked the coals and methodically put things in order, setting the crucible aside to finish cooling before it went into the rubbish heap. Just before leaving, she took out the stub of a candle—carefully hoarded since she'd obtained it from the altar at Saint Leonhard's in Prague—and lit it from the remains of the fire. With the door closed behind her, she worked a brief mystery over the heavy iron lock. Saint Leonhard was the patron saint of prisoners, but the curious logic of patronage gave him responsibility for locks and locksmiths as well. The brief prayer, sealed with a drop of the consecrated wax, would keep out the ordinary run of lock picks. A faint, flickering light ran across the iron telling her that the saint had answered.

She glanced up and down the street to see if anyone had noticed. Heidelberg had worked free of the worst of the religious battles of the last centuries, but her Lutheran neighbors still looked askance if one worked the saints' mysteries in public. She pinched the wick out. She had only one more of the candles when this one was used up. Experiments with remelting it into ordinary wax to extend the effectiveness had proven useless. For the thousandth time she wished she could master the more powerful version that would allow her to sense when the lock was being meddled with. The apparatus for that was harder to obtain, calling for a true relic of the saint and a text written in the presence of his altar. She hadn't the time to experiment and see if substitutions could be made. But if she'd had just that much warning, she could have brought more possessions away with her from Prague. At every move she left more behind. She gave a mental shrug. She'd saved everything that mattered.

As she worked her way up from the riverside and along the Hauptstrasse toward the heart of the students' quarter, the streets were beginning to fill and Antuniet elbowed her way through the tide, heading for a narrow alley off the Heumarkt.

If she had at least three students today she could purchase a new crucible. If she could hold off the landlady until next week. And if she didn't eat. It was tempting to accept Gustav's persistent offer to take her for dinner at the Golden Falcon. Most of the students who came to her for tutoring were there to be drilled in Greek and Latin. Gustav von Lindenbeck also used it as an opportunity to lay siege to her virtue. She'd known so many young men like him back in Rotenek: rich, privileged, accustomed to being granted whatever their whim of the moment might be. When she'd been Mesnera Antuniet, niece and then sister to a baron, she'd found his sort merely tedious. Now it was a delicate balancing act. Not so rude as to drive him away, but not the slightest hint that she would bend to his will. For him it was a game to greet her with ever escalating offers of gifts and luxuries. It was clear he doubted her claims to virtue—virtuous young noblewomen did not traipse about Europe on their own, earning their bread by tutoring—but her refusals were no game. If just once she stepped across the line that lay between her and Gustav, it would be impossible to redraw it. No, she could put off the new crucible until next week and spend the time trying the alternate method of calcination.

She could recall when tight budgeting meant cutting your guest list from eighty to fifty, and when utter poverty was remaking last season's gown rather than buying new. Now, last season's gown could pay for two months' rent and outfit her workshop from scratch. That's what they had gone for, one by one, in Prague. The last of her finery had set her up here in Heidelberg. The letter of introduction from Vitali had been meant to do the rest. Since then, it had been hand to mouth. Alchemy couldn't pay the rent or put food on the table. Even if she'd been willing to waste her time transmuting metals, that drew exactly the sort of attention she needed to avoid. Without the protection of a powerful patron it was too dangerous to be known for practicing the esoteric arts. In Alpennia, name and rank had protected her; that and the license that Rotenek society allowed to known eccentrics. But she was a stranger here. Invisibility was her only ally.

The rooming house stood hunched between two taller and more modern buildings, and the plaster was peeling in places to show the brickwork underneath, but the rent was cheap. More importantly, it stood not a hundred paces from the heart of the university and her tutoring there enabled her to scrape together the coins to pay that rent. And, if she were lucky, to pay for new equipment sometime soon.

Her students would be waiting in the coffee room below, but she headed around to climb the rickety back stairs for a chance to wash up and collect her books. Frau Schongau saw her pass by and leaned out the window to rail at her incomprehensibly. Antuniet's German could manage Goethe and Kant but fell short of Frau Schongau's Swabian when she was in an agitated mood. All she could decipher was *Out! Out!* That meant it was the usual empty threats over the lateness of the rent. She shrugged and answered back in Alpennian just to annoy the woman.

The door from the stairs to the narrow hallway stood ajar, but that wasn't unusual. The first sign of disaster came farther in when she saw the splintered joist where the extra iron hasp had been installed. She pushed it open with no thought for what might lie within. The sight that met her held no immediate meaning. Every stick of furniture had been upended and torn apart. The bedding—or was that clothing?—lay in heaps of rags. Her books…oh, her books! They were drifts of scattered pages. She closed the door behind her and leaned against it, overtaken by dizziness. Slowly she sank down to the floor, staring blankly at the ruin.

Who…? Had *he* followed her all the way here? The man she'd fled Prague to escape? Eight months and she figured she was safe. If he'd tracked her down anew then she was dealing with more powerful opponents than she'd thought. Or was it ordinary thieves? Or fanatics who'd learned of her work…but then why here and not the workshop? No, this wasn't merely a search; this was fury at not finding what they sought. If she'd been here… Her heart began racing. They'd expected her to be here. She would have been, except that her assistant hadn't turned up and the working couldn't wait. Was Altmann in league—? Had they—? No, it was too complex to untangle at the moment. She scrambled back to her feet, leaning against the wall at another wave of dizziness. There was only one possession of hers that could inspire this zeal. She knew he wanted it, but not that he had the connections to reach this far or the desperation to move this ruthlessly. Each attempt to wrest it from her only confirmed its value.

She rushed to kneel in front of the hearth. The andirons had been tossed aside—one had been thrown into the wall hard enough to dent the plaster. But the stones themselves were still in place. She traced a complex figure across the mortar lines and the charm that held the largest stone in place gave way. The satchel was still there behind it, and the book within.

Panic could only be conquered by action. Her thoughts turned to practicalities. The jar that collected her earnings was smashed with no sign of the contents. That was to be expected. So all she had was the handful of coins sewn into the hem of her jacket. The ones she successfully pretended did not exist every time Frau Schongau came knocking or the coal bin was low again. And that was all she had to get her away from Heidelberg to somewhere safe. It wasn't enough. It could buy a seat on the common stage but that would be too public. If he were here and watching for her at all she'd never make it out of the city. A private carriage would be safer but she might as well wish for the moon. Perhaps she could slip out into the countryside on foot and then…

She flinched, thinking she heard a step on the stairs. He'd be coming back. Soon. They might be ransacking her workshop even now. She needed to leave and—

A knock sounded like the crack of doom. Her heart stopped, but then a familiar voice called out, "Madame Kätzlein? Are you there? We waited for you but you never came."

Gustav! She'd forgotten about the waiting students. She cracked open the door and peered through, preventing him from seeing the chaos within. His long, cheerful face was an incongruous invasion of the present disaster. He lifted his beaver hat briefly in salute and returned it to those perfectly coifed yellow locks. Antuniet blinked and returned to the present. "I was just about to come down."

"Bah! Don't bother," he said. "The others are gone. We could be so much more cozy up here."

"No," she said.

"I could take you to a private room at the *Falke* and we could practice our *amo, amas.*" He assumed her refusal but played the game out. "Or I could sweep you away to my cousin's hunting lodge at Uhlenbad and make wild love to you under the gaze of every stag the Lindenbecks have ever killed."

The moment seemed frozen in time. Antuniet thought over all her options one more time but nothing else offered. "Yes," she said.

He gaped at her as if she had answered in Chinese. "Pardon?"

Antuniet imbued her shrug with every scrap of world-weary boredom she could pretend to. "My experiments have all gone sour and I'm sick to death of this place. I want to go somewhere else—anywhere. Now. This minute."

She could see the hope leap in his eyes and hated what she was doing.

"But, my Kätzlein, I would need to send word ahead, and you need to pack your things. Perhaps a pleasant dinner and then we set out tomorrow…"

Antuniet shook her head. "Now. This very minute or not at all." She ducked back inside just long enough to throw on her cloak and grab the book satchel. "Well?" she demanded on finding him still frozen in place.

A slow grin spread over his face. "If you would, Madame," he said, offering her his arm.

He led her down the inner stairs and through the coffee room. His company took her past Frau Schongau unscathed but the landlady had shrunk to a very minor demon in her hell.

It took all her self-control not to start at each strange face between the rooming house and the livery stable where Gustav hired a phaeton for their excursion. A phaeton…well, at least it wasn't an open curricle and he didn't quibble when she insisted on raising the hood to give some protection from curious glances.

Even if he had provided a closed coach with the crest of the von Lindenbecks standing between her and her unknown enemy, she would not have felt entirely safe. But they came out at last on the Rohrbach Road still with no sign of pursuit, and the tension began to drain out of her as he urged the horses to a trot. Gustav saw her relax and leaned toward her, beginning, "Liebling—"

Antuniet stifled a well-timed yawn. "I was up all night working and if I'm to be good for anything, I need some rest."

"Yes, yes, of course," he replied in a disappointed tone as she turned away and curled into the corner of the hood. "You sleep now."

And much to her surprise, she did.

* * *

Antuniet woke to dusk filtered through trees and the absence of motion. Without conscious thought, her hand went to the hard outlines of the book within its bag, tucked inside her cloak. Reassured, she looked around. The horses had been unharnessed and the glow of lights drew her eyes to a stone and timber building lying in the shadow of the tall pines. She considered and discarded the thought that this had all been a grave mistake. The panic of the moment had sped her decision, but longer consideration would have brought her to the same place. No way out but forward. She stepped down, shifting the book satchel to her shoulder and holding her cloak close against the chill.

She had only a general idea of where she was: south of Heidelberg by half a day on indifferent roads. She had woken briefly when they stopped to change horses and enjoy a bite to eat before taking a narrow, unpaved track into what passed for wilderness. Closer by half a day to Alpennia. This wasn't how she'd meant to return: fleeing, near penniless, with no more progress on her Great Work than the promise that it would one day succeed.

Gustav came out and took her by the hand to lead her inside. "I thought to let you sleep while they made things ready. Come, come, there's a fire built up and the wine is poured and soon there will be dinner." He led her through an echoing foyer lit only by a few flickering candles. It stretched up into a darkness relieved by rows of pale, antlered skulls mounted on every surface of the walls. That part about all the stags the Lindenbecks had ever killed had been no joke.

Antuniet found to her dismay that the fire and the small dining table beside it had been prepared in a room dominated by a large canopied bed. Well, what had she expected? She let Gustav remove her cloak but then took it from him to wrap casually around the book satchel. She laid it on a chair in a corner beside the hearth, where it had a hope of being overlooked by any housekeeping impulses the staff might have. Judging from the dust on the mantel, those impulses were few. The fire drew her, but when Gustav approached to hand her a wineglass, she cast about for an excuse to keep moving.

"It's such a delightfully gothic building! Do show me around. Where did you find the wainscoting? It must be two hundred years old at least." Architectural details bored her but she knew enough to put on a good show.

Evidently they bored Gustav even more, for he shrugged, saying, "It's my cousin's place. I really have no idea." But he gamely set about showing her through the rooms, providing stories that centered primarily on the details of how the featured hunting trophies had been taken.

When they came around again to the room with the fire, supper had been laid and a sour-faced man stood in attendance to serve them. That provided one more hour of respite, but at last the servant cleared away the covers, poked up the fire one more time and disappeared. Gustav lifted Antuniet's fingers to his lips and asked, "Tell me why, after so many times of no, this time it was yes?"

She gave him a small piece of the truth. "I'm leaving Heidelberg—I've left Heidelberg. I'm not going back."

"Ah," he said. "And you no longer care what the gossips say."

She shrugged. He could believe whatever story pleased him. "Tomorrow I would like you to take me to the nearest public coaching inn."

"But Kätzlein…" he protested.

She fixed him with a gaze that belonged to the old Antuniet—the one who was accustomed to having her way. Would he refuse? She'd gambled much in coming here.

He rose and came to stand behind her. "Tomorrow," he echoed.

She felt him take the pins from her hair to let it tumble down her back. Her stomach clenched at his touch. There was still time to tell him it had all been a mistake—a ruse. Surely he wouldn't insist…*Don't be a fool*, she told herself. *What does it matter?* Her future held no virginal wedding bed. What was she saving herself for? For honor? Well, honor demanded that one paid one's debts and she had taken this one on with eyes open. With mechanical precision she unbuttoned her jacket and shrugged it off. He took her by the shoulders and turned her toward him. She stared over his shoulder at the flickering fire in the grate and allowed his embraces and practiced attentions.

* * *

When the pale dawn had grown enough that she could cross the room without stumbling, Antuniet gave up on the pretense of sleep and slipped from the bed. Gustav stirred sleepily and she froze until he quieted again, then gathered her clothes. There was a dressing room behind a door almost hidden in the oak paneling. She washed as thoroughly as she could in the basin and dressed. It would likely be hours yet before the sour-faced caretaker would be up. She found a seat by an east-facing window in the entry chamber where the light was sufficient to read and wrapped her traveling cloak closely around her.

The object of her obsession, the hope of her salvation, the bone the dogs were hunting, lay open in her lap, its worn red binding soft in her hands like the touch of skin. *Concerning the Mystic Marriage of the Earth and Sun to Beget Works of Great Virtue and Power*…The title went on for another half page.

Two centuries it had waited to come into her hands, hidden away from the ravages of war and neglect, superstition and greed. Surely that was a sign? She turned to the passage that had first caught at her heart that day in the little bookshop behind the castle in Prague. The crude cipher used in the introductory chapters had become as familiar to her as Greek. *And with these secrets the sharpened mind can work such wonders as will earn the acclaim and gratitude of even the highest Earthly Princes, and the virtuous heart will purify the spirit to receive the Prince of Heaven.* Purity of spirit was long since out of reach, but the other…that she could aspire to. *The acclaim and gratitude of princes.* The words had reawakened the vow she'd sworn standing over the graves of mother and brother, the one a suicide and the other a traitor. *This will not be the final judgment on our line. I will redeem it.*

* * *

Gustav had come looking for her hours later with a tinge of concern coloring his satisfaction. Well, if he had regrets they were his own burden to carry. And he was as good as his word, delivering her to an inn where a southbound coach would pass. Two coins from the hem of her jacket would see her as far as Basel. Two more, to Rotenek. That left three to live on until she could make arrangements. No, not the homecoming she had planned. He even offered to stay with her until the coach arrived but she refused. At the last, he leaned down from the phaeton and took her hand for one final kiss. "Farewell, dear Madame Kätzlein."

Annoyance finally overcame forbearance. She pulled her hand back saying, "The name is Chazillen. It was once a noble and honorable name and God willing I'll make it so again. I'll thank you to use it!"

He nodded stiffly. "Then God keep you, Madame Chazillen."

That had been unkind but she had no room in her heart for kindness. She had no room for anything except the path that lay ahead. She turned away so that she wouldn't see the carriage disappearing behind her.

CHAPTER TWO

Margerit

Margerit Sovitre gazed around the royal council chamber trying to keep two things foremost in mind: that she truly belonged here, in the presence of Her Grace, Princess Anna Atilliet, and in the company of the renowned *dozzures* of Rotenek University and of Archbishop Fereir himself…and that she would do well to keep silent until she was addressed. Four years ago Margerit would have had no trouble holding her tongue. Four years ago her godfather, Baron Saveze, had not yet named her his heir in pursuit of his own tangled plans and given her the chance to seize what a woman could claim of a university education in Rotenek. Four years ago she hadn't yet discovered how the visions she'd experienced since childhood gave her the skill to develop new holy mysteries. Four years ago she couldn't have imagined that she would sit here, named by appointment as the royal thaumaturgist. But being here, now, among those notables, she found it hard to hold her tongue. The impatience helped tamp down her trepidation.

It went beyond daring to present her case to this audience. It wasn't as if she were taking an actual degree at the university, where her studies would be guided and given imprimatur. A schoolgirl's dabbling in mysteries wasn't even worthy of attention, much less of disapproval. If she'd confined herself only to studying, her work would be of no more concern than the charm-wives who sold blessings in the marketplace or the ceremonies of the fraternal guilds that were more social fêtes than religious worship. But the princess had proposed that the Royal Guild celebrate her thaumaturgist's first new mystery at the feast of All Saints this year, and for that Archbishop Fereir's consent was necessary. If she were to fulfill her appointment in truth—to serve openly as Princess Annek's thaumaturgist—she needed, if not the sanction of the Church, at least its open disinterest. *Princess Anna*, she corrected herself silently. Everyone called her by the fond pet name Annek in private, and she was said to be flattered by it. But it would be a dreadful faux pas to use it here.

Dozzur Alihendin, the most prominent of the teachers of theology at Rotenek University, had been droning on for half an hour. He was pompous, condescending, dismissive of her talents…and he was there as her advocate. "As you know, we have found that young girls often have a…a sensitivity regarding the mysteries that can be put to use. There is a danger that these sensitivities may verge onto hysteria and it's important not to place too much stress on the child. But she has been examined by a number of learned men and we are satisfied that her visions are true and reliable and that they are of God and not mere phantasms. As to the accuracy of the specific observations she reports, there is less consensus. As I need not remind you, Your Excellency, the divine manifests itself in many ways. Several reliable individuals were asked to report their own visions during the Great Mystery of Saint Mauriz recently celebrated, and though the generalities were in agreement, none perceived the level of detail that Maisetra Sovitre claims to have seen."

She might have hoped for a more effusive recommendation, but that wouldn't have served as well. The archbishop was known for taking his own way despite tradition and advice. That was what had begun this matter after all: his changes to the text of the Mauriz mystery. His eyes turned finally to her, fixing her from under black brows that contrasted incongruously with his white hair. It gave his face a sinister cast that Margerit knew came entirely from her own imagination. She felt her hands tremble. Would he even give her a hearing? At worst he could forbid her work entirely; that was the gamble. With no other preamble, the archbishop asked, "What have you to say, then?"

She understood suddenly what drove LeFevre, her business manager, to shuffle papers ostentatiously before a presentation. It focused the attention and marked a beginning. She fought off the urge to imitate him and began laying out the sheaf of diagrams and drawings that sat beside her. This would be the proof of her talent and skill: the observations she'd made of how divine power flowed through the ceremony, and how it stumbled and faltered at the points where the ceremony had been revised. It was not enough to know all the esoteric vocabulary of the field; she must convince him that she understood it, and that her understanding did not stray too far from the orthodox. There was no turning back now. She glanced up once at the princess for guidance, but Annek only gazed silently with those dark, hooded eyes that marked her as her father's daughter. The slight play of an approving smile at the corners of her mouth was all the encouragement she gave. Margerit took another deep breath and began.

"When I first came to Rotenek and witnessed the celebration of the Mauriz *tutela* in the time of Prince Aukust—God rest his soul—several things struck me as odd about the way the *fluctus* manifested, particularly at the *markein* and the *concrescatio*. At the time, I was only beginning my studies and had no way to describe what I was seeing." She laid out a sequence of pages, each marked at the top with a section of the mystery as it was performed. As the pages progressed, the diagrams of the cathedral layout were washed with colors and marked with small symbols indicating how she had perceived the *fluctus*, the presence of divine grace within the course of the ceremony. For the first time in her life, Margerit regretted that her education had not included the use of watercolors or even drawing, beyond the most basic skill. The rough paintings were nothing like the true substance of her visions. But would technique have told the story more clearly? The colors weren't true colors, only impressions of them. And the patterns of movement often felt more like the swelling of song. So perhaps the crude indications were better to convey the idea than something more refined would be.

She led them through what had appeared to her: the way the divine light responded to the words of the priests, the actions of the royal celebrants and the responses of the congregants. "Now here," she pointed, "is what first caught my eye." She indicated the constricted flare of the *charis*, marking the saint's response, at the conclusion of the rite. "At first, all I knew was that it felt... wrong. But later, when I'd had a chance to study the text of the *expositulum*, and then when I witnessed the ceremony again, I noted the way the *fluctus* convulsed every time the celebration shifted from the older text to the new."

There was no response from those watching, so she moved on to the second set of drawings. "Now this is the ceremony the first time that Her Grace presided using the new version based on the Lyon rite exactly as written. You see here and here and here—" she pointed out the sections where the two differed most strongly "—the effects are clearest. Those are the parts where the lay presider—" she nodded in Annek's direction "—details the *markein*, giving the physical scope of the requested blessing. The places where the language is most changed from the older version that Prince Aukust used."

She rushed through the next set of examples hoping to pass over the political aspects of what they had done. When Aukust had refused to change the words he'd spoken all his life, it could be chalked up to an old man's stubbornness. "And this is from the ceremony just performed, when Her Grace returned to the older language for her parts." And that had caused no end of fuss. Whatever the reasons she had given publicly, it had been because she, at least, had been convinced the structure of the mystery was damaged. "We can see that the differences in effect come from the ceremony itself and not from changes in the celebrants."

The archbishop finally raised his hand to interrupt her. "This is all very fascinating, but not much to the point. Do we know that the results of the new ceremony are different from those of the older one?"

"It's true that I never witnessed the older version in whole," Margerit admitted. "But mysteries from the Penekiz tradition are used widely in local celebrations. All the Penekiz *tutelas* have the same general form. And I've found at least two village churches dedicated to Saint Mauriz that use a version of the same text as ours—without the elaborations, of course. Akolbin is near enough that I was able to witness theirs on Mauriz's feast day this year as well as our own." She began setting out the last sequence of diagrams. "Here and here are the key points, especially the conclusion, the *missio*, when the *charis* is granted." She indicated the swirl of exploding colors in the new image. "Saint Mauriz is supposed to solicit God's grace to encompass the entire parish the way it does here. Instead, in the Rotenek ceremony, the *charis* sinks away beside the altar. I believe the change in wording directs the *charis* to encompass only the buried relics of the saint."

The archbishop was signaling for her silence again. "I meant," he said emphatically, "that you have not demonstrated that any difference in the forms of the celebration would change the results. Do you think divine grace comes and goes at our command?"

Margerit hesitated, fearing a trap in his words. This wasn't a question she had expected to answer. Was he suggesting that the visual manifestations of mysteries were meaningless? She recalled Barbara's comments on why the ancient scholar Fortunatus had couched all his more daring conclusions in the subjunctive. She said cautiously, "If it were only necessary that God look into our hearts, then prayer and worship would be unnecessary, wouldn't they? If it matters that we give spoken voice to our petitions, then why shouldn't the form of that speech matter as well? And if the form of speech matters, then wouldn't it be well to use what tools we have to know what would be most pleasing?" She watched his face carefully, but he gave no sign whether her answer had been acceptable. She reached for an analogy from her readings. "Any arrow you loose will hit something, but if you want to hit the mark, it matters that you can see to aim."

The archbishop said dryly, "I see you have been studying Gaudericus."

Once again she looked for a trap—she recalled the stares and questions she'd received when hunting down that particular book. "It would have been difficult to do this without his work," she acknowledged. Gaudericus and his circle had nearly caused a schism between those who viewed the mysteries purely as worship and those who saw them as granting power. Strangely enough, it had been the Protestant rejection of thaumaturgy that had saved Gaudericus from being condemned outright as a heretic. But there was still a fine line drawn between the mechanists and those with even less acceptable philosophies.

The archbishop gathered the several series of diagrams into a stack and placed them at his right hand. "I will examine these further," he said.

Margerit stifled a protest. There were details, analyses that she couldn't easily reproduce from memory. The notes from that last ceremony that Aukust presided over would be impossible to duplicate. She wished she'd thought to make copies. And yet this was what she'd hoped for: to be given a hearing and have her work acknowledged and tolerated. There had never been a reasonable expectation of more. The flaws in the Mauriz *tutela* would continue to haunt her, but she was learning to choose her battles.

"Was there anything else, Your Grace?" The question was directed at Princess Annek.

Her answer was deliberately casual and she waved one long-fingered hand as if to dismiss the matter. "Nothing of great importance. The Guild of Saint Adelruid would like permission to celebrate a new mystery in the cathedral."

The request should have been only for form's sake. The Royal Guild was the most exclusive and prestigious of the lay guilds—certainly the most important of those sponsored by the cathedral. There would need to be good reason to deny it. Their private mysteries were their own affair, unlike the Mauriz *tutela*, which belonged to the cathedral.

"And what would be the nature of this ceremony?"

"Do you recall that unfortunate matter of the Atelpirt *castellum*? The one that caused such a fuss back before I was confirmed as my father's heir? We've reworked it. Or rather Maisetra Sovitre has. The basic structure is sound and it seems a good addition to the royal mysteries."

Margerit knew it was tactful of everyone not to mention the part she'd had in designing the original, treacherous version of that ceremony. The one that had ended with Iohennis Lutoz banished and Estefen Chazillen executed. This was her hope of redeeming that disaster: the adoption of the mystery as part of the divine protection of the realm.

"As you wish," he replied.

It seemed an anticlimax: all the preparation, the courting of the *dozzures* to support her presence, the careful analysis and diagramming of her visions. But there had been two goals and both had been achieved. She had been presented to those who mattered as the princess's thaumaturgist, with her work not dismissed outright, and her first great mystery would have its place on the calendar.

* * *

Finally released from the council chamber, Margerit looked around to find where Marken would be kicking his heels, waiting to escort her home. Her armin would have preferred to fulfill his duties by standing behind her throughout her ordeal, but that would not have been proper. His mandate did not extend to the council chamber, only to the streets and ballrooms where an unmarried heiress might need protection for her reputation and her person. But instead of his stolid bulk she saw a tall, slim figure in mannish riding clothes, rising from the window-bench opposite the door. The sight made her heart leap every time, even after so short an absence. "Barbara! I didn't realize you were back."

"Only an hour or two. Did you think I'd leave you to face the dragons alone? I told Marken I'd see you home." Barbara kissed her lightly on the cheek and Margerit raised a hand to tuck an unruly lock of tawny hair back under Barbara's low hat. It always felt daring to make those gestures in public, even though any close friends might have shared such a salutation.

"And Marken allowed it?" Margerit inquired teasingly. The armin took his watch over her very seriously—more seriously than was necessary only for propriety. Barbara had preceded him in that duty back in the days before she had become Baroness Saveze, but he was disinclined to cede it to her these days. And he looked askance at Barbara's own preference for going about unescorted. In his eyes, a baroness owed something to her own dignity.

"I insisted," Barbara said. "I thought we might stop at the Café Chatuerd for a bit. The moment we walk in the door at Tiporsel House there will be a thousand claims on your time, and I wanted to have you to myself for a while."

Moments later the doorman at the café bowed deeply to Barbara, murmuring, "Baroness Saveze, we are honored. Maisetra Sovitre, will you be joining friends?"

At a shake of her head they were shown to a table upstairs, where it was quieter and where a spot by the bowed windows gave a view out across the Plaiz without putting one on display for passersby. The café had been named for the old palace watchtower that had once stood on the site, but the name fit, for it still served as a vantage point over the heart of the city. Barbara waited until a plate of delicate pastries and the small steaming cups of coffee had been brought, then took her hand and asked, "How did it go? Have you restored the ancient wording of the *tutela*?"

Margerit laughed. She hadn't realized how much the hearing had weighed on her until that weight was gone. "I never hoped for that! But he listened, and that is enough for now. And the Royal Guild will perform my castellum. I'm trying to remember that advice Mother Teres once gave me about pride. Alpennia will not stand or fall on the basis of my mysteries. And what of your errand, was it successful?"

Barbara shrugged. "Well enough. I'll be glad to stay home for a while. Except—"

"Now we come to it! Except for what?"

"I have a royal invitation. Efriturik asked me to Feniz for his hunting party. I don't care to say no to an Atilliet. May I go?"

It was a game they played—the asking of permission. The expiation of a time when there had been too much silence and too many things taken for granted. There was less need for it now. The world knew…well, what the world knew and what it suspected were two different things. But society understood that an invitation from Tiporsel House came under the seal of Saveze. And it was known that if an invitation to the baroness did not also include the name Sovitre, then it was likely she would be otherwise occupied. Beyond that, what the world knew was that the woman who had inherited Marziel Lumbeirt's fortune and the woman belatedly acknowledged as his daughter who now bore his title had their lives bound together too tightly to ignore. And if gossip went further than that? There was always gossip, and most people chose to see only what was convenient. Once Rotenek society had granted a woman the label of Eccentric, it required only that she be discreet and entertaining.

Barbara was still waiting for an answer, amusement glinting in her pale eyes. "You can hardly say no to Princess Annek's son," Margerit said. "And whatever would I do at a hunting party? I don't even ride!"

The amusement turned into a wide smile. It was another private joke between them, one of the threads weaving the tapestry of their lives. "In truth, I think Efriturik only asked me in hopes of learning all the best coverts. It was one of the baron's properties, you recall."

Between them, he was only ever "the baron," never "my father." Margerit was one of few who knew the depth of hurt and anger behind that. That, too, was a thread that bound them. She looked out over the Plaiz, watching the ever-changing river of people passing by in the square that lay between the cathedral and the palace. The season had begun only a few weeks ago— the feast of Saint Mauriz marked its formal start—but already it was as if the summer exodus had never happened. A figure caught her eye and then disappeared into the crowd before she realized why her attention had been held. A movement, a way of walking, the turn of a head—it couldn't be. She leaned toward the window as if that would help to find her again.

"Margerit?"

She hadn't been attending to what Barbara had just asked. "I'm sorry, I thought I saw…Never mind. What was it?"

"I was wondering what this evening's to-do is about."

"A musical soirée," she answered absently. "Uncle Fulpi asked me to sponsor a composer with some connection to one of his business associates. I don't know much about the man but I have so few chances to make my uncle happy. And if he takes, then I'll have the glory of having discovered him. And there's a very talented soprano that Jeanne recommended."

Barbara grinned. "No doubt a very beautiful and talented soprano."

That brought a laugh. "And have you ever known the interest of the Vicomtesse de Cherdillac to fasten on anyone who was not both beautiful and talented?"

"I seem to recall that she was interested in me for a time," Barbara teased.

It was precisely that parade of beautiful singers and artists in Jeanne de Cherdillac's life that had cooled the jealousy Margerit once felt toward Barbara's first lover. "It wouldn't be very handsome of me to accept that as a contradiction to my claim! But I will admit that you're not in her usual style."

"She's deeper than you might think," Barbara said thoughtfully. "And she's stood a good friend to us when we needed her."

"And that," Margerit said, "is why I'm more than happy to hire her latest ladybird for my entertainment."

CHAPTER THREE

Jeanne

The visitor's voice was too quiet to hear well, but Tomric's voice, denying her, was icily clear even in the front parlor, where Jeanne was dutifully attacking her correspondence.

"Are you expected?"

The butler's dismissal evidently was not sufficient, for the visitor's muffled reply was countered by, "The Vicomtesse de Cherdillac is not at home."

Who could possibly be that persistent? She could recall no bills that were so far overdue as to warrant rudeness. Benedetta wasn't expected, and the servants knew better than to refuse her entrance in any case. Curiosity stirred, but there was no point in encouraging importunate visitors by giving in. Jeanne rose to abandon her letters until such time as she could work undisturbed. Then a startlingly familiar voice echoed clearly in the foyer. A voice she hadn't thought she'd hear again. One that expected to be obeyed. "You will tell the vicomtesse that Mesnera Antuniet Chazillen wishes to see her and will wait until it is convenient to be received."

She could hear the man's hesitation in the face of that commanding tone. He would remember the scandal—everyone did. "Mesnera…Mesnera, I do not believe the vicomtesse would be advised to receive you."

"That's hardly your decision to make, is it?" Antuniet snapped. "Announce me!"

Jeanne relieved her butler's dilemma by emerging from the parlor. "Antuniet, *ma chère*! How delightful to see you again!"

It was easy to see the cause of Tomric's confusion. She herself wouldn't have recognized the figure in the well-worn traveling suit of gray serge without prompting. Even beyond the clothes, the past two years had greatly altered her visitor. She was thinner—gaunt even—which only emphasized her imposing height. The cool, distant gaze that had once been thought haughty now seemed haunted. Her straight dark hair was still pulled back in a severe, practical bun, but now a few threads of silver told a tale of more hardship than twenty-five years should have seen. And yet, now that Jeanne looked closer, there was no mistaking the piercing dark eyes and that famous blade of a nose. They had never been bosom friends—differences in age and taste had seen to that. Had Antuniet Chazillen ever had bosom friends? But still, one knew everyone to some degree in Rotenek society. And beyond her enduring interest in the scholarly set that Antuniet had favored, their lives had intersected in the person of Barbara Lumbeirt, Baroness Saveze. "Where have you been keeping yourself all this time?" she asked, as if it had been only two months and not two years and more.

"Here and there." Antuniet's forceful entrance retreated into diffidence. "Prague. Heidelberg most recently. I thought it was time to come home for a while."

"And you're still doing alchemy, I see," Jeanne added, glancing briefly to where the other's skirts were pocked with small, even holes and washed with pale stains.

Antuniet followed her gaze and Jeanne could have sworn she saw her blush. Except that Antuniet Chazillen never blushed at anything. "Yes, I'm still doing alchemy. And that touches on why I wanted to see you."

Jeanne would have received her for no reason other than curiosity and boredom, but this added spice. "But of course. Come in and sit. I was writing some tedious letters and you've saved me from the chore for now." She turned to Tomric, who waited in some trepidation to learn how his judgment had erred. "Have some tea sent in, and—" She looked Antuniet over in quick evaluation. "Tell Cook to send up some cake and sandwiches, or whatever she can manage. I was too busy to eat earlier and now I'm famished."

It was a bald-faced lie. He knew it, the cook would know it and Antuniet could certainly guess. Jeanne saw a mixture of mortification and gratitude sweep across her face. "How long have you been in town?" Jeanne asked, leading the way to the green-striped settee by the bow window. "You must be starved for news."

"A few weeks only."

"Then you'll know we lost Aukust a year and more past, God rest him." She chattered on of marriages and deaths until the refreshments had been brought and the doors closed again. "Now tell me," she said with a sudden change of mood, "whatever brings you knocking at my door?"

Antuniet finished eating a slice of almond cake with careful small bites, then settled her hands in her lap and looked Jeanne in the eye. "Because you know everyone. And because, given your disregard for convention, of all the people I know in Rotenek, you seemed least likely to feel the need to deny me."

"*Et voila!*" Jeanne responded with a gesture of welcome. "But that tells me only why it was *my* door and not why you have returned at all."

"And why shouldn't I return?" Antuniet countered. "My exile was my own choice, not demanded by law."

Jeanne waited patiently for her to recall that she had come for a larger purpose than verbal fencing. "You mentioned something about alchemy?"

"Yes." And then, with the air of a rehearsed speech, Antuniet explained, "I was engaged in some very promising work in Heidelberg, but now I find myself in need of a patron. I hoped that you might be willing to act as a go-between, given that there are certain…difficulties in approaching prospects myself." The mask slipped a little. "And you aren't the sort to dismiss the idea out of hand—of a woman alchemist, that is."

That was the Antuniet she knew: plunging into business with no pause for preliminaries. Jeanne sipped her tea slowly to sort through possible replies. Alchemy. Not at all within her usual métier. Opera parties and boating expeditions were more in her style. And yet she could see why Antuniet had approached her. This called for the same sort of diplomacy and strategy as launching an ill-favored debutante. "It seems to me that there is one obvious candidate for a woman seeking a patron for her studies. Have you asked Margerit Sovitre? It's likely she's forgiven you by now." Jeanne could only guess what might have passed between those two in the disastrous collapse of the Guild of Saint Atelpirt. Antuniet's brother had tried to have Margerit condemned. Perhaps his own life had fully paid that debt.

"But I have not forgiven her," Antuniet responded in a tone as smooth and hard as marble.

"No? If you don't care to speak to her directly, there's always your cousin the baroness. You know the two of them are—" She placed two fingers side by side and waggled them suggestively. At Antuniet's startled response, she wondered if she had been too indiscreet.

"No," Antuniet repeated, less coldly but just as firmly.

Jeanne shrugged. "As you will. I can think of several men who might be interested in such an investment, but they'll want more details of what you plan."

"I would prefer," Antuniet said carefully, "a patroness rather than a patron."

Jeanne threw up her hands in a shrug. "Now you're being foolish. It's the men who have the money and it's the men who take little risk to their reputations in associating with a Chazillen…or an alchemist. That's how the world works."

"I know well how the world works. Should I seek a male patron…" Antuniet's shrug was more sedate. "I have neither the aptitude nor the inclination to please a man in exchange for his support." She left the implications hanging between them.

"And yet you come to me, knowing my reputation," Jeanne said with a smile. "Dare I flatter myself to think you wish to solicit *me* for a carte blanche?

Oh, Toneke, if you could see your face!" She couldn't tell whether Antuniet was more flustered by the gibe or the nickname. "No, no, sit down. If you're going to come to me for help you must learn to bear with my teasing! Truth to tell, I think you would be too expensive for me. My purse isn't deep enough to support an alchemist even if my name could bear the weight of being tied to one." She tilted her head to one side as another thought struck her. "Have you considered disavowing the name Chazillen? Your father's cousin did, I hear. It would greatly increase your prospects."

The response came with Antuniet's legendary coldness. "My cousin Sepestien is a coward. Lack of imagination is the only thing that saves him from being as great a fool as my brother was. When the name of Chazillen is redeemed, he'll have no share in it."

"So you have a plan for this redemption? And—dare I guess—it involves alchemy. Tell me more."

At first Antuniet's face closed up like a shutter, but then she seemed to relent, perhaps realizing that some bait was required when fishing for patrons. There were gaping holes in the story she told, but the essence came through. Not the usual transformations of metal, but something more subtle, more complex. A gift for the crown of Alpennia more valuable than mere wealth. Lost techniques—or, if not lost, kept secret so long they had gone out of knowledge. And how had she come upon them in the space of a year or two? That answer was not forthcoming.

"There's no true benefit to simple working in metals," Antuniet explained. "Master the transmutations and in the end all you do is cheapen what was valuable. But to create something that enhances Princess Anna's ability to rule—that could be worth a family's honor. There's nothing of fraud or sorcery in it, I swear. Nothing that would put anyone's soul or reputation at hazard."

"Why not approach the princess directly then? It would be the safest route." Given the events of two years past, Jeanne thought, secret projects— even for the good of the realm—would be looked at askance.

The suggestion was dismissed with a wave of the hand. "A gift, not a commission. And what reason would she have to put that trust in me until the work is proven? You know the poor repute of alchemy. The work is sound; I know it. But I don't care to puff it off until there's something to show. No, I don't want to approach her until I can present a gift valuable enough to redeem our name."

"Is this all for family honor, then? What did the name of Chazillen ever bring you that you owe it so much?" Jeanne said, shaking her head sadly. "You would have left it behind at marriage—you may yet. Work for your own future, not that of a tainted name."

Antuniet stood abruptly and said, "I thank you for your time—and for not throwing me out on the street at sight."

"Tcha, there's no need for that. I'll ask around, if you wish. I might find someone who will take you on. Give me a week or so to try. What is your direction?"

There was an awkward hesitation. "My plans are not yet certain at the moment."

Jeanne saw through the evasion, and all the humor and affectation dropped away. "Antuniet, how badly in need are you?"

She shrugged, which was answer enough from one once nicknamed "the proud."

Jeanne crossed to her writing desk and drew out a box to count over a few notes. Antuniet bristled when Jeanne pressed them into her hand. "But *chérie*," Jeanne pointed out, "you came here looking for a patron. This is nothing. Are you willing to swallow a horse but turn your nose up at a flea? Come back a week Tuesday. We can have a cozy little supper just us two and I'll tell you what I've been able to manage."

* * *

It was never Jeanne's habit to sit quietly in contemplation, so after Antuniet left she sent for Marien to help her change into a walking dress. There was no time like the present to begin, and she had a few ideas of whom to approach first. How very interesting the Rotenek season had suddenly become!

There was no reason to hire a fiacre as long as she kept north of the river, and the day was fine for walking. She was approaching the Plaiz along the Merketrez when a carriage pulled up beside her and a pink-cheeked face framed by a precise row of tiny ringlets peeked around the lowered hood.

"Wherever are you going in such a hurry?"

Jeanne stopped and smiled. "Was I hurrying, Tio? I wasn't paying attention. I'm off to Mesnera Chaluk's."

"May I come along?" Tionez asked. "I haven't seen her since I arrived back in town."

Jeanne said, with a carefully insouciant air, "It's only tedious business, I'm afraid. You'd be bored to tears. But you may take me up and we'll have all the way to the Plaiz Nof to chat."

Tionez seemed little heartbroken by the refusal, for the moment the horses started up again, she moved closer on the seat and leaned over to whisper in her ear, "I'd rather have five minutes alone with you than an hour in company anytime." Her eyes gazed up from under brows too straight and thin for the coquettish look to be truly successful, but Jeanne took the invitation and toyed with Tio's gloved hand, kissing each of the fingertips in turn. Tio would never go further than such flirtation, but she loved to think of herself as scandalous. And there were few things more safely scandalous than to be rumored to be one of de Cherdillac's amours.

"And where were you off to when I crossed your path?" Jeanne asked.

"My dressmaker. I'm having a daring new riding habit made. You've heard that Efriturik is taking a hunting party down to Feniz? You simply must get me an invitation! My husband is wild to go and I want to go with him."

"But Tio," Jeanne protested, "I know almost nobody in his set. Easier to get you tea with the princess! And I rather doubt it will be the sort of expedition where women are welcome."

Tionez pouted. "Saveze is going."

"Barbara is another matter entirely. But—" She considered the possibilities. One could propose the argument that including only Baroness Saveze was too particular an exception and that the addition of a handful of other women, respectable married women... she couldn't repress a bubble of laughter at the thought of giving Tionez that label.

"Is the picture that humorous?"

"I have an idea. No promises, but I think it may succeed. In return you must take me to visit your grandmother tomorrow. Don't worry, you needn't stay! I have a matter I want to discuss with her and I'd rather it seemed by chance."

"You're all full of secrets and errands today," Tio said, but her pout had faded. "I saw your friend Benedetta singing at Maisetra Sovitre's the other day. She looked so much older off the stage; forty if she's a day!"

"She's thirty-eight, or so she says," Jeanne replied tartly. "And I'm a few years more than that, you know."

"Never! Surely in your heart you're still seventeen."

From another, Jeanne might have thought it mockery. Tio might not be serious, but she was sincere. And she couldn't know she'd touched an old scar that could still give pain. "My heart will never be seventeen again," Jeanne said, thinking on those days. "An eternal twenty-five, perhaps." She gave Tio's fingertips another lingering kiss. "You remind me a great deal of myself when I was twenty-five." Tio had that same reckless passion, however misdirected it might be. Nothing was as attractive as that inner fire and she was drawn to it as a moth to flame. "Here we are, and now I must leave you." She lifted Tio's fingertips to her lips once more as the carriage steps were let down.

Alchemy, Jeanne thought, returning to her purpose as she climbed the steps to Emill Chaluk's door. How in the world did one even begin to broach the subject without seeming a fool?

CHAPTER FOUR

Barbara

An invitation—or perhaps, more accurately, a summons—from the Dowager Princess did not carry the same weight it once had. When young Aukustin, her son, seemed likely to be named his father's heir, Elisebet, his mother, had been a power in the court. But when the council threaded the shoals of the succession controversy by electing Annek, Prince Aukust's widowed daughter by his first wife, Elisebet's star had been eclipsed. Many of those who had once supported her now kept their distance, but Barbara saw no reason to ignore her request. Elisebet was still an Atilliet and mother to one of the potential heirs. There was loyalty owed for that, despite the conflict they had come into during the succession debates.

Barbara arrived promptly at Elisebet's private apartments at the stated time, and was surprised to see they were to be alone.

"Mesnera," she said, curtseying with the proper degree of respect and trying to guess from the strained expression on the princess's face what would be asked of her.

There was a time when Elisebet Atilliet had been counted a beauty, but the years had coarsened her features. The delicately pink cheeks were now merely ruddy and the dark-eyed glance that was said to have pierced hearts had turned sharp. Even before she had watched the crown slip from her grasp, the confident pride had become a brittle haughtiness. Persuading others to her plans had never been one of Elisebet's strengths. If it were, likely Aukustin would sit the throne today. So it was no surprise that she began with no preamble and no subtlety. "I understand Friedrich has included you in this expedition to Feniz."

It was a small thing, the insistence on calling Annek's son by his Austrian name and not the Alpennian version he now used. A small thing and it only made her look petty rather than reminding others of the boy's foreign birth. "Yes, Efriturik has done me that honor."

"He asked Aukustin to accompany him and I didn't dare refuse."

"Surely your son is of an age to enjoy riding to the hunt. How old is he now? Fourteen?" She spoke of him as if he were still in leading strings.

"I would like...I would ask...could you watch over him? See that he comes to no harm?"

"Mesnera, if you think your son still needs a nursemaid, then you would be advised to keep him at your side. And if you think he needs the protection of an armin, then hire one. I don't follow that profession anymore."

Elisebet's eyes darted back and forth and she leaned closer as if fearing spies even here in her own chambers. "Saveze, my son has enemies—I dare not name them. The sudden hiring of an armin just now and at his age would be tantamount to an accusation. Many things can happen during a hunt."

Barbara's patience with her had long since worn thin, but it had not yet shredded entirely. And it would take more than shredded patience to push her past hard counsel into naked rudeness. Respect was due to the princess's rank, if not her sense. "You do your son no favor by teaching him to fear his cousin. Some day—God forbid it be soon—one of them will sit the throne and Alpennia will be better served on that day if they are friends, not rivals."

"On that day all I ask is that he still be alive."

Barbara sighed. The threat might be illusory, but her fear was real. What harm could there be in easing it? "I'll keep my eye on him, but I can't promise more than that." She was embarrassed that Elisebet caught up her hand and kissed it in gratitude.

Lake Feniz was a small lapis jewel, caught up in a fold of rising ground on the skirts of the mountains. There had been a time when adventurous souls had tried to scratch a living on its shores, leaving a small cluster of cottages where the narrow road—barely more than a track—came in from the valley below. But the stony fields had long since been abandoned back to trees where they would grow, and patchy meadows where they would not. In the summer, the cottages were taken up by herdsmen bringing goats up from the valleys. And with the returning forests had come red deer and cunning wild boars and smaller game, picking their way through the ruined stone walls and feasting in the bones of abandoned orchards. They had brought a new crop to the land: a scattering of hunting lodges ringing the shore. In the autumn, when the goats had been sent back down, the goatherds' sisters and daughters moved into the village to tend to the cooking and cleaning for those who rode out from Rotenek for the pleasure of the hunt.

The baron had purchased one of those lodges. It was useful to have a private space to entertain those whose attention he wished to have to himself for a spell. The property had passed on to Margerit, but on the advice of LeFevre, her estate manager, she had found a buyer. Hunting was not in her style and the place produced no other benefit. Count Mainek had purchased it and now he, too, used it as bait to gather up the rising, the bold, the quiet decision-makers, those who might be of use now or in the future.

The expedition to which Barbara had been invited was Efriturik's party only in name, for he had no property of his own yet. It was awkward for him, having no title to give him status beyond being Annek's son. But title-lands didn't fall from trees and though there were several dormant titles held under the crown, it was a more delicate matter to negotiate fixing one of them to Efriturik's person.

Barbara wondered sometimes what he truly thought of the whole affair. It had been his Austrian foreignness rather than his youth that the succession council had found hard to swallow. And now he seemed to have staked all on the hope of becoming Alpennian by the time the matter would be considered again. It had been one thing for Annek to return to the Atilliet surname. Had it been his choice or hers that he had traded Friedrich von Maunberg for Efriturik Atilliet? Had the attractions of being a younger son in his brother's shadow back home been so few, or were those of someday becoming Prince of Alpennia so great?

It was odd to come to Feniz as a guest, Barbara thought. The luggage and horses for the hunt had been sent ahead and this time there was no need to participate in the complex dance of arrangements and security that such an endeavor required when those of high rank gathered, even for what was purely a pleasure trip. And that was what this was—as much as any activity around the court could be for pleasure. The guests had arrived throughout the previous day in twos or threes, though the call-up at dawn was the first time they were all assembled together. Most were young. These were men who might someday be Efriturik's allies and advisors—or Aukustin's, for that matter— and a sprinkling of the more adventurous of their young wives. It was not an event calculated for flirtations; she found herself the only unmarried woman to be included. And Aukustin was the youngest, clearly struggling between the excitement of his first grown-up hunt and the desire to behave with dignity.

Barbara watched carefully as Efriturik greeted his cousin, addressing him familiarly as Chustin with apparent affection, tousling his hair as one might a younger brother. And when Chustin grinned back she could see something like hero worship in his eyes. Well, there was one answer for Elisebet's concerns. They could have been brothers to all appearances—half-brothers perhaps. Old Aukust could be traced in both faces, in the straight line of the nose and the slight cleft of the chin. But Chustin had his mother's heavy brows and dark hair, while Efriturik... Barbara could only guess that it was his father's blood that leavened Annek's brooding features on him and left a touch of gold in his hair. Even without the attractions of rank he was a handsome man, though it seemed not to have made him vain or self-satisfied. He leaned closely to Aukustin to say something for his ears alone and the boy flushed slightly and nodded. No, there was nothing of concern on that end. From what she'd seen of Efriturik, he might be impetuous and inclined to careless pleasures, but there was nothing of duplicity in him.

The scouts had been sent out into the hills before dawn to find signs of quarry worthy of their sport. The hunt itself would be carefully planned and directed. There were no formal boundaries up here claiming territories for the lodges, but there were still customs and courtesies to be followed.

As the light grew toward sunrise, the courtyard began to fill with pairs of panting hounds held in close check, and grooms busying themselves with the horses. There were carriages for some of the women and a few of the older men that would carry them more easily to where the kill was planned. A stag hunt at Feniz was far more choreographed than most of the guests might be aware.

Barbara rechecked the girths and shoes of her own hunter purely out of habit before swinging up into the saddle and circulating among the other mounted guests. She made her courtesy to Count Mainek and then to Efriturik before looking around to see who else she knew. There was Count Peskil and his son and old Chozzik. She knew Count Mainek's friends well, for they had been in the baron's circles. But there was a new wave come into the court. Efriturik's closest companions were not old enough to feel the pressure to marry, nor yet for the most part to have come into titles and lands. And then there was a scattering of those nearer her own age, falling between the two groups. She saw a bias in Mainek's selection for the diplomatic set: all of them the young noblemen who would soon be taking up government posts and gaining the experience to serve in Efriturik's government, should that day come.

She sidled close to greet Iohen Perzin. "I thought you were off to Paris," she said, searching through her memory for what she knew of his duties. His long, oval face looked too serious for the pleasures of the day. He wasn't one of Efriturik's inner set. In fact, she knew of no ties he had to either of the competing parties.

"No, it's been put off until spring," he replied. "Albori says the French mustn't think we're too eager. And I confess I'm scarcely eager myself to leave Rotenek so soon." Warmth transformed his expression as he looked past her, and she followed his gaze to where his young wife was settling on her own mount as he continued, "I understand you're to blame for Tio's new ensemble."

Tionez Perzin wore a bold fashion indeed. A tall beaver hat topped her round face, made even broader by a fringe of small, precise curls, but it was her habit that caught the eye. The dark gray serge was sober enough and the cut fell short of the almost masculine style that Barbara affected for active pursuits, except in the lines of the coat, but Tio's skirts were cut full enough for riding astride and high enough to show off a pair of bright red Hessian boots with a glimpse of breeches underneath as a nod to modesty. Barbara covered her dismay by quipping, "As long as that color doesn't warn off the quarry!" But she made time, as the guests continued to gather, to seek Tio out and comment quietly, "You're ill advised to take my wardrobe as a model. You have your husband's dignity to think of."

"Oh, pooh!" Tionez said dismissively. "In truth, Iohen says he finds it dashing." She was one of those women who had been told that her pout was attractive, and she employed the expression liberally.

Barbara was not moved. "What he says and what he thinks may be different things."

"And you're a fine one to be scolding me on proper behavior!"

It was hard to blame her for bristling at being lectured by someone her own age. Barbara couldn't have pinpointed her unease. She herself was forgiven some outrageous behavior because of her past and her rank. But it was another matter entirely to be accused—even in jest—of leading others down the same path. That was less forgivable. And if Tio didn't care for her own sake, it wouldn't do to raise the hackles of society in general. Tionez had lately been flirting at the edges of Jeanne's set and Jeanne was not at all innocent of leading respectable women astray.

The sight of Aukustin settling himself on a restless gray hunter brought her promise to the Dowager Princess back to mind, and she watched him with a frown creasing her brow. He was handling the horse badly as it shifted and sidled and his seat… No, that wasn't it. She urged her own mount over beside him and swung to the ground.

"Mesner Atilliet, if I may?"

His pale face looked startled, as if he were unused to being addressed as an adult, but at her gesture he moved his leg aside for her to check the girths. Loose, as she had suspected, and one end of a strap was twisted up and under. No wonder the horse was twitchy. "Groom!" she called sharply. When Aukustin's attendant appeared, she merely pointed to the maladjusted equipment.

He turned pale and stammered, "Mesnera, I swear, I saddled him myself! I don't know how—"

"I don't care how," she replied brusquely. "Just fix it." She believed him. He must have stepped away for other chores and left the horse unattended. She didn't want to call too much attention; there was no harm done. Likely it would have meant no more than an embarrassing tumble. But on rough ground? Who could say? And here was proof that Elisebet was not simply imagining dangers. Someone had redone the girths with ill intent. With difficulty she kept herself from looking around to see who might be watching. No need to give away the advantage. Let them believe she thought it nothing more than a careless servant.

The times she had ridden here before, her attention had been entirely focused on keeping watch over the baron, staying back far enough for invisibility yet never more than a few seconds from his side. This time was turning out not so different. The terrain at Feniz could be challenging, even treacherous, depending on the path, with enough leaps and scrambles to test the skill of the best riders. But Mainek guided them to more sedate pathways.

This was to be an entertainment, not a steeplechase. And no doubt he had in mind the need to keep safe the two closest heirs to the throne. So they set out on easy slopes for the first hour, winding through the old fields and orchards, watching the mist rise off the jewel-blue waters of the lake and listening for the distant sound of the hounds.

When her path lay alongside Efriturik's for a space, Barbara asked, "Is the hunt what you expected?"

"Not at all. Back home…that is, back in Austria, we would have used guns on the open hills. This seems almost barbaric." He raised the spear he carried, a self-mocking smile twisting the corner of his mouth. It was a match for those carried by Count Mainek and another of the older men.

Barbara laughed. "That's meant for a mark of honor. The hounds will do most of the work, but whoever is awarded the kill at the end will be given a spear for the finish. The cover's too close for shooting here at Feniz, but you might try hunting pheasants out along the lower parts of the Rotein. Listen, I think they've picked up the scent." She turned her ear to try to catch where the sound was coming from.

Efriturik spurred his horse ahead, followed by his companions. Barbara saw Chustin attempt to follow and crossed over to stay more closely at his side. "Take the lower path," she called out to him. "They'll spend more time crossing the ridge and we can meet them around the other side." She thought he threw her a grateful look. Aukustin was a good enough rider for a boy his age, but he'd never had the freedom to become truly skilled. His mother had seen to that. Half the party followed them on the lower path. Some had already fallen behind and slowed to a gentle walk. It hardly mattered; they would all come together in the end when the quarry came to bay.

She lost the sound of the hounds for quite some time. The ridge was in the way, but more likely the huntsmen had sent them out around to drive the stag back toward the riders. The chase had wandered near to the Ovinze's lodge, and courtesy called for a diversion. The small party around her stopped to listen in silence for the horns and baying.

"There!" the younger Peskil said, pointing across a small arm of the lake. "How did they get so far?"

"It's a trick of the echoes," Barbara called out. "Wait a bit." And sure enough the sounds shifted and now were coming from a deep draw running up from the arm of the lake. The riders in the carriages would be disappointed, she predicted. The plan had been to bring the stag to bay on one of the bald knobs that lay along the edge of the woods where the cart track ran. But the beast must have slipped by them and turned down toward the water rather than climb the hill as expected.

Two men rode ahead eagerly as the belling grew louder, but the others looked to her and followed more sedately. Now she could hear the whinnies of approaching horses, protesting as their riders urged them down the steep ravine. That must be Efriturik's group, having caught up with the hounds just as the hunt turned. Beneath it all came the shouts and calls of the huntsmen urging the hounds forward.

The stag burst out from a thicket before them so suddenly that the foremost horses reared and plunged in terror. Barbara saw Chustin go down as she struggled to reestablish control of her own mount. He had regained his feet by the time she reached his side. The stag was past and gone, with the hounds close on its heels. And from the crashing in the bushes, the huntsmen weren't far behind.

Seeing Chustin safe, Barbara set off to catch his horse where it danced nervously at the far edge of the clearing. She'd barely caught the reins when the crashing of more riders emerging from the brush spooked it again. She swore and looked back in exasperation. Her heart stopped.

Somehow in the mad descent they'd roused a boar from its lair. It stood in the middle of the clearing, twitching its tail angrily, not ten yards from where Chustin stood frozen. If it charged, it would be on him before she could cross half the distance, and her with no more than a hunting knife to stop it. As her mind calculated furiously, there was Efriturik, forcing his horse between the two and swinging to the ground with his spear at the ready.

You fool! That's no boar spear! He'll run right up it! The beast stamped and snorted. But whether it had past experience with the hunt or was too sleep-groggy to want a fight, the boar snorted one more time, then wheeled back into the brush. She let her breath out and whispered a prayer of thanks to Saint Hubert, who watched over huntsmen. Fighting a wave of guilt, she returned to the task of catching Chustin's horse and brought it over to where the two Atilliet cousins waited, surrounded by the relieved congratulations of the other riders.

In the distance they could hear the horns signaling that the stag was down. Efriturik helped Chustin up into the saddle, saying, "We've missed the kill but I think we'll have the better stories to tell. Yes?"

Barbara's mind raced as the group slowly made its way toward the hunt's conclusion. Had it been planned? Impossible. There was no knowing exactly which way the chase would go. No, the boar couldn't have been predicted. This was the ordinary luck of the hunt—and luck it had been. If the boar had charged… If Efriturik had been slower to act… If he had needed to trust that pretty ceremonial spear to turn the beast…

* * *

The narrow escape gave the evening's festivities an edge of frenetic bravado. Barbara found herself in a more sober mood than most, thinking what she would say to Princess Elisebet. She picked back over every minute of the hunt, trying to find some flaw, some sabotage. There was nothing. Her training as an armin had taught her to look for any subtle nuance but she could find no moment in the day's events that was more than ill chance—none except the matter with the girths before they set out. Yet if the worst had happened, no one would have believed it was happenstance.

Charlin, the count's son, had won the privilege of the kill but he had ceded the honors of the evening to Efriturik. Now the celebration was fading as the evening deepened. There were two more days of hunting planned with lesser game and morning would come early enough. Barbara had noted when Aukustin headed for his rest and considered herself free now to seek her own bed. As she crossed the courtyard she could hear voices from the lakeshore in that muffled tone of men in their cups trying to be discreet. More faintly came the hollow sound of a small boat knocking against the pilings. She could guess where they were going. It was said that cooking and cleaning were not the only services available from the village women if one knew whom to ask. Pray God they were enough in their senses to lose no one overboard. She was on the verge of turning away to continue to her room when she saw Efriturik crossing the courtyard behind her in the direction of the dock.

"A moment if you please, Mesner Atilliet," she asked formally.

He glanced at the waiting cluster by the boat but paused with a vaguely guilty air. Well, his entertainments were none of her affair. But it was unlikely he'd thought the matter through. "I wanted to thank you again," she said, "for what you did with the boar. That was bravely done."

He seemed embarrassed and shrugged. "One does…what must be done." There was an impatient sound from his waiting companions and Efriturik said, "Forgive me, I must be going." With the conspiratorial air imparted by too much wine, he offered, "Charlin knows two lovely sisters in the village…" He trailed off, realizing it was hardly a suitable thought to share with a lady.

"Do you think that's wise?" Barbara asked mildly. She felt uncomfortable, as if she had been thrust into the role of tutor over him. "Have a care how you treat the daughters of your people," she urged. "The villages here have long memories and you should be careful what little souvenirs you might leave behind." *And with that face, there will be no lack of willing daughters.*

He made a dismissive noise. "Charlin says it's understood how these things are handled."

"Count Mainek's son has no expectation of being the next Prince of Alpennia," Barbara retorted but she turned away and let the matter lie. If the princess left him running loose then it wasn't for her to try to leash him. It would strain her resources enough to explain the day's events to Elisebet without terrifying her more than she was already.

CHAPTER FIVE

Antuniet

Antuniet paused for a few moments in front of de Cherdillac's small brick townhouse before climbing the steps. This time her heart didn't pound as she lifted the knocker. The place was, if she recalled correctly, one de Cherdillac had inherited from her family. Her long-dead husband had brought little more with him than his title when he fled France in the chaos of the revolution. The vicomtesse might affect a French accent and manners but she was Alpennian born and bred.

The house's location was respectable but far from fashionable: on the northern side of the Rotein, but neither directly along the river where the oldest families lived, nor at the city's edge where the new money had built. Close enough to the Plaiz that a woman careless of proprieties might walk to the cathedral or the opera house or other entertainments if she didn't care to keep her own carriage, but far enough that the houses allowed for breathing space between them. One could catch glimpses of tidy gardens and carefully trained fruit trees through the side passages. A family would have filled the house to a cheerful chaos. De Cherdillac had no brothers or sisters that Antuniet knew of. Well, no, there would have been no brothers or she wouldn't have inherited the house or the comfortable competence that allowed her to play queen bee to an eccentric social set of mildly questionable reputation. Antuniet knew the vicomtesse's public face, played out in the *salles* and concert halls and the country homes of her wealthier friends, but today was business and private. She wondered if de Cherdillac had chosen to meet her at home rather than a public café to preserve her own reputation or to preserve her guest's dignity. No matter, it suited them both.

There was no bar to her entrance this time, rather a bland and dignified, "Mesnera Chazillen, if you would…?" and a gesture leading her past the dining room back into the small breakfast parlor that looked out over the garden. It was early to dine, unless one were going out later in the evening. Antuniet made a mental note to watch for signs of impatience. Better to make a dignified retreat than put de Cherdillac to the embarrassment of dismissing her. Places were set for two, and there would be no need to shout across the length of a long table to be heard. That could be excuse enough for using the smaller parlor without touching on how out of place she would look among the crystal and silver of the formal dining room.

The man took her coat and bonnet, and she crossed to the windows to wait for her hostess to be informed. A thick, gnarled vine climbed along one edge of the view and disappeared above, testifying to the house's age. How many generations of boys had used that route to escape for nighttime adventures? There had been a twisted ilex of similar function behind her own house. No, it hadn't been her house, not then and certainly not now. The house she had grown up in—that was as much as she could call it. And she recalled the tree's spiny leaves had held a penance for the transgression.

De Cherdillac burst into the room as if she were walking on stage. Antuniet wondered idly if she paused before entering to gather herself to assume the role. She was as striking as ever with coal-black curls peeking out from under a turban of gold silk and setting off the creamy perfection of her skin. That perfection, Antuniet knew, owed something to the powder box, but the vicomtesse was enough of an artist that you scarcely noticed. You forgot the question entirely as soon as her dark eyes fixed upon you in delight and she unexpectedly clasped you for a quick peck on both cheeks. "*Ma chère* Antuniet! I'm so glad you could come! You're looking well."

By which Antuniet assumed she did not look as if she'd been sleeping under a bridge. "Well" was stretching matters. "Do you have any news for me?" she asked.

"Tcha, we'll come to business later. I have a lovely dinner planned. My cook has managed to find the most succulent duckling you have ever tasted and she won't say where she gets them because she thinks I'd tell all my friends and then she wouldn't be able to buy any more. Which I would, of course." She laughed.

So it was to be the fiction of a purely social call for now. Well, it wasn't as if she had any other appointments this evening. Antuniet took the indicated seat and started composing a praise for the meal that would sound appropriately artificial. Somehow "It's been ages since I dined this well" struck the wrong note in her present situation. And she was trying not to bring to mind that last private dinner.

As the evening wore on it was easier than she thought to slip into the rhythms of her old life, especially with someone so skilled at the game. The food *was* delicious. And the conversation covered harmless, inconsequential topics. De Cherdillac was a superlative hostess. Almost, she could imagine that the meal would be followed by a concert and then she would return to Modul Street. And her mother would inquire in her acid, pointed way whether she had met anyone interesting. And then, later in the night, she would be awakened by some minor uproar when Estefen returned home.

Reverie and reality merged in the sound of a raised voice elsewhere in the house, the tapping of quick footsteps and the bursting open of the door. De Cherdillac's butler was serving at table, so the unexpected guest was trailed by a parlormaid, apologizing profusely, "I'm sorry Mesnera, but she insisted on seeing you and—"

"And you are always welcome in my house, Benedetta. Thank you, Ainis, you may go. But darling, as you see, I have company."

The intruder was a tall, curvaceous woman, wearing a pelisse in the Italian style of deep garnet sarsenet. The elaborate coiffure and the boldness with which her long, oval face was painted advertised her profession as a performer. A singer, Antuniet guessed from the honey-rich tones of her voice, which were at odds with her waspish words.

"I expected you two hours ago."

De Cherdillac rose and, with a brief gesture of apology, took the conversation out into the hallway. It made no difference, as neither woman took the trouble to whisper.

"Didn't you receive my note, Benedetta? I have other plans this evening."

"And I wanted to see for myself just who these other plans were."

"*Chérie*, you know I adore you, but this jealousy is so unattractive. You embarrass me in front of my guest."

"And you embarrassed me in front of my friends. I promised Hannek you would join us for a drive. You have made me a joke."

"But *chérie*, you should not have promised in my name! Here is a promise for you: I will be there for the performance tomorrow. And afterward we will go to Café Chatuerd."

"Who is she?"

"An old friend. Really, Benedetta, this is growing tedious."

And then the voices became less distinct and there was the sound of a door closing. Antuniet rose when the vicomtesse returned to the dining room. "Perhaps I should come again when it's more convenient."

"No, no, there's no reason to go. I do apologize; she has a lovely voice but such low-class manners. Who would have thought she'd turn jealous when they're only here to perform for a month? But she sings with such fire! I have a weakness for passion and talent." She gave a little forced laugh. "I confess I'll be glad after tomorrow when the company moves on. I've grown bored of the constant tragedies."

Antuniet had no idea what one said to that, but some change of topic seemed to be called for. "Perhaps we could discuss my search for a patron."

"Ah, yes. Tomric, bring us some Madeira in the drawing room and then that will be all."

* * *

De Cherdillac settled herself on the edge of a chair and leaned over to touch her gently on the wrist, as if in apology. "There's no point to beating around the bush. I fear I haven't had any luck yet in finding someone to sponsor your work. It isn't…" There was an awkward hesitation. "It isn't the matter of your brother. But alchemy…" She shrugged helplessly.

Antuniet wondered why her heart sank so. It had been a long reach from the beginning. "I wonder that you didn't simply leave word for me and save yourself all that." She gestured to take in the earlier quarrel.

"But then I wouldn't have had the pleasure of your company this evening."

Almost, she could make it believable. It was easy to see why de Cherdillac was invited everywhere, despite…everything. She had that way of focusing her attention, as if you were the most fascinating person in the room. *Never mind that I'm the only person in the room*, Antuniet thought. She had never been the target of that charm in the old days. She could see how it might be intoxicating. No one had ever considered her worth charming, even during her first seasons out in society. "Whom have you approached?" she asked, bringing her mind back to important matters.

The vicomtesse rattled off an assortment of names. It covered all the likely possibilities. "Of course you forbade me to speak to Sovitre or your cousin, which would come to the same thing."

"I would prefer," Antuniet said more stiffly than she intended, "that you not refer to Baroness Saveze as my cousin. I rather doubt she acknowledges the relationship."

"But do you?"

She shrugged. "Does it matter?" In truth, Baroness Saveze was a stranger to her. She had known Barbara No-name, her uncle's ward, the strange, intense child always keeping quiet in the shadows. And she had known the ruthlessly competent duelist she had become, always at her uncle's side, and after his death left along with the rest of his property to the Sovitre girl. But Barbara Lumbeirt—revealed as her uncle's bastard daughter, the one granted his title after Estefen's disgrace and execution—that latest Barbara was a stranger to her and she was more than a little frightened of her.

De Cherdillac had been speaking again, mentioning those she still planned to approach. "Don't bother," Antuniet said abruptly. "I can see it was a foolish hope. There are other roads, they're merely slower." And had more hazards, but that was no one else's concern. "I thank you for your efforts on my behalf."

She rose, but the vicomtesse protested, "Surely you aren't leaving yet? I'd hoped for a longer visit once business was out of the way."

"Mesnera de Cherdillac," Antuniet said tiredly, "I have work to do in the morning. Business is never out of the way." She curtseyed formally, giving the other no choice but to return the gesture and see her to the door. But at the last, she turned and said, "Thank you for letting me forget, for a few hours at least."

* * *

She dreamed again that night. The sort of dream that had haunted her since the flight from Prague. Dark spaces, locked doors, and beneath it all her mother's insistent voice: *What do you have to show for yourself? Is that all? You could have made a good match if you'd tried at all. Instead you waste your time with books and mystic nonsense.* But a good match would have done nothing for the Chazillen name now. Marriage would only have provided an excuse to turn her back on the family disgrace. It was the alchemy that was their chance at redemption, but only if she could scrape together enough money to begin again.

The immediate problem had been to find some students. In Heidelberg she'd had the small advantage of being an exotic curiosity. In Rotenek she was merely an embarrassment, but at least she knew her ground. The university district had been her second home for years, and she knew its rhythms and gathering places. She had found some work already—enough to put a roof over her head. It would never be enough to support the Great Work, but there were those she knew who dealt in money for the right return. She remembered Estefen's fury over his debts and one name more than others on his lips: Langal. None of Estefen's rages had suggested that the man cut more than the usual corners in his financial dealings or that he would cheat anyone who didn't deserve to be cheated or that the subject of alchemy would deter him. Estefen had raged at anyone who came between him and what he wanted. Oh, not always outwardly, but rage had driven him all the same and that had been his downfall. Watching him, Antuniet had vowed never to let love or hatred cloud her sight. Only once had she allowed herself the luxury of hatred. At the end of that long, dark night full of death, on the last occasion when she had come face-to-face with Margerit Sovitre, she had let it spill over. *This time you have blood on your hands; this time I do hate you.* No, she would not go beg anything from Sovitre, not when two deaths stood between them.

As with de Cherdillac, Langal lived in a part of the city where Antuniet's shabby clothing marked her out more strongly than the fact that she traveled on foot. The difference was that his neighbors were quite accustomed to seeing him receive visitors whom fortune had treated badly. She knocked boldly on the front door at an hour far too early for social visits but quite acceptable for business. The man who opened it to her had too much of the ruffian about him to be a footman and not enough crisp professionalism to be an armin. In addition to combining the duties of reception and security, he seemed to have sufficient authority to assess her name and person and instruct her to follow him without further consultation. He preceded her into Langal's office, announcing, "Mesnera Antuniet Chazillen to see you."

Langal looked up and removed a small pair of spectacles, gazing at her from under bushy eyebrows with a face that gave away nothing except in the length of the silence that hung between them. At last he addressed her escort, "I believe you have been misinformed. This is *Maisetra* Antuniet Chazillen."

Antuniet struggled to match his bland demeanor. It would have come to this sooner or later. The vicomtesse might be too polite to take notice, but it was to Langal's advantage to point out that she no longer enjoyed the rights and privileges of the nobility. They stood at the same social level now. The taint her brother had brought on the Chazillens had stripped her of all her birthrights. The courtesies of address and title were the very least of it, but she still felt it as a slap in the face.

"As you say, Maistir Langal," she said with a formal curtsey. "The world has turned."

"And turning, it brings you to me. I'm trying to imagine what possible use I could be to you."

There was a chair placed facing him and she settled herself in it without waiting for permission. There was a fine line to be trod between confidence and arrogance. "I am engaged in a certain project." She weighed how deeply to delve into the details, but complete vagueness seemed unlikely to bring him to the table. "An alchemical project. I have had some small initial success." No need to mention all the failures since then. "And the results will produce both wealth and influence." She reached into her purse and drew out a knotted cloth. Unfastened, it revealed a blood-red carnelian, the only one of the gems worth keeping that was still in her possession. The rest had been lost in the flight from Prague. But if it were true to its nature, it would bring her what she needed. He picked it up between a stubby thumb and forefinger and examined it with the same bland expression as before. She watched for any sign that the stone affected him, but as his face still gave nothing away, she continued, "In my present situation the work goes slowly and I find myself short of patience. I need a workshop, equipment, supplies and perhaps an assistant or two."

Langal frowned and dropped the gem back onto the cloth. "The last time someone tried to pay me in alchemical gold it was nothing but gilded copper. He swore it was an instability in the transformation and that it had been pure gold when he gave it to me, but it came to the same thing. I have no interest in being made a fool when I try to sell cut glass and rock crystal. And this—" He nudged the stone where it lay. "Don't insult me by trying to pass it off as ruby."

If he hadn't the wit to look beyond glittering jewelry…"The stone's value lies in other properties than the obvious," Antuniet returned evenly.

"Oh, no doubt. I'm sure you can produce some clever conjuror's trick to convince me of its power. But what of the ones you plan to give me in payment? I'm no infant in the world. I've seen all the tricks before. But in any event, you seem to be misinformed as to my trade. I'm not a moneylender."

Antuniet blinked at him. The man's reputation was known to all. What was the point in denying it?

"Ah, I see your confusion," he said. His thin lips failed to manage a smile despite the amusement in his voice. "I'm not a moneylender, I only broker existing debts. I have, on occasion, been known to venture a mortgage or two. But the true profit lies in relieving amateurs of the burden of collecting on the notes they've been so imprudent as to accept. If some other person were unwise enough to extend you credit, that debt might find its way into my hands. But no, I have no interest in investing in your little alchemical charade."

"My brother Estefen—"

"Yes, your brother. Shall we discuss your brother? I made the mistake of holding his notes and he, at least, had expectations. What do you have? Would that cousin of yours be willing to stand surety for payment? Ah, but no. If she were, you wouldn't be here talking to me, would you?" He leaned forward across the desk with a pugnacious scowl. "Here's my offer: pledge yourself to pay back your brother's notes and I will undertake to find you an investor."

For one brief moment she considered it. But no, that road led nowhere but ruin. Better to build up slowly from her tutoring fees. It might take years to come back to the starting place she'd had in Heidelberg, but she could make it work. She rose and said, "I do apologize for wasting your time, Maistir Langal."

But when she reached to tie the stone back up in its cloth, he stopped her and picked it up to examine again. She held her breath, watching for signs that the amulet was working its influence.

His face settled back into a thoughtful look. "Alchemy, you say? There's a possibility that occurs to me. I give the advice freely because I'm in a strangely generous mood and it takes nothing out of my pocket. And perhaps because I admire you for being too sensible to accept my offer. In this business one hears things. One never knows when information might become valuable. I will tell you only that if you went and talked to Monterrez, the goldsmith on Zempol Street, you might hear something to your advantage."

Antuniet recoiled. "I'm not that desperate yet," she said, retrieving the gem from him and tying it up securely.

"Truly?" Langal asked in amusement. "Now how might I have taken the impression that you were? But Monterrez isn't a moneylender either, if that's what concerns you. Not in the ordinary way of things. He…let's say that I think he might be interested in your project for his own reasons."

* * *

If she had any other prospects, Antuniet would have discarded the suggestion as one more cruel joke. But without making any conscious decision, she followed a path back to her room in the university district that bent to take in the neighborhood centered around Zempol Street.

The shop gave little indication of its trade, only a counter overseen by a serious young man and a half-finished project lying on a table behind him among tools for polishing and delicate repairs. No doubt the wares were brought out only for customers. The man at the counter was too young to be the owner of the shop and Antuniet briefly wondered if she had come to the right place. "I'm looking for Maistir Monterrez," she said.

He might be young but he seemed to have evaluated her in a single glance. "Perhaps the Maisetra has some jewelry to sell?"

The jewelry had gone long before the gowns had. "I have a business matter to discuss with him."

The man pursed his lips and regarded her carefully. Then, without letting her leave his sight, he stepped back to a doorway and called out something rapidly that Antuniet couldn't follow. A woman's voice answered and he nodded at the response. "He will be with you shortly, if you're able to wait," he told her.

Antuniet said nothing, only stepped to one side as another customer came and went. The goldsmith emerged a few minutes later, looking as though he had hastily traded his work apron for coat and neckcloth, for there was a smudge of jeweler's rouge on one cuff. Evidently the summons had conveyed the information that there was no need to fetch a fresh shirt and don a hat. "How may I assist you?"

Antuniet had considered and discarded several approaches and in the end she simply brought out her one perfect gem and offered it to him to examine. He sent a sharp glance at his assistant, as if to reproach him for disturbing his work for a simple appraisal, but then he took the stone over to the window and peered at it more closely, drawing out a small glass to assist him. A frown furrowed his broad, balding forehead. It wasn't the admiration of a work of art but the consideration of a puzzle.

"Where did you get this?" he asked at last.

"I made it," Antuniet replied.

He looked up at her expectantly and she felt her way toward her question. She risked revealing more than she ever had previously. "I was told you might… that is, your name was suggested to me…I…I have been working with certain properties of stones and how to create and enhance them. I created that one in Prague." That would mean something to him, perhaps. "There were others, but I lost them. I want to set up a workshop here in Rotenek. But I need…" She shrugged. "I need everything. I was told it might be useful to speak to you, but not why. I can offer no security, no bond except my word. I—"

He held up his hand to stem the flailing. "You made this?" he asked. And then, more pointedly, "*You* made this." And again, "You *made* this, you were not simply working with a natural stone?"

She nodded.

"If I may ask, whom did you study under?"

"Rutufin, here in Rotenek, and then Vitali in Prague. But the stone, that was my own work. I found…" No, she didn't want to reveal too much. "I found some hints and formulas in an old book. Some of the techniques of DeBoodt."

That clearly did mean something to him. "I see. I think I know why you were sent in my direction, but forgive me…ah…Maisetra? I believe I missed your name."

"Chazillen. Antuniet Chazillen."

She saw recognition in his eyes for the name at least. He returned the gem, saying, "I need to think on this matter carefully. Could you return in the morning?"

What matter? He didn't seem to be speaking only of business affairs. But at least Langal's hint hadn't led to a solid wall. She nodded and left.

* * *

On her second visit to the goldsmith's shop, her host was more formally attired and she was led into a small parlor behind the store proper. Not a part of the residence, but no doubt a place where favored customers might be entertained in privacy. She was offered a seat but no refreshment. She had gone outside the limits of her ability to read such signs.

He began with little preamble. "Maisetra—you will forgive me?" From the hesitation it was clear that he had acquainted himself with her history and with her fall in status. She nodded in acceptance. A few more repetitions and the *burfro* title would cease to sting.

"Maisetra Chazillen, I have a daughter. God help me, I have four daughters. It was the husband of my eldest you met in the shop."

It was a mystery why she was being treated to this familial explanation, but Antuniet settled her mind to patience. She tried to look interested.

"My youngest but one, she has long had a mind to study alchemy, like you. Ordinarily it would be out of the question, of course, but...four daughters! What is one to do? Perhaps it might be best to give her a means of making her own way in the world, if the need arises, and if she has the talent and the interest. And an alchemist in the family could be useful. But there are difficulties, as I'm sure you know. I have done what I could and she has studied what she may, but looking forward, the usual roads are barred to her."

"The university allows..." Antuniet's thought trailed off. They lived in entirely different worlds. Did the university allow women of her sort...? Her own studies had been hard enough back then—piecing together scraps of philosophy and chemistry—until Rutufin could be convinced to take her on. How much more difficult...

He had watched her closely as she worked through the problem. "Whatever the university may allow," he said, "I cannot allow it. In my own home, in our own community, I have respect. I can protect my daughter as I should. But outside that? If she ventures so far outside what is considered proper for her? There are too many men who would consider that she had stepped outside the protections of modesty and respectability."

And that was even before one came to the question of alchemy. An absurd possibility was presenting itself. Antuniet stilled her impatience and asked, "And what would all this have to do with me?"

"If you would contract to take my Anna on as an apprentice—to teach her all the skills and secrets she would need to become a mistress of the art—I will arrange to provide the place and the materials and whatever else is necessary for it."

Was it possible? That he had the resources was clear from looking around. His custom must be drawn from the elite of society to maintain this style.

But an apprentice? She could only imagine the burdens of shepherding the pampered daughter of a goldsmith through the rigors of the art, even merely as a student. How much success would he require to fulfill the bargain? If it were the only way…"Perhaps I should meet her before deciding."

"Of course," he said and went to the door to call, "Anna, come here."

From the rapidness with which she appeared it was clear the girl had been waiting on the other side.

Antuniet's first reaction was dismay. *She's too old; it's too late. She needed to have started years ago!* But then she realized it was an illusion of the girl's height, the soberness of her clothing and the way her dark hair was braided up in a crown under a cap more suited to a matron than a young girl. Her eyes, staring from under delicately arched brows—they spoke more truly, with a mixture of shy deference and hopeful expectation. She dipped in a formal curtsey and Antuniet rose to meet her, asking abruptly, "What is your age?"

"I have fourteen years, Maisetra," she answered softly but with confidence.

"And what ancient languages have you studied? Latin? Greek?"

She nodded. "I have some." It was hard to know whether that was modesty or a deficiency. "And Hebrew, of course."

"Modern languages?" Antuniet continued. The usual assortment in smatterings. "Mathematics? Astronomy? Chemistry?" Her answers gave a patchwork picture. Well, that wasn't at all unusual given her background. Margerit Sovitre had been the same, delving deeply into what interested her and touching barely on what didn't. The deficiencies could be made up if she were willing to work.

"You realize I need an apprentice, not a schoolroom miss," Antuniet said sharply. "You'll be grinding ores and tending furnaces."

In the first spark of something more than obedience, she replied, "That sounds no worse than baking days."

Antuniet covered a doubtful laugh by demanding, "Let me see your hands."

The girl held them out before her and Antuniet turned them over one at a time. Nowhere near as rough as her own had become, but the hands of someone accustomed to work. And the telltale stains of ink around the nail; at least that was true. She turned to the goldsmith. "Shall we discuss the details of the contract?"

CHAPTER SIX

Margerit

It was worse than her coming-out ball, Margerit thought as she frowned over the gown that Maitelen had laid out and wondered if it were too frivolous, too young-looking. At twenty-three, she was scarcely ready to give over the trappings of youth for those of a confirmed spinster—to trade curls bound up carelessly in a fillet for a matron's lace cap or turban—but there was a certain dignity to be maintained. At her own debut she had scarcely noticed her dress. She'd felt like a boat on the flood, uncertain where the tide would carry her. But tonight was for the debut of her creation, her child. And while she was more certain of the outcome, she also cared far, far more.

It was usual for the mystery guilds to enjoy a formal dinner before their own special observances. Princess Annek had gone further and chosen to hold a full diplomatic ball on the eve of All Saints, with every foreign visitor and dignitary of rank in Rotenek present to hear of the working. Only a few of those guests would be invited to witness the *castellum* itself. It would be enough that they carried away the knowledge that the nation of Alpennia, small as it was among the great players, was still to be taken seriously.

And she, too, hoped to be taken seriously. She turned to Maitelen to question the choice of gown once more but was forestalled by a tapping at the door that the maid hastened to answer.

"Margerit dear, are you still not dressed?"

"Just starting, Aunt Bertrut," she replied, putting away her qualms.

Her aunt had been both relieved and disappointed that her services as chaperone would not be required tonight. Balls and concerts were one thing, but this event was outside the world Aunt Bertrut knew. Last year her aunt had finally agreed to let Uncle Charul present her at court and that was as high as she cared to go. She had married into the aristocracy, but she was still only Maisetra Pertinek and content to remain so. Yet she couldn't help fussing over the proprieties.

"I wish you had asked Charul to escort you. This isn't just a party among friends. How will it look for you to come alone, with no *vizeino*, no chaperone?" Worry pinched her pleasant face.

"I won't be alone. Barbara will be there, and Marken of course, though I know that's not what you mean."

"The baroness can't be a proper escort," she protested.

Margerit sighed. Bertrut had long since settled into a stiff formality with regard to Barbara, for all that they lived under the same roof for much of the year. It wasn't even the scandalous nature of their relationship that bothered her aunt as much that Margerit had chosen it over the hope of a brilliant marriage. Neither she nor her aunt would ever push matters far enough to destroy the balance of the household. Bertrut's presence—and more so Uncle Charul's—gave a respectable foundation to her life, one that turned aside questions and suspicions. She, in turn, avoided reminding them that it was her fortune that paid the bills. But that was neither here nor there tonight.

"The invitation was for me alone, Aunt. This isn't a social affair." And that argument was unassailable. She wasn't invited as an eligible young woman who needed a chaperone against any stain on her reputation. She would be there in her own right, as Annek's thaumaturgist and the author of the mystery to be celebrated. It was intoxicating beyond anything she had imagined, and not even Bertrut's fussing could dim the glow. She turned to Maitelen and held out her arms to begin dressing.

The next time the door opened, no knock preceded it, only Barbara sweeping in wearing a gown of cerulean blue, her hair pinned up in an old-fashioned braid but ornamented with an aigrette of sapphires and peacock feathers. Barbara dropped a kiss on her cheek without disturbing the finishing touches Maitelen was giving to her chestnut curls. "Dearest, it's time to go. It won't do to be tardy!"

They were announced into the hall, made their curtsey to Annek and were whisked off to be introduced to the Spanish ambassador, a fussy little man who seemed far more interested in shipping agreements than politics. Margerit had been tutored deeply on the subject of the shipping trade by her business manager, LeFevre. It was a source of no small part of her income. But she chose to forget what she had learned and tried to assemble an interested expression for the ambassador without the need to comment. When Mesner Felzin came up and entered into the debate with more enthusiasm, she took the opportunity to look around. Rotenek society was not so very large that she hadn't met most members of the Royal Guild at some point. There were a few exceptions: Ehing never went out in society for mere pleasure and Solz had been traveling abroad until very recently. She had worked closely with those who would take the principal roles in the ceremony, but the ordinary members had simply been given the *expositulum* to learn and been rehearsed in the basics. There was little hope that this first celebration would go well enough to find the ear of the saints and draw the response it was meant for. Perhaps next year. For now, it was enough that it was celebrated at all.

The Spaniard had drifted on to another audience. Now Efriturik was approaching purposefully with yet another foreign stranger in tow. She had noticed them by the mantelpiece, discussing something with great interest. The other man's gaze was never still, looking this way and that as they crossed the room, as if he would poke his sharp, narrow face into every conversation they passed.

"Mesnera Lumbeirt," Efriturik began, addressing himself first to Barbara, "may I introduce Herr Kreiser…that is, Mesner Kreiser, an emissary from Emperor Franz's court? Mesner Kreiser, Baroness Saveze, and Maisetra Sovitre, who presented my mother with tomorrow's ceremony."

He barely glanced at her and turned to Barbara, lifting her hand to his lips. "Saveze?" he asked in clipped tones. "I met your predecessor in that title once in Vienna." He was all sharpness, from his long, narrow fingers to the thin sweep of his side whiskers.

Barbara looked surprised. "I hadn't known Estefen had time to travel that far abroad. Or was this longer back? I recall there was a tour of some sort."

The diplomat looked surprised in his turn. "Estefen? I thought his name was Marziel. He was there for the congress, of course. Who is this Estefen?"

"Ah, I see the confusion. A cousin who held the title briefly, Estefen Chazillen."

A strange look came over the man's face. Margerit thought it was like the moment when a falcon saw prey. As if he were sighting down his beak-like nose and gauging Barbara's likely response. His next question was couched as mere curiosity. "Is Chazillen a common name in this land?"

Barbara answered dryly, "Not quite as common since his execution for treason."

The man's mouth twitched at one corner, the only sign of more than idle interest. "There was a woman of that name whose work came to my attention. I was hoping to gain an introduction to her. Antonia…Antoine—"

"Antuniet?" Margerit blurted hopefully before she could think better of it. He fixed that falcon gaze on her. "A friend of yours?"

She had misstepped. Barbara came to her rescue with an air of affected disinterest. "The sister of the unfortunate previous baron. You'll look far to find an introduction. She hasn't been seen in Alpennia for quite some time."

"You will forgive me for contradicting you," he replied. "My sources tell me that she has been in Rotenek this past month and more."

The talk moved on to other matters and Margerit tried to regain her composure. *It was her, that day in the Plaiz. I wasn't seeing ghosts.* But why was her return not widely known?

* * *

When the signal eventually came to go in to dinner, Margerit waited as the majordomo sorted out seating partners. Guild members were being matched with the high-ranking guests and Barbara had gone on ahead, for Saveze carried membership as a right. Beyond the birthright members, other nobles might be invited as it suited the monarch's purpose. When those had been seated, the rest of the guests would sort themselves out into the lower tables. Margerit expected that someone had been appointed to escort her in, but before that introduction could be made, the Austrian emissary came up beside her, offering his hand. "You must forgive my boldness but I only now recalled that Friedrich said you were the author of tomorrow's mystery. What other chance will I have to learn so much about it?"

Margerit looked around to see if he were disrupting plans already in place. The majordomo nodded at her to indicate the pairing fell within his rules, and Margerit allowed herself to be led into the dining hall. "Not the only author," she demurred, "but perhaps you might say the composer."

Discussion of the mystery occupied the first course. Not a deep, technical analysis, though he seemed interested in far more detail than a light dinner conversation might call for. Margerit remembered that hawk look that had come over him. He was a foreigner and therefore, in theory at least, one of those the *castellum* might be protecting against. She wasn't such a green girl not to know that diplomats and spies were one and the same. Over the second course he spoke for a while to the woman on his right and Margerit in turn answered the curiosity of her other neighbor. But when the pastries and fruits were brought in, the Austrian brought his attention back to her.

"This Antoinette—how is it you say it? Antuniet Chazillen? She is someone you know? A friend of yours?"

Margerit regretted her unguarded tongue, but she longed to hear news, to hear that she was well. "We studied together at the university." She attempted a disinterested shrug. "One knows everyone in a place like that. Where did you meet her?"

He waved a hand as if to brush away the question. "I haven't."

An awkward silence stretched between them. Margerit sensed that he was waiting to see what she might reveal. She damped down her own curiosity and said, "Rotenek is not so large a city. No doubt you'll meet her someplace."

"But not in the sorts of places where my business for the emperor takes me, evidently."

Margerit thought about that. "No, there are few houses where she would be received now."

"Is she considered complicit in her brother's crime, then?"

It was a question Margerit had long pondered for herself, but that went beyond what she cared to reveal. "It hardly matters what people think. The Chazillens were disenrolled."

He stared at her blankly. "You will need to explain."

"The family no longer carries noble rank. Barbara—Mesnera Lumbeirt—would be able to explain it better. She's studied law. Those who bear the name can petition to join a collateral branch and retain their status, but if Antuniet is still going by Chazillen…"

"And yet one may move in society without noble rank," he noted, gesturing toward her with a smile.

"But not without one of the three *f*'s," Margerit responded. When he raised a brow, she elaborated. "Without family, it must be fortune or friends."

His face took on a thoughtful expression: no longer the hunting hawk. "With none of those, one wonders why she returned to Alpennia at all." He waved dismissively. "But as you say, Rotenek is not so large a place. I'm sure to encounter her somewhere."

* * *

The cathedral was still chilly and nearly empty when Margerit arrived to prepare for the ceremony. There was little for her to do, in truth. The course of the mystery was out of her hands and all she could do would be to observe and take notes for later. She found the corner of the choir assigned to her and laid out her notebooks and sketching materials while Marken scouted out the least obtrusive place to stand guard over her. There was no more need for her to watch discreetly from shadows, striving to hold the visions in memory lest a sketchbook bring disapproving attention. No more warnings from Barbara to be careful who overheard her as she dissected and critiqued the structure of the rites. Barbara would arrive later, when the guild processed in. Despite the quiet movements of the priests and sacristans making their own preparations, the space felt empty. It wasn't so much the absence of people as the absence of ritual. Even the private worshippers had been cleared in preparation. Having trained herself to notice even the faintest trace of *fluctus*, it was like sitting in a darkened room at midnight. The feeling was strangely restful. She closed her eyes and found herself praying—not for any response, only for worship.

The mood was broken soon enough, attendants bringing in the assorted apparatus for the mystery, cushions and kneeling pillows being arranged at the seats for the royal family, and then singers practicing phrases out of sight somewhere in the inner rooms. There was no music in the *castellum* itself but, as with all of the cathedral-sponsored guilds, the lay ceremony would be followed by Mass. It sometimes felt, Margerit thought, as if it were meant to reclaim the space for the church. She took up her sketchpad and charcoal and traced outlines of the nave and choir on the first few sheets, ready for scribbled notes should anything unexpected happen.

She had only ever seen the full ceremony in her mind's eye. Rehearsals in bits and pieces were no substitute. As the attendants opened the doors and the priest welcomed the princess, followed by the guild processing through in pairs, it was hard to know what to expect. It seemed like only another rehearsal. There was a gap in the line as they came in and Margerit tried to remember who should fill it. Not one of the principals, she hoped. That would make it no more than a rehearsal indeed. As the guild members took their assigned places, the gap resolved itself, leaving the seat at Annek's left empty. Efriturik. No wonder Annek looked troubled. He wasn't a member of the guild proper, but it was customary for all members of the royal family to participate. Elisebet was there and Aukustin at her side; that was part of the careful balance. Margerit tried to read the faces but she was far less skilled than Barbara would have been. Then Annek's eyes flicked toward the doors and Margerit saw a figure slipping past the carefully ordered rows and around the back of the chairs on the dais to take his place. Efriturik looked the worse for a hard evening and it must not have begun until after the guild dinner was complete. Whatever had possessed him to go carousing last night of all nights?

The ceremony began out of balance but the rhythms of the repetitions slowly pulled it into alignment. As each of the themes built up—each of the "towers" that defined a particular protection for the land—the patterns of the *fluctus* became more clearly defined. They were pale and weak compared to the visions evoked by an old, established mystery, but the drifts of light and sound followed their intended courses for the most part. The pattern held; it would do for now. Margerit's hands worked deftly to sketch and note the flaws and errors. Some were in the execution, some in the design. She longed to have another set of eyes on the work. Antuniet would have had useful things to say, despite her lesser sensitivity. How long had it been since the Royal Guild had taken up a new mystery? Not in this generation, certainly. It had been a long time since there had been any reason to allow an outsider to witness.

By the time the towers were complete, there was more chaos in the structure. It was too long, Margerit thought. Too complex. Not too much for the band of eager young scholars it had been designed for, but for the Royal Guild? The focus had been lost. She would need to think on that. At the *concrescatio* she watched the *charis* wax throughout the nave and pour through the walls to seek the borders of the land—the circuit defined in the *markein*. That much succeeded. It was enough.

CHAPTER SEVEN

Jeanne

It wasn't easy to discover where Antuniet had been keeping herself. There was no overlap in their orbits—no hope of a chance meeting unless perhaps in the streets around the Plaiz. Anyone else might have let her be. It was what one did when an acquaintance fell from grace. But Jeanne was bored. The brief thrill she'd felt when Antuniet mentioned her work still haunted her. The passion of an artist was a blaze of fire, but passions of the mind ran deeper and burned longer. Alchemy: it had been out of fashion for quite some time in this modern age. The wheels and devices that drove industry required a more consistent approach. One person in a thousand might be able to produce reliable results from the esoteric arts, the way that people like Margerit Sovitre did with the mysteries. But if the rewards for charlatans in the realm of thaumaturgy were mixed, those for alchemy had destroyed the reputation of the field. It had become the refuge of mystics and upper-class dabblers who would disdain turning their curiosity on anything that smacked of trade. Those who lacked the protections of rank for their dabbling found the old prejudices against the art daunting. One couldn't pass it off as worship in the way one could for even the most practical of mysteries. For every alchemist accused publicly of fraud, there were three whispers of devils and sorcery.

Yet Jeanne had no doubts of Antuniet's sincerity; there was no one less likely to deal in false coin or mystical nonsense. Had she found a patron after all? Where did one set up shop as an alchemist in Rotenek? She rather imagined it would be in one of those corners of the city unfrequented by any of her friends. Any except…well, and why not? She'd only promised not to approach Barbara about the money. There had been no promise not to speak to her at all. With that thought, she added a visit to Tiporsel House to the next day's plans.

* * *

Jeanne carefully hid her disappointment when the parlor at Tiporsel held only two women of her own age: Margerit's aunt and someone she didn't recognize at all. That meant that somewhat more formal introductions were called for.

Bertrut Pertinek rose promptly as she entered. "Vicomtesse, we're honored. May I present my friend, Maisetra Lufise Chafil? Lufise, the Vicomtesse de Cherdillac."

Jeanne nodded to acknowledge the greeting but with a brief evaluation of Maisetra Chafil's origins, she declined to make the woman free of her Christian name. And as she had clearly interrupted the tête-à-tête of old friends, she also declined to sit and exchange pleasantries. "I was hoping to find Baroness Saveze at home."

There was a brief hesitation. "I believe she's in the library."

Jeanne overlooked the absence of an invitation and found her own way through.

"Barbara, *ma chère*, I do believe that woman disapproves of me!"

Barbara rose from the table, not needing to ask whom she meant, and allowed a light kiss on the cheek. "Don't take it to heart. She doesn't entirely approve of me either. But we rub along together, so be kind to me and don't tease her."

"I wouldn't dream of it." Jeanne wandered over to the windows overlooking the river. A light drizzle was starting.

"So what are you here for today?" Barbara asked, sitting once more at the book-strewn table.

"Is it impossible that I might have come for a visit?"

Barbara shook her head. "I know you. You visit people in the way a gardener visits flower beds. Now it can't be to stir up mischief, because there's no mischief here to be stirred. But you always have a purpose."

"Perhaps I'm merely bored. Nobody seems to have any need for me at the moment. You know how restless I get when I have no projects. Did you know that Antuniet Chazillen is back?" She said it as casually as if she were remarking on the impending rain, and watched for Barbara's reaction. There was, perhaps, a slight tightening of the mouth. That was all. Barbara was still good with masks.

"Yes, I'd heard."

Jeanne sat in the second chair at the table and leaned forward to peer at one of the open books. "I don't suppose you could tell me where she's settled in. We met by chance when she first arrived, but she hadn't a direction yet at the time."

Barbara smiled, as if at the salute of a fencing match. "And why would you think I could tell you that?"

"I know you," Jeanne echoed. "You've never been certain she had no part in Estefen's little plot against Margerit. You were certainly relieved when she left town after the execution. And you've never really given up playing the bodyguard. I remember back when you were Marziel's armin: you always knew exactly where his enemies were, waking or sleeping. There's still enough of the armin in you that you'd want to know where Antuniet is."

Barbara nodded as if to acknowledge the touch. "And why would you want to know? You were never a close friend of hers that I recall."

"But she has so few friends now," Jeanne replied with a little shrug. "I seem to have risen to the top of the list." She met Barbara's skeptical stare with her best imitation of a bland and innocent look, feeling oddly disinclined to admit to her interest.

"Oh, very well," Barbara said at last and scribbled out a few instructions. "Would you like to borrow a carriage?"

It was tempting, but— "No, I think the sight of your crest might hurt my welcome."

* * *

Jeanne glanced down at the directions one more time to be sure the driver hadn't erred. Trez Cherfis. Even the name reeked of trade and grubby warehouses, harking back to a time when breweries on the south bank rolled barrels down to waiting barges on the river. She might have declined Barbara's offer of a carriage, but both the drizzle and the neighborhood made some sort of transport essential. Eccentricity might excuse traveling on foot north of the river, but safety was another matter entirely. In such a neighborhood as this, propriety demanded the company of a maid as well, though she begrudged the time spent to return home for Marien. When they found the street, she asked the driver of the fiacre to wait until he saw her enter, then went to knock on the door indicated in Barbara's description. Several voices could be heard indistinctly from within, too muffled to follow the words, but the tune of the conversation could be guessed: an order to answer the knock; an excuse; a third voice offering; a sharp refusal; then quick, impatient footsteps. When the door finally opened, Antuniet stared at her in surprise.

"Do invite me in," Jeanne said when the moment had stretched out to an awkward length. "It's miserably wet out here."

"Of course, Mesnera de Cherdillac," Antuniet answered. "I hadn't been expecting guests."

"Tcha, if you don't start calling me Jeanne I'll think you don't care for me!"

The polite mask held, but she replied, "Jeanne, then, since you will."

Jeanne looked around as she untied her bonnet strings and unbuttoned her pelisse, handing them off to Marien when it was clear that no one else would step forward to relieve her of them. The place might have been a cookshop or the stillroom of some great estate. Through the open door to the next room she could see pots and vessels of all shapes, half unpacked from crates. In one corner, well protected from accidental jostling, stood a glass alembic, nestled on its trivet like a jeweled ornament on a mantelpiece. A standing furnace warmed the room pleasantly despite the stone floor, and from somewhere out of sight came a rhythmic pounding. Down a corridor there was the clatter of something heavy being moved and a man's muffled cursing. "So you found a patron," Jeanne concluded.

Antuniet didn't bother to confirm the obvious, asking instead, "How did you find me?"

"Oh, you know how it is in Rotenek: one always knows someone who knows something. And I owed you a visit—two, in fact. You've gotten busy quickly. How is the work going?"

The pounding from the next room had stilled, and a young woman wearing a heavy leather apron over work clothes peered curiously through the doorway, inquiring, "Maisetra?"

"What luminous eyes," Jeanne exclaimed. "I could quite drown in those dark pools!" She quirked an eyebrow questioningly at Antuniet.

Antuniet sighed and motioned the girl to come forward. "Jeanne, this is Anna Monterrez, my apprentice. Anna, the Vicomtesse de Cherdillac."

The girl stared at her in open wonder and dipped a deep curtsey.

Jeanne reached out to clasp the girl's hand briefly, then tilted her chin up with the touch of a finger when she looked down with a blush. "Charming! An apprentice, now why did I never think of that?"

"Jeanne!" Antuniet said warningly. Then to the girl, "Anna, go back and finish the grinding. It's not done until it all goes through the finest sieve."

Jeanne watched in amusement as the girl scurried away and closed the door behind her. "Jealous?"

"Leave her alone," Antuniet said coldly. "She's under my protection and her father is my patron. And she's only fourteen," she added as an afterthought.

Jeanne pouted. She'd seemed older. "A bargain: show me your work and I'll let your little apprentice alone."

"No! This isn't a game!" The cool mask slipped a little. "Jeanne, I appreciate your friendship, but I *need* his patronage. If you won't behave yourself, you aren't welcome here. If I expose her reputation to the slightest whiff of scandal—"

I've done it again. "I'm sorry," she said. "You know how I am. An imp of mischief takes the reins and I'm off. I swear, I'll treat her as if she were my own daughter." She searched Antuniet's face to see if she believed her. Antuniet only shrugged. "But please, do tell me about your work. It's started to pour outside and who knows how long it will take for me to find another carriage."

"I could have Iakup fetch you one," Antuniet offered.

"Not yet. Please?"

There wasn't even a shrug this time as Antuniet turned to open the door to the back workroom. Behind them, Marien settled onto a chair by the door, a picture of patience.

* * *

Jeanne found herself hanging on Antuniet's every word. Not for the explanations themselves. The basic theories she knew already and the rest went far over her head. It was for the fire that lit Antuniet from within when she described the experiments, the initial successes, the maddening failures, the slow teasing apart of myth and fact. There were gaps, holes. Somehow the exact nature of her Great Work was never mentioned. The quest for perfection, for purity—it was all in abstracts despite the grimy reality of her labors. And why had she left Prague when the work had been going so well? What had happened in Heidelberg that had left a shadow anyone could see? And this marvelous book that lay behind all her hopes, how had it come into her hands to make the work possible? That, at least, was a safe question.

Antuniet looked embarrassed. "It's only a foolish game I play in bookshops."

Now there was a curious image: Antuniet playing foolish games. "Tell me."

Antuniet turned away and began setting tools in order on the workbench as she answered. "My old nurse…you know those silly fortune-telling mysteries that girls play at floodtide? The ones for predicting your true love or your future husband?"

"Mmm-hmm?" Jeanne encouraged. It had been a long time since she'd been young enough and silly enough to take anything of the sort seriously.

"My old nurse knew one that—well, let's say that it worked better than a lucky guess. You brought everyone together in a circle around the fire and wrote everyone's name on a slip of paper. There was a great deal of fuss with symbols and herbs, wax from the altar and water from a sacred well. Not all of it seemed to matter. But you folded it up in a billet and threw the contents in the fire and if that person's true love were present, the sparks and smoke would pick him out."

"And your true love was a book?" Jeanne asked.

Antuniet laughed despite herself. When she laughed she became another person entirely. "Close enough I suppose! I changed it around a bit. I see visions you know—nothing like Maisetra Sovitre does, but enough to know what works and what doesn't—and I changed it into a charm to find the object in a room that you will find most useful."

Jeanne had almost stopped listening to the words. She'd never seen Antuniet so animated before; had she simply never looked?

And then, as if Antuniet realized it herself, her face shut down once more to that cool, sardonic mask.

"Can I see the book?" Jeanne asked.

Antuniet shook her head. "It's in a safe place. Maybe some other time."

And then the moment had passed. Iakup was called up out of the cellar, where he'd been stacking crates and sacks, to brave the storm and hail a fiacre for the mesnera as Marien helped her into her pelisse and bonnet once more. "May I come again?" Jeanne asked at the door.

"I can't match your hospitality, I'm afraid," Antuniet said, which was neither yes nor no.

"Next week sometime," Jeanne said. "Expect me."

Jeanne rested her hand briefly on Antuniet's shoulder, disappointed when she turned away with no further word.

CHAPTER EIGHT

Barbara

As she stepped out into the narrow courtyard where the groom was waiting with the horses, Barbara glanced up at the thin afternoon sun. Enough hours of light to get to Urmai and back and enough in between to examine the books Chasteld was said to have on offer if there were no delays. But with Chasteld there was no guarantee. Perhaps it would be better to take the town-chaise instead, despite the delay. No, Bertrut would have taken it already. On a better day she might have considered hailing a riverman to row her downstream. Chasteld's place had its own frontage and dock on the river. But though the trip down would be swift, it would be slower coming back when there was more chance of rain. Her errand scarcely warranted the trouble of a coach and four, and she preferred to ride in any case.

If Eskamer's information were accurate she might return with a delightful surprise. The pawnshop owner was better known for less savory merchandise, but he had a talent for finding unusual books, and Margerit had been searching everywhere for more of Tanfrit's writings. Her work survived in bare scraps and quoted correspondence, for the most part—bare glimpses of what a female philosopher might have accomplished in the time of Gaudericus. In Tanfrit, Margerit saw a reflection of what her own life might have been like in an earlier age.

As she paused to draw on her gloves, Barbara saw a woman entering hesitantly through the arched gateway to the street. With the reflexes of her former profession, she drew a few quick judgments. The visitor's dress was good, but scarcely fashionable. Provincial—dowdy, even. Yet she wore it with the air of having put on her best. One of Margerit's country cousins? No, not on foot and unannounced. An older woman, or well into middle age at least. Freshly come to town and not yet aware that it wasn't at all the thing to go visiting on foot. An old acquaintance of Bertrut's, most likely. A guest of some friend in the city taking the opportunity to renew ties.

She smiled politely at the woman as she swung into the saddle and touched her hat in the masculine habit she fell into when wearing riding clothes. "I'm afraid you'll find Maisetra Pertinek away from home. But leave your card with the footman and she'll know you called."

The woman stared at her in confusion and began, "Thank you, but I—" The sound of hooves on the cobbles masked what she might have added as the groom fell in behind. Whatever the woman wanted, someone would see to it.

In the end, the errand was for nothing. Chasteld had been away from home and no one could say if he'd be back before dark. They had no instructions about any books. She'd do better to let Eskamer handle the matter. But it wouldn't be the same as if she'd brought them home in triumph herself.

Barbara had forgotten about the stranger entirely by the time she returned to Tiporsel, so she stared at the card with curiosity and confusion where it lay on the sideboard beside yet another thick letter from Margerit's cousin Iulien. Maisetra Heniriz Chamering. It was no one she recognized. Perhaps one of her tenants from Saveze? No, at least the name would have been familiar in that case and there wouldn't have been such formality. Well, either she would call again or she wouldn't.

* * *

In the baron's day, the invitations that went out from Tiporsel House were first of all about power and only clothed in the garments of art and pleasure. In the first years of Margerit's residence, there had been no invitations sent out at all except for the most intimate of informal dinners. An unmarried woman of no great name had no standing to host balls and soirées. Now, under the name of Saveze, the invitations were flowing again and Margerit delighted in using their combined influence to wield her own sort of power. Balls she had little use for, but music was another matter. And through a chance meeting in the university district came the opportunity to play hostess for a different sort of performance.

Barbara's first impression of Miss Collfield had placed her in that species of mad Englishwomen who went traipsing across the face of Europe in pursuit of adventure and art, accompanied only by one stoic and inarticulate servant. She had fit the mold from the soles of her laced boots to the brim of the weather-beaten straw bonnet that topped her severely drawn-back hair. But that mistaken impression had been corrected in the course of a dinner and a long evening's conversation.

Margerit had come across Frances Collfield in the midst of an argument with the porter of the university's library. The argument had, at that point, not yet touched on the fruitlessness of Miss Collfield's request to view the collections but rather was stalled on the man's inability to comprehend the flavor of French learned in English schoolrooms. Margerit intervened and her patience in disentangling the matter had been rewarded by the story of the visitor's travels and details of her botanical research, and that was what had led to the dinner invitation. Traipsing across the face of Europe was, indeed, what had browned Miss Collfield's face and given her movements a loose-limbed, purposeful stride that set her out of place on the city cobbles. But it wasn't the usual quest for picturesque vistas or moldering ruins that drew her.

"Lichens," she explained, as if discussing the ornaments on a new gown. "And the occasional moss, but primarily lichens." The stoic and inarticulate servant, in addition to carrying the usual sketchpads and painting supplies, was burdened with several voluminous pressbooks of samples, carefully annotated as to location, elevation and substrate. "I have a theory regarding the distribution of the *Lecanorae*," she continued. "I don't care to map the entire mountain range on my own and I'm told your university has an excellent geologic atlas by Leunerd. Is there no way at all to see it except with the escort of some man? I suppose I should have written ahead and brought letters of introduction, but I never plan my travels more than a few weeks at a time. If it weren't for your kind invitation I wouldn't even know where I'd lay my head tonight."

"But of course you must be my guest as long as you like," Margerit urged. "I think I can convince one of the *dozzures* to sponsor you."

"You shouldn't need to beg!" Barbara objected. A thought came to her, complicated but far more satisfying. "Margerit, why don't we host a public lecture for Miss Collfield's studies and invite Princess Annek as our honored guest." She saw Margerit grin as she caught her meaning. If the ploy were successful, it was certain that some means would be found to bend the university's rules.

* * *

"Public" was a relative matter, of course, but Margerit had insisted on letting the women of the Poor-Scholars house know that they were as welcome as the regular university students. More important to the success of their plan was that portion of high society that had either the interest or the ambition to attend. And since Annek had deigned to come, it seemed the choice of the *Salle-Chapil* as a venue hadn't been overambitious after all.

The only part Barbara regretted was that, having lent her name as hostess, she was expected to take a far more public role than she preferred. While Margerit escorted Collfield and saw that all was prepared for the lecture, she waited by the doors, welcoming those whose status demanded personal attention. Jeanne took pity on her early in the evening and joined her, perhaps only for the chance to share whispered gossip in the brief quiet moments. Guests who felt no need for ceremony in their entrance had filtered in through the side doors, so it wasn't until she felt the weight of being watched that Barbara noticed the woman from the courtyard staring at her from a corner of the room. She stood apart, with no sign that she'd come as anyone's guest, but this was a public affair, after all, so there was nothing odd in that. It was the stare that was disconcerting.

Barbara leaned closer to Jeanne. "That woman over by the column—the dowdy one—do you have any idea who she is?"

Jeanne flicked her fan to disguise her own glance. "Goodness, no. Why should I?"

"Evidently the name is Chamering. I don't know why I should know her either but she left her card for me the other day and I can't puzzle it out."

Jeanne laughed. "You should be used to all and sundry petitioning you for things. I've almost sent a few people your way myself. She does have a bit of a hungry look."

It was true. Not in the sense of wanting for food, but Barbara felt drunk in by her gaze, as if she were the woman's hope of salvation. Another guest of note entered and she looked away to perform her duties. When she looked back, Maisetra Chamering had taken a seat at the edge of the *salle* and was examining the program closely.

The lecture was everything they'd hoped it would be. Collfield's slow, schoolroom French made her topic easy to follow, despite the odd turns of her studies, and a dry sense of humor came through to entertain the crowd after a few initial stumbles. At the end, Princess Annek had a kind word for her in public and in private a reassurance that the university collections would be at her disposal, as a special favor. That made all the trouble worthwhile: to see the *dozzures* required to bend and not to wait on their charity.

The Chamering woman had lingered as the audience began dispersing and Barbara, with a sigh, excused herself at last and approached her. "I'm sorry for the confusion the other day. I had no idea it was me you'd come to see."

Maisetra Chamering ducked her head with a fumbled curtsey. "It's no matter. I didn't recognize you and I wasn't sure—"

"Then we haven't met?" Barbara asked. "I've been trying to think whether I've heard your name before."

"No, that is…it's somewhat complicated."

Barbara tried to put her at ease. "Perhaps you could start at the beginning."

The woman looked around, as if afraid someone might be listening. "Oh, no, not here. I must speak to you in private."

"So this is a matter of business?" Barbara's eyes narrowed. Business with random strangers generally meant requests for either money or influence. And if not from her, then through her from Margerit. Best to deal with it promptly. "Come by the house tomorrow morning. I'll be going over accounts with my agent until well past noon, so you're certain to find me home."

* * *

Maisetra Chamering knocked on the door of Tiporsel House promptly at nine, which was far earlier than Barbara had expected, but perhaps she kept country hours. Or perhaps she was impatient. Barbara had barely begun reviewing the next quarter's budgeting with LeFevre. He had kept the baron's accounts since long before her birth and continued the same service now with those properties split between her and Margerit. She left the two of them to sort things out for now, leading her guest into the library. It wasn't where she would have chosen for such matters, but the library fires were always kept up and the parlor wouldn't be presentable yet. Barbara gestured to the chairs by the fire as her visitor gazed around at the room.

"You have a beautiful house," she said, seating herself tentatively. "It's good to see you've done so well."

Barbara frowned, trying to guess where she was leading. "It's not my house," she said shortly. "I live here as a guest. I own nothing at all in Rotenek." It was overstating the case but might bring her to the point.

The woman looked disconcerted. "But you are…that is, I thought…you *are* Barbara Lumbeirt? Baroness Saveze? That's what the woman said last night at the lecture."

Barbara nodded. "I am."

"But I thought…"

"It's clear what you thought," Barbara interrupted, losing patience at last. "You thought I was a wealthy woman. What isn't clear is how you thought to turn that to your advantage. Let us not mince words here. What is it you want?"

She made a very convincing show of looking aghast. "No! You misunderstand! I don't…you mustn't think…oh, this is all so difficult. I don't know where to start." She pulled a handkerchief from her reticule and dabbed at her eyes. "My sister—"

"Ah, your sister. Now we come to it. What is it your sister wants, then?" Barbara interrupted.

"My sister has been dead these twenty years and more," Maisetra Chamering said quietly.

Barbara didn't know which of those words sank into her stomach like a stone, but she felt the shiver of someone walking over her grave. She waited, all senses alert, her heart pounding in her ears.

In that silence the stranger continued. "I thought you might have recognized…but no, why would you? It was so very long ago and you were an infant. And of course there's no reason why the name Chamering would mean anything to you. But I was born Heniriz Anzeld."

"Anzeld," Barbara repeated.

She nodded. "Elisebet Anzeld, my sister, was your mother."

Barbara felt the stone turn to a flood of rage, welling up into her mouth. She stood abruptly. "Get out."

Maisetra Chamering shook her head. "Please—"

"Get out!" Barbara repeated, shouting now. "How dare you come here with her name on your lips? How dare you think I owe you anything after what you did to her?"

"I don't understand—" she began. But the shouting had drawn attention. Ponivin had entered on the briefest of discreet knocks and employed a butler's skills at extracting unwanted guests swiftly and quietly.

Barbara followed into the hallway, still shaking with rage. Margerit and LeFevre stood in the office doorway staring in concern. Barbara heard the distant thud of the front door closing.

"What's wrong?" Margerit ventured.

Barbara turned to them. "Evidently my mother had a sister. Did you know that, LeFevre?"

He frowned slightly. "I believe I did. It's been a very long time. Yes, a sister, but none of that would have been any of my concern until after you came into the household. And by then, the Anzelds had long since vanished from society. What did she want?"

Barbara shrugged. "I don't know. Money most likely. She was quite disappointed to learn that I didn't own this house."

"But Barbara," Margerit said, "to discover you have family—isn't that a wonderful thing?"

"Family?" The word tasted of gall in her mouth. "We all know my mother's story. How her family as much as sold her to Count Turinz for the sake of his title, then cast her off when his ruin threatened them as well. We know how they treated her."

"Do we?" LeFevre asked quietly. "We know the story the baron told— perhaps the one he truly believed. But there may be other stories."

"What else is there to know? They let her die with Turinz in a debtors' prison." She turned on both of them. "And I don't want to hear that you've gone to Maisetra Chamering behind my back to try to make peace."

"I wouldn't do that, Barbara." Margerit sounded hurt. "We promised each other, no secrets."

"No, no secrets." Barbara drew her hands slowly over her face. They were still trembling. "I'm sorry. I'm going to be of no use to either of you until I get out and shake off this mood. Will you forgive me if I leave the accounts to you for a while?"

LeFevre waved her off and Margerit touched her cheek briefly. It was permission enough.

After a change of clothes, Barbara headed to Perret's fencing academy, not to spend her anger in action, but because it was one place where anger couldn't exist. She had only to walk through the doors and hear the rhythmic sounds of quick footsteps and clicking blades, smell the sharpness of sweating bodies, for her mind to find that old familiar place of purpose and…not calm, but balance.

Perret himself broke off his bout to welcome her. "Mesnera, it's been too long. You'll lose your edge."

She'd once thought of him as impartially strict with all his students, but with the changes in her life there had been a shift beyond simply the forms of address. She wasn't merely a skilled and dedicated student now; she was a point of pride for him. "I still do my passes most mornings, to get the blood warmed up. But I didn't mean to interrupt your work. I'm not here for lessons today, just some sparring to keep in practice."

He bowed slightly. "I would be honored to engage with you, if you wish."

In the old days, the honor would have been all on her side. Now? Now she accepted graciously.

They worked easily at first, loosening up and trading banter.

"You still haven't hired an armin of your own, I hear," Perret said.

"Now you sound just like Marken!" Barbara returned. "He thinks I don't show proper respect to my own rank, running around town with no one but a groom except for the most formal of affairs."

"He's right. And it goes beyond respect. It isn't fair to burden him with standing behind both you and Maisetra Sovitre."

Barbara hadn't considered that side of things before. Just because she'd never asked for more than the trappings of ceremony didn't mean Marken didn't take his job more seriously. But she laughed lightly in response, saying, "And I suppose you have some eager student who's looking for a position!"

She made the touch to end the bout and Perret shook his head as he stood down. "No one I can think of at the moment, but if you like I'll ask around."

Barbara pondered the idea. "I wouldn't be an easy charge."

"And the old baron was?"

She laughed again. "But he trained me up to exactly what he wanted. I suppose I could do the same, but it would take years! I wouldn't stand for being bullied and sheltered like some innocent girl. But it would need to be someone I respected enough to obey if there were a genuine danger. And then there are the complications of my household…" An armin ended up being privy to most of his employer's secrets. How easy would it be to find someone who would take hers in stride?

Perret nodded as if following her thoughts. Whatever his own feelings might be, this was business. "Shall I keep my eyes open?"

Barbara considered the offer. "No," she said at last. "I'm still not convinced of the need." She glanced at the long clock at the end of the practice *salle*. "I should be getting home. Thank you for your advice."

* * *

The practice had dispersed her anger enough that Barbara felt only a slight twinge of annoyance when she found a small letter-casket waiting for her on returning to Tiporsel, accompanied by a note written on the back of another one of Maisetra Chamering's cards. *Your mother left this with me when she went to join her husband in prison. I never opened it. Do with it as seems best to you. I will not trouble you again. H.C.*

Lifting the box, she could feel a slight shift of the contents that spoke of a large volume of paper inside. There was no outer latch, only a keyhole. Unless the previous holder had had the key, her claim that it was unopened seemed true. Strangely, no curiosity stirred in her, only trepidation.

She took the casket into the library and tucked it into a space next to a volume of Desanger's *Logica*. It could wait.

CHAPTER NINE

Antuniet

Darkness. Darkness everywhere and thick silence. She was looking for…what? She needed to find it; she couldn't return empty-handed. A thin crack of light, like the slightest opening in a wardrobe door. She moved toward it, seeking a way out. Show me! *The demand was like a watchdog's bark.* Have you done it? Show me! *Her reticule hung heavy at her wrist, dragging it down. She fumbled at the strings and poured out the contents into the outstretched, expectant hand. Instead of brilliant, glowing gems it was nothing but dirt and pebbles. The hand closed into a fist then jerked sharply downward to cast the work aside. The door slammed, erasing that line of light and a key snicked in the lock. All was darkness again.*

Antuniet woke with a start, thrusting her hands out against the dream-door. Thin threads of light shone through the shutters from the first streaks of dawn. She rose, still exhausted, and went to throw them open to chase out the shadows.

The attacks in Prague and Heidelberg had come with almost no warning. Here at home it was easier to notice things out of place and wonder: the man who seemed to follow her home from the market one day, the shadows lurking more openly down in the street when she'd climbed up to the gable window at midnight to check the zodiacal watch against a sighting on the star Aldebaran. Were the curious stares in the street only for her rumored occupation or was there a deeper interest? What of the man who stood on the corner opposite for three afternoons in a row? But then on the fourth day, a young woman ran out of the baker's shop to join him and they walked down the street hand in hand. She felt a fool for being afraid. Was anyone watching her? Or was she seeing spies in every loiterer? She'd never seen the men who searched her rooms in Heidelberg. Would it matter if she had? Likely they'd been hired riff-raff. One face she knew: the man in Prague who had seemed in charge. Vitali's assistant had pointed him out and repeated the questions he'd been asking. And then when she'd seen him ransacking Vitali's laboratory—the one where her work was done—she'd turned and fled the city that same day.

But there would be no leaving Rotenek. There was nowhere left to go. She'd seen that face again, crossing the Plaiz Vezek. She wasn't certain, but his features had stood out against a river of Alpennian faces. She'd turned away quickly when he glanced her way and then he was gone when she looked back. Who was he? And why had he tracked her here? Beyond the obvious, of course. Back in Prague, Vitali had seen him coming and going from the castle, but that told her nothing that she couldn't have guessed.

And now at the chemist's shop, where she bought minor supplies and admired the intricate glassware she had no excuse to order, the proprietor brought the fear back to the fore when he said, "There was a fellow asking after you. One of those German sorts. Must be one of the new *dozzures* at the university."

Antuniet barely had time to wonder at that when his assistant countered, "Not German, Austrian. I told you we'd start seeing more of them with the princess returned. I know because he bought that *sublimatorium* you were looking at," he added, turning back to her. "Had it delivered to the ambassador's house on the Plaiz Efrank. I don't much think he's going to use it though. Looked at the piece like it was a vase for the mantel or something."

The old panic leapt up fresh, though his chattering gave her time to renew the mask. *What did he ask?* she wanted to demand. *How much does he know?* It would only draw attention. The chemist no doubt had guessed the nature of her work, but it was in his best interest to ask few questions. She could assume the Austrian knew her direction and habits…or would soon enough. If he were connected with the embassy then her worst fears were confirmed. Here was no jealous scholar seeking the book for his own purposes. She thought she'd been careful, during those early days in Prague, when she first realized what she'd found. Yet word had gone around. That had been unavoidable even in the secretive community of alchemists. And somehow her work had come to the attention of men with power, men who wanted her discovery for their own masters.

But what would he do? Would he move as directly as he had in Heidelberg? Here on her home ground? He was connected to the ambassador. Had he maneuvered ahead of her and gained Annek's ear? Until she had successful work to show, it would be hard to compete with the promise of an emperor's gratitude in return for one little book. There was nothing she could do beyond the precautions that had become second nature. The book was concealed, even more securely than in Heidelberg, taken out only in the depths of night when she was sure of being alone to copy out pages of cryptic notes for the next experiments.

Her hands were still shaking when she returned to the workshop. Anna called out a greeting from the inner room as Antuniet closed and locked the door behind her. She leaned against it for a moment, drinking in the sense of security, before answering, "Are you finished with the distillation? Set out the materials we'll need for tomorrow and make sure there's nothing else running short."

* * *

Whatever dreams there may have been didn't survive into the soothing rituals of the next morning's routine. The working couldn't start until the stars had achieved the specified angle and nearly all the preparations were complete. The knock came as she was measuring out the caustic. Antuniet jumped and barely kept it from splashing. At the second knock, Anna called out from the other side of the room, "Shall I see who it is?"

"No!" she answered sharply as she stoppered the jug and set it aside. Coming into the front room, she scolded, "I've told you a dozen times, you aren't to be answering the door to strangers. If I'm not here and Iakup isn't here then they can come back later. Go back to your work." Anna scurried off. She'd trained the girl well enough to obey a direct order without question.

She stood frozen at the door, unwilling to betray her fear by demanding a name, until the third knock came and she lifted the bar and worked the latch. But it was only Jeanne framed in the doorway. She was trailed by her maid carrying a large hamper. Antuniet closed her eyes briefly in relief and leaned against the jamb.

"Is something wrong, *chérie*?"

Antuniet felt Jeanne's hand touch her cheek and brushed it away along with her concern. "I wasn't expecting you this early."

"I do hope it's not *too* early," Jeanne said as she swept inside. "I thought I'd bring a luncheon today. Can the work be paused enough for you to enjoy it?"

That was just like her, Antuniet thought. It wasn't that she was unconcerned with other people's convenience, but it didn't enter into her planning until necessary. It was oddly comforting, as if Jeanne's very presence banished all the shadows. "I can make time," she answered. It was worth the interruption for that illusion of normalcy Jeanne brought in her wake. She turned to where Anna was peeking out from the inner workshop. "Go tell Iakup to bring the table down from my room. And another chair from wherever he can find it."

When the table had been placed and a cloth laid, Jeanne turned to Anna while the dishes were being set out. "Do join us. Toneke, tell her she may."

"I don't think…" Antuniet began.

Anna offered, "I have my own dinner to eat later, Mesnera."

"I brought plenty," Jeanne assured her. "We needn't stand on ceremony today."

Antuniet interrupted, "Jeanne, let her be. She isn't permitted to eat Christian food."

Confusion gave way to understanding. "Oh! I hadn't realized—" And then both reactions were driven out by curiosity. "But how does that work, Antuniet? I thought that alchemy was like the mysteries, that it requires the aid of God and the saints. How—?"

Antuniet saw the defiant flash in her apprentice's eyes and hid a smile. "Anna, are you ready to stand your first examination? Come join us and explain to the vicomtesse how it is that Jews and Christians may join together in the practice of alchemy."

Once urged past her sudden shyness, Anna filled their ears with the history of the Great Work. Watching Jeanne focus her attention on someone else was enlightening. Was her charm calculated like the movements of her fan? Or did it come as naturally as breathing? Antuniet couldn't recall ever seeing the act laid aside for more than a startled instant. And yet it never seemed false. Watching them, she would have sworn that Jeanne knew no more fascinating subject in the world than the paths that traced from ancient Egypt through the tangled web of knowledge and enlightenment.

Anna seemed willing to recite the entire history of the field from Maria Ebraica to Saint-Germain, but Antuniet stopped her before it would become tedious. "That will do for now. Go finish measuring out the materials for this afternoon's work, then take your own dinner." When the girl had disappeared into the back and closed the door, she asked, "And what do you think of my apprentice now?"

"She suits you," Jeanne said thoughtfully. "I wouldn't have guessed you had the patience for students."

"How did you think I've been earning my bread?"

Jeanne made a dismissive gesture. "People like me don't give a single thought to earning bread!"

"Don't you?" Antuniet asked. "I think it's just a different type of bread." But she didn't follow the thought. She pulled out Vitali's watch to check the alignments. The conjunction wouldn't be for a little while yet. "I can only spare you another half hour. Tell me what the gossip is." In truth, she cared nothing for gossip but it kept the illusion in place a bit longer. On days like this, she wondered how long she could last without the glow of Jeanne's illusions chasing out the shadows.

* * *

Antuniet watched Jeanne being handed up into the fiacre and waved briefly as it pulled away. She stared after the vehicle, wishing that… From the opposite side of the street, a stare caught her attention. Too long for idle curiosity; not long enough for recognition. As the man turned and strolled off slowly, worry settled back into her belly like a small, burrowing creature. She barred the door again and went through to the workroom.

Anna looked up from her jars and powders and asked, "Maisetra, why does the vicomtesse visit you?"

Antuniet considered the easy answer: that she was an old friend. But it wasn't true. They'd barely been passing acquaintances before her return. "She's bored and she finds me amusing," she said at last. It was likely to be close to the truth and it seemed to answer the girl's curiosity. But the question nagged at her.

She felt…cultivated. Courted, almost. Back when their paths had crossed in the old days, she'd watched Jeanne pursue connections for the sake of her little games of influence. That was the bread she earned: the balls that couldn't be held without her advice, the hostesses who relied on her to secure the most prestigious guests. Did Jeanne have so much confidence in the eventual success of the Great Work to consider her worth the trouble to attach? It hardly seemed likely. But that left only the possibility that Jeanne had an interest in *her*. And that was too absurd to entertain for more than a passing moment.

* * *

For days there was nothing new to worry her. Then one morning she needed to open up the door to the lane behind the shop so that Iakup could bring in the coal without trailing dust through the front rooms. And in the wood around the latch there were deep, fresh scores, as from a knife searching for a crack. She was certain they hadn't been there before. The locks were strong and she still worked Saint Leonhard's charm over them for whatever good it would add. As Heidelberg had proven, those protections only mattered when her enemies hesitated short of force. And even the best locks could be defeated with enough skill.

She didn't mention the attempt to the others. It was her they were after, her and DeBoodt's book. There was no need for Anna to be as worried as she herself was—though it was impossible to keep her concern entirely hidden— and it went beyond Iakup's duties to play watchman. He was there to escort Anna from home and back and to do those little tasks that required a man's strength. It would be worth more than his life to be found carrying a weapon, even at her request, and he had his own family to return to at night. This was her burden alone. She tested all the locks and the bolts on the inside of the shutters. It became a nightly ritual to make a circuit of all the rooms to satisfy herself that all was fastened and secure. Sometimes she made it twice, after lying sleepless for an hour trying to remember if she'd checked everything.

But now every sound in the night was full of menace. Was the baker's dog barking at rats or at furtive shadows? Was that the creaking of the furnace cooling from the day's work or was some intruder walking across the floor? Sharp winter winds tumbled litter down the streets and against the doors and rattled the shutters. Sleep rarely came until well past midnight and left too early. She filled the dawn hours by slipping down to the neighborhood chapel to give thanks for another night of safety and to pray for protection.

She brought Maistir Monterrez a selection of the small stones she'd succeeded in producing so far to discuss how they might be set for use. So small, and none of the nobler gems had succeeded yet. "These are mostly only ordinary stones, of course," she told him, "with whatever properties they might have naturally, though the purity makes them stronger than most." Only that first stone—the one she'd carried away from Prague—had come successfully through the further transformations, the ones that moved her work beyond mere craft. "We need to be sure the gems themselves are flawless before the next steps, but it isn't too soon to think how they might be set. The stone itself should be both visible and in contact with the bearer's flesh."

"A ring would be the first choice," Monterrez said, setting a loupe to his eye to examine one of the gems more closely. His brow furrowed and he set it down to look her hard in the face and ask, "Are you well? It won't serve either of our purposes if you work yourself to death. I'm content with my daughter's progress. Her trade won't be learned in a day or a month no matter how long the hours."

Antuniet shook her head. "I have bad dreams, that's all. Yes, rings would be ideal, I think, but how will it hold the stone securely if both top and bottom must be bare?"

He took the hint and left the matter alone. "I have some thoughts. Let me try a few designs and you can test them." He picked carefully over the gems she had brought and selected the carnelian. "This one. It should do for practice." He held it up to the light. "This is the first one you showed me, isn't it?"

That was a good sign, Antuniet thought. The stone should have called to him and it had. And while he had it in his keeping, it would bind him more closely to her and her work.

"Will it change the properties if I cut it? The shape is rather awkward."

Antuniet shook her head. "Cutting should do no harm, but best to do it at dawn when both the sun and Venus are in the sky and their influence is balanced."

"And if I may," he continued as he separated out two of the deepest-colored jaspers. "If these are not essential for your work, may I take them in payment for the gold for the ring? I have a commission that they would suit. That precise shade of color is unusual."

"Yes. Yes, of course," Antuniet said. "I hadn't...I have no need for those in particular." To her chagrin, she hadn't given a thought to the cost involved. Monterrez had paid the expenses of the workshop with never a question and she had begun thinking of him more as a distant partner in the work. This was business. It was important to remember that.

* * *

Antuniet didn't like leaving the workshop entirely empty for long, but it was unavoidable when Anna and Iakup kept their Sabbath. Once, on returning, she thought the clutter of research notes in the workshop was disarranged. What had they been working on last? Surely it had been the winter alignments, not the notes on measuring furnace temperature that now lay on top. She made her circuit of the doors and windows but all were latched and barred. *Am I simply going mad?* she wondered. There were ways, both mechanical and mystical, to refasten a latch from the outside. But why conceal the search so carefully? *They don't know whether it's here!* she thought suddenly.

Her Austrian shadow had never seen the book himself, only hints and reports of its existence from others. He knew some of what shape her work was taking and could guess from that. But every time he'd caught up to her and searched her belongings, he'd come up with nothing. And then she'd disappeared and he'd had to track her again. That alone could be reason for his caution—waiting for her to make some mistake, to let down her guard. Afraid to set her on the run again. He couldn't know she had nowhere left to go, could he?

The gems had come out of the matrix flawless and perfect in color for three firings in a row—the jaspers at least. The onyx by the same method was still inclined to craze and crack during the congelation. But they were ready to set systematically to work on the next steps: the nourishing of the first gravelly seeds into larger growths. More diagrams and formulas needed to be copied out. Anna and Iakup had left for the evening and there was time to work undisturbed. Antuniet checked the doors and shutters once more, then took a supply of candles down into the cellar.

At one end of the flag-paved chamber, between the sacks of coal that fed the furnace and the baskets of ores and minerals waiting to be processed, she stood in front of the timber and plaster wall and set the candle down on one of the boxes. The natural place to put a locked chamber would have been under the wooden stairway where rough planks shut off a cramped storage area. The day after she'd moved her things into the building she'd had a carpenter set a door into the planks and fasten it with a strong lock. That was for the deliverymen to see and gossip about. But at the opposite end of the room the wall concealed a small forgotten space. Whatever its original purpose had been, some previous inhabitant had paneled it over. With additional careful paint and plaster work, the door became just another panel and—like the hearthstone in Heidelberg—with the working of a mystery for hidden things, even the knowledge that it had been a door was erased from the memory of the materials.

Antuniet worked the revealing and pushed the panel inward, then took the candle in and closed the door partway behind her again. A traveling desk was set on a table at one end of the space, and she lit half a dozen candles and set them around it in the stumps of old wax standing there. Ink, pens and paper came out. Then at last the book, lifted from the iron-bound box that kept it safe from gnawing things. She weighted it carefully open to the section she needed and began to write.

She didn't need a full copy, only sufficient notes to remind her of the steps and signs to follow and the diagrams recording DeBoodt's observations. The alchemist had recorded his experiments in meticulous detail. If the seed-stones were set in a flux at this spacing…if the layers in the crucible were made to this depth...if the work were begun at this hour. The instructions were couched in arcane codes and allusions as well as the cipher. Half the work was simply to make sense of them. Her own results had been somewhat different from DeBoodt's, but she kept working from his parameters as a touchpoint. Several variant recipes for the flux. She had a favorite that had worked well for the carnelian and jasper, but they shared the influence of Venus, so perhaps that was the fault in the onyx process. Perhaps the second recipe that partook more of Mars. She tamped down the impatient voice that urged her to tackle the more ambitious gems. Step by step. Master the first successes and build on them.

Time was measured only in the ink filling the pages. Ten close-covered sheets were done and at least two more to go when a brief, sharp noise brought her head up, ears straining through the darkness. Long minutes passed. Only the house settling. She raised the pen to continue, when a second sound pulled at her attention: a soft shuffling, as if someone were carefully feeling his way across a dark room. The scratching of the pen would have masked it entirely. There was someone in the house above. Antuniet laid the pen carefully aside and snuffed the candles. She'd tested, to see there were no chinks in the floorboards that would betray the light. But if he came down the cellar stairs... She eased the concealing door closed. No chance to work anew the mystery to hide it. The plaster and woodwork would need to suffice.

The darkness was absolute, as if in her nightmares. The blood singing in her ears threatened to drown out the soft sounds from above. There! The familiar creak from the fourth step up to the over-story where her bedroom was. She tried to remember: the door would be open and even the closed shutters let in enough moonlight to see that the bed was empty. But did he mean to murder her or was he only searching? The same creak again. Not a search, then. Only long enough to see she wasn't there. They'd never tried entrance when the house was occupied before. Perhaps even now they thought it empty. They...he. She thought there was only one intruder above. A long hesitation, then the faint whisper of the workshop door. Less cautious footsteps now. Yes, he thought he was alone. Antuniet imagined him rifling through her things, sifting through notes, poking at the half-complete work laid out on the bench. Had he lit a lamp? There was no way for her to see. The footsteps returned to the corridor. A longer silence. Had he left? How had he entered? Not the front door—that was barred too solidly. Nor the back, though it gave the most privacy. That door stood right at the top of the cellar stairs and the sound that first alerted her had come from a different angle. One of the windows then, opening on the cramped space between the buildings. The latches were strong but latches could be defeated more easily than bolts. She imagined him boosting himself up over the sill. A small man, thin and wiry. Not the Austrian in that case, but a hireling. What had he been told he was hunting?

The silence was still complete. He must have left by now. Surely it had been a quarter of an hour since she'd last heard anything. Antuniet felt around and laid her hand on the latch of the hidden door. Another creak cut through the dark and she froze. This time he was on the cellar stairs. She heard him descend. A faint spill of light traced across the floor of the hidden room where the door failed to meet the flags. If the candles had still been lit, they would surely have betrayed her. Couldn't he hear her heartbeat? She heard tapping at the boards closing in the under-stairs and a series of small metallic tinks as he tried something with the lock. A snick and a creak of hinges. Well, she hadn't meant it to be more than a decoy. A faint oath. He was getting careless. He was close enough now that she could hear the scrape of his shoes on the flagstones as he circled the small room. Just when she thought surely he would find the hidden door there was a whistle, sharply, from outside. Another oath and quick steps up the stairs.

Antuniet waited in the darkness, daring to breathe again but not to move. The minutes stretched out. Was he gone? She'd thought so before and nearly betrayed herself. The darkness swam before her eyes, like a sinister echo of the visions she sometimes saw during the mysteries. Each time she started thinking that surely she was alone, the building would creak. She could no longer tell the natural sounds from signs of danger. Had it been an hour or only a few minutes?

* * *

At a shout and clatter Antuniet sat bolt upright. The dark—it came back to her. The sound resolved itself into the ordinary noises of the street. It must be morning. She moved stiffly and cautiously to open the door to the hidden chamber. She had no lamp but even the faint light spilling down the stairs seemed like day after that darkness. She took the time to strike a flame and light one of the guttered candles in order to work through the mystery to conceal the door again.

After searching through every corner of every room to make sure no intruders lingered, she examined the window shutters one by one. Yes, there it was: the faintest scratches between two boards where some intricate tool had been slipped in and around to draw the latch. She would have sworn it was proof against mere physical means. But if a housebreaker's tools were all she had to counter, then iron bolts were her next defense. With luck, it could be done before evening.

But even the newly installed locks couldn't keep away the gnawing fear. As night closed in again, every sound in the street was a potential intruder. Antuniet clung to one hope: they didn't want her to know. They'd never broken in when someone was present to see. If they knew she was there and awake they would wait for a better chance. She lit the lamps in the rooms where the light would show through the shutters. Still, sleep wouldn't come and she went back down to the workroom and puttered at those tasks that wouldn't be ruined by clumsiness.

If the work were only a bit further along—if she had more than those few stones that could prove success—she could risk going to Princess Annek. It wouldn't be the full array she had planned, but it might do. It might be enough to gain approval for the work and some measure of protection—protection not only from her enemy but from the suspicions and whispers of her neighbors. Much could be forgiven one with royal patronage. It wasn't what she'd hoped for: the triumphant presentation of her gift. In three weeks—two if all went well—she might be ready to risk a petition. But not like this. She was a wreck and she knew it.

She didn't fear for herself; she'd been through worse. It was the fear that he'd seize the one thing that made the work possible. If she could be sure the book was beyond his reach...Could she? It was a mark of her desperation that she even considered the idea. She had enough working notes copied out to see her through to the immediate goal. Success would be a matter of technique, not discovery, for this small part.

There was one person she knew in Rotenek who would both know the book's value and have the resources to guard it well. One person who she could trust to be honest enough to return it on demand. If the book were safe, she could sleep again.

CHAPTER TEN

Margerit

During the night, the light drizzling rain had turned to snow. Not the crisp, pretty snow of Chalanz that Margerit remembered from her childhood, but a moist slush that collected on street corners and settled in heavy clumps in the branches of the trees around the Plaiz. The short carriage ride to the cathedral for Mass became a morass of crowding vehicles and swearing coachmen. Even those whose dignity permitted them to walk to services on a Sunday morning had chosen to ride, and the drivers jockeyed for the closest spot to the steps to save fine shoes from the muck. Barbara had urged an early start, her old instincts anticipating the crush of the crowd, but even as small a household as theirs couldn't be hurried so easily, and they arrived in the worst of the confusion.

So it wasn't until Marken shifted—in that way an armin had that both warned of and warned off trouble—that Margerit noticed the woman working crosswise through the crowd on the porch, coming toward them. Her movements were vaguely familiar despite a worn cloak wrapped tightly around her, hiding her face in shadow. When she came close enough for Marken to step deliberately into her path, the familiarity resolved itself.

"Antuniet?" Margerit exclaimed, pausing in the flow of worshippers. At her back, she felt Barbara turn sharply, while Aunt Bertrut and Uncle Charul moved on toward the doors, unheedingly.

Antuniet tried unsuccessfully to step around Marken, looking daggers at him when he laid a hand lightly on her shoulder in warning, but she knew better than to persist. Margerit stepped forward, on the verge of calling him off, but Antuniet glanced around wildly, then drew a package from under her cloak, thrusting it into Marken's waiting hands. Margerit knew Antuniet's words were meant for her ears as she said urgently, "Keep it safe! Whatever you do, keep it safe!"

And then she was gone, back into the crowd. How long had she been waiting there for them? Margerit wondered. And what was she afraid of? She held out her hand to Marken for the package and saw him exchange a quick look over her shoulder with Barbara.

"Later," Barbara said in her ear. "Let's get inside first."

Whatever fear was haunting Antuniet seemed to have infected the others, and Margerit let herself be carried along into the nave to find their places before repeating the request.

It was a battered leather satchel of the sort used to carry valuable books for travel. And by the weight and shape of the burden within, that seemed to be the contents of this one. She undid the straps enough to peek. It had an old, thick binding, corded across the back and worn rough at the corners. She started to pull it out then some instinct stopped her, as if she felt eyes upon her, watching. No, not here. Recalling the look in Antuniet's eyes, she handed the satchel back to Marken. "You heard her, keep it safe. And out of sight," she added as an afterthought. Time enough later for questions. He shrugged an arm out of the sleeve of his greatcoat to slip the strap over his shoulder and tucked the bag away in its folds behind his back.

The weather was not the only sign of the turn of the seasons. Next Sunday would begin the Advent services, a reminder that winter was truly come. Margerit looked over to the seats reserved for Princess Annek and others of the royal family. Back in Prince Aukust's day they'd rarely been occupied, at least by the time she'd come to the city. He'd been too frail and Elisebet had preferred the private palace chapel. But Annek was there to be seen most Sundays and at all the special services. It was, perhaps, a calculated choice, but the others in the royal household followed her lead and the palace was always well represented these days. Advent would bring another such change, for Annek had announced that the Royal Guild's Christmas mysteries would be public for the first time in anyone's memories, leading up to the New Year's court and all its pomp.

Margerit cared little for the court itself. Barbara had taken her during the two years past, and the intricate web of intrigue and power-balancing that played out on its stage had only confused her. Barbara drank it in like mother's milk, watching the slightest changes in greetings and courtesies, hearing what was said in corridors, teasing every scrap of meaning out of the princess's actions and the court's responses. Barbara was the one who had found deeper meaning in the change to the Advent mysteries. Margerit only knew that it was a new chance to study the compositions of Tinzek without need for special pleading.

It seemed special pleading would not have been needed in any event. In the confused lull after services ended came an informal summons to Annek's presence in the name of that very topic.

"You were planning to attend?" she asked, evidently in no doubt of the answer.

Margerit nodded with a small curtsey.

"Then I was hoping you might take some notes. I have no plans to change the ceremony itself, of course, but I'd like to have a better understanding of the purpose and effects. I'd like to do that for most of the Guild's work eventually—saving only those of the Great Mysteries for which we have no present need. And I'd like to know if having spectators affects the work. Secrecy and privacy have their place, but…"

Margerit knew the rest of it from frequent repetition. The people should see how they were governed and what their rulers did for them. Secrecy bred irrelevance. The old guard was scandalized by Annek's approach, but it was a new age. "I'll need a copy of the text," Margerit began.

"Yes, yes, of course," Annek replied, already turned to the next petitioner. "Come to the palace tomorrow. My secretary will have a copy you can borrow."

On their return to Tiporsel House, it was like those early days in Rotenek when nothing had seemed more important than slipping away to the library to study a newly acquired book, with Barbara leaning close at her elbow. How slow she'd been to realize that Barbara leaning close had been as important as the books! There was no need for coy, accidental touches now.

Barbara stood over her as she slipped Antuniet's puzzle out onto the round table in the center of the room and pulled a chair close to study it.

The pages were covered with what seemed like gibberish, though the diagrams and symbols made the contents clear. "Alchemy. Well, that's no surprise," Margerit said, feeling something akin to disappointment. "I heard that was what she's been working on. For all the fuss I expected something more dangerous."

"Dangerous enough to have frightened her," Barbara countered. "And you have no idea what the book really holds." She traced a finger along the first few lines of text. "A simple substitution in the vowels, I think. See here? *De gemis itaque ac lapidibus.* That's clear enough even without knowing the symbols. But it would take some time to work through and I suspect there are other codes. You don't know, and ignorance is dangerous. Don't forget what happened the last time a Chazillen left papers in your hands. That time they were meant to brand you a traitor. You'd do better to hand the book off at once."

"To whom?"

Barbara shrugged. "Someone better equipped to weather those dangers. Who's to say what's hidden in here? Take it to the palace. If you give it to Annek at once, no one can accuse you later of conspiring in whatever comes of this."

"But she gave it to me. Keep it safe, she said. I'll tell Her Grace about it, but there must be some reason Antuniet entrusted it to me."

Margerit heard victory in Barbara's sigh. There was one more warning. "Don't assume that reason is to anyone's benefit but Antuniet's." But she sat down and pulled the book over to examine it more closely.

After two hours of study, Margerit was only a little more enlightened than she had been by those first few pages. The book was wide-ranging and detailed, with formulas and diagrams at every step—more the working notebooks of a practitioner than a text meant for the instruction of students. If Antuniet had been keeping ribbons in the sections of particular interest to her work, those markers had been carefully removed. She closed the covers at last and looked questioningly at Barbara. "Safe?"

Barbara gestured around them. "What could be a safer place to hide a book than in among the rest?"

It hardly seemed to answer Antuniet's sense of concern, but without knowing what specifics she had feared, there was no telling how to counter them. Safe from thieves? From damage? From some more invisible hazard? She looked up at the shelves for an open space. Not among works of similar topic. In the end she slipped it in between two volumes of a commentary on the *Statuta Antiqua* whose bindings were similar in age and color. Nothing would draw the eye. "I wish I knew—" Margerit began.

"I intend to find out," Barbara countered. "I should have been keeping a closer eye on her since the day I knew she'd returned."

"Barbara, do you really think this is some revenge aimed at me? It doesn't smell like a trap. And why be so obvious?"

"At you? No. But that business with the Guild wasn't aimed at you either. Not really. It was aimed at your fortune. And at Efriturik and his brother. That didn't mean you were in any less danger. The Chazillens have always acted for their own interests first. They don't much care who falls under the carriage wheels. That's what worries me."

Keep it safe. The words haunted Margerit's dreams that night. The Antuniet she remembered from their time as students together had never been that haunted, that desperate. What had she seen in the years since she'd left Rotenek that had stripped away the old confidence and—yes—arrogance? Margerit checked that the book was still in place the next morning before setting out to the palace. *Keep it safe.* It still whispered at the back of her mind when she took the borrowed *expositulum* for the Advent mysteries to the Poor-Scholars Hall at the edge of the university district and asked who might be available to do a bit of copying.

"It's a bit of a rush, I'm afraid," she told the older woman who had met her in the visitors' parlor. Margerit had never seen more of the building than that room. Whatever their lives had been before being taken into the Hall, the young women there were watched over as strictly as any well-born debutante or convent-bound novice until the day they left to take up the careers that the scant edges of a university education might fit them for. All too often, Margerit knew, their futures held nothing higher than keeping accounts in a shop or tutoring the daughters of ambitious *burfroi* families. It seemed a paltry thing to bring her copy-work to them, but Margerit had fallen into the habit of coming here by preference.

"I'll fetch Mefro Mainus," the woman replied. "She'll know who might be available."

"Akezze? Is she still here?" Margerit was surprised. She hadn't seen Akezze Mainus since the breaking up of the ill-fated Guild of Saint Atelpirt. She must have found some position outside the city. The woman shrugged and left the parlor. She was only a portress and chaperone. It wasn't her business to know the whys, only the wheres and with whoms.

Akezze's eyes lit up when she entered the parlor. She had clearly come direct from her work, for a smudge of ink stood out against the pallor of her cheek where she must have tucked a stray coppery curl back under her muslin cap. "Maisetra Sovitre! I hoped I might see you again! How may I serve you?"

Her greeting was a reminder that the illusion of equal fellowship had dissolved with the Guild. Margerit kept the other woman's Christian name off her tongue and gave her the dignity of formal address and a scholar's rank. "Maisetra Mainus, I have a bit of copying to be done. I'm afraid I'm in a bit of a hurry and some discretion is called for. Ceremonies of the Royal Guild. I know there's a scriptorium here at the Hall but I can't really let the papers out of my hands. The work would have to be done at my house. Do you have anyone who could be spared?"

"*I* can be spared," she answered crisply. "Is it bound or loose? Would it help to have several hands? There are two or three girls who might have time at the moment. You'd have to pay extra to have one of the matrons come with them. I'm afraid I'm not respectable enough to serve the purpose."

Margerit smiled in amusement at that. Akezze was one of the most proper people she knew, but the matrons also had widowhood as a shield for their reputations. "Are you still studying?" she asked. "I'd thought—"

A troubled look crossed Akezze's face. "No, I'm only passing through between positions. There was space to lend me a bed for a few months and I've been overseeing the scribbling to pay for my keep." Her brisk tone didn't invite further questions.

Margerit nodded, returning to business. "Whoever you can spare, then. Starting this afternoon, if possible, when lectures are over. I need to return the *expositula* to the palace by Saturday. And—" A sudden thought came to her. "—I have another job in mind after that. Similarly discreet and requiring some very careful work."

Akezze echoed her nod, then said more warmly, "It's good to see you again. I heard about your appointment and…the other matter. The baroness."

And which part of *that* did she mean? But there was no hint of anything but friendly interest, and surely the simple matter of Barbara's inheritance was all she intended. Margerit answered vaguely, "Who guessed how the world would turn?"

"And are *you* still studying?"

Margerit grinned. "Always and ever. As much as they'll let me." Neither of them had ever been matriculated students, of course. Whether Poor-Scholar or well-off dabbler, female students were allowed to attend lectures from the gallery as long as sufficient fees were paid. But even apart from no hope for a degree, there were limits. Margerit allowed some of her frustration to show. "How did you ever get so far with Kant? I remember you outpaced even Choriaz in working proofs but I've met walls at every turn. I can't trust to luck that one of the men will ask the same questions I'm puzzling over, and you know how Grossler is. Even a royal command couldn't get him to bend on the subject of tutoring women. Not that I'd ask Her Grace to interfere, of course," she added hastily.

Akezze took the question seriously. "It was still Agnelli when I was there. He wasn't quite so stiff on the matter. And I had a cousin who was a scholar. He was always willing to speak for me." She shrugged. "And mostly I just read what I could and worked it out for myself. Disputations might have sharpened my skills. But those arguments we had with Choriaz and Perfrit over the design of the *castellum* ritual always seemed more like lessoning schoolboys than serious debate."

"To you, perhaps!" Margerit said ruefully. "I always knew what I was trying to explain but it was hard to convince anyone until you led them through step by step. I wish I could have *you* as a tutor." Their gaze met as if the same thought had occurred to both at once. Margerit could see Akezze's hesitation and knew the proposal was hers to make. "Would you? Tutor me, that is? Or are you contracted already for the spring?"

"Nothing certain yet," Akezze said slowly. "I pledged myself here through March. One of the older girls has been promised the scriptorium post when the Easter term starts. I'll need to have something in place then."

"And I won't be staying past floodtide this year. You could come with us to Chalanz and then to Saveze and then I wouldn't waste the summer in idleness."

Akezze looked dubious at that. "I can't imagine you'd need me more than an hour or two every day. And the opportunities for other work would be few in the provinces. I've been hoping to save up enough to start a school in Falkoiz. It's where my father's people are," she added by way of explanation.

Margerit saw the problem and reached for a tactful offer. "If I'm going to drag you all over Alpennia to be at my convenience, of course I'd guarantee you full wages. Shall we say two quarters' worth, for the period from April to September? What's your usual rate?"

"At my last position I was to have been paid forty-five marks per quarter. With room and board included."

A pitiful amount. And *was* to have been paid? There was a story there but not one she could ask after. "I'm afraid you'll have to settle for eighty," Margerit said.

"For the full term?" Akezze asked warily.

"Per quarter. I'm hardly going to pay you less than I do my lady's maid."

Akezze nodded. It seemed all the contract they needed. "Shall I bring the copyists over at three? Will you have supplies enough or should we bring our own?"

CHAPTER ELEVEN

Jeanne

Surely it was not possible for Beethoven to sound as deadly tedious as this singer made his music seem. Where had Mesnera Arulik found him? The earlier tenor had been the same. She'd heard more engaging performances from street urchins in the Plaiz. The entire season had been remarkably flat, but one couldn't sit at home endlessly staring out the window. Jeanne raised her fan to hide a yawn.

Count Chanturi caught her movement and leaned closely to whisper, "You need a new lover." His dark eyes glinted with amusement below arching brows that had broken many a heart when they both had been young. From any other man the comment would have gone far beyond permission, but Rikerd was scarcely offering himself; they both knew that.

Jeanne snapped the fan shut and rapped him on the knuckles just for form's sake. "What I need is a new tenor."

He dropped his voice even softer. "What you need is a new soprano. Confess," he continued. "You've been as dull as lead all autumn. When will we see our de Cherdillac sparkle again? You always sparkle when you're in love. Will you be going to the ball the ambassador is holding in Efriturik's honor? It's sure to be teeming with sweet young things."

Jeanne sighed. "The sweet young things they're dangling in front of the young Atilliet will be well guarded against the likes of me. Give them a few years to grow tired of married life. Then I can see which ones are inclined for my little games."

"Like Mesnera Perzin?"

"Oh *la*, no! Tio isn't tired of marriage, only of propriety. In our day, she would have been a revolutionary only to make people stare. But yes, I'll be attending the ball, a demure widow, chatting with the *vizeinos*." She fluttered her fan coyly to belie the description. "Everyone will be there and I've been remiss at keeping my hand in."

It was true, all true. She *had* been letting her distraction show. If it started being whispered that de Cherdillac had grown tedious and dull, the invitations would decline. Hostesses would find someone else to advise and assist them. Perhaps it *was* time to look around for a new flirtation. That would put the world right side up again.

* * *

The second snowfall of the year had stayed, building little drifts against stone walls and laying a blanket over gardens and parks. Jeanne turned up the collar of her pelisse more firmly, anticipating the chill when she stepped out the door, as Marien went down to the corner, where there was always sure to be at least one fiacre waiting for fares. The driver recognized her. Handing her up the step he asked, "Where shall it be today, Mesnera?"

"Charner's library." On impulse she added, "And if you don't mind waiting, take me to Trez Cherfis after that." That was the thing to lift the tedium. She wanted to see how Antuniet's work was coming along. And she was worried. On the last few visits, Antuniet had been distracted and drawn-looking. She was impatient with the work—that was clear—but it was more than that.

If it hadn't been for the smoke rising from the chimney in quantities indicating a firing, Jeanne might have thought they were gone for the day. The windows were all shuttered tightly and her knock went unanswered for long minutes. At a second knock, Antuniet's voice called out sharply, "Who's there?"

"It's Jeanne. Do let me in; it's freezing out here."

The door cracked open enough to let her enter, then while Marien was helping her out of her coat and bonnet, Antuniet refastened a set of elaborate locks. Her face was pale and the shadows under her eyes looked near to bruises.

Jeanne threw propriety aside and took Antuniet's face in her hands and turned it toward the light. "Toneke, what's wrong? You look awful. Do you mean to work yourself to death? Why all the locks?"

She shook her head and backed away. "It's for them. They're waiting out there, watching. They're always watching." She turned and started back toward the workroom.

Jeanne stopped her with a hand on the arm. "Who?"

This time she didn't flinch at the contact. "My enemies. They want to steal my work. They follow me everywhere now."

With too many questions on her lips to even begin, Jeanne followed Antuniet into the back room, where Anna was tending bellows and coal tongs to keep the fire at just the right heat. She glanced up briefly, then returned to her task. Between the unnatural dark and the furnace's glow Jeanne could imagine herself plunged into the tale of Faustus. Antuniet had returned to the equipment and was adjusting vessels and tubes that fed through the head of the furnace.

Jeanne wandered idly about the room, poking carefully at the various materials laid out on the bench. Enough time passed in silence that it seemed impossible that the work required so much uninterrupted concentration, but at last Antuniet straightened up and wiped the sweat from her brow and offered what was clearly meant to be a smile.

"There, that will do for now. I'm so close. Another three or four days, I think." She paused a moment to check on Anna's work and said a few words of quiet encouragement. "The ceration shouldn't take more than a few more hours and then it can be left for the congelation to proceed on its own. Let me know if you grow tired."

"I won't be tired, Maisetra," Anna responded, not looking up from the furnace.

This time the smile was genuine, though the apprentice couldn't see it. Antuniet untied her work apron and washed her hands at the basin then led the way back into the front room. "She's dedicated to the work, there's no question of that."

"Could we open the shutters?" Jeanne asked abruptly. "It's like a tomb in here."

Antuniet shook her head and the smile faded again. "They come in that way. It's too much work to go around and undo the locks every day."

"You've had thieves in here? Why didn't you...Antuniet, this is madness. Why didn't you ask for help?"

"Ask whom?"

Jeanne could only guess at what lay behind that bleak question. "I don't know. Ask the city guard?"

"And have them poking around in all my things? They'd only tell me to lay a charge if I have a name. Even if I had a name to give them, I can't prove anything on him."

"Then what about your patron, Monterrez?" She knew better than to suggest Barbara again.

Antuniet looked over her shoulder toward the workroom and lowered her voice. "I can't ask him to put himself forward. You know what a delicate position he'd be in. It's too dangerous."

"But surely there's someone—an old family friend?—someone who would take up your cause."

"If there were, where were they the night my mother died? Where were they when our house was seized and I was left on the street with nothing but two traveling trunks?"

The bitterness hung heavy between them. Jeanne tried to remember those days after Estefen's execution. She'd barely known Antuniet then; now she wished she could go back and take her in. "What about me?" she asked. The question left her feeling exposed, and she waited for a rebuff.

Antuniet stared at her. "And what could you do? Can you hire guards to stand watch at all my doors night and day? Can you secure me royal protection? Can you have my enemies banished?"

"At least let me take you around the corner for some food and daylight," Jeanne said, a sense of practicality returning. "This can't be good for you." The gloom was beginning to make her share Antuniet's fears. It bred strange noises in the dark. She could see Marien waiting in a chair by the door, looking nervously about, infected by the mood.

"No, I don't want to leave Anna alone." Antuniet's mouth twisted in wry apology. "I'm not much of a hostess today, am I? I couldn't spare you as much as an hour even if it were safe to leave. One more week and it may be better."

"And then what?" Jeanne felt her imagination caught up in the hints and mysteries.

"Then…" Antuniet hesitated for long moments. "Then, God willing, I'll have enough of a gift to offer to Princess Annek to ask for her protection. Something real and solid as an earnest of my work, if my enemies haven't poisoned her against me or stolen it."

"Stolen what?" From anyone else, Jeanne would have thought it all mad raving. But not from Antuniet, not the Antuniet she'd come to know.

"Would you—" Antuniet hesitated as if fearing refusal. "Would you be willing to keep something for me? Just for a week? Just until I'm ready?"

Jeanne nodded. "Anything you ask." Antuniet motioned her to wait and disappeared briskly down the corridor. She returned long minutes later with a small purse. Jeanne felt it pressed into her hand.

"Just until I ask for it. I don't want to risk losing all my labor. I don't think they're looking for this in particular, but better to put it out of their reach."

Jeanne could feel the contents through the rough cloth; a handful of gravel it might have been, but she could guess its true nature. "Just until you come to fetch it," she assured her.

And then there seemed nothing else to say. No sharing a pot of tea, no quizzing Anna on her studies, none of the amusements she had come to enjoy on her past visits. None of that seemed important. There were worse fates than a dull season.

When the door closed behind them and Jeanne heard the bolt sent home, Marien asked plaintively, "Mesnera, is it safe for you to keep coming here?"

Jeanne looked down the street, noticing a man who seemed to be taking a deep interest in Antuniet's visitors. "Of course it's safe." But she went in the opposite direction to hail a passing carriage.

* * *

In the privacy of her dressing room, Jeanne opened the purse and spilled the contents out into a tray. The stones were mostly rough and dull with flecks of darker matrix embedded where the surface was irregular. Several had been polished to show the varied colors inside and a few glowed green even in the pale winter sun. Three had been shaped more carefully but only one had been set into a plain gold band. She picked it up and held it before the lamp's flame, momentarily losing herself in the translucent red of the stone. Impulsively, she slipped it onto a finger, then shifted it to another where it fit better. The carnelian felt almost warm against her skin. Instead of the standard cabochon, it was a more of a double-lens shape, curved underneath to press closely against her finger. *I'll wear it just to keep her in my mind and prayers*, Jeanne thought as she scooped the other gems back into the purse and locked it away in her jewel case.

She dreamed that night, unsettled by the haunted look in Antuniet's eyes and the gloom pervading the workshop. Faceless shadows pursued her and a cold voice demanded endlessly, *Where is it hidden?* She woke suddenly once, in the small hours of the night, surprised to find herself whimpering. A soft voice called out from the dressing room where Marien slept, "Mesnera, are you well? Do you need something?"

"Only a nightmare," she answered. "Go back to sleep."

* * *

The flavor of society in Rotenek had shifted in the past year. It had been more than a generation since the marriage market had encompassed a member of the house of Atilliet. Annek's own match had been a hurried diplomatic bargain, years before an ordinary girl would have been out. Her brothers had been swept up in the French wars with no time for idle entertainments before their deaths at Tarnzais. Then for the last twenty years Princess Elisebet had been the center of court life and all the gossip and intrigues had centered around her set and her favorites and their interests. That was a field of play that Jeanne knew well. But now all eyes—and many hopes—were on Efriturik. And if his circle of boisterous young men were not exactly the leaders of fashion, they must be accommodated and courted if one's entertainments were to be a success.

As Jeanne watched the currents of people flow through the ballroom, she contemplated what place she could make for herself in this new round of the game. The politics were beyond her reach and outside her concern. It was clear the Austrian ambassador had instructions to make sure of Efriturik's interest for the hope of future influence. That was only to be expected. Efriturik himself was harder to read. Jeanne's thoughts turned to what pleasures he might be enticed by that her friends were able to provide. Drunken revelry and loose women were out of the question but sport…

Recalling the soft fall of snow on the brief ride earlier, a vision came to her. A skating party. Scope for young men to exert themselves and display their skills. An opportunity for them to guide the young women in more sedate exercise. The same informality as a hunting party without the need for travel. But where to hold it? One couldn't depend on the Rotein freezing hard enough; that had only happened five times in her memory. But a shallow pond on one of the properties at the northern edge of the city? They were sure to freeze by sometime in January. Now who might benefit from the suggestion?

Jeanne cast her eyes over the assembled company and made her way over to a woman standing slightly apart for the moment. "Maisetra Saltez! How is dear Chazerin doing? I haven't managed to spot her yet."

"Vicomtesse," she murmured. "Very well, thank you. There she is, in the pale gold."

Jeanne followed her gaze and said all that was proper. The girl was only in her first dancing season, so her parents might host ordinary parties but not yet a formal ball. And she was scarcely a contender for Efriturik's attention. Jeanne knew better than to dabble in serious matchmaking. But she could peddle dreams and fancies. "What a pity you haven't managed to lure the young Atilliet to any entertainments yet. Wasn't your son one of his guests at Feniz?"

"Oh yes, but only through young Peskil. It won't be enough of a connection to allow an invitation after the New Year's court." She lowered her voice in the way one did when sharing a secret that everyone knew. "They say Her Grace will be granting him a title at last. He'll be above our touch then."

It was just that complication of the social rules that Jeanne was depending on. "But what if you invited him now? Before the court?"

"Don't be absurd!" Maisetra Saltez laughed. "There's no room to squeeze in so much as a luncheon before then, and we could hardly ask him too particularly. It would need to be a sizable affair."

"I had in mind a skating party. To be held whenever your little lake freezes. But that's the beauty of it, you see. Because of the uncertainty, you send the invitations now. The season is always a little slow late in January."

She saw her eyes light up. "What a clever idea!"

"And you could set up a pavilion for the refreshments with little braziers for keeping warm." Jeanne smiled as Saltez nodded eagerly. It seemed she hadn't lost her touch after all. "Let me know if you need any advice on the planning, though I'm sure you'll have it all in hand."

With a flourish of her fan and a nod she moved on. Now who else might benefit from a word and a little push? She felt a twinge of guilt at spending her talents in frivolity when she could think of no way to apply that influence to help Antuniet. But the world turned and one must turn with it.

She spotted Margerit Sovitre lingering at the edge of the ballroom floor watching the dancers with a wistful look, and followed her gaze to see Barbara leading a set with one of the Pelniks. She drifted over as if by chance and whispered, "Someday we should hold a private little ball where we can all dance together without comment." She saw Margerit blush as intended but the idea unexpectedly took hold in her mind. "We should! What are your plans for floodtide?"

"I…I couldn't say," Margerit answered. "We rarely go far because of the university, but I'm not planning to follow lectures in the Easter term. We were thinking of spending it in Chalanz this time."

"But that would be perfect!" Jeanne urged. "It would be lovely to take a company there. It's been ages since I saw it. Only give that dragon of yours a holiday. I doubt she'd approve."

"Dragon? Oh, you mean my Aunt Bertrut. No, I suppose she wouldn't be comfortable with the house overrun by your set. But they always spend floodtide with the Pertineks, so you needn't worry."

Jeanne noted that the plan had shifted from *I couldn't say* to *You needn't worry*. That was enough for now. She would have moved on, but one of the foreign guests was approaching with the look of someone desiring an introduction. She wracked her memory. His narrow, fox-like face looked slightly familiar but the name failed her. Margerit seemed to recognize him, though the look that crossed her face wasn't entirely welcoming.

He bowed slightly to Margerit, murmuring, "Maisetra Sovitre!" and briefly taking her fingertips in salute.

With an almost apologetic glance, Margerit turned to her, saying, "Jeanne, have you met Mesner Kreiser? He's some sort of aide to the Austrian ambassador, I think. Mesner Kreiser, Jeanne, Vicomtesse de Cherdillac."

He bowed again. "An imperial emissary, more precisely. I've been hoping to meet you."

Jeanne hid her surprise by exaggerating it. "Me? Oh la! I can't imagine what interest you would have. My only claim to fame is the success of my little parties, and it's clear you need no help on that score." She gestured around at the company with her fan.

His expression reminded her of a skilled card player considering which suit to lead. "My interest is in one of your friends. I understand you've been making regular visits to that unfortunate Chazillen woman."

Jeanne would have been put on guard even without the frantic look Margerit gave her from out of his line of sight. Was this the man Antuniet feared? "Good heavens, have our stale scandals risen to the level of diplomatic attention?"

He made a dismissive gesture. "It's a minor matter. We have no interest in whatever it was that drove her out of Alpennia, only what she may have brought back with her. You will forgive me if she is, indeed, a friend of yours, but we believe her to have taken something the emperor considers to be his."

Then she *is* being shadowed, Jeanne thought. She allowed only a patient curiosity to show and made no response.

"I don't suppose she's given you something to hold for her. A book, perhaps?"

Jeanne saw Margerit's face turn pale and snapped her fan open to keep the man's eyes on herself. Feed him a crumb to distract him, she thought. "A book? Mercy no, only some jewel—jewelry. The merest trinkets, really, hardly worth melting down for the value." The gems themselves might be too close to his interest. She frantically invented a plausible trail to throw him off. "I suppose her good pieces were all sold long ago, but she asked me to see if I could find a buyer for these. It's a sad thing when a woman is reduced to selling her last brooch and ring." She was suddenly aware of the band with the carnelian displayed on her finger. Would he recognize it as one of Antuniet's creations? Too late to conceal it now without drawing more attention. "If I'd known how many visits it would take to settle the matter I would have refused. My maid quakes in her shoes every time we go down there. She thinks alchemy is only a step from summoning demons! But Maisetra Chazillen asked and I agreed out of pity and so I must see it through." She was too accustomed to social lies to feel more than a twinge of guilt. And the guilt was for maligning the friendship, not for the falsehood.

Margerit had yet to compose herself fully. Really, she must learn a little acting! Jeanne reached her hand out to Kreiser and said, "If you want to know all the Rotenek gossip, I demand a dance in exchange. Will you oblige me?"

There was nothing he could do except smile and accept.

CHAPTER TWELVE

Barbara

The stone bench down at the bottom of the garden by the small private dock had long been Barbara's favorite spot to contemplate problems. But on a day like this, sharp and cold with the clouds alternately threatening snow or rain, she settled instead for staring down at the scene from the shelter of the back parlor. The library would have been too comfortable for the topic that gnawed at her and she hated to disturb Margerit's work with her pacing. Her steps tapped on the polished floor as she turned on her heel once again. It was one thing, Barbara thought, to see a runaway horse galloping down a crowded street and another thing entirely to be in the right place with the strength and skill to stop it.

So Antuniet's book belonged to Emperor Franz. Or at least he claimed it did. Or at least *Kreiser* claimed it did. Was Kreiser's position at Annek's court entirely a blind to pursue the book? Had he learned of it only after being posted in Rotenek? Or was something more complicated than that in play? If it were truly a simple question of theft, the matter would have been settled long ago. At least it explained whose men had been playing cat and mouse with her own hired shadows in the streets around Antuniet's workshop. But why hadn't Kreiser simply demanded that Annek take action to retrieve his master's property? Barbara had seen enough of the book's contents to guess the answer to that. If it were more than the scribblings of a charlatan, it was a valuable tool indeed, in skilled hands. Too valuable to risk being brought to the attention of a rival. Not that Alpennia was in any way a rival to Austria, but on such small turns of cards lay the fate of empires. Antuniet's interest could rule out the possibility that the book's author had been a fraud. So many alchemy texts were nothing but empty boasting and clever allegories, but she was no fool to be taken in.

Antuniet—now there was the problem. The runaway horse was barreling down on her full speed with little room to dodge away. Or—to change images—she thought to draw off the pursuing wolves by throwing the bait in Margerit's direction. There might be no malice behind it at all, only desperation, but the danger might be just as real if they weren't careful. Her concern was the danger to Margerit, of course; Antuniet had brought her troubles on herself.

But even if she wanted to move on her cousin's behalf, what could be done? Very little indeed unless Antuniet wanted her help. And if she wanted it, why hadn't she asked? The city guard…There was nothing they could do unless Kreiser's men acted first. The palace had more latitude, but they would do nothing unless it touched directly on the House of Atilliet. It was no small matter to interfere with an embassy.

Yes, what could be done? If it weren't that Margerit had asked, she'd be content to watch and wait. But Margerit had asked and so at least she would talk to Antuniet. She could take the carriage down to Trez Cherfis and be back long before dinner. It was too cold and wet to make the prospect enticing. A gust whistled past outside and rattled the windows, briefly obscuring her view of the river with a flood of rain against the panes.

The sound muffled a distant pounding on the door. The pounding only impinged on her attention when it was answered with a burst of shouting voices. Old instincts were stronger than new ones and Barbara hitched up her skirts and met the footman running to fetch her before he'd gone three steps.

"What is it?" she barked at the chaos in the entry hall. Ponivin had arrived at the same moment she had, but the butler—exchanging quick glances with her—deferred to her command. Bertrut was near to hysterics in the doorway from the front parlor. The servants were alternating between outrage and terror. The new arrivals were two of her hired shadows, dripping rain all over the carpets and laying down a large burden that looked terrifyingly like a body. "Report!" Barbara barked again, this time directed at them. Behind her, Barbara could hear Margerit gasping in fear.

"They broke into the workshop—staged a carriage accident to cover the noise and came in through the back, I think. We didn't know until we heard the screaming."

"Antuniet!" Margerit cried and dodged around Barbara to kneel by the motionless bundle and peel back the cloak wrapped around the bloodied figure. But the face revealed was younger and unfamiliar.

"The apprentice girl," he continued. "There was also a serving man. He's dead. We saw no sign of Maisetra Chazillen. Either they carried her off or she wasn't there." He looked guiltily at his fellow. "I never saw her leave but there was some time—"

Barbara cut him off and joined Margerit at the girl's side long enough to determine that the need was for a surgeon, not an undertaker. "Send for Muller. No, not you." She turned and pointed at the man she most trusted for the job. "You, quick as you can. And Iannik," she continued, turning to the waiting shadows, "back to your post and find Maisetra Chazillen. Call in anyone else you need. I want her found and I want her safe."

She turned her attention back to the girl. "Any bones broken?" she asked to the air, then shrugged. "Well, we can't do any more damage getting her someplace warm than has already been done." She stepped back and let Ponivin direct several of the footmen to lift her gently, using the cloak as a litter, and carry her into the back parlor that had been filled with contemplation only moments before.

* * *

For an hour, the household was a stirred-up anthill. *Was it like this the time I was attacked?* Barbara wondered. It had been pouring rain that night too when she was ambushed in pursuit of her father's debts—not her true father, but the man she had then believed to have sired her. She remembered far more of the sword fight on the bridge than its aftermath. Now only the scar remained. She rubbed her fingers absently over the mark on her forehead, just hidden under her hair. She had been a less cooperative patient than Antuniet's apprentice was.

Anna—it was a good sign that, when she roused briefly, she had been able to tell them her name—lay quietly under Muller's no-nonsense ministrations. He'd been an army surgeon in the French wars and had an excellent reputation among the armins, but he made no allowances for a young girl's delicacy and modesty. There were bruises and possibly a cracked skull, though he thought it unlikely. Worst of all, a long deep cut, deliberately sliced across one cheek. In her lucid moments, her first words had been, "I didn't tell them, Maisetra. I didn't tell them anything." Barbara tamped down her rage at hearing that. Someone would pay.

Margerit had stayed by the girl's side through it all, even holding her hands tightly while Muller took tiny, even stitches through the wound until the girl surrendered to a swoon. Margerit herself looked pale enough to faint as well. Through the haze of memory, Barbara remembered Margerit holding her own hand through the surgeon's ministrations and declined to send her away.

The afternoon had passed and it was growing dark before Muller left to let them wash the girl gently and dress her in one of Margerit's own shifts and make her more comfortable on a cot brought down from one of the servants' rooms. Mesner Pertinek had come by to say that his cousin had sent over a woman who was skilled at sick-nursing and they were welcome to keep her as long as needed, which told Barbara that the uproar would soon be known all up and down the Vezenaf.

That uproar was now muted but continued on. Hard on Pertinek's heels came Ponivin with the message that a Jewish gentleman named Monterrez was at the door asking for Baroness Saveze and that he would not be put off. After a brief moment's confusion, Barbara looked more closely at the sleeping girl, and light dawned. She hurried to the entryway, now cleaned of all traces of the chaotic invasion. The bleak expression on the man's face confirmed her guess.

"Mesnera—" He faltered and started again. "Mesnera, they tell me my daughter was brought here…"

"She lives," Barbara assured him quickly. "She lives and, God willing, will continue to do so."

His face crumpled and he buried it in his hands, murmuring something she could not follow but could easily guess at.

"Come," Barbara said softly and led him back to where the girl lay. In a few brief sentences she explained what she knew and some of what she guessed about what had happened.

He knelt beside his daughter and took her hand, murmuring, "My poor child, my precious girl." The bandages obscured the worst of the damage for now. At last he looked up in confusion, asking, "But how do you come into this, Mesnera? Why was she brought here?"

Barbara wondered how much he'd known of Antuniet's doings. "Maisetra Chazillen is my cousin," she began.

"Yes, I know," he said. "And I have guessed you were not close, seeing that she looked elsewhere for a patron. Then why should you come into the matter at all?"

She glanced over at Margerit, warning her to keep some matters yet secret. "I had men set to watch her. Maisetra Chazillen sought to draw us into her intrigues and I wanted to know what those intrigues were. I feel some responsibility here—" she gestured down at the girl "—because I knew there was danger and I hadn't thought that it might fall on the innocent."

"You know who did this?" he asked urgently.

Barbara shook her head. "Only the man behind them. I'll pursue the matter. I can't promise you justice, but I'll do what I can. The bullies who attacked are nothing and easily dealt with, but their leader may be difficult to touch. Leave him to me."

He sighed and folded in on himself a little. "I would like to take my daughter home. When can it be arranged?"

Margerit made a gesture of protest. "She shouldn't be moved, not for some days yet. The surgeon will be back tomorrow and we have an excellent sick-nurse and—"

"My people have physicians too," he said, raising his head stiffly.

"Of course," Margerit answered in some confusion.

"And there is the matter," Barbara added, "of her safety. If Antuniet's enemies still think she knows something…" She let the implications sink in and saw the bleak look return to his face. "Better to wait a week or two and see what falls out."

And then there were further interruptions. with a maid coming in to tend to the fire and Bertrut asking whether the cook should wait dinner and another question from the cook as to what she should prepare for the invalid.

Monterrez answered the last, unexpectedly. "I will send one of my elder daughters to care for her and bring her food. You needn't trouble yourself over that."

Margerit began to protest that it was no trouble, but Barbara countered, "An excellent idea. Margerit, she's his daughter; he has the right to see to her care." She called out into the hall for the footman on duty there. "Have the town carriage brought out and tell the coachman he's needed." When the footman poked his head in to be sure of his instructions, she added, "Maistir Monterrez will be using it for the evening. See that he has every assistance."

* * *

It was another hour before the searchers came back to report, quietly slipping in through the side entrance this time and insisting that word be sent up directly to the dining room. Barbara excused herself and hurried to meet them, Margerit trailing after anxiously.

"We searched the whole quarter with no sign of her," came the report. "The others were out there looking too, so I doubt she's been taken. Either she's deep in hiding or she's fled the city. What do you want us to do?"

Barbara frowned in thought. "Tell the men to keep their old schedule. If she turns up it will likely be at the workshop. And get names, if you can, of the other watchers. We may have enough to take to the city guard, and if not there are other means." And she sent them away, leaving the puzzle: "But where could she be?"

"Jeanne might know," Margerit ventured.

"Jeanne?"

"Kreiser—he said she'd been visiting Antuniet. Jeanne had some story about being asked to sell some jewelry for her, but I didn't believe it. I don't know whether he did." And then, with sudden fear: "Do you think she's in danger too?"

"No, he wouldn't dare threaten anyone with standing. Not directly. But she might know something. Give my apologies to your aunt and uncle; I'm going out."

Barbara didn't care to wait for Monterrez to return with the carriage, so she sent word to saddle her horse and went off to change into riding clothes, bracing herself for a damp evening.

Jeanne was out, but her butler allowed himself to be coaxed into revealing that she was dining at the Penilluks'.

Barbara found their staff less sanguine about her sudden arrival. "Are you expected?"

"Oh good heavens, do you think I've come to invade their dinner party like this?" Barbara assured the footman at the door. "Please take word in to Vicomtesse de Cherdillac that I need to speak with her urgently, in private." And she was instantly tucked out of sight in the cold front parlor to wait.

Jeanne came in all haste, her eyes wide with concern. "Whatever brings you out like this?"

"Jeanne, I need you to answer as honestly as you can. Do you know where Antuniet is at this very moment?"

"Antuniet…?" For a moment it looked as if she might faint, and Barbara guided her to one of the chairs. "What's happened? What have they done?"

So. She knew something. "Her place was broken into. Her apprentice was attacked and badly hurt. Antuniet has disappeared. Do you have any idea where she might have gone?"

Barbara could see Jeanne's mind racing as she swallowed heavily and fidgeted with the rings on her fingers. "I don't know," Jeanne said at last. "There's nowhere, no one…if she'd had anyplace left…"

"Why didn't she come to me?" Barbara demanded. "Why didn't you?"

Jeanne managed a bleak smile. "Because she made me promise not to."

Barbara stifled an oath that had no place between ladies in a parlor. "I have men out searching for her, watching all the places I think she might show up. If you receive any word from her, any sign at all, tell me. Her enemy thinks she's alone and friendless—"

"And isn't she?" Jeanne interrupted.

"Only by her own choice. And she's dragged me into the mess unwillingly so she'll have to put up with my interference. Send me word the moment you hear anything."

Jeanne rose, her composure returning. "If she comes to me, I'll do as I think best for her safety." She offered her hand formally in dismissal, adding lightly, "You really are something of a bully, you know."

Barbara was taken aback and brought her fingertips to her lips in reflex. "Am I?"

She would have protested further, but there was truth enough to sting. Yet what was the point of pleasantries when action was needed? Too many lives had been damaged at this point by Antuniet's games.

CHAPTER THIRTEEN

Antuniet

She'd only stepped out of the workshop for a moment. Only a few steps down around the corner to see if the lime had come at the chemist's. And she'd checked, before slipping out the door, to see who was on the street or loitering at the edge of alleyways. For once, no one seemed to be watching. But that had been the mistake, of course. They hadn't been waiting for her to leave; they'd expected to find her there.

It seemed the chemist had taken shipment of a small collection of lodestone and wanted to know whether to set some aside for her. So it must be checked and tested and the price haggled over. And then, returning, the commotion in the street. She'd kept to the shadows, fearful of the crowd, and swung several blocks wide to slip in from the back.

That was when she saw the splintered door and heard—

Antuniet crammed her hands over her ears to keep the sound from ringing still in her mind. This was worse than Heidelberg; that only haunted her dreams, not her waking. She'd stood frozen, stabbed through by the screams. She didn't remember running. But now here she was, crouched in the shallow arch below the back stairs of the old brewery. Every footstep, every shouted voice meant pursuit. The rain muffled those warning sounds. She'd ventured out once and returned, shivering, with heart pounding, when a cart came out of nowhere, driving past the end of the alley. Night. She must wait for dark and then…where?

She should go to Monterrez and tell him…tell him what? She didn't even know. She quailed at the prospect. Cowardice burned like acid in her belly and she shook in a sudden spasm. She should have been cold, but she only felt numb. At some point in her flight the rain had soaked her coat clear through and the stones where she huddled were icy, but the narrow alley gave some protection from the wind. Was the sky growing darker? How slowly time passed!

Where should she go? Where would be safe? To Jeanne? Jeanne had said *Anything you ask*. Antuniet could almost hear her light laughter and feel the way her presence banished all that was dark and uncertain. But Jeanne had also said that her name couldn't bear the weight of being tied to an alchemist. And how much more of a danger would it be with this new trouble? No, she couldn't bring all this down on the head of the one person in Rotenek who had been kind to her, the closest she'd ever had to a true friend. Was it time at last to go crawling to Barbara and beg her protection on the slender thread of kinship? Her body spasmed again, as if to reject the very thought. And yet...

No doubt Barbara would relish a chance to play the grand lady over her. The old baron had delighted in flaunting the power of his purse over less fortunate relatives. She'd never danced to his tune herself; it was better not to want what he had to give. But she'd watched Estefen engage in endless battles to claim some small piece of his expected legacy. Estefen had been a fool. With each skirmish he thought he'd won, he'd only dug his own grave a little deeper. No, she would beg nothing from Saveze. Nothing except the return of her property. Whatever else she did, she must venture to Tiporsel House to reclaim the book. But perhaps she could offer something in exchange: the chance to be rid of her and the scandal that couldn't help but spread like ripples from this disaster. Safe passage to her next refuge? The money was all gone but she could still work. Paris, perhaps? England might be better still. She knew little of the language and the rules of society there, but she'd heard stories enough to think that an aristocratic foreigner who dabbled in the esoteric might be able to play out enough of a charade to get by. Her imagination spun off scenes of possibilities.

* * *

She couldn't have slept. How could it be possible? And yet when she came back to herself again it was dark. Tiporsel House, yes, and then a way out of the city. Her mind set forth but her body was slow to respond. Would it be better to wait a few hours? She was so tired, and the cobblestones under the arch were strangely comfortable. But the rain had stopped and there might be no better time. It took three tries to find her feet and then she leaned against the side of the stairs until she trusted her legs to hold her.

Tiporsel House. That meant crossing Pont Ruip if she didn't mean to go well out of her way. If they were watching for her the approach to the river would carry the most hazard. *Think*. How far would it be if she went up to the East Gate and doubled back? A couple hours' brisk walk in fine daylight, but now? She wasn't sure she could make it that far. So tired.

It took twice as long to get to the river when keeping off the larger streets. When she reached the small square at the south end of the bridge she hung back in the shadows, watching the drifts of passersby as they hurried on their way, no doubt hoping to reach their goal before the rain started again. A lone chestnut seller had set up his cart at the foot of the bridge and was crying out his wares in counterpoint to the splash and calls of the rivermen passing below. It looked so ordinary. The foot traffic was mostly coming south, people returning home from the shops and day-work serving the better part of town. There were fewer groups walking north for her to hide among—lone stragglers and the occasional carriage. It would only get worse the longer she waited.

Three students, slightly the worse for drink, passed by the corner where she lurked and Antuniet took her chance. Not so close that they would notice her presence; not so far back that she wouldn't seem part of the group. She staggered a little from the stiffness in her legs, adding to the illusion. But she hadn't wasted the weeks sharpening her vision for any hint of her watchers. A man, there, buying chestnuts. His head came up in her direction and he moved purposefully. No point in bluffing it out now. Antuniet turned to the left and hurried around the bridge embankment and down the sloping steps to the waterside. Please, God, let there be a waiting boat! The river would take her the wrong direction, but with luck she could lose her pursuers in crossing to the other side.

She brushed past three chattering women who were ascending the path and tumbled into the waiting craft. "Downriver. As quick as you can," she tried to say, but the words came indistinctly and muffled through violent shivers. "Go! Go!" she managed at last, hearing shrill protests behind her as someone else pushed the group of women aside.

The riverman gave her a hard look but shoved off, muttering, "You'd better have more coin than it looks." They were out in the middle of the slow current when he asked impatiently, "Where to?"

Antuniet tried to think. Downstream there'd be more chance of shaking off pursuit, but farther to return. Upstream and they'd make such slow time that her enemies could pace them on foot and wait at every landing. She could never convince the man to leave her at the Tiporsel dock. It was worth his license to touch the private landings without a commission.

"Well?"

"T—t—take…" Her mouth refused to form the words. The riverman was peering at her strangely. He must have dropped the oars, for the craft was spinning around in the tide. Or was it only her head? Now he was staring down at her. She felt a hand touch her face then jerk back with an oath. Then the sound of the oars, working furiously. Had she told him where to go? She must have. Perhaps she could risk closing her eyes for just a little while. She was so tired.

She roused only briefly when the boat stopped and she felt strong hands lift her up. Had they found her? As if from a great distance, she heard the riverman's voice. "Didn't know where else to bring her. She'd no sooner stepped in than she swooned in a heap. Didn't even have a chance to give me direction. Don't know who she is. Or what."

And in response a man's voice. "That doesn't matter, we'll see to her."

"Is it…I remember last time, when it seemed the whole city was sick. Is it that again? That's why I didn't just leave her on the next landing."

"That and for the sake of charity, I would hope. And God bless you for that. No, I don't see the signs of river fever."

Who could they be speaking of? Antuniet wondered. But it mattered very little. Her mind drifted away again for a long time.

CHAPTER FOURTEEN

Margerit

The morning Anna was to return home—when Barbara had deemed it safe—Margerit succumbed to her request and brought a mirror. She expected tears, watching Anna crane her head this way and that to view the healing scar. Her dark eyes kept their secrets and she handed the mirror back, saying only, "Thank you. I needed to know." She wouldn't likely have grown into a beauty; her mouth was too wide and her nose too strong for that. But now who would look past the angry red cord that traced from the corner of her eye down across her cheek and almost to the line of her jaw? Margerit bit her lip to keep from offering cruel sympathy. Once or twice she had cracked through the girl's shy reserve, but it seemed unlikely there would be a chance for more. At the last, when Anna and her sister Iudiz had been handed up into Barbara's carriage for the ride across town, Anna pleaded, "If you hear anything—anything at all—about Maisetra Chazillen, send me word? I don't know that my father will tell me."

"Of course," Margerit assured her, stepping back as the horses were given office to move.

There had been no word, not the slightest trace of Antuniet or clue to her whereabouts. Barbara continued to keep a few watchers in the places where Antuniet might return. And those watchers noted other watchers as well, though never with enough certainty to act. Margerit counted that a source of hope, that Kreiser was still searching too. Barbara was of the opinion that Antuniet had fled the country completely, but Margerit couldn't stop thinking of the book that still lay hidden on the library shelf. Would Antuniet truly have left behind the object of all this intrigue? All this tragedy?

Every day, Margerit prayed for Antuniet's safety. Ordinary prayers. She had searched for a mystery that would apply to the case but found only one for the safety of a fugitive that had requirements she couldn't meet. And she wasn't the only one praying. Drawing up the analysis and notes from the Advent mysteries took her back to the cathedral for several hours on most days and twice she had chanced upon Jeanne there, kneeling with beads in her hands, her lips moving silently and the traces of tears on her cheeks. And once, when they met in their comings and goings, Jeanne asked searchingly, "Any word?" Margerit could only shake her head.

* * *

They called it the New Year's Court but it was the secular echo of Epiphany, closing the celebrations of Christmastide. The previous time when Margerit had attended—trailing in Barbara's wake, staring at the splendors like some country cousin—she had been oblivious to most of the undercurrents. This time she swam in those currents. It was a season for gifts, and the gifts that Annek had had the power to give carried more meaning than their value: rewards for loyalty, first steps toward new alliances, statements best made tacitly. Margerit would have been glad enough to remain only an observer, but that was denied her. No sooner had she delivered the last of the commentary on the Advent mysteries than another summons followed, and Margerit found herself ushered into the chamber Her Grace used for informal business.

"I need a small ceremony," the princess said briskly with no preamble. "Perhaps I should have given you more notice, but I'd thought there might already be some traditional form that would do." She looked up from the correspondence before her and gestured for her to sit. Annek's dark eyes were bright with pleasure today; the shadows around them seemed only ordinary weariness and not her usual brooding watchfulness.

Margerit perched on the edge of the damask-upholstered chair and waited for further instructions as the princess's secretary exchanged one set of correspondence for another in the array before her.

"Not a mystery, as such," she continued. "But I want it to have some of the flavor of one and it seemed to me that might fall within your talents."

"I'll do my best," Margerit ventured, since some sort of response seemed called for.

"I suppose you've heard that my son will be named Baron Razik at the New Year."

Margerit nodded. The information had meant little to her except as an opportunity for Uncle Charul to expound on the intricacies of title and inheritance. The passing of Ambors Atilliet—not unexpected given his age—had solved a conundrum. His title returned to the crown, not to his heirs, being held only for his lifetime and granted by tradition to the offspring of a reigning prince. Ambors had received it from his grandfather as a boy and now it would pass in turn to Annek's son, giving him standing and a household of his own, both key assets in the path planned out for him.

Efriturik should have been enrolled with a title of his own a year past when he came of age, but there had been no crown titles to hand. The princess had waited, hesitant to spend the capital of independent title-lands for what might seem self-serving purposes. Margerit drew her mind back to the matter at hand. "You would like…a ceremony? For the enrollment?"

"Exactly. A bit of pageantry, if you will, to make it clear this is not simply a routine grant but a matter of planting his roots in Alpennian soil. I want his taking of the title to mark his commitment to this land, no matter what the future may bring. And to that end, there are a few individuals to whom I would like you to give roles. Make whatever arrangements you need in my name." She slid a small sheet of paper across the desk.

Margerit took it up and glanced over the list. Her heart sank at one item there. "Mesnera, I may not be the best person to seek your cousin's assistance in this."

"And yet you are the person I have asked." Annek's voice was sharp with asperity. "Do you refuse the commission?"

"I'll do my best, Mesnera." Indeed, what else could she say? That she'd thought the appointment as thaumaturgist would mean more of scholarship and less of politics?

* * *

In some ways, the ceremony would have been easier to draft if it had been a true mystery. There were set forms and models; success would be proven when the saints granted the requested miracle. Barbara found time from her own affairs to make a few suggestions based on previous ceremonies she'd seen, but the approach Annek wanted was entirely new. It was tempting to design it as a mystery and then step back from what touched on the sacred but that felt too perilous. What if she succeeded too well? Efriturik's commitment was to be symbolic only. Who could tell the consequences if the ritual wove bonds that couldn't be broken? And not only on Efriturik's part. He had no special claim yet on the succession. She must take care to avoid even the appearance of binding the loyalties of those around him. It didn't matter that the ceremony would be held in the court hall and not a sacred space. The saints found their own way of working, if they chose.

So she used only the phrasing and cadences of more formal workings, leaving aside the trappings of prayer and candle or the use of names. Telfin Zuremin, a granddaughter of Ambors, would hand over the keys and stewardship of the title-lands of Razik to Princess Annek. She, in turn, would grant them to Efriturik and direct Lord Ehing to enroll the grant in his function as Chamberlain. That was the essence of the business. The additions must be worked in around that skeleton. Efriturik was to request…

not the title and lands themselves, as if it were a right, but a stake, a sense of homeland, an exchange for what he had relinquished in leaving behind his father's name. And the representatives of Alpennia's titled lords would not simply acknowledge and record the grant but would receive him into their company as a cousin and equal.

That was the part Margerit dreaded negotiating. It was not Princess Elisebet herself whose name had been on that list of participants, but young Aukustin, acting as Efriturik's kinsman, to make the petition. But it was Elisebet who must assent to his participation. And in the two years since the matter of Estefen Chazillen's trial and execution, Elisebet had avoided any public notice or acknowledgment of her existence. It had been an easy enough matter to pass over before. Elisebet could scarcely admit the grudge without admitting that Estefen had been her proxy.

Back then, Margerit had been content to be of no notice or importance in the court. Now she was no longer entirely nobody. The carefully worded note soliciting the favor of Princess Elisebet's time had not been answered yea or nay and Margerit dreaded having to beg Annek for a more tangible sign of her authority to complete the task. Every day she delayed it, hoping for a response, until there was no time left to take account of any changes Elisebet might demand. No time for anything but to instruct the participants on their roles.

The holiday season left the entire city simmering with activity. Only Annek's borrowed authority brought a hearing for her belated requests for appointments, and she had packed them into one long day. So the schedule looked to be thrown into ruin, when Marken of all people put a hurdle in her path. He'd known the outline of her plans, but on meeting her in the entryway while they waited for the carriage to be brought around, he balked. "I'd thought Maisetra Pertinek would be joining you."

"She's out visiting. This is all palace business so I didn't ask her." Aunt Bertrut would have come if she'd asked, of course, but why not spare her the trouble?

Back when Barbara had served her as armin, there had been a type of hesitant pause that had invariably signaled some bar she was not to cross—a quirk born out of a training that hadn't allowed for more direct refusal. Marken's moments of silence bore the same meaning, not from any reticence but for the time it took him to convert his instincts into words. Margerit connected the line from his question past his silently pursed lips and protested, "Surely I don't need a *vizeino* on Her Grace's business. You never suggested it before."

"Begging your pardon, Maisetra," he replied, in a tone that belied any expectation that pardon was needed, "but that was all in public. Guild meetings and dinners and whatnot. As long as you had the right to be there, no one can whisper about what happens under Princess Annek's nose. But going alone to a man's lodgings? That's more than my position's worth."

Not alone. You'd be there, she wanted to protest, except for a fragment of conversation that floated back from memory. *An armin would have counted as an escort? No, an armin would have gotten her out of there.* Marken's role was to prevent the possibility of scandal, not ameliorate it by his presence.

"If it were just Lord Ehing I wouldn't fuss," Marken offered. "Him being old enough to be your grandfather and his wife sure to be there. But the young Atilliet? No. I can't allow that."

Margerit realized there was more to it than her own good name. Efriturik's reputation was at stake too, for all that a man's was far less fragile. The thought nearly made her laugh. "But they've all gone out already! There's no one I could ask to come along." Even Barbara was away from home, though she might not have served for the purpose. "I suppose we could try to track down Aunt Bertrut. I've already made appointments for today."

Marken cleared his throat. "Mesner Pertinek might be a better choice. More...suitable. I know where he'll be."

And what might *that* mean, Margerit wondered as she waited in the carriage while Marken ventured into the back rooms at Uncle Charul's club on Peretrez. Because these were his people? Or because he would lend the image of a man's protection? As her uncle climbed into the seat beside her she said, "I'm so sorry to have interfered with your plans for the day."

"No trouble at all my dear," he replied. A smile crinkled the corners of his eyes. "It's been explained. I'm happy to be of use. Indeed, I sometimes wish—" He broke off as the carriage lurched in starting and didn't complete the thought as he settled back against the cushions.

But Margerit knew she could finish it. *I sometimes wish I could be useful more often.* And he was, in subtle ways, by lending that image of respectability. But it must needle him to be reminded how rarely it rose above the mere image.

Today she couldn't deny how much his presence smoothed her path. Mesnera Zuremin was greeted as an old friend, and Lord Ehing seemed far less likely to balk at her youth after Uncle Charul's introductions. When they sought out Efriturik at the palace, Margerit felt suddenly shy, as if the presence of a *vizeino* suggested the need for one. And Efriturik traded the practiced courtesy he had always shown her in public for a teasing banter that threw her off balance for a few moments. Uncle Charul had the wisdom to stay quiet and stand back—a matching bookend for Marken—as she struggled to maintain the dignity of her office and turn the talk to business. This was her task to master and Efriturik would hardly be the worst of those she would need to impress in time. She turned away to lay out the text and diagrams of the ceremony on a table. Confidence returned with the familiar motions.

When they emerged again into the maze of palace corridors, still decked with garlands of the season and teeming with unknown errands, Uncle Charul asked, "Is that the last of it?"

"No. That is, there's still Aukustin's part to deliver and explain but Princess Elisebet hasn't answered my requests for an appointment yet."

"Ah." And she heard in that *ah* an understanding of what lay behind it all. "As long as we're here, we might as well see if she's receiving visitors." He leaned close for a conspiratorial whisper. "If you assume that her response has gone astray, she can hardly contradict you by admitting that she's refusing to bow to Her Grace's request."

Now that was something she might not have had the nerve for by herself. "I was going to ask Barbara for help, but I think she would have suggested a more subtle and complicated approach."

He laughed. "She does love the intrigue for its own sake, I think. Shall we venture into the dragon's den?"

Elisebet was receiving and didn't deny them, though she looked as if she wished she dared. There was a long wait while those who had come before them chatted and revolved slowly from expectancy to notice to dismissal. But when Margerit came at last to the fore and began explaining the order of the ceremony, Elisebet put out her hand to take the notes, saying, "My son is suffering from a slight chill today; I won't have him disturbed at the moment."

Margerit hesitated. There had been no acquiescence, no promise to see the matter done. "I hope he'll be well recovered by the day. Perhaps I could return tomorrow to go through his lines with him."

"Aukustin knows well enough the ways of a court. He doesn't need your tutoring."

Again, the turning aside, but it was clear she'd get no further at the moment. Margerit could feel the eyes of the other guests on her. This was not the place to make a stand.

There was no need to linger for the sake of courtesy. When the door had been closed behind them, Uncle Charul offered, "That was as well done as it could be, I think."

Margerit sighed. "And yet I still have to hand the matter back to Her Grace incomplete. It was a test, you know," she confided.

"Of course it was, but for whom? For you or for her?" He nodded back toward Elisebet's apartments.

That hadn't occurred to her. "Perhaps—" She felt her way through the possibilities. "Perhaps I'll ask Barbara for advice after all."

* * *

Margerit was not entirely disappointed when Barbara volunteered to approach Elisebet the next day on her behalf. That evening over dinner, she reported some measure of success.

"I think I've convinced her—she had an idea that the intent was to bind Chustin's loyalty to his cousin."

"To bind...you mean as a mystery? But I explained all that at the start," Margerit protested.

Barbara glanced at Aunt Bertrut and Uncle Charul. It was only the four of them this once, but Barbara still seemed to be calculating the need for discretion. "I think you must forgive Elisebet for considering you to be Annek's creature. You are her thaumaturgist; how could Elisebet not expect deeper currents? She takes these things very seriously, you know."

"But she trusts you? Even knowing…" Out of courtesy for household harmony she left the rest unspoken.

"Not trust, but—" A hesitation. A moment of decision. "I think I told you she's come to me a few times before. She's concerned about Chustin's safety. There have been some odd events…" She shrugged. "The first time was that hunting trip. She may have asked me, thinking I could put on my old profession again. Or perhaps she had nowhere else to turn. She has friends at the court but no true allies any longer, not outside her own household. And even there, I think Mesnera Sain-Mazzi is the only one of her old guard who's still loyal." Sain-Mazzi had presided over the princess's household almost since the day of Elisebet's marriage to Prince Aukust. It would have been something indeed if she were to turn away.

"But she thinks you're loyal?" Margerit asked.

"I am," Barbara said fiercely. "To the Atilliets: to all and each of them. And just now, Elisebet needs me and Annek doesn't. But Elisebet doesn't deal in nuances; to help her is to be her partisan. Someday I will need to disabuse her of that, but for now it means she listens to me."

Margerit saw Uncle Charul hiding a look of amusement with a cough. *Intrigue for its own sake.* But she disagreed. Barbara had survived so long only by reading every hidden motive in the old baron's circles. To stop now would be like ceasing to breathe.

* * *

For all that her responsibilities were complete, Margerit experienced the New Year's Court only in briefly remembered glimpses between the confusion. The clothing—that was something to remember. The women's gowns were glorious, as always: from the stiff, archaic robes of those closest to the royal family to the daring fashions of the young matrons to the more modest confections of the unmarried girls. But even the men turned peacock tonight: the older ones in the satin knee breeches of a previous generation and gaudy military uniforms wherever one turned. On an occasion such as this, every man of noble birth carried a sword, whether he had pretensions to any skill or not. Though it was all for show at the moment, it was said that before dawn came there would be more duels fought—in person or by proxy—than on any other day of the year.

Barbara had claimed the privilege of an Eccentric and sported her own blade as an accent to a gown braided and buttoned like a Hussar's jacket. Though her aunt and uncle had chosen ordinary evening wear, Margerit had caught the spirit of the event and commissioned a creation evoking a scholar's robes in wine-colored stuff. Not the sort of silken confection affected by the fashionable girl-scholars for gossiping at lectures, but more elegant and dignified.

And then there were the ceremonies: the endless parade of gifts and presentations. Margerit could later recall the details only of the one that mattered. Efriturik took the matter with proper seriousness now, and young

Aukustin stumbled only once over his lines. Margerit let out a sigh of relief as Princess Annek proudly presented the new Baron Razik with the letters and signet that marked his rank.

Beyond that it was all confusion. Long waiting and chatting in the galleries, entirely too brief moments to snatch supper from the buffets laid out in the side rooms. And later, when all business was done, there was dancing for the young and more sedate entertainments for their elders and less mentionable delights for those who drifted away into the streets and across the Pont Vezzen to the south bank of the Rotein. Margerit tried to taste all of it as her path repeatedly crossed and parted from the rest of her party.

Only Marken was a constant presence through the evening, never close but never out of sight. It was odd how time had made her more, not less, aware of the armin's presence. It had become second nature to pause in doorways and walk more slowly at corners to give him time to follow. She had enough experience now to appreciate his purpose and methods. Barbara had always been much more...present. But that hadn't been the fault of her skill. And Barbara's career at her back had begun more dramatically. Now she was conscious of how much trouble and annoyance was quashed before it even began by the message Marken's presence carried.

Eventually Aunt Bertrut plucked Uncle Charul away to make an early evening of it, but Margerit lingered, tired though she was, until the dancing began to thin and Barbara suggested they make their best attempt to find their hostess for farewells and then be off before the streets became too rowdy. They had seen Annek moving through the corridors earlier, never settling for long but speaking with any who approached her, high or low. It took some searching to find her now. Finally Barbara caught the sound of her voice coming from an alcove at the end of the mirror gallery and they spotted the scattering of attendants standing by at their prescribed distances as if by chance.

They waited discreetly, hearing voices raised, but there was no mistaking Annek's response. "This is not the place to speak of such things, but since you've chosen it, you may tell your emperor I'm disinclined. When my son is of an age for it, his marriage will be for the good of Alpennia and to bind his loyalties here, not to tie him to his past."

Barbara turned with an eyebrow quirked and whispered, "Poor Efriturik! No sooner titled than they want to see him wed. No wonder he wants to sow his oats madly."

But the interview was at an end and Margerit was unsurprised to see Mesner Kreiser coming past them with a scowl. What *was* his mission at the embassy? As far as she could tell he seemed to be minister of long noses, poking into all manner of wasp nests. On seeing them, he composed himself abruptly and paused long enough to ask, "And have you found that lost thing you were searching for?" But he continued on without waiting for an answer.

They went farther on then, curtseying and approaching when noticed and exchanging all the pleasant nothings one did on such occasions.

"It went well, don't you think? The ceremony?" Annek asked.

Margerit nodded but deferred with, "If you think so, Mesnera."

"Very well. It occurs to me on this occasion that I haven't yet found a suitable way to show my gratitude to you for your work. Perhaps you could give some thought to that matter."

"Now there's an offer that requires careful consideration," Barbara commented later when they stood on the porch near the palace gates waiting for the carriage to be brought. The pavement was crowded with arriving vehicles. Out in the Plaiz they could hear shouts and laughter and in the distance came the clash of metal where questions of honor were being settled in rings of torchlight. Barbara continued, "What will you ask for?"

"Nothing, I think. I've gained more simply from her notice and attention than I could have desired. Would she take it badly if I asked for nothing more than her continued favor?"

She could hear the grin in Barbara's voice. "That sounds too much like empty flattery. Better to say nothing at all. But I—" She broke off, staring back at the doors. "Mother of God, what now?"

Margerit turned to follow her gaze as Marken shifted, concluded the matter was outside his notice and returned his attention to the Plaiz. A woman was hurrying toward them—one of Elisebet's ladies—and there was no mistaking her goal.

"Mesnera! Thank God I've found you before you left. The princess needs you, come quickly."

"For what?" Barbara asked with no movement to follow.

"Aukustin has gone missing."

Margerit thought she saw some flicker of concern but Barbara remained rooted. "Am I his nursemaid? Surely there are many people at call who could search for one young man."

"Please," the woman pleaded. Margerit thought she seemed more fearful of bringing back a refusal than for Aukustin's unlikely peril.

"Very well."

They trailed after her one and all to where Elisebet lay sprawled in dramatic collapse on a chaise tucked into one of the small side parlors. Her normally florid face was pale and she clutched a vinaigrette offered by Mesnera Sain-Mazzi, her chief waiting woman. Elisebet raised a hand at their approach, saying, "Ah, you've come."

Barbara's response was more conciliatory now. "Mesnera, surely there's no need for this fuss. Have you sent the palace servants out searching?"

"I don't dare raise the alarm. Chustin was seen—seen leaving the palace with his cousin. It would mean to accuse—"

A little of the no-nonsense tone returned. "I can think of nothing less likely than that the new Baron Razik would choose a fourteen-year-old boy as a companion for his celebrations. And I can hardly go chasing all over the city at this time of night."

The woman who had run to fetch them offered, "Aukustin was seen following Friedrich and some of his friends out to the Plaiz." She glanced up at Mesnera Sain-Mazzi apologetically. "You know how boys are. They might not have known…"

Margerit could see a little of the tangle. Elisebet might be genuinely concerned for her son's safety, but to suggest that Efriturik might be at fault, even through negligence? Even if she believed it, the insinuation would do her no good. And for whatever reason, she trusted Barbara's discretion, hence the plea for assistance.

Behind them, the normally taciturn Marken spoke up, pitching his voice for Barbara's ears. "Mesnera? I was talking with Maier earlier—he does for Count Mainek's son. Said they were planning to go to the Black Bull later, or maybe the Barrelhead. And he would have been part of that party."

Elisebet caught enough of the exchange to look hopeful. "Could you go—?"

Barbara and Marken exchanged a look. Margerit could guess that she was involved in some of the calculations and to forestall the possibility that she might be left in Elisebet's care, she responded, "Of course we can go just to check." To Marken, "I promise I'll stay in the carriage no matter what happens."

* * *

She could guess what sort of place the Black Bull was, simply from Marken's tone and the gossip she'd heard of what sorts of New Year's entertainments were popular among the young men. So it was no surprise the instructions grudgingly followed by the coachman took them across the Pont Vezzen to thread their way through the riverside streets toward the very edges of the wharf district. The festivities were well underway, if one could include as festivities a collection of bodies spilling out into the street in what resembled a small riot. Barbara gave one last admonishment: "Not one step outside the carriage, and the coachman knows to leave if it gets bad." As she stepped out, she kilted up her skirts slightly through the fancy sword belt and commented, "A fortunate choice of costume tonight, eh, Marken?" If the armin replied, Margerit couldn't hear it.

They quickly disappeared into the surging crowd, moving like a practiced team. Margerit peered anxiously through the lowered window in the carriage door. How would they find their targets in such confusion? How long would it take to discover if they were even there? They reappeared at last with the suddenness of a duck emerging from the bottom of a pond. Margerit barely had time to draw back from the door when it was pulled open and three bodies tumbled or were pushed in. Barbara had lost the little braided cap that matched her jacket and her tawny hair had come half-unpinned. Efriturik's mouth was bloodied and his collar hung half-loose from his cravat. He looked completely bewildered. Only Marken had emerged completely unscathed.

Barbara pushed a finger into Efriturik's chest, demanding, "Where is Aukustin?"

The bewildered look deepened. "Chustin? Is that what this is about? I sent him about his business before we ever left the palace grounds. Look for him wherever he goes to sulk, for he was none too pleased about it."

Barbara leaned back with a relieved sigh. She awkwardly sheathed the thin, decorative sword she was still holding and then rapped on the roof of the carriage for the driver to start.

There was silence for a block or two, then Efriturik burst out, "Do you think I'm so great a villain as to take a boy his age to that place?"

"And yet," Barbara said coldly, "you're so great a fool as to go there yourself unaccompanied."

"Unaccompanied?" he protested. "There were five of us. And Charlin and Henrik both had their—what do you call—their armed men."

"And where are your friends now? And those armins? Their duty was to extract their charges from danger, not to look after you. Which they did. No one grudges you your amusements, but I told you before there are rules to the game and you need to take care for your position. Do you expect anyone else to respect your rank when you don't respect it enough to be properly attended? Hire yourself an armin, a good one. One that understands there are more hazards for you in Rotenek than tavern brawls. If something has happened to Aukustin, who do you think will be blamed?"

He looked taken aback at that but said only, "You're a fine one to lecture me about following the rules. I thought you, at least, had moved past all these gothic rituals and restrictions."

There was a muffled sound from the opposite seat, where Marken had once again become invisible. It might have been laughter.

Barbara said coolly, "I have no expectation of inheriting a throne."

But the argument sounded weak and there was no further conversation until they returned through the palace gates and were greeted with the news that Aukustin had, after all, been found safe in his bed when checked a second time.

CHAPTER FIFTEEN

Jeanne

The entertainments were far from slowing when Jeanne returned home but she found it hard to pretend to a festive mood. Sleep came fitfully as it had so many nights.

When she woke in the darkness there was nothing to tell whether minutes or hours had passed. Had there been a noise? She strained her ears listening to the creaks of the house, the faint whistling of the icy wind, the occasional pop from the hearth and through it all the soft snoring of Marien from her bed in the dressing room next door.

Jeanne pulled the covers closer and turned to find sleep once more, when the sound came again: a tapping from the French doors to the narrow balcony that overlooked the back garden. Too regular for a branch in the wind. The wrong time both of year and night for a bird entranced by its own reflection. She rose, pulling on the dressing gown that lay across the end of the bedstead, and went to draw back the curtains.

A ghostly head floated before her, gaunt and pale, its lips moving soundlessly. Jeanne shrieked in the terror of having all her fears confirmed. In the next moment, even as she heard Marien calling out from the next room, she pulled open the doors with a glad cry. "Antuniet! Whatever are you doing there?" The spectral head was explained by a dark, high-necked dress, but the gauntness and pallor… That was real. Jeanne grasped her by the shoulders and quickly drew her in. "Did you climb up by the vine? But why? You could have rung. Tomric would have let you in."

It took a few minutes in the warmth of the room for Antuniet's teeth to stop chattering enough to answer. Enough time to reassure Marien and send her off for a glass of brandy. "I didn't want to be seen coming here," Antuniet said at last. "They're still watching for me. There was someone at the end of the street; I don't think he saw me come around the back. Didn't want to make trouble for you, but—"

"Don't be absurd!" Jeanne countered. "I've been worried sick. Where have you been?" She guided Antuniet into the chair by the hearth and rubbed her hands together as Marien returned with the brandy and poked up the fire.

Antuniet looked up, asking, "How much do you know of what happened that day…when I disappeared?"

"I know Kreiser's men broke into your house and—"

"Anna," Antuniet asked suddenly. "Is she—"

"She's…better," Jeanne said hesitantly. The details could wait. "They killed poor Iakup. And there was no sign of you. We all thought…Barbara had men out searching for days. She still has them watching for you anywhere you might turn up. I'm sure that was who you saw out on the street. But where have you been?"

When Antuniet was warmed and fortified by the brandy, the story emerged, in fits and starts. "I was out of my head with a fever…I don't know how long. A riverman—I don't really remember how he found me but he took me to Saint Iulin's hospital, downriver just outside the city walls. They cared for me with no questions asked, but eventually I had no excuse to stay longer. This seemed the best evening to move about the city unnoticed. If I could just have a place to sleep for the night? I promise I'll be gone in the morning, but I need to retrieve my property from Tiporsel House."

"Gone?" Jeanne asked. "But why? You can stay as long as you need."

"I don't want to make trouble for you."

"You said that before and it still makes no sense. What trouble could—"

"I bring disaster on everyone and everything I touch!" Antuniet burst out. "Just let me go and be well rid of me!"

There was no question of that, but Jeanne knew there was no use arguing at the moment. Morning would bring more sense. "Of course you can sleep here tonight. And then tomorrow I can take you anywhere you need to go. Marien?"

"We'd need to make up a bed and a fire in one of the guest rooms," Marien offered, "but if Maisetra Chazillen doesn't mind she could take my bed and I'll go upstairs to sleep. She looks so done in that I'd hate to make her wait."

Indeed, Antuniet had begun shaking again and practicality took over from hospitality. "Then that's what we'll do and thank you for the offer." Of course, it meant Marien could also save another wakeful hour spent seeing to the room. "Come," she said, holding a hand out to help Antuniet up from the chair.

Antuniet stared at her finger. "That ring…"

Jeanne glanced down. "Oh!" She'd almost forgotten it was there, that it wasn't hers. "I hope you don't mind. I—I wanted to keep you in my thoughts and—" She twisted it off and held it out. Antuniet took it and looked back and forth from the ring to her. "I didn't mean to keep it," Jeanne apologized.

"It doesn't matter," Antuniet said, handing it back. "Keep it. Keep all of them."

Jeanne slipped the ring back on, vowing to return it to the bag of gems in the morning. "Come, get some sleep. Things will look better in daylight."

* * *

There was screaming in the dark. Jeanne stumbled out of bed and lit a lamp to see her way into the windowless dressing room. She set the lamp down and shook Antuniet by the shoulder. "Wake up! Wake up, it's only a dream." A thunder of feet came down the stairs and along the corridor and she looked over her shoulder to reassure Marien. "It's nothing. Go back to bed."

Antuniet cried out once more and jerked upright. "No!"

"Hush, hush, Toneke, it's only a dream. Only a nightmare." Jeanne sat on the edge of the bed and took Antuniet in her arms as if she were a child. "It isn't real."

"It is. It was." She spoke as if still lost in sleep.

"Shh, what did you dream? Telling it aloud will break it."

Antuniet twisted in her arms. "I saw my mother...accusing me. I was locked in the dark; I couldn't get away. And she was there beside me, all stiff and cold. And then her hand raised and pointed at me." There was a deep shuddering breath. "She—I found her, you know, after she...when it was all over. She made certain I was the one who would find her. She didn't think the servants should have to—"

"Shh, that's all past. She isn't here now." How many ghosts were haunting her? How long had she kept all this without a soul to share the horror? "What could she accuse you of? You've done nothing."

"But that's it: I've done nothing." Antuniet's voice came muddled through the edge of sleep. Likely she'd remember none of this in the morning. "I've done nothing of what I promised her. I promised—I swore over her body— that I'd wipe out what Estefen had done. I'd bring honor back to the family. And I've done nothing—worse than nothing." Her voice caught in a sob.

Jeanne held her even more tightly. She remembered Iosifin Chazillen well. Remembered the look on her face when she gave the final damning evidence at her son's trial. Remembered the shock, but no surprise, at the news of her suicide. What must it have been like to have a mother who valued honor over her children's lives? Over her own life? To the rest of the world it had seemed tragically noble, but such a ghost to have haunting one! "You've done everything you can, Toneke. You've survived. And your work will succeed; I know it."

She started to loosen her hold, but Antuniet cried out, "Don't leave me alone! Don't leave me in the dark!"

"Hush, I won't leave you," Jeanne said. "Go back to sleep. I'll stay and keep watch over you."

She laid Antuniet down again and tucked the covers closely around her. In the soft glow of the lamplight her face gradually relaxed into sleep once more. The fear faded away and only the weariness remained, but in that face Jeanne could still see the bones of the sharp wit and sardonic humor that had always attracted her, the spark of passion that was only released in the safety of her studies. She leaned forward to brush a strand of hair out of Antuniet's face and froze.

When had this happened? When had teasing and idle flirtation deepened into something more? She sat back, searching her memory. If she had foreseen it, she would have guarded her heart more carefully. There was nothing for her here. Antuniet wasn't some nobody to be courted or seduced and then sent on her way with a parting gift—that wasn't how Jeanne wanted her. Nor could she be approached as a knowing and experienced lover. Antuniet hadn't found her flirtation offensive, only embarrassing. But a serious declaration of love… that would be a different matter. Could she learn to be the friend that Antuniet needed and to be no more than a friend?

She recalled the last time she had misjudged her heart and fallen unwisely in love. That summer with Barbara… The ache had faded eventually and they were friends now—it could be done. And Antuniet… She had barely begun to trust the offer of friendship; might she someday accept more? Oh, they always crept up on her unawares, the ones who were far more than a pretty face and a pleasant armful. She sighed at her own folly. In echo, Antuniet moaned and turned as if trying to escape the demons in the dark. "Shh, shh, I'm here. I won't leave you," Jeanne whispered. She lay down on top of the coverlet beside her and held her close until she quieted. "I'll keep you safe tonight." Eventually, she too slept.

Morning arrived stiff and cold. Jeanne carefully unwrapped herself from around Antuniet and slipped out to seek her own bed. It would embarrass them both for her to be found there.

CHAPTER SIXTEEN

Barbara

After the excitement of the night before, it wasn't a morning for early rising. Barbara rolled up onto one elbow in the bed and leaned across Margerit to pour another cup from the chocolate pot on the little side table. She paused to leave a kiss in passing.

"Mmm, you could have asked me to pour," Margerit said.

"But that wouldn't have been nearly as much fun." The pastries had long since disappeared into a few lingering crumbs and the sounds of the household below tolled an approaching end to their lazy intimacy.

Margerit's expression turned from playful to thoughtful as she returned to last night's events. "Efriturik was right, you know. You can hardly scold him for not maintaining the dignity of his rank when you give so little care to your own. Someone else will have to convince him of that."

Barbara sighed. "My reputation is built on eccentricity. And it's not as if I need someone else's protection—"

"—except when you go charging into tavern brawls wearing a ball gown. You always tell me to trust Marken's instincts and you know what he thinks."

The arguments were all true. She thought back to the times she'd borrowed Marken even briefly for show or safety. That wasn't fair to him or any of them. And yet…"I dread the thought of bringing someone new so closely into our lives. An armin isn't like hiring a new kitchen maid. It may not be his place to approve or disapprove, but I need to be able to trust him. He'll know all our secrets and have your good name in his keeping as well as my own. Marken knew us back before. That makes a difference."

Margerit drew a hand down along Barbara's cheek to acknowledge the point, and Barbara pressed it against her lips. "Just promise me you'll think about it," Margerit said.

"I'll do better than that." She rolled out of the bed and pulled the bell. Maitelen answered with an alacrity that suggested she thought it past time to be moving on with the day. "Lay out my riding clothes, the breeches and the blue coat." She turned back to Margerit. "I'll go off to Perret's this very morning and after my practice I'll ask him to start looking for possibilities. He'll know who's good and who's looking for a position."

Margerit sat up in bed and watched her dress, adding, "As long as you're turning respectable at last, why not hire your own maid and stop stealing mine!"

"Now that would go too far!" Barbara returned. "How could you ask Maitelen to give up being lady's maid to a baroness?"

The subject of their conversation made a noise something like a snort and said, "Never you mind about me, Mesnera. I knew the day I met you back in Chalanz that I'd do well to stick by you and you weren't a baroness yet then!"

They were nearly dressed when Maitelen answered a tap on the door and returned to announce, "The Vicomtesse de Cherdillac is waiting for you in the front parlor. With a guest." The faintest of frowns told what she thought of untimely visitors.

Margerit urged, "Go down and see what she wants, Barbara. I'm nearly done and likely it's you she wants to see anyway."

When Barbara entered the room, Jeanne turned to her with a strained cheerfulness, saying, "Look who turned up on my doorstep last night!" And then, with a smile that spoke of secret jokes, "That is, not the doorstep precisely."

When the other woman also turned, Barbara's face hardened into a scowl. Someone should have warned her! No. Who among the ordinary servants would have recognized her like this? And Jeanne...must have had her own reasons.

Antuniet curtseyed stiffly, murmuring, "Baroness!"

An awkward pause stretched out as Barbara fumbled through the possible salutations she could return. In the end she settled for nodding silently.

"Forgive me for the hour," Antuniet continued. "I don't mean to trouble you further. I've only come for my property."

"It seems to me you've been trouble enough already. I—"

But Margerit came through the door in that moment and her glad cry of "Antuniet!" brushed away what would have been said.

Antuniet shrank into herself and Margerit paused at the rebuff. Antuniet repeated, "I've come to retrieve my property."

"Of course," Margerit said in a more subdued voice, looking back and forth between all of them as if sorting out the tension. "I'll go fetch the book."

Silence fell while they waited. Jeanne had stepped back and was watching closely but had said no word after the start. Barbara could hear voices out in the hallway: Bertrut questioning, Margerit answering. The last thing they needed was awkward interruptions. Margerit returned at last, carrying the book in the same satchel it had arrived in.

Barbara laid a hand on her arm when she would have offered it to Antuniet. "I've worked my way through a fair amount of that book," she said. "An interesting text. Dangerous, in the wrong hands."

"I've gone to some trouble to keep it out of the wrong hands," Antuniet said evenly.

"I was wondering about yours," Barbara countered. "What exactly are your plans for this work of yours?"

"That's hardly your concern." It was clear her veneer of patience was fraying to shreds, but Barbara's own patience over the matter had worn out long ago.

"You made it my concern when you thrust my household into the middle of it willy-nilly. I still remember the last adventure your family led us into. Swear to me that you had no part in your brother's plot and you can have your book."

Antuniet's chin went up in defiance. "If you need to ask, then you wouldn't believe me no matter what oath I swore. Will you return my property to me or are you a thief?"

Barbara bristled, but whatever hot words she might have returned were cut short when Margerit shook off her hand and stepped forward. "You gave it into my keeping and I return it to you safe and sound. But what will you do now? Nothing is changed. Mesner Kreiser…yes, we know about him. You need to take someone's protection. I could—"

"No!"

"Or you could go to the palace. Ask Annek—"

"No." Antuniet opened the case and drew the book out just far enough to ascertain its identity. The gesture might have been meant as an insult but it had more the feel of reassurance.

"What will you do?" Margerit repeated. "Where will you go?"

Antuniet shrugged and unbent enough to answer. "I'll see what can still be saved from my workshop and then I'll flee Rotenek, like a thief in the night, before Kreiser can get word of me. It doesn't much matter where I go. I've started from nothing before and I'll do it again."

Jeanne took a half step forward as if she would speak at last, but her silence held until Antuniet had strode from the room with no farewell and they heard the echoes of the heavy front door closing behind her. Then she turned with a look of fury, crying, "Damn you, Barbara! Damn the both of you for your stiff-necked pride! She needs help and you stood by and let her walk away."

"If she wants help, then she needs to ask for it."

"Ask you? Ask the person who represents everything she's lost?" Barbara couldn't remember ever seeing Jeanne this angry. "Do you know why she wouldn't go to Annek for help with Kreiser? Aside from no longer having the right? Because the work was meant to be her gift to Alpennia…her gift to redeem the honor of the Chazillens."

That rang true, but Jeanne's fierce defense did not. "Why do you care so much?"

"Why do you care so little?" Jeanne countered. "Does it mean nothing to you that Antuniet is the nearest kin you have still living? And that you stand the same to her?"

Barbara had never gotten used to thinking of Antuniet as family. Fate had conspired against there ever being goodwill between them.

Jeanne must have seen some softening, for her voice dropped to a more coaxing tone. "You cared enough to have men watching my house for the last month in case she returned, so why not—"

Barbara felt a cold shiver. "I never set anyone to watch you."

The same realization crossed all three minds at once.

"Dear God!" Margerit exclaimed. "Kreiser. He knows she's back."

There were reflexes trained into Barbara's body that time would never entirely erase. She was moving toward the door before a plan had fully formed in her mind. It was one thing to leave Antuniet to her own folly and another to help betray her to her enemy. She called out to the footmen in the hall as she passed: "Marzo, Sikipirt!" Not the men she necessarily would have chosen to have behind her in a fight, but young and strong and *here*. And if her foreboding were true, time meant everything.

Crossing the yard at a run, she added one of the grooms. If Antuniet were heading for her old workshop, she'd have gone down the Vezenaf to Pont Ruip. The bridge was the worst place to be trapped; she knew that lesson well. Barbara ran as if before the hounds and heard the footsteps of the others falling behind. What would Marken say now! Traffic was sparse on the road but still too crowded to see whether Antuniet had made the turn yet. It wasn't until she turned onto the bridge herself and began the rise that Barbara saw the struggling knot of people she'd been searching for. No one figure could be discerned as they surged against the parapet, but all of a sudden a dark object arced over the rail and hung suspended against the sky before falling into the river below with a splash.

Every actor in the scene stood frozen watching it fly, released at last by a harsh shout, "You stupid bitch!" as the knot convulsed inward again. Hearing footsteps and panting breaths close at her back again, Barbara surged forward with her own shout and waded into the fray. There were fewer of the others than it had seemed at the first and they had no stomach when it turned to a true fight. Even so, when they fled they left Sikipirt nursing a bruised head and Marzo sporting a bloodied nose and a triumphant grin. Antuniet had sunk to a huddled ball close up against the bridge parapet. When Barbara crouched down beside her, the only word she could make out was, "Gone."

"Yes, they're gone," she echoed reassuringly.

Antuniet raised her head at the familiar voice. Her eyes stared blank and hollow. "Gone. It's all gone." With a sudden motion she rose and scrambled onto the low stone wall. Barbara grabbed for her, barely dragging her from the brink by the skirts of her dress. "Don't be a fool! It's sunk into the mud by now. You'd never find it."

Antuniet twisted wildly in her hands, shouting, "Let me go! Let me go!" as Barbara took a stronger hold and pulled her back. "You don't understand. It's gone! It's all gone. There's nothing left. Nothing."

With a shock, Barbara realized she hadn't meant to go after the book but to be lost beside it. She pushed Antuniet down onto the pavement and held her in a grip of iron as she called out to the men, "Go find us a carriage, a wagon...anything! No need to be a spectacle for all the city!"

As they scattered to obey, she took Antuniet's face in her hands and forced their eyes to meet. "You told Margerit to keep it safe," she said in a tone that pierced through the despair. "What is the surest way to keep a book safe?" She saw the faintest spark kindle in that darkness.

By the time they returned to Tiporsel, Antuniet had left behind her frenzy. Indeed, she seemed to have left behind everything but mute obedience. Barbara ushered her past the curious eyes in the front hall and nodded at Margerit and Jeanne to follow as she led the way back to the privacy of the library. Jeanne had been crying. Margerit, more practically, had initiated preparations for all possible outcomes of the chase. With a few brief words Barbara told them what had occurred.

When she came to the fate of the prize that had set it all in motion, Margerit looked quickly at Antuniet's bleak expression and went to retrieve a thick bundle from her working desk. She placed it in Antuniet's lap, saying, "I had two done separately, as a check on errors because of the ciphers. I haven't had a chance to have them bound yet." Antuniet touched the ribbon that bound the pages together but made no move to untie it.

"Not a gift," Barbara said, quickly forestalling any impulsive generosity Margerit might feel. "For use. If you accept my conditions."

CHAPTER SEVENTEEN

Antuniet

Antuniet woke to the pale winter sun filtering through the shutters and spent long minutes untangling true memories from fever dreams.

For the last week, every day had begun the same. It was the voices drifting up from below that sorted out truth from phantasm—that and the numb absence of terror. Left in its place was a deep weariness. She was back… No, she could hardly think of this place as home. It wasn't hers now, if it ever had been. She had a new patron. And a staff—to watch over her as much as to watch out for her—but they answered to Margerit, not to her. The voices below weren't Anna and Iakup beginning the day. Her mind shied away from that path.

No. She had always hated cowardice. Iakup was dead because of her. Because she had thought only of her own danger and not that others might fall defending her. He had been defending Anna, not her, but it came to the same end. And Anna—her message there had gone unanswered and no blame to Monterrez for that. Disaster came to everything she touched.

Footsteps echoed on the stairs and a knock rang on the door. Mefro Feldin. Not quite a housekeeper—there wasn't much house to keep—but here to keep things in order, along with Petro to do the man's work that Iakup used to cover and the two rough men whose names she hadn't sorted out yet but whose sole purpose was to advertise that Antuniet Chazillen had a patron who would see to her protection. None of them lived in—there wasn't room for that and Feldin, at least, had starkly refused—but she was never left alone.

The knock came again and she realized she hadn't answered it. "Enter."

The woman looked her over with a silent sniff. Margerit had gone to some trouble to find a housekeeper willing to dare the uncertain peril of an alchemist's house. There had been emphatic assurances that she wouldn't be asked to touch any of the equipment. And beyond that, it wasn't any part of her duties to play lady's maid. She sniffed again. "I was going to the market, Maisetra, and wondered if there was anything in particular you wanted."

"No." Was there anything she wanted? What good had it ever done to want things? She wanted her old life back: the house on Modul Street, to own more than a single garment, to have the company of minds worth talking to. She wanted her work back. She wanted her book: that mystical talisman that her hands remembered like a lover's touch, the scent of years rising from its pages like incense. It had meant more than the text inscribed on the pages; it had been *hers*, the proof of her talent and the promise of her success. Now there were only marks on a page and even that came from someone else's charity. In those last weeks, when fear had haunted every step, at least the work had been all hers. The hope of triumph had been there, drawing her on. There would be no triumph now, only the failure even to fail.

She turned restlessly. Mefro Feldin had left some time ago. Hunger finally bored deeply enough to drive her up to dress. No one would be bringing dainties on a tray to coax her appetite. She found bread in the small pantry, fresh from the bakery across the street. That was enough for now.

Two hours later she had gone no farther than to move jars around on the bench in the workroom. There was a handful of notes in a stack, retrieved from the concealed room where they had lain hidden the last month. She could begin again on the last experiment without needing to go beg entrance at Tiporsel house to review DeBoodt. Someone had consulted the chemist for what supplies she needed when no list had been forthcoming from her own hand. She hadn't had a chance to see what remained from before and what had been spoiled or lost in the attack. There was the trace of a bloodstain still on the floor next to the furnace. She stared at it until the outlines shifted into monstrous visions.

That was where Jeanne found her later, bustling in with her maid in tow just as if nothing had happened in the last month. "I dropped by because I was thinking about your appointment at the palace tomorrow and I was wondering—"

"Is that tomorrow?" Antuniet asked, rousing herself to the present. "I'd lost track." That had been one of the conditions. Margerit could hardly be blamed for insisting that she couldn't sponsor work such as this secretly, not in her position. But whatever Annek had been told, she'd wanted more. An invitation—a summons, really—to attend on her with explanations. This wasn't how it had been meant to be.

"I was wondering," Jeanne repeated, touching her lightly on the shoulder when she saw that her attention had wandered, "whether you might like to borrow something a bit...nicer to wear." She gestured to her maid, who laid a muslin-wrapped bundle across the table and began untying it. "I think we're close enough in size, except that you're taller, but there's enough hem to let down for that. Marien is quick with a needle and she can have it ready by tomorrow."

Antuniet fingered the fabric, evaluating the quality. The choice had been calculated carefully: a fine brown wool with rows of dark braid, but nothing too luxurious. Nothing to make it feel like a masquerade. "Thank you," she said quietly.

She let herself be led upstairs to her chamber and pinned and tucked into the gown. There would be more work than only the hem. Had she grown so thin? Years of pointed comments had left her thinking of herself as Amazonian in proportions, but the bodice hung loosely, and not entirely by comparison to Jeanne's more womanly figure. She had never been vain, but she was glad, of a sudden, for the lack of mirrors in the place.

As the maid bundled up the gown again, Jeanne handed her another smaller package. "I also thought…well, you could hardly just borrow a chemise or stockings or that sort of thing, so…"

Antuniet felt her face grow hot. It was such an intimate thing to have considered, and startling to have it considered at all. "Jeanne—"

"Oh, it's perfectly selfish, I assure you," she replied. "I was hoping you'd join me for a bite to eat at the Café Chatuerd after you're done at the palace tomorrow and you know what sticklers they are for appearances!"

"So I'm to be rehabilitated into society?" Antuniet asked, forcing a wry smile.

She expected a joke in return, but Jeanne's expression was serious. "Toneke, we thought…that is, Margerit thinks she may have been at fault in letting Mesner Kreiser believe you were entirely without friends in Rotenek."

"But it's true," Antuniet said. Jeanne looked so stricken she wished she'd held her tongue. "Jeanne, why are you doing this? All this?"

Jeanne reached out to take her hand and pressed it between both of hers. "When you become accustomed to the idea of having friends again, you won't need to ask that question. But for now, just remember that your talent may be alchemy but this is my talent. Put yourself in my hands, and the next thing you know you'll have invitations to balls and the opera."

It was utterly absurd—dancing at balls was the last thing she wanted—and a burble of laughter made it halfway to her lips. And that seemed answer enough for Jeanne, who squeezed her hand once more and took her leave.

* * *

It was impossible not to remember the last time she had entered the palace gates in the shadow of Estefen's execution and her mother's death. She had been too numb for anything to touch her: the dissolution of the Guild of Saint Atelpirt, the pardon for all but Lutoz. But she still remembered that chance confrontation with Margerit as she left and the bile she had allowed to spill. *This time you have blood on your hands; this time I do hate you.* And yet Margerit could pretend there was no wall between them. At least she'd had the tact to delegate Jeanne to accompany her today.

Jeanne left her at the doors to the royal apartments. She would wait in the corridor with those who hoped for a moment of the princess's time. Antuniet continued on, privileged by the escort of a palace page. This was no formal audience in state. Annek looked up from the work on the desk before her and beckoned. Antuniet approached, curtseyed and said, "I am come as Your Grace requested."

Those perceptive eyes looked her up and down and Antuniet was suddenly even more grateful for the borrowed dress. Princess Annek must be of an age with Jeanne, she thought, but looked much older. They shared the same raven hair but where Jeanne's eyes always seemed bright with laughter, Annek's were hooded and guarded, giving nothing away. Antuniet couldn't help but see an echo of her own mother in the princess's rigid posture. Annek pursed her lips as if in disapproval.

"You aren't quite what I expected. From all the uproar around you I'd expected someone older."

"I am five and twenty, Your Grace."

"No matter. Forgive me, but I don't believe we've met before."

Antuniet thought back to all those long days of the succession debates when they'd occupied the same room. But there had been hundreds in that hall. "No, not formally." Was this to be all pleasantries and social nothings?

"I understand that you dabble in alchemy."

She bristled. Was that what Margerit had said of her? "I don't dabble; alchemy is my work."

"You've been making your living by it?"

"I make my living by tutoring students at the university, when I can. Few people have ever made a living by alchemy, except frauds."

The princess turned more fully to face her and tapped a finger idly against the desktop. "Maisetra Sovitre has come to me with an odd request. As a token of gratitude for the services she's done for me, she asked that I place your work under my protection. You seem to have impressed her a great deal."

"I think," Antuniet said carefully, "that it was in the way of paying a debt she felt she owed me."

Eyebrows raised. "Indeed? Then perhaps I misunderstood. Tell me about your work."

Antuniet swallowed heavily. The room was tilting and she reached for the back of a chair to steady herself. "Forgive me, I've been unwell." Had she eaten that morning? She couldn't remember.

At Annek's gesture she was guided into the chair. "A glass of wine for Maisetra Chazillen, if you please."

It gave her a few minutes to assemble her thoughts. The time was past for holding her plans close. As before, there was no way out but forward. She opened the small purse that hung at her wrist and drew out a knotted cloth. "My work concerns the properties of precious stones."

It all came out, bit by bit, interrupted by Annek's questions, for she had a sharp and perceptive mind. She described the initial experiments, the glimpse of success, the setbacks and—like a splinter drawn from a wound—what she hoped to gain in exchange for the gift.

Annek made no comment to that, only picked up the carnelian ring once more and turned it in the light. "Not a holy relic, nor yet the work of the devil, but you say it has power. If you wore this, what would happen?"

"If I wore it? Very little, I expect. That one draws between two poles, one set during the fixation, the other where it is worn. Or where it touches. Sometimes simply its presence will influence those nearby, but it was designed for contact. If I wore it, both poles would point to me." She nudged the small pile of gems on the corner of the desk between them and fished out a jasper and one of the best black onyxes. "With these, the effect is fixed as a vector, only from the stone to the bearer. The process for enhancing those is more complex and so far I've only produced a weak effect. The carnelian—it only involved a single ceremonial role, so it was my first project in Prague."

"And if I wore it?"

Antuniet hesitated. It would be hazardous to overplay the stone's effects even though she'd seen them in action. "Then there would be a…a connection between us. It would strengthen any sense of agreement or affection. It would guide you into sympathy with my desires. The natural stone carries a variety of properties but the fixation focuses on enhancing specific elements."

Annek smiled but Antuniet noticed that she shifted her grasp to touch only the band. "Agreement or affection. A love charm, then?"

"Nothing so crude. The effects are subtle and rarely rise to the level of compulsion. You might say that it increases any impulses the wearer already feels." In her mind she saw the stone glowing against the pale skin of Jeanne's forefinger. That could explain much.

"Interesting," Annek said at last, returning the ring to the pile. "It seems harmless at the very least. We have yet to see how useful it might prove." She stood in dismissal and Antuniet hastened to rise and scoop the gems back into her purse. "I'm not prepared at this time to lend my name to your work," Annek continued, "but I think Maisetra Sovitre's request can be met. The Austrian emissary has been informed that his welcome in Alpennia has worn thin and his…ah…associates understand that they will be held responsible if any harm comes to you or those who work for you. Is there anything else you wanted?"

Those who work for you. Was she finally allowed to want something again? Perhaps…"Your Grace, I want my apprentice back."

* * *

Café Chatuerd was much as Antuniet remembered it, bright and noisy in the crowded downstairs room. The upstairs was quieter, but Jeanne was determined that they be seen as much as possible. The food was light and dainty and only enough to wake her appetite. No, she must not have eaten that morning. She needed to be more careful about that.

Jeanne, as always, made conversation easy and pleasant without seeming effort. It helped to cover the stares of those who recognized her. None of them approached the table to talk or did more than greet Jeanne quickly in passing. If rehabilitation were the goal, it would take time. Time… She glanced over at the ornate ormolu clock on the sideboard once again.

"Is there somewhere you need to be, Toneke? You almost make me think I weary you."

"No, not at all!" She touched Jeanne's hand in reassurance. It felt awkward but she was rewarded by Jeanne's smile. "That is, it seems I do have another appointment today. Would you mind…"

"But of course I can accompany you, if you like. When must we go?"

That hadn't been what she meant to ask, but the company would be appreciated and it would be convenient if Jeanne would provide the transportation. It was a long walk down to Zempol Street and she was still feeling shaky. "Not for another half hour, I think."

* * *

They waited in the hired fiacre until the second carriage arrived, disgorging a lady, veiled as a widow, with her attendant. Without a word, Antuniet led the way into the shop. It was the same young man behind the counter that it always was. He took in the small crowd curiously but the others held back, as if waiting their turn by chance. Antuniet could tell he recognized her. He pulled the bell that rang farther back in the house even as she said, "I would like to speak with Maistir Monterrez."

There was no easy way to begin. What apologies could be made had been in her letter—the one he hadn't answered. She saw a slight movement in the shadows past the half-open door to the living quarters and the glimpse of a pale face. "Maistir Monterrez, I made a contract to teach your daughter alchemy. And though I understand that you hold the contract to be broken on your end, I consider my part to be a debt of honor. Will you allow Anna to return to her studies?"

"No." That one word and nothing else.

The topic of their conversation slipped out from the doorway. She held her shawl close across the left side of her face. "Papa, please! Let me—"

"Go back in the house, Anna. Don't argue with me in front of strangers."

Antuniet tried again. "You have my word that she will be safe from all harm."

His face was sorrowful but his expression hard. "I failed my daughter once by trusting you. You will forgive me if I consider your word to be of little weight and no worth."

Antuniet heard a rustle of silks behind her and a soft voice asking, "And what of my word?"

Annek had stepped forward and drawn the widow's veil back from her face. There was no one in the room who didn't recognize her. Monterrez bowed deeply and silently.

"You haven't answered my question, Maistir Goldsmith. Will you accept my word? If you allow your daughter to return to her apprenticeship, she will be under my protection."

Antuniet could see the struggle on his face, but he bowed once more, saying, "Then she has my consent." There was really no other answer he could give.

Anna's face was glowing as the princess stepped close and raised her from her curtsey with a finger lightly under her chin, saying, "So we share a name? Work hard and do honor to it." And then, with a further rustle of silks, she left.

Monterrez sighed deeply. "It's for the best, I suppose. Better you should have a profession. Now more than before."

"Thank you, Papa," she said, embracing him.

Antuniet saw how his eyes skipped away, never resting on that marred face. There was a deep debt owed here. "You can begin tomorrow," she said. No point in delay. And it would give her a reason to leave her bed in the morning. That would be useful.

CHAPTER EIGHTEEN

Margerit

When she returned from scouting out the next term's lectures Margerit heard cheerful voices in the front parlor. Once she'd been divested of coat and bonnet she went to put in an appearance before Bertrut's friends. There was value in such an investment, no matter that their conversation rarely turned to anything of interest. She was mistress of the house and any guests were her guests as well. She would put in half an hour of listening to the latest matchmaking speculations and tales of soirées past and balls to come.

"Maisetra Saltez had a great triumph with her skating party," Ailis Faikrimek reported. "What an idea! Everyone thought it a great lark and though some of the antics went beyond what must be thought proper, the young men all turned up in numbers that you wouldn't find at an ordinary party. They even managed to lure Baron Razik, at which I was amazed, for he's quite outside their circle now."

Margerit smiled, recalling Jeanne's entertaining explanation of how she'd dropped that hint. Jeanne was quite the artist in her own way, and Margerit had plans to make use of those skills.

"He'll be snapped up soon enough," Lufise Chafil added. "Maisetra Sovitre, you should put in a play for him. Fortune's been known to win before, but not if the pretty faces get there first."

"I beg your pardon?" Margerit asked, having lost the thread of the conversation.

Aunt Bertrut said quellingly, "Lufise was making the rather unseemly suggestion that you might set your cap at the heir to the throne."

"Oh, but he isn't the heir yet," Lufise said. "That makes it possible. You might give it a thought."

Margerit shook her head. "I have no ambitions to marry Efriturik Atilliet or anyone else. It would interfere too much with my studies. Speaking of which…" She rose, calculating that she'd put in enough time to be polite.

Bertrut followed her out into the foyer and closed the door behind them. "Margerit, I was wondering…that is, I thought you might give that woman a hint. I know she's some sort of cousin of the baroness, but for weeks now—"

"You're speaking of Maisetra Chazillen?"

"Coming and going at all hours and in such clothes. I thought you might let her know that it would be more appropriate if she came in by the side."

By the servants' door. Margerit stifled the sharp answer that came first to mind. "Aunt Bertrut, I'm sorry if you were embarrassed in front of your friends, but Antuniet needs to do her research. You know that we thought it safer to keep the papers here for now. She has my invitation to come and go at her own convenience, and I hope you haven't said anything to make her feel unwelcome." It had been hard enough to convince her of that welcome in the first place.

"But the front door? Looking like some workhouse girl? You've spent enough on setting her up; surely some of it could go for clothing!"

Margerit shook her head. She'd lost that argument already. Whatever rules Antuniet had set in her own mind, they didn't encompass letting others pay for her personal things. She had her tutoring money for that, she'd said. And Margerit had let it alone. "Don't badger her about it, Aunt. Please?"

"Of course, if you insist, dear," Bertrut said doubtfully.

Margerit hesitated before opening the door to the library. She'd meant to do some reading, but would Antuniet take it as a sign to retreat? Antuniet looked up from the spread papers and carefully set her pen aside.

"Don't let me disturb you. I only have some correspondence to read. Would you like to have tea brought in?"

"Not while I'm writing," Antuniet said shortly.

"Of course. Perhaps later?" Margerit found the latest packet of letters and poetry from her cousin Iulien and settled into her usual chair by the window, kicking off her shoes and tucking her feet up under her like a little girl.

She'd given up waiting for an answer when Antuniet spoke again, more quietly this time. "Thank you, that would be pleasant."

For the next hour there was only the rustling of pages and the thin scratching of the pen. The news from Chalanz was all the usual, filtered through a girl's eyes. Iuli was the only one who wrote to her about the family. Uncle Fulpi wrote only on business: a client who wished for an introduction in Rotenek, a request for a book that her cousin Nikule needed, arrangements to be made for Sofi's coming-out ball at the end of next summer. Beneath it all was the sense that these favors were the price she paid for not being disowned entirely.

Reading Iuli's letters was like returning to the chatter of her childhood, full of half-overheard gossip and descriptions of their favorite places. And then there were the poems. The privilege of reading them was made clear by the inscription at the top of the page, "Show to No One," amended by the awkwardly inserted allowance, "except the Baroness." Iuli's staple offerings were solemn and gothic odes to the ruins in Axian Park or meditations on historical figures she had no doubt been set to study by her governess. But in among them was the occasional gem: the description of a nightingale heard through an open window on a late summer evening; a surprisingly mature contemplation of the unreliability of memory. At first, Margerit had responded only with mild praise, guessing how tender Iuli's pride was likely to be. But lately she'd started sending back comments on a particular turn of phrase or choice of words. Since it hadn't stemmed the flow of verse, it seemed Iuli didn't mind.

Margerit kept part of her attention on the other occupant of the room and when Antuniet finally cleaned her nib and sorted the papers out into three tidy stacks, she rang the bell, giving Antuniet no opportunity for a change of mind.

"The copyists did their work well," Antuniet said when the cups had been poured and the silence hadn't had time to become awkward yet. "Making two copies as a check was a good idea. I've only found a few common errors, though the diagrams were clearly more difficult. They did an excellent job on the ciphers and the Greek is accurate but I suspect they had little knowledge of Hebrew. I may need to have Anna come to help me sort things out sometime."

"I'd like that," Margerit said eagerly. "I've hoped for a chance to see her again."

"You could have come down to the workshop."

"I didn't know if…I didn't want to intrude too much into your life."

Antuniet gave a bitter laugh. "You've already intruded into every part of my life, so why stop there?"

How to answer that?

Antuniet set her cup down and leaned forward. "Manners are like ice on the river: a smooth and polished surface, but brittle and treacherous if it needs to bear weight. I accept that you never meant to destroy my family; you only meant to survive. And yet, here I am. And there you are. I won't set a price on that guilt but I'm willing to acknowledge that you are paying it."

Margerit was taken aback. "Did you think this was out of guilt? I would have helped you for the sake of friendship any time you were willing to accept it."

Antuniet shook her head. "We can never be friends; there's too much distance between us."

"No," Margerit answered firmly. "Barbara said the same thing when she and I first met and I made the mistake of believing it for entirely too long." She, too, leaned forward in challenge. "Do you know how few people there are in this world that I can meet mind to mind and soul to soul? And I can never forget how much help you were to me when I first came to the city."

"Help?" Antuniet sounded genuinely puzzled.

"When you set me on the trail of Gaudericus. When you gave me hints on how to get what I needed from the *dozzures* at the university. That day you showed me that mysteries could be designed by trial and experiment. Simply letting me know by your existence that it was possible for a woman to be a serious scholar in Rotenek. If that isn't friendship, I don't know what other word to call it by."

Antuniet was silent for a long time and would not meet her eyes. She began, "Barbara—"

"It may surprise you," Margerit interrupted, "that Barbara and I don't always think alike. You'll have to make peace with Barbara in whatever way seems best to you, but for my part, my hand is there if ever you choose to take it." She laid it out on the table, matching action to words. It was an offer halfway: not so far that refusal would be pointed.

"I...I don't know," Antuniet stammered. "I don't..." Her voice trailed off and she bit her lip. In anyone else, Margerit might have expected tears. At last she sighed and said, "Come down to Trez Cherfis sometime. I'd like to show you how the work progresses. And perhaps you could talk to Anna about some of the more ceremonial parts of the practice. I feel like the blind leading the blind there. I don't know whether she has any sensitivity to guide her or whether she'll need to learn by rote the way I did. She'll need more teachers than me."

It was neither acceptance nor rebuff. It would do for now.

They met Barbara just arriving in the courtyard as Antuniet set forth with the day's work. Antuniet acknowledged her with a deep curtsey and murmured, "Baroness!"

Barbara returned, "Cousin," with a briefer nod.

Well, stiff formality was better than spitting like cats, Margerit thought.

* * *

Margerit found it hard to seize a chance for private conversation in the evening, even when they stayed in with no guests. It seemed unkind simply to disappear and leave her aunt and uncle to their own company. And when retired at last to bed at an hour still young, there were better things to do than rehearse the events of the day. But later, rolled closely in Barbara's arms, she felt the need to unburden herself before sleep would come.

"Antuniet invited me to see her work. I thought I might go down to her workshop sometime soon."

"You hardly need an invitation," Barbara muttered impatiently.

"But I do," Margerit said. "I know it seemed the obvious answer to us—for me to be her patron—but you're the one always talking about the Chazillen pride. I think she would truly prefer to have died than to lose her work, even to me. I don't want to push too far, so I wait to be invited. And in defiance of Aunt Bertrut's feelings I won't insist on buying her a new wardrobe. Maybe someday she'll believe my offer of friendship."

"Now there you're barking up the wrong tree. Antuniet has never had friends."

"And why is that, do you suppose? I don't think it's pride. I think—" How to explain? "I think no one worthy of her friendship has ever tried hard enough."

Barbara snorted in laughter. "Well, bloody your knuckles knocking on that door if you please."

Margerit judged it time to let the matter be. "Weren't you supposed to bring home a new armin to try out today?"

A sigh. "He didn't suit at all."

"I thought Perret was an excellent judge?"

"For skill, yes, but he has his blind spots." Humor threaded through Barbara's voice. "I told the man the first part of his interview was to spar a few bouts with me and he refused outright. Wouldn't fight with a lady, he said. Not a good sign. So it's back to the beginning again. There was one other possibility Perret mentioned but Efriturik seems to have snapped him up already."

"Then at least his problem is settled."

* * *

Trez Cherfis was neither close enough to the wharf district to be thought rough, nor close enough to the university district to be considered bohemian. And it was a world away from the fashionable neighborhoods north of the river. Margerit watched the passing houses from the carriage window, trying to imagine what Antuniet must feel to have come to this. It was a street of shops and craftsmen and the poorer edges of the Jewish district. Likely not one in ten rated a higher greeting than *Mefro*.

A brief note from Antuniet had suggested a day and time, and the directions brought her to a squat brick and timber building with the fading traces of a trade sign over the door. On entering, she could imagine a shop in the front with storage behind and cramped living quarters above. The first room was more stark and spare than she expected but the back held the familiar clutter of work in progress.

Antuniet ushered her in with the air of a hostess showing off her garden… or perhaps more aptly, a farm manager answering to the landowner. "I thought you might like to see the process as a whole," she said briskly, "so we've left bits of the work at every stage. And then the firing is set to begin around noon. Do you mind if I have Anna explain things to you? I never seem to have time for her examinations."

"Of course," Margerit said. She crossed the room to greet the girl with a brief embrace, to Anna's startled surprise. After the time she'd spent at Tiporsel, it would seem odd to return to distant formality. "I'm glad to see you back at work." She noticed how Anna ducked her head sideways to hide her scarred cheek from view and decided not to ask how it was healing. Instead she offered, "They say Kreiser has gone back to Vienna."

"In the middle of winter?" Antuniet sounded understandably skeptical.

Margerit shrugged. "Annek's warning seems to have been taken to heart. Or perhaps, having failed, he had no further business here. In any event, he's

left. I suppose he must have gone south to take ship at Marseilles. I'll still keep
the guards on duty though."

Now it was Antuniet's turn to shrug. "As you wish. I can't say there's much
need for the both of them. Anna, perhaps you could begin over here."

They started with the jars of fine powders, ground and sifted and laboriously
purified. Anna described the separations and calcinations, the dissolving and
filtering, drying and careful mixing. "Some steps are only mechanical," Anna
explained, waving at the mortars and sieves and clearly relishing her role,
"but the quartz here was put through a minor exaltation at the last stage—
working under a specific alignment of the stars and with Maisetra Chazillen
and I taking different roles—to enhance the…the drawing of the—" She
looked at Antuniet for guidance but was motioned to continue. "To enhance
the influence over the sleeping mind." She looked back again. Evidently the
explanation had been correct. She moved over to the workbench, where a
crucible stood, already filled with a muddy-looking mixture. "The mystic
marriage isn't just a matter of measuring and mixing. The *materiae* are put in
layers, suspended in the correct solvent, but each must be added by the proper
role and sometimes with words as well."

"The proper role?" Margerit prompted. "I remember reading something
about how Mercury will do this and Jupiter will do that and the Virgin will
cause the Lion to eat the Sun, but I thought those were just poetic descriptions
of the stellar alignments."

"Sometimes, but some of them mean the people performing the process.
Mercury is usually the principal alchemist, though sometimes it means the
transmutation itself. The lion and sun are different parts of the heating
process. But the virgin, the twins, Mars and Venus, the king and queen usually
indicate roles for people. We can only do processes that need one or two, of
course."

As she continued on, Antuniet interrupted only occasionally to correct
or expand on a point. "The roles and words…" she explained. "They aren't
mysteries because they don't call on the saints, though some alchemists use
the Great Work to perfect the soul as well as the physical world. The processes
use all sorts of heathen names from the ancients, but only to stand for forces
and properties of the world, or to mark the alignment of the planets and
describe the precise phase and position of the moon, or to indicate the roles of
the participants, as you see."

Anna took up the thread again at her signal. "You could say the same thing
in ordinary language, but the ancient writers preferred to conceal their secrets
from those outside the craft. And sometimes the more poetic descriptions
make things easier to remember."

Margerit looked over the diagrams that described the rituals. She could see
a resemblance, slight though it might be, to the drawings she used to describe
her visions during mysteries. "But I don't understand why it's necessary to go
through all this," she said, gesturing at the array of equipment. "Can't you
start with natural stones and—what was it you said—exalt them?" She could

tell it was a good question from the glint in Antuniet's eyes as she took over the explanation.

"The properties inherent in the stones have long been known and cataloged and a great deal of work has been done attempting to enhance those properties. DeBoodt's genius was to perform the enhancement—the exaltation, we call it—on the *primae materiae*…the raw materials, if you will. Then the physical transformation and the exaltation operate in harmony. Like all the alchemists of his time, he kept his methods closely secret. His public writings concerned only the description of the properties. All that remained of the other after his death were rumors and a handful of gems added to the crown of Saint Wenceslas that slowly lost their potency over the years. And the book, of course, though it was lost by then. But it isn't only the exaltation of the *materiae* that matters; the purity and perfection of the gems amplify the effect. It's always been known that a perfect stone is stronger than a flawed one. In theory, by using DeBoodt's processes, it should be possible to create much purer stones."

"In theory? If creating jewels were easy, surely every goldsmith would do so."

"They try," Anna broke in. "It's not really worth the trouble for ordinary stones. The gem merchants hold to their monopoly, so you can only make them for your own use. That's why my father allowed me to come learn from Maisetra Chazillen. But alchemy takes long study and discipline and the results aren't always dependable. Most attempts only produce a very pretty sand. And the untrained can't manage even that." Her pride was clear in the glance she gave her teacher.

Antuniet led the way to where the results of the firing were displayed. "Here's what she's talking about—and most of what we've been producing so far. Almost anyone who's studied the masters can produce this." She stirred the contents of a dish with a fingertip. "Too small even to set as pavé and their properties have no strength at all even with the enhancement. It takes forever to pick them out of the matrix. They can be used as a starting point for further work, though, especially for the formulas I was working out in the autumn. The firing is the key to making larger ones—the time, the heat, above all the position of the furnace and the hour you begin. I have endless notes on which combinations work best, but there's a great deal more to learn. Every time I move my workshop, it seems as if everything I've learned becomes useless." She took out a pocket watch and consulted it briefly. "Anna, continue, the alignment is approaching."

Margerit stared in fascination as they clamped the lid on the waiting crucible and sealed it with clay and symbols. Antuniet was right: the actions and words had the feel of a mystery ritual. There'd been no stirring of her visions when reviewing the static work, but now wisps of sound and light played about the edges of the vessel. "What happens if you don't mark the seal?"

Anna looked surprised at the question. "It won't work. This isn't gold or silver to fuse by the heat of the furnace alone. The salamander must be bound both by the crucible and by the signs before it will loose its fire."

"Do you see something?" Antuniet asked. "I sometimes think…No, later." She took up the crucible with long iron tongs and waited for Anna to open the furnace door.

As the work was slipped inside and turned to align the symbols with the door, Margerit thought she saw something like a *fluctus* moving within the waves of heat. Then Antuniet pushed the crucible farther in and it winked out. "Why is your furnace set aslant from the room?" she asked curiously. "Is that—"

"DeBoodt gives the requirements," Anna answered promptly as she adjusted the drop-weights for the clockwork bellows. "It needs to be aligned to the stars for the particular stone and purpose. He has endless calendars giving the proper time to start every type of conjunction throughout the year. We have to reposition it for each firing. DeBoodt had a great iron wheel under his to turn it."

"I remember that from the drawings," Margerit said. "It would certainly make the movement easier." So that explained the odd location, and the long beams at the side of the room for moving the massive athanor. But something niggled at the edge of her mind. She gestured at the tongs. "Do you mind if I try something? Would it ruin the work to open the furnace again?"

Antuniet tilted her head curiously and shrugged. "They're all just experiments at the moment. As long as we record what was done…" She nodded to Anna, who retrieved her thick gloves and unlatched the door.

The tongs were heavy and awkward and Margerit had only a faint idea of what she wanted to try, but she teased the crucible around, turning it in place only a degree or two at a time. The heat of the coals made her eyes water but through it she saw again that faint twist of *fluctus*. More carefully now, a hairbreadth, then another. As brilliantly as a lightning flash, the currents swirled to encompass the crucible and encase it in a ball of iridescent light. She heard Antuniet gasp behind her and signaled Anna to close the furnace again. "So you saw it?" Margerit asked.

Antuniet was shaking her head, not in denial but in wonder. "The peacock's tail. I told you once before, I can see enough to know *when* something happens but not why or how. That was the sign that the conjunction has begun." She turned to her apprentice. "Anna, did you notice anything odd there at the end?"

With a bewildered look, she answered, "No, nothing."

"Ah, well, there's no shame in that. Not one in a hundred are *vidators* and the work can be learned without it. But how could DeBoodt have been so mistaken? The book is most specific about the positioning of the furnace and the alignment of the seals."

"Maisetra?" Anna asked hesitantly.

"Yes?"

"Is it possible...it seems to me...what if the position of the stars only matters to align the furnace precisely?"

"Of course," Antuniet said with a trace of impatience. "But that still means the alignments are wrong."

"Or different," Anna said. "The calendars use the position of the zodiac, but he doesn't usually say much about the influence of the stars other than for timing. The theoretical discussions all focus on the planets and the sun and moon. The alignments to the planets and the moon are checked directly by sightings, but what if the sun itself is the key alignment for the conjunction?"

"It could be..."

Margerit could tell that Antuniet had followed the thought but couldn't see it herself yet.

Antuniet's eyes took a faraway look, as if she were calculating in her head. "DeBoodt was working over two hundred years ago. The precession shift could put all his tables off by a couple of degrees, but that shouldn't make so great a difference. Sunrise would only differ by a few minutes. But it might explain why only the jaspers and carnelians proved true; they're more forgiving of the precise alignment."

Anna had caught her enthusiasm. "But there's the difference in geography as well. You were working at much the same latitude in Heidelberg, but we're farther west and more south here. The angle..."

"Perhaps. It's worth a try." Her voice took on the crisp tones of a university *dozzur*. "Calculate a new calendar of alignments, corrected for the shift and, since you think it important, for latitude. No, calculate three tables. One for each effect and one combined."

Anna looked daunted but said only, "Yes, Maisetra." The triple calculations seemed excessive, but Margerit suspected they were meant for practice.

"If we had years to work and a skilled *vidator* always at hand, we could simply draw up the tables by experiment, but that would be impractical. Once we have the new calculations, Margerit, perhaps you could find the time to verify the alignments the first few times?"

"Of course," Margerit said. It was the same simmering excitement they had known back in the days of the guild. She ventured, "So am I forgiven for intruding into your work?"

For a moment she wasn't sure Antuniet recognized it for a joke, then she burst out in the first genuine laugh Margerit had heard from her since her return. "Forgiven! Though I should hold out for one of DeBoodt's iron wheels as a penance."

They'd been too focused to note the knock on the door until Jeanne came through into the workroom. Looking up, Margerit caught the barest glimpse of an odd look—envy?—before it vanished to be replaced by a smile.

"Have I missed the festivities? Here I thought you were always hard at work."

Antuniet welcomed her into the room, saying, "Margerit has stumbled onto a flaw in our calculations. I could almost scream for all the time I've wasted, but—"

"—but you wouldn't have listened to me before," Margerit pointed out. "Everything comes in its own time."

"And clearly I've come in mine," Jeanne finished. "Margerit, since you're here, you simply must help me convince Antuniet to come to Mesnera Chaluk's concert next week. She refused me for the skating party and she refused the Nantozes' little soirée, but I'm determined to prevail this time."

"I wasn't invited to any of them," Antuniet pointed out with the air of a continuing argument.

"I had leave to bring any guest I chose."

"And how much longer would you continue to be given that leave if you brought me? The name Chazillen is still an embarrassment in most homes in Rotenek. I won't enter anyplace I haven't been invited by name."

It wasn't only a matter of invitations, Margerit knew. Antuniet had been close to the Nantozes in happier times and now they didn't speak at all. "There's one invitation I can guarantee," Margerit offered. "Jeanne, I've been meaning to ask your help. I want to sponsor another lecture."

"Is your mad English botanist back in town?"

"No, this time it will be Akezze Mainus—Antuniet, you remember her, the poor-scholar who could tie all the men in knots of logic—and I need to get the right people there to hear her."

"And who might the right people be?" Jeanne asked. "Fashion or influence?"

"Neither. People who would pay to have her as an instructor. I've hired her to come with us to Saveze for the summer to tutor me, but there's no hope of keeping her in Rotenek in the fall unless she has enough students to make it worthwhile. And I'm not talking about schoolgirls. She's a better scholar and a better teacher than half the *dozzures* at the university. But I need people to see that for themselves and the ones I want wouldn't come just for entertainment. That's where I need your help. It's all entirely selfish, you know."

Antuniet turned from where she'd been setting the workbench in order. "The both of you have very strange ideas of selfishness."

"Now there's a challenge," Jeanne said, tapping a finger against her lips in thought. "Do you know what she'll be speaking on? It would help if there were some practical use—"

"The rhetoric of public debate," Antuniet suggested. "If she's willing. Don't aim for the well-born students. It's the ambitious *burfroites* you need to attract and mostly they'll want knowledge they can apply in their careers. Geometric proofs are all very well, but teach a man how to win an argument in sessions and he'll be willing to learn it even from a woman."

"An excellent idea. Margerit, will you hire the *Salle-Chapil* like last time? Or perhaps someplace in the university district would make more sense."

When she left an hour later, Margerit was confident that the lecture would have its best chance of success.

* * *

When the day arrived, the lecture was indeed looking to be successful, at least within the modest ambitions she'd set for herself. The *salle* was growing full, or nearly so. There was a sprinkling of the powerful to give the affair approval, but largely the crowd consisted of students, eager to hear something outside the limits of their formal lectures or simply curious. It seemed that her own name was enough to stir that curiosity when it was attached to the event. Barbara had insisted, even to the point of staying home, *This is your venture. Have faith that you can carry it off.* It had made sense when she'd said it, but she wished for Barbara's presence for comfort, if not for courage.

This time she stood alone, welcoming those who would expect special notice or who were close friends. Jeanne and Antuniet arrived together, but she had no time for more than a brief nod. It seemed Antuniet had decided to spend a mark or two on new clothing after all… No, she'd seen that outfit before on Jeanne. So perhaps the pride could bend a little when there was no complication of patronage to provoke it. With no time to think further on the matter, she turned with a glad cry to greet Amiz Waldimen and Cheris Riumai, but it was Cheris Enien now. "I scarcely expected to see you here. Amiz, have you decided to give up balls and return to the university?" They all laughed, for Amiz had never been more than desultory at her studies, attending lectures out of boredom while waiting for her turn to be out.

"I saw the notice and thought it would be a lark to see what you were up to. And I dragged Cheris along so I wouldn't need my mother as *vizeino*. I don't know that she'd entirely approve."

There were others present from the loose community of girl-scholars: the ones hungry for what scraps the university allowed to fall their way and the ones, like Amiz, who had attended lectures as a permitted license from their sheltered lives. Margerit knew she'd become something of a legend among the younger girl-scholars and there were some shy and longing glances from under the shadow of their escorts. But welcome though the girls were, the most important audience for the lecture would be men. They were the ones who could pay for tutoring, whether for their children or themselves.

It was in greeting the noble guests that she most longed for Barbara's presence. Barbara knew everyone, with a minuteness of detail that astounded. Margerit more than once found herself scrambling to recall a name or title and falling back on a hurried, "Mesner, welcome to my lecture," before moving on to the next. She was startled to see Efriturik come through the doors, just before they were set to close. "Baron Razik!" she said. "I'm honored that you chose to come."

He bowed in that funny foreign way he hadn't managed to shake—or did he keep it as a charming affectation the way Jeanne cultivated hers? "Maisetra Sovitre, my mother sends her hopes for a successful venture. She wishes me to say—" He paused, as if trying to recall the exact words. "—that she is pleased to see the pleasures of the mind leavening the frivolity of the season. Me," he added, "I prefer the frivolity."

"And that makes me the more grateful you came. I didn't know you were interested in rhetoric."

He shrugged, looking out over the crowd. "My mother wishes me to find some useful occupation. I don't have it in me for a scholar. And they won't let me take up a commission in the cavalry yet. So I look here and there. Perhaps I will make a career in politics."

Afterward, she couldn't have said whether the lecture went well or ill. It was all a nervous blur. But the buzz of conversation among the departing audience told her she had accomplished her desired end. Once was a novelty, twice success. And when everyone returned at the end of summer, she'd try a third. After that, the lectures would be considered an institution.

CHAPTER NINETEEN

Jeanne

"Jeanne, what are your plans for the day, other than choosing some new books?" Alenur had met her as they both entered Charner's library. "Helen says there's a hill out past the west gate where the snowdrops are already blooming. We're going out to see if we can find them. Do come along; I've hardly seen you since the turning of the year."

"Snowdrops?" Jeanne asked.

"Any excuse for an outing. The weather's been so miserable these past few weeks and this will be the third fine day in a row. I have space for you in my carriage. Helen's is full already and Verneke is bringing her girls and you know how they chatter."

For a moment Jeanne was swept up in the vision: carriages full of laughing companions, a drive in the crisp bright air, a lighthearted treasure hunt. Someone would bring champagne and then they'd stop at that tavern a mile out on the western road to dine. She shook her head reluctantly. "I'm promised to a friend for luncheon. You couldn't wait for tomorrow?"

"Pooh! A luncheon? What's that when the snowdrops might be gone by tomorrow. Your friend will understand."

"No, but you might offer the place to Tionez. She could use an outing to cheer her up now that her husband's been posted off to Paris. She's been languishing, the poor dear."

* * *

But on arriving at Trez Cherfis, the housekeeper met her at the door with a finger on her lips, saying, "The maisetra said they weren't to be disturbed until they're done," with a jerk of her head toward the closed door to the workroom. And the presence of Margerit's armin, rising discreetly from the anteroom's only chair, told her who "they" comprised.

Jeanne tried to keep the dismay from her face. "Ah, I must have mistaken the time," she whispered and directed Marien to put the basket with the food on the table. It was never any use to try to coax Antuniet out to eat—even to the cookshop on the corner—when there was work to be done. "I can wait here," she said, settling into the newly vacant chair.

The woman shrugged and disappeared back down the corridor. From the other room came the sound of rhythmic voices, too low to distinguish the words. Silence and footsteps, then a voice again. She could recognize Margerit's tones this time but couldn't follow what was said. She tried to envision what actions that rhythm accompanied. What was it that needed such seclusion and took so long? The work Antuniet had shown her in the past had all been physical, more like the work of a kitchen than the churchlike rituals this evoked.

An hour passed. Marien ventured to ask, "Mesnera, perhaps we should leave?"

"No, I'm sure it can't be much longer." But it was another hour before the inner door opened with a burst of excited voices.

Antuniet spotted her with a look of almost comical dismay. "Oh, Jeanne, I'm so sorry! I entirely forgot! We had such success yesterday that I couldn't wait to try the full process. The alignments were going to be perfect and—"

"—and everything else flew out of your mind. I know how well that can happen!" Jeanne brushed away her annoyance and put on a smile as she rose. "I'm afraid the food's all gone cold, but there's plenty for three," she said with a nod to Margerit.

"Oh, no, I'm already late getting back," Margerit countered. "We're promised to Lady Marzim for dinner and I'll need hours to make myself presentable." She gestured at the grimy smock thrown over her clothes and scrubbed at a smudge on her cheek, only worsening it. "But Antuniet, tomorrow? May I return to see the results?"

"Of course. Jeanne, truly, I am sorry. Can you wait for me to wash up? Anna, bring one of the other chairs out here."

A little more waiting would scarcely matter, but it was annoying when an elaborate plan went awry. And how long had Margerit been a partner in the alchemy? Jeanne directed Marien to begin laying out the hamper of food. Jealousy was such a pointless thing. And she wasn't jealous of Margerit, not really. Not even of her fortune—though how differently things might have gone if she herself had been able to stand as Antuniet's patron last fall! No, it was the work itself that was her rival. And there was no answer to that except to embrace them both. Without that work, the woman she loved wouldn't exist.

Antuniet showed a gratifying attention to the food. Jeanne chattered of inconsequential things while they ate, but when they'd come to tea and biscuits she asked, "What is it that had you all excited this morning?"

"We finally worked out the process for a batch of the chrysolite. I couldn't manage it before with just Anna and me. This is a chance to really test the strength of the exaltation. With so many of the properties it's as bad as looking for signs of miracles from a mystery: did the saints hearken or was it only chance?"

"And why is this one different?" Jeanne asked.

The barest flicker away of Antuniet's eyes spoke volumes. "It's…it banishes evil dreams. If it works, I'll know."

"The same dream still?"

Antuniet looked confused.

"You had bad dreams that night you spent at my house at the New Year. Something about your mother." She could tell from Antuniet's response that it was not a subject she cared to discuss. "No matter," Jeanne said, dismissing it with a brief touch on her arm. The chance to comfort her wouldn't be worth the distress. "Tell me what you did this morning."

It was so easy to listen as Antuniet poured out the details, the plans and the expectations. So easy to be lost in the animation of her eyes. This was the wine she came here to drink. But she tried to take it in more deeply, to ask questions that showed not only interest but understanding. And when Antuniet noted for the third time how much more progress they'd made now that there were more participants for the roles, Jeanne said quietly, "You could have asked me as well."

Antuniet looked startled. "I didn't think…it wouldn't…Jeanne, this isn't the ceremonies of a mystery guild. It's dirty work. The roles—they aren't just symbols. They represent tasks in the processing and enhancement."

"I suppose I should get myself some sort of gardener's smock like Margerit's," Jeanne said, dismissing the objection. "And gloves, or…would gloves interfere?" She looked down at her hands, preserved against time and weather with such diligent care. Was she mad? But it would always be a barrier between them if she held back.

"Gloves, of course," Antuniet assured her. "Are you sure? I'd love to have more help, but you're always so busy."

"With morning visits and soirées and pleasure drives out to look for elusive snowdrops. I'm sure I can be spared on occasion."

Antuniet paused in looking over the sweetmeats. "Snowdrops?"

Jeanne launched into the tale, making it both more amusing and less attractive in the telling than it had been in life that morning.

* * *

And the work *was* dirty and sometimes tedious. But then there were times when she was swept up in the excitement of creation. There were parts to learn and roles that sometimes seemed more like a holiday masque than a scientific process. One by one they worked through the formulas that Antuniet had chosen for the demonstration of mastery.

"What came before were only the elements. Oh, I made a few enhanced stones to confirm it was possible, but this is the real work." She sorted through the piles of notes and diagrams that carefully documented the essential details not elaborated in DeBoodt. "It'll take years to learn the techniques for every stone and every property he describes and we don't have the participants for most of them yet. But here's the list I want to produce before—"

She left the rest unsaid, but Jeanne knew: before she went back to Annek to present her gift. Curiously, she reached over and took up the book. Antuniet had her own copy again now, bound in dark green leather with gilded edges. That had been her own gift—that binding. Too ornate, perhaps, for a working text but she'd been unable to resist. She read through the handlist tucked between the pages. "What about this one? 'To protect travelers and make the stranger welcome.' That would be useful."

Antuniet gave her a rueful glance. "There was a day that would have been more than useful! But it needs someone for the Mars role." She sighed. "I don't want to bring in outsiders until we've had more practice."

Margerit looked thoughtful. "Does the role specifically require a man or simply a warrior? I was wondering: might Barbara be able to try it?"

"For that I don't know. It might be interesting to see, but the baroness hasn't offered."

A thread of tension stretched through the room. Had Barbara been asked and refused? Or had she simply washed her hands of her cousin's life again once the crisis was past? Jeanne skimmed down over the list of formulas, looking for those with no more than four female roles. "I like this one. 'To ensure that the true worth and beauty of the bearer is seen.'" Her gaze flicked briefly to where Anna was working. How many women could benefit from that power!

Antuniet glanced over at the handlist, then looked through her own papers. "I don't think we can manage that one at the moment. It requires a mirroring of the *virgo* role. Anna usually takes that one but—"

"Couldn't Margerit take the second?" Jeanne asked. "After all, it isn't as if—"

Antuniet cut her off with a gesture and turned to say, "Anna, go fetch water to fill the copper. It will be nice to have it hot for washing up."

Jeanne watched the girl leave. "Was that necessary?"

"I'm responsible for what she learns under my roof," Antuniet said briskly. "DeBoodt is fairly explicit in the definitions of the several types of roles. For the *virgo* he says it must be 'one who has not known carnal embrace.' And Margerit, I doubt you meet the requirement."

Margerit turned a pretty shade of pink and said, "Yes, I suppose so. But couldn't you take it?"

"No," Antuniet said sharply and pushed away from the table to busy herself with something on the bench.

And what was that about? Jeanne wondered. The answer had scarcely invited further questions. Antuniet had spent nearly two years wandering the face of Europe alone. It would be no wonder if… Her imagination failed her, not knowing whether it should lead to curiosity or pity.

"I had another thought for the male role," Margerit offered into the lengthening silence. "I want to explore it further before mentioning names, but it wouldn't be an outsider. Not exactly."

Antuniet only shrugged and said, "As you please," as if she were weary of the conversation.

Jeanne lingered when the others had left, seeking a chance for a question that couldn't wait, but uncertain of Antuniet's mood. "Toneke, you've disappointed me," she began at last.

"And what have I done now?" Her voice was tired.

Jeanne knew instantly that the teasing had been a mistake but it was too late to begin again. "You promised that you'd come out with me if you were invited by name. And I know that Margerit asked you to the opening of Fizeir's new opera. And I know that you refused."

Antuniet sighed. "Jeanne, I have nothing to wear. Not to the opera. I can't go on always borrowing your gowns."

"Which is why I've made an appointment for you with my dressmaker tomorrow. I made sure it was in the late afternoon because I know you have work planned in the morning, but she'll need a week to do her best and that doesn't leave much time." She saw Antuniet preparing to refuse and pleaded, "Please let me do this. I know you let Margerit buy you that rock crystal crucible and it must have cost twenty times what a ball gown would."

And once more she knew she'd managed things badly when Antuniet colored and looked away, mumbling, "That was for the work."

"I don't know what's come over me today; everything I say is wrong!" She reached out to take Antuniet's hand and said earnestly, "I try to understand. I really do. But I can't help you the ways that Margerit can. You take so little time for yourself and that's where I *can* help." She searched Antuniet's face, trying to see if she had redeemed herself and finally released her hand when Antuniet stopped trying to pull away. She added more cheerfully, "And I won't enjoy the opera nearly so much if you aren't there beside me."

A war fought itself out in Antuniet's face but at last she said only, "Thank you. And thank you for asking Margerit to invite me."

* * *

An opera night always called for more than ordinary care in dressing but it didn't usually entail the mountain of gowns that had been considered and discarded and lay waiting for Marien to return them to the wardrobe. And it rarely called for more than an hour to be spent over the selection of jewelry and the application of powder and paint. Jeanne brushed at her cheek once more with the haresfoot, then leaned toward the mirror. She pulled at the corner of her mouth, smoothing out an imagined line. *Someday soon I'll become as ridiculous as an aging roué. Please God, not for a few years yet.*

Why had she ever thought—even for the moment of denying it—that Antuniet might grow to feel more for her than gratitude and friendship? Every time she tried to reach out she became as clumsy as a green girl. And for what? As she kept reminding herself, there was no future for her there. It was time to let go of that fantasy before Antuniet found her attention tedious. And yet she was drawn again and again like a moth to the moon, simply for the pleasure of her company and the taste of bittersweet dreams. So it ever had been. She had no power to deny herself even the shadow of pleasure. But giving up didn't mean letting herself go. She addressed her image in the glass in stern tones. "When you admire a woman, it is a virtue to make yourself attractive *for* her, even if it isn't possible to make yourself attractive *to* her." She took up the haresfoot again and dipped it in powder to brush across her cheek.

Marien tapped and entered, carrying her feather-topped turban, freshly arranged into crispness. "Your guest is here, Mesnera."

"Tell her to come up, I'm almost ready."

She finished the last touches and stood as Antuniet was shown into the dressing room. "Oh, Toneke, it's beautiful! Dominique triumphs again!" She had known the rose shade would set off Antuniet's dark coloring, but the dressmaker had transformed her steadfast refusal of lace and ribbons into an elegant texture of pleats and tucks. "You look lovely," she added in the face of clear skepticism. "Now help me choose a shawl. I keep coming back to this hideous thing." She held up the offending garment. "Tio convinced me that striped fringe was all the rage, but…" She shuddered in mock revulsion.

"You're coming to me for advice on fashion?" Antuniet asked in amusement. "Which one do you like the most?"

"Ah, that would be this one," Jeanne said promptly, holding up a length of mauve cashmere, its borders decorated with a design of peacock feathers. "But the color is impossible with this gown. Although…" She held it up speculatively against Antuniet's shoulder. "Perfect! You simply must borrow it for tonight," she urged before any protest could be made. "With that vision before me I can bear the striped fringe." She held it up and circled around behind Antuniet to drape it across her arms and shoulders. A wave of heat ran through her. The wisps of hair trailing across the back of Antuniet's bare neck invited kisses. She closed her eyes, only to have her senses filled with the scent of her. No, this would never do! If she didn't find some distraction soon, she'd be betrayed into doing something unforgivable.

Margerit had offered a light supper before the affair but Jeanne had demurred. "I hope you don't mind, Toneke," she offered, "but I thought you might prefer a quiet bite here with me." And she would have the pleasure of Antuniet's company all to herself for a time. She was different in public, even with just the few of them at the workshop; there only the work brought out her inner fire. But here at home…"Tell me more about Prague," Jeanne urged when the soup was served. "Once you promised me the full story of how you found your treasure with a true-love charm!"

Antuniet leaned forward, but her eyes were distant. "There's an ancient wall by the castle where long ago people built houses into the spaces of the archways. Back in King Rudolf's day, when he gathered alchemists from across the face of Europe under his patronage, it was known as a gathering place. I don't know whether it was a bookshop already at that time or if it was DeBoodt's workshop, or one of his student's. But somehow his greatest work came to fall behind a case, against the wall. I was in the shop one day, a tiny place crammed so full of books you could hardly turn around. When I worked the finding charm it kept leading me to the back of a cabinet, even after I'd emptied out all the shelves onto the floor. And when I tapped on the back there was one spot that didn't echo like the rest. It took most of the day to convince the owner that I was ready to buy whatever it was, sight unseen. He had to chisel open the back of the cabinet because it had been plastered to the walls ages ago. The book must have fallen down from on top and been utterly forgotten for over two hundred years."

It was like an ancient fairy tale with romance and adventure, chance and destiny. She could imagine Antuniet standing there among the shelves and corridors, lighting her tiny candle and sprinkling the dust of the charm over it to see which way the sparks pointed her. And she was grateful that in the course of time they'd pointed her back to Rotenek. Antuniet had brought new fire into her life even if it could never go beyond moments like this.

The opera itself was only ordinarily entertaining. Maistir Fizeir was known for his historic tragedies, but tragedies had become less popular than farce. His attempts to join the two made for an odd assortment. The guests, too, were an odd assortment: the aunt and uncle and some assorted older Pertinek cousins; a countrified-looking gentleman who might be some connection of Margerit's Chalanz relatives. Jeanne suspected that Margerit was using the occasion to pay off a collection of social debts that hadn't balanced out in the ordinary course of things. She should put a word in her ear about how to manage these things more elegantly.

It mattered little. An excellent performance could have been transporting, but tonight it was enough to enjoy having Antuniet at her side and to exchange small witty comments with the other guests. Antuniet seemed to have expended most of the store of her conversation over dinner, but she gave every sign of enjoying the music and the company. "It's different," she said at one quiet moment. "When my mother dragged me to the opera it was always to be on display. And then there would be a quarrel when we returned home because I hadn't spoken to this one, or was unfriendly to that one. There was no chance simply to listen."

"I've never thought of conversation as a burden," Jeanne said. "What you must think of me! I made you talk all through dinner."

The music swelled and prevented a response, but when the song was finished Antuniet continued, "I didn't mind. You make it so easy to talk. It's different when it's just us. I miss—" She hesitated uncertainly. "It may seem strange to miss anything about those awful months last fall, but I miss our little picnic lunches. There never seems to be time for that now."

Jeanne was tempted to retort about whose fault that was, but instead she pressed Antuniet's hand silently. She let go more quickly than she'd planned as the heat rose again. But it was gratifying to know that she'd been able to provide those bright memories.

They walked about the galleries at the interval, though Antuniet declined to do more than nod to old acquaintances in the hallways, and then returned early enough to Margerit's box to catch the last of the visitors there.

"I was wondering where you'd wandered off to," Count Chanturi greeted her, rising from where he sat beside Barbara. "I'm holding a small celebration afterward to congratulate Fizeir on the new work. I've been hoping you could come because there's someone I'd like you to meet. Will you grace us?"

"So kind of you to invite us, Rikerd," Jeanne replied, looking pointedly at Antuniet, still close at her side.

Chanturi added, "Maisetra Chazillen is welcome too, of course." Antuniet nodded hesitantly, but she couldn't say she hadn't been specifically included. He turned back to kiss Barbara's hand and bow farewell to their hostess.

The opera ended in a muddle of deaths and triumphs, with the lighter elements falling somewhere by the wayside. Jeanne doubted it would be performed again after this season.

They were a smaller party to join the celebration afterward. The Pertineks and several others had made an early evening of it. Margerit's country friend pleaded business in the morning and perhaps sensed that he would be out of place in the Count's crowd. But the rest descended to the smaller concert hall that Chanturi had hired for his festivities.

There were speeches and congratulations from the composer and his patrons, all hearty and insincere. The principals were toasted and then the guests were released to the scattered tables of food and drink, with small groups of performers entertaining between them. At first Jeanne feared they might be regaled with a repetition of highlights from the evening's work, but it seemed the singers and dancers had been directed to bring out favored bits from previous seasons. She recognized snippets of the overtures and a few of the arias. But the entertainments were the least of the evening. Maisetra Ovinze offered a wealth of gossip regarding performances they could expect in the fall, and when Tionez claimed her attention to tell all the fashion news her husband had written from Paris, a crowd of eager listeners buzzed about them. Antuniet drifted away while Tio held forth and Jeanne watched her worriedly with half an eye until she fell into conversation with Margerit.

When the swarm around Tio dissipated, Rikerd pulled her aside to point out a group of dancers in an energetic performance halfway between a tarantella and the tumbling of acrobats. "She's quite talented," he said archly, directing her attention to the smallest figure in the group. "I'll introduce her when they've finished the set."

Jeanne took a moment to admire the blond dancer's skill, then raised an eyebrow at him, not in question but in understanding. He smiled and nodded and moved on to the next group of his guests. Well, perhaps this was what she needed: distraction without any lasting entanglements. In the brief breathing space, Jeanne looked around for Antuniet and found her standing by a string quartet who were playing at the far end of the room so as not to compete with the singers.

"You're being very quiet," Jeanne said, coming up beside her. She seemed to be listening to the music more as an excuse for retreat than in true interest. "I hope you aren't sorry you came."

Antuniet gave a careful answer. "The evening has been pleasant enough, but I was up at dawn to set up the firing and tomorrow will be all day cleaning up the result to study."

"Surely it could wait another day if you're tired?"

She shrugged. "It could, but until I know how the stones came out I won't know whether the adjustments to the congelation worked. And then I wouldn't have the new procedure worked out in time for the next alignment. Margerit promised to find me someone to take the Mars role, so it will waste everyone's time if I'm not ready."

Even here her thoughts were back in the workshop. She hadn't meant the additional invitation to be a burden. "You could have said no to this."

"Oh, Jeanne, I don't mean to complain. I didn't want to drag you away. You've been working so hard to find people who will receive me. I don't want to seem ungrateful, either to you or to the Count. Don't worry over me. Go enjoy yourself." Someone else might have come up with a polite lie, either to escape the party or to excuse her mood. Antuniet didn't deal in polite lies but neither was it her habit to apologize at such length.

Jeanne frowned. "Are you sure? Say the word and we could go. We've been here long enough to honor Chanturi's invitation."

"Thank you," she said. "But I'm enjoying the music for now. It's only the people who make me tired."

Jeanne couldn't think of how to answer that except to let her be. She saw Rikerd beckon to her from across the room and, with a light touch on the shoulder in place of the missing words, she left Antuniet to the viols in the corner.

"Jeanne, I thought you might enjoy meeting Luzild," he said as she approached, gesturing at the petite dancer. "Luzild, this is the Vicomtesse de Cherdillac. She's a great patron and admirer of the arts." And with that, he stepped discreetly away to find other amusements.

Jeanne had thought at first glance, from her diminutive height, that the girl was young. The dance companies were generally chosen to be well-matched in size. But it was only that she was compactly built, combining a womanly body with the lithe athleticism of a cat. "How long have you been dancing with the opera?" she asked. It seemed an easy opening to draw her out. "I'm trying to remember whether I've seen you perform before."

"Only for a year now," she replied. "They needed someone to dance the role of the monkey in *La Turca* last March and one of the musicians remembered seeing me performing in Iuten at floodtide, and Maistir Fizeir thought I'd be perfect for the role." The woman's mobile expression reflected her every emotion. "And of course once I was here in Rotenek I was hardly going to let myself be sent back to the provinces! But I don't appear in any of the main dances, only in the back of the chorus. That's why you don't remember seeing me. They say it's because I'm not good enough yet or because I'm so short, but—" She leaned forward conspiratorially. "—they're as bad as a flock of hens for not letting new people in. I think they're just jealous." Her eyes sparkled and a wide grin split her face. "Fizeir says he may write a child's dance for me in the next one, and of course if they need the tumbling they come to me. That's what I was doing in Iuten before."

She chattered on at length, hardly needing prompting to tell the story of her life and career so far. Jeanne was amused at her complete absence of self-consciousness, but to stem the flood of trivialities, she asked, "So how does a monkey dance?"

The woman looked up at her sideways with speculation. "Perhaps you'd like to see?" she asked. "I think there's a hallway back behind the promenade where there would be enough room." And few people about, Jeanne thought, as the dancer led her out past the wide entryway and around the corner.

The place was empty and unlit, though the glow from the promenade beyond left enough to see by. Luzild slipped off her shoes and stretched and twisted briefly to loosen her muscles. Her face was stiller now as she bent and curved in clever contortions: now standing on both hands with her back arched, now lifting one leg and then the other to tumble in one spot like a slowly rolling wheel. Her wide, flowing skirts followed her muscular limbs like water, always promising but never revealing what lay beneath. She finished by bending her legs up over her head to set herself down nearly at Jeanne's feet then rose up in a slow, controlled stretch to stand before her, close enough that Jeanne could feel her panting breath. The dancer fixed her gaze and said low, "Count Chanturi tells me that you might be interested in a companion for the evening."

It was a delicate but unmistakable offer. A flood of warmth ran through her at the promise in those tones. Jeanne answered with similar delicacy, "Count Chanturi is an old and dear friend who is very familiar with my tastes."

Luzild stretched up on her toes and leaned forward boldly. Her hot breath tickled Jeanne's cheek as she whispered, "Or for the night?"

"Very familiar," Jeanne repeated as the woman's lips brushed hers. Hunger ran under her skin. One hand came up without thought to guide the kisses to the corner of her jaw, the hollow below her ear, the nape of her neck. Her other hand moved across the woman's back and lower, enjoying the play of muscles beneath the curve of her hip. A brief wash of guilt whispered Antuniet's name in her mind but Luzild pressed closer and more insistently. It had been too long…too long. Jeanne felt a draft of cool air on her leg as her skirts were drawn up and gasped in pleasure at a touch on her most intimate parts. That brought her back to her senses. She moved away a fraction. "Shh, not here, not now."

"Where and when?" The warm lips pursued her. "Tonight?"

"Tonight…" No, tonight was impossible. "There is a friend I must see safely home tonight. Tomorrow?"

"I perform tomorrow night. We practice all afternoon."

Jeanne saw a petulant look creep over the dancer's face. No doubt she feared if the moment of passion were allowed to pass, the opportunity would as well. Her own heat longed to burn itself out. She touched the other's lips. "Don't pout. Something can be arranged."

Luzild nipped playfully at the fingertip and her mouth settled into a lopsided and knowing smile. "Arrange it soon."

"We should return to the *salle* now. Someone may come looking for me." She hoped the woman would have the tact to wait before following, but Luzild entered the crowded room hard on her heels. Jeanne turned back, just enough for a brief shake of her head and a shooing motion of her fan, before drifting farther out into the room. She thought she'd seen Antuniet over by the sideboard when she first entered, but now there was no sign and Tio claimed her ear for a lament on the life of a diplomat's wife.

When she was released once again, one of the servants approached with an apologetic cough. "Mesnera de Cherdillac? I was asked to give you a message from Maisetra Chazillen. She wished you to know that she has accepted a ride home from Maisetra Sovitre. She said she didn't wish to disturb you."

"Oh. Thank you." She'd said she was tired… Perhaps Margerit had offered at an opportune time. The guilt came back more strongly.

The man continued, "She left an item that she said was yours. A shawl? I placed it with your other things."

"Thank you," she repeated absently.

While she stood there in thought, Luzild passed by, sending a wink and a smile in her direction. In sudden decision Jeanne called her over. "It seems I'm free for the evening after all."

* * *

Jeanne rolled over sleepily and came more fully awake at the soft sound of snoring. She opened her eyes. The little dancer from last night. A slow smile turned to a moue of irritation. The woman really had no conversation. Last night their mouths had been far too busy with other things for it to matter, but the thought of her empty chatter stretching over breakfast… She slipped out of bed and pulled on a dressing gown. Luzild turned over and reached out an arm toward her. Jeanne kissed her own fingertips, then pressed them against the woman's lips. "I'm sorry for the rush but I have appointments to keep this morning." It was a polite fiction, but the woman would understand its meaning. "You don't mind seeing yourself out? Tomric will arrange for a carriage."

There were customs for this sort of thing. A gift was called for. Not money, of course—that would be an insult. A small gift was an invitation to meet again. A very expensive gift was the opening negotiation in a contract. But one that was neither large nor small signaled an amicable end to the matter. With as much warmth as she could muster, Jeanne said, "The evening was lovely. As a memento, perhaps you might accept—" She looked around for inspiration, wondering what would be suitable. Her eyes fell on the heap of clothing she'd discarded in the heat of the night before. "—you might accept the shawl I was wearing when we met." She gestured where the garments lay across the back of a chaise. With a smile and a wink she slipped into the dressing room, where Marien waited discreetly and closed the door behind her.

By the time she'd finished dressing, the dancer was gone. The fringed shawl still lay tumbled across her crumpled gown. That was an unusual move. If she hoped to bargain for something more she'd be disappointed. Jeanne shrugged and opened her jewelry case to contemplate the day's ornaments.

Marien moved about the room picking up the scattered garments. As she folded the shawl away into a drawer, she asked, "What's happened to the mauve cashmere, the one with the peacock design?"

"I lent it to—" No. Antuniet had returned it last night. Where had she put it? On the... She glanced back at the chaise. So that was it. She'd taken the wrong shawl. How annoying when it had matched Antuniet's gown so perfectly. "I gave it away," she finished.

* * *

The weather had turned foul again, wavering between rain and icy sleet. That alone might have explained Antuniet's mood, but what she railed against was the inexplicable lateness of everyone involved in the new working. Jeanne cut short her own excuses upon realizing she was the first to arrive.

"Margerit promised to bring someone for the Mars role but she hasn't seen fit to tell me who," Antuniet continued. "She takes too much on herself. And I have no idea what's happened to Anna." But the last had more of worry than irritation.

"She might be waiting to see if the rain passes," Jeanne offered.

"It never stopped her before," Antuniet muttered as they fell to setting out the equipment.

A clatter of carriage wheels outside heralded the answer to one set of questions. *Now that should not have been a surprise*, Jeanne thought when Margerit was followed through the door by Efriturik Atilliet. The front room was becoming quite crowded, given the shadowing armins as well. She could see the same thoughts crossing Antuniet's face as the formalities were dealt with.

"You know the Vicomtesse de Cherdillac, of course," Margerit said briskly. "And...but I don't know whether you ever had a formal introduction to Maisetra Chazillen back...before."

He made that charming foreign bow, saying carefully, "I am unlikely to forget any of the Chazillens."

Antuniet responded with equally stiff formality and Margerit plunged onward, "I remembered what Baron Razik said at Akezze's lecture—that he was looking for some useful occupation—but I didn't know what Her Grace might have to say to it, so I didn't want…Well, it doesn't matter. She thought it a fine idea and…and here we are."

"I am no scholar, like you or Maisetra Sovitre," he offered, "but my mother thinks I could be of some use here."

Antuniet looked as if she might have words in private for Margerit later, but said, "Then we have only to wait for my laggard apprentice and we can begin. Has Margerit told you anything of what we actually do in these workings? Good, that will save us some time. Perhaps you might read over—"

She was interrupted by a clatter of running feet outside and the sound of Anna's hurried farewell to her escort as the door opened once more.

"Maisetra, I'm so sorry," she said, hurriedly doffing her coat and bonnet. "The house was in an uproar this morning and—" She faltered, seeing the strangers present. Her face was flushed red from the run and the thread of her scar stood starkly white against it.

"Dear God, what an ugly thing!" Efriturik exclaimed into the sudden silence.

Anna looked wildly from one face to another, then plunged on past into the workshop, slamming the door behind her. The muffled sound of sobbing came through the boards.

He can't have meant that as badly as it sounded, Jeanne thought desperately.

"I meant the mark; it startled me," Efriturik said in confusion as all heads turned angrily.

Antuniet advanced stiffly toward him, stopping at a carefully calculated distance as if it were only the presence of his lurking armin that kept her from laying violent hands on him. "That scar," she said coldly, "is as much a medal of courage and loyalty as any soldier's tinsel. And if you ever again give her cause to weep or so much as blush over it, you needn't return."

"I meant no harm," he protested.

She seemed to believe him. "Then go apologize and we'll say no more of it."

There he balked, glancing toward the workshop door. "Apologize to a… an apprentice?"

"To my apprentice, yes. Or leave. It makes no difference to me."

What inducements had Annek laid on him to come? Whatever they'd been, it seemed refusal was not allowed. He slipped inside, closing the door again after him and emerged several minutes later followed by a silent but dry-eyed Anna.

* * *

In the weeks that followed, the work progressed better than its inauspicious start might have suggested. Efriturik had a flair for learning the lines and gestures, Jeanne observed critically. If, as she guessed, he had not come entirely of his own volition, at least he entered into it with a will. But he disrupted their cozy circle. From Antuniet, there was a tension; from Anna, a mortified reticence. And gone were the days of closing out the world with the workroom doors, for propriety demanded they be open for witness, though the armins paid little enough attention. At the second session they began a complex game of dice that picked up with no pause each time their duties brought them together. And as the days passed, with the work growing ever more successful, Antuniet had little time to spare. The cozy picnic lunches of their early days became a faint memory.

But surely today work can't be an excuse, Jeanne thought as Tionez bustled into her parlor in a carnival costume bordering on the outrageous, even for her. She had taken inspiration from the Parisian dandies, layering a garish waistcoat over close-fitting breeches and topping the whole with her husband's caped driving coat.

"That will turn heads!" Jeanne laughed. "Whatever would Iohen say?"

Tionez pulled her friend Maisetra Silpirt after her, more tamely costumed *à la bergère.* "Oh pooh! He wouldn't care. And he can't expect me to spend my days sulking at home while he's in Paris, can he, Iaklin?"

The other woman giggled nervously. Jeanne guessed that she was less sure of the limits of her license. Their husbands had met in the diplomatic service and Tio had taken the woman under her wing, to her greatly expanded education.

"Iohen won't be back until June, he says," Tionez continued. "And then it's the country for the rest of the summer and by the start of the season I'll either be too far gone to travel or have a little gift to look after." She laid a hand casually on her belly, confirming the truth of that rumor, at least. "I'll be a boring matron before you know it."

"Well, we need to see you properly entertained in the meantime, then," Jeanne said. "I have a scheme in mind for floodtide that I think you would enjoy. But enough on that for now. The plans aren't fixed yet."

Jeanne caught up her own cloak and mask and fastened it around her neat curls as they all settled into Tio's carriage. "I hope you have room for one more."

"Anything for you," Tionez said, rapping on the roof to catch the driver's attention.

"Then I'd like to go by Trez Cherfis and see if Antuniet will join us. I invited her last week." And she'd turned the subject without saying no or yes. Perhaps it would be better to let her be, Jeanne thought.

But Tio replied, "That odd duck? Whatever do you see in her?"

Jeanne returned, with the slightest touch of asperity, "My friends are quite a flock of odd ducks, as you well know. But if that bothers you, I'm sure I can find other guests for my little plans at floodtide."

"Oh, Jeanne, you wouldn't! Very well, invite the Chazillen. But I'll feel as if I'd brought my mother-in-law along."

It was no gamble at all to expect that Antuniet would be home, but she might be working, even on the last day of carnival. That question was answered when the door opened almost as soon as she knocked, but Jeanne saw with dismay that Antuniet had on the brown walking dress and was throwing her traveling cloak over it. "Oh dear, were you going out?"

"No. That is…I thought you'd asked me—" Antuniet hesitated in embarrassed confusion.

"Of course. Why else am I here?" Jeanne said. "But you never gave me an answer, so I thought I'd need to carry you off by force. Why the change of mind?"

"I…I don't know," she stammered.

Waiting at the door with coat in hand and she doesn't know? Perhaps, after all…"Well, never mind. Come join us. They've raised a pavilion in the parade ground out past the Tupendor, with dancing and entertainments of all sorts. We'll find you something worth renouncing for Lent."

There would be private balls later, of course, but they wouldn't have the excitement and abandon of the public festivities, where even respectable ladies might venture under the shelter of pretended anonymity and whatever degree of chaperonage their condition and status might require.

The road was choked, as all manner of carriages and hired hacks disgorged their passengers and another stream of traffic flowed up from the little wharf on the Rotein where the rivermen plied their trade. Those without even a *teneir* to come by boat straggled along on foot. The field was lined with market booths and groups of entertainers competing for attention and coins. In the center, a vast canvas hall, lit precariously with torches and warmed by small stoves, provided the opportunity to dance under shelter and jostle for the tables set up around the edges.

Iaklin was too shy to dance at first and Antuniet never danced, so Jeanne accepted Tionez's gallant bow of invitation and let the faux-chevalier draw her out into a country jig. The floor was not so crowded as it would be later and there was less chance of needing to fend off drunken invitations. That was all part of the daring: throwing off the chains of convention behind cover of a mask and the license of the festival. It was unwise of Tionez and her friend to have come without any male company at all, but who was she to judge? They were both married women, so their reputations could only be marred by acts, not by mere rumors, and that was a matter between them and their husbands.

They returned to the table that Antuniet had secured, flushed and laughing at the exertion. A parade of hawkers offered trays of food, and Jeanne sent a boy off to fetch a bottle of champagne. Thus fortified, Iaklin found the courage to take the floor and was led away. The crowd was increasing, growing noisy and boisterous, and there was little chance for conversation as the dancers swirled past, but Antuniet seemed content just to watch.

Jeanne leaned close to be heard over the din. "So, Toneke, have you chosen your vice for the day?"

"Isn't it daring enough that I'm here? I've never been to a public carnival before," she said with a trace of wistfulness. "Mother never would have allowed that risk to the family honor. Not even with an armin at my back and Estefen at my side—if he could have been bothered. The family honor!" she added more bitterly.

Impulsively, Jeanne took her hand. "Would you like to dance?" Antuniet was startled and shook her head. But her expression as she looked down was more bashful than affronted.

In another moment, Jeanne thought, she must choose between pressing forward or letting go. She leaned closer again just as Tionez returned, loudly intoning, "It's become such a crush in here. Shall we go out to see the entertainments?"

With the weather cold but dry, the field had turned to a market fair as well. They wandered between the stages where guilds were presenting scenes from the Passion as well as the usual Lives of their patrons. Unlike the more staid mystery guilds of the well-born, these were less ritual and more entertainment, filled equally with pious verses and coarse humor. Every empty space between the booths also had its juggler or hurdy-gurdy player competing for the generosity of the merry crowd. With all the masks and inventive costumes, there were times when the distinction between spectator and performer was erased entirely.

Tionez was playing her disguise to the hilt, a picture of swaggering bravado with a lady on each arm. Jeanne tried to soften the pointed exclusion by reaching for Antuniet's hand, but it was elusive. Jeanne watched closely for signs of discontent. For now, Antuniet seemed pleased enough just to be at her side. They watched an unintentionally hilarious performance of Peter's denial at cock-crow by the poulterer's guild, then bought a cone of roasted chestnuts and pretended to admire a display of gaudy jewelry that would have been too vulgar to take notice of on any other day.

"Oh look!" Iaklin exclaimed suddenly, tugging them toward a gap in the crowd. "Gypsy dancers!"

Tionez used her height to advantage as they worked their way through to the front. "It's just some girls from the opera company," she said quellingly. "I recognize the costumes from *La Turca* last year."

Tio was right. The dance was only bits of the choreographed figures from the opera, though the music accompanying them from a mandola was more raw and fiery. First one, then another would embellish the steps with a venture toward the crowd to flirt with the spectators. The musician had caught a few coins in a hat at his feet but the dancers seemed to have joined for their own amusement. As the shortest of them spun around, Jeanne recognized the shawl tied around her hips—far more tastefully elegant than the rest of the ensemble—and recognized those hips as well. Luzild caught her glance at the same moment and detached herself from the others. She twirled and clapped before Tionez, playing up to the masquerade, then came to a stop facing their group. Jeanne noted with a touch of trepidation that the woman was well into her cups. It hadn't shown in her steps, but there was a mischievous gleam in her eye as it caught her own. Luzild reached out to seize her hand and turn it upward, asking in a thick stage accent, "Would the fine lady like her palm read? I see the past; I see the future."

No harm in playing along. "What do you see? Give me a good fortune and I'll see you rewarded."

She made a show of examining the lines. "Ah, Mesnera, I see a mysterious stranger who longs for your gaze. Who pines for your touch. Does that fortune please you? Will you reward me with fine gifts—" She smoothed her hands possessively over the shawl tied about her waist. "—or perhaps with a kiss?" She leaned up against her familiarly.

Jeanne laughed and looked around at her party for advice. But a stricken look on Antuniet's face drove all frivolity out of her mind. She was staring past her at nothing, as if lost in thought, or as if she had seen someone in the crowd. "Toneke, what's wrong?"

She shook herself and said, "I think I should go home."

Jeanne drew her a few steps away from the others. "Are you ill?" In sudden concern she looked in the direction Antuniet had been staring. "Did you see someone? Are you in danger again?"

"No, no. It's…I just…I should go."

"Tionez can send for her carriage. It'll only be a short while."

Antuniet shook her head again. "No need; I can go by boat. I'll only have a few blocks to walk at the end. I don't want to interfere with your entertainments."

She pulled free and slipped into the crowd before there could be further objection. Jeanne started after her but Tio come up beside her. "I told you it was a mistake to invite her," she said sourly. "Now shall we go back and dance some more?"

Jeanne bit back a sharp reply. Tio was too good a friend to offend lightly. She looked around at the growing boisterousness of the crowd and said, "I think Antuniet has the right of it. We've had our amusement, now it's time to go home. In another hour we'll likely be subject to some very rude offers and while you might consider it good fun, I doubt Maisetra Silpirt would enjoy it quite as much." Indeed, Iaklin had been looking more and more as if she regretted her adventure. No doubt she hoped that any acquaintances who might have seen her here would forget the matter by the time her husband returned. "There'll be plenty of dancing at the palace ball tonight. Though not with you," she finished with mock despair, clutching Tio's hand to her bosom. It was the touch needed to bring her around and back to good humor.

CHAPTER TWENTY

Barbara

It was still too early in the year to be walking in the palace gardens for pleasure. The paths were caked with dead leaves and hidden clumps of ice in the shadows of the hedges. The gardeners wouldn't yet consider it worth their time to begin cleaning, but there were shovels at work here and there, setting out new trees or repairing the lay of the drainage. It was an ideal place to meet for a private conversation, if one had sufficient excuse to be there at all. Princess Elisebet needed no excuse, but Barbara had chosen to use the lightly-peopled walkways to exercise her favorite bay mare without the trouble of riding out past the city gates. The princess had done her an awkward compliment to single her out again for mysterious private errands.

Nothing had ever been asked that wouldn't bear the light of day. Yet it said much about how far Elisebet's star had fallen that a woman who once had scores of partisans hanging on her every word would turn so often to someone outside her own household for assistance. Of the coterie that had surrounded her when Prince Aukust was alive, only Mesnera Sain-Mazzi, her chief waiting woman, remained close. And though half of Elisebet's fears had turned out to be groundless, there had been too many odd events happening around young Chustin. If they had concerned anyone else, they could have been called coincidences. But Aukustin Atilliet might still someday be Prince of Alpennia. And for that reason, if no other, Elisebet could command her assistance.

Barbara had seen Elisebet walking along a side path with one of her ladies, but she cantered past twice more before dropping the horse to a walk and approaching as if by chance. She dismounted for a salute worthy of a dowager princess and fell in with her, leading her mount, to share pleasantries as the attendant fell behind.

"It looked to rain or worse; I didn't know if you would come," Elisebet said.

Barbara squinted at the sky. It might yet rain. "I'm not likely to wash away. I would have been riding out in the afternoon, in any case. I still keep up my sword practice, you know, and that was my excuse for coming out alone without a groom. Your note was quite insistent on that. Is Aukustin well?"

"He suffers from a slight chill in the lungs. The physician says there's no serious concern, though Maistir Escamund thinks a pernicious spirit has taken hold and must be banished. But that isn't why I asked you here," she added hurriedly, as if fearing that the mention of consulting a thaumaturgist would bring Margerit into the conversation. Elisebet chose to overlook that connection, though it was Margerit's service to Annek that made it awkward. Barbara had long since deflected any other suspicions in that line and Elisebet was not one to look beyond the obvious.

"How may I serve you?" Barbara asked. It could take Elisebet long to come to the point without prompting.

Elisebet looked back over her shoulder. Her lady was still well beyond earshot, so the gesture only served to emphasize a surreptitious purpose to their meeting. "It concerns my son's tutor."

Barbara searched through her memory for a name. It had been mentioned somewhere and she rather enjoyed her reputation for recalling names and faces. "Maistir Chautovil? What of him?"

"What have you heard?"

"Nothing at all," Barbara returned blandly. "As far as I know he's one of hundreds of adequate young scholars hoping to earn their bread now that their studies are done. A bit young, I would have thought, for a position of such importance."

"The last man was…I thought a younger tutor might be more sympathetic, might catch Aukustin's interest more easily."

Barbara guessed at part of what lay under the choice: not a pompous old schoolmaster, but a more dashing figure who might compete with Chustin's cousin for his admiration.

As if picking up her line of thought, Elisebet continued, "Too interesting, perhaps. Sain-Mazzi has heard it whispered that he has republican sympathies."

Barbara laughed. "Every *burfroi* with a bit of education comes to contemplate the Equality of Man. He could scarcely be a revolutionary if he took service in your household. Is it anything but rumor?"

She hesitated. "Aukustin has been…repeating things. Asking some odd questions."

"If it bothers you, turn him off. I'm sure you could find a reason."

Elisebet protested, "But he's an excellent tutor! And Aukustin is very fond of him. I only want to be sure—"

"How may I serve you?" Barbara repeated.

"You were a student at the university some years ago."

"After a fashion."

"But you know the district. You must know the people. If you could ask… find out who his friends were, what he was known to think?"

It was, in a way, the sort of snooping that had been part of her duties as the baron's armin. "Didn't you ask questions before hiring him?"

Elisebet shrugged. "He came with references from…well, from reputable people. But now I wonder if…Might someone have thought to cause trouble through my son?"

Barbara picked her way through the twists and turns of the explanation. "If I am to be of use, I need all the truth. Who gave him references? And whom do you suspect?"

The story was extracted with difficulty. The Dowager Countess Oriez had presented him for consideration through her daughter, who was one of Elisebet's ladies. But the connection was more distant: a favor owed, the complexities of patronage back in Helviz. At the end of the trail, Elisebet wasn't sure who had first mentioned Chautovil's name; she was suspicious, but suspected no one in particular.

As always before, Barbara came to reluctant agreement. "I'll see what I can discover. It may take time—weeks, perhaps. Especially if you don't care for word to get back to him."

Elisebet clearly wished for speedier news but acquiesced. "Thank you. It's good to know whom I may rely on in this city."

It was barely noon when Barbara left the palace grounds. Her usual appointment at Perret's *salle* wasn't for hours, but it made no sense to go home and change clothing twice. She could take potluck at finding someone to spar with.

Seeing Count Peskil's son arrive as she handed the mare off to Perret's groom, she called a greeting and claimed the promise of a bout or two if time allowed. "Though I'd rather find someone who can give me a challenge," she teased. Peskil could be counted on to take it in good part. Not all of the regulars were willing to forget her sex in the fencing *salle*.

"Mesnera," Perret called across the busy room at her entrance. "I hadn't expected you until later!"

Barbara waved away the apology. "It was an impulse to come early. Don't trouble yourself."

But Perret beckoned her over and looked toward the far end of the *salle*, calling out, "Tavit! I have a match for you!"

Barbara saw a head come up: a slightly-built young man—not much older than herself, if that—in a worn broadcloth coat and knee breeches in the archaic mode that suggested he was in service, or had been lately. As he left off the broom he'd been wielding, Barbara looked skeptically at Perret. "A new candidate?"

He answered her unspoken question. "He came to town with nothing in his pocket but an introduction from an old friend of mine, so I've been letting him work for his board. His last position was a bad business all around, from what I've heard. The less said about that the better. But I think he might suit you."

Barbara looked back to the approaching figure. Slight, yes, but wiry. A bit of a dandy in his appearance, despite the clothing. Close-curled black hair in a fashionable crop framing a beardless face. Spanish blood, perhaps, or a touch of Gypsy. The cast of his skin nearly hiding a fading bruise all along one side of his cheek. A brawler? Not if Perret vouched for him. Perhaps only that "bad business," whatever it had been.

Perret's only introduction was, "Tavit, perhaps you could give the Mesnera a few passes."

A narrowing of his eyes betrayed surprise but he made no demur at the request and only went to shed his coat and fetch practice blades for both of them. He fought cautiously, not in disdain of her skills, but as if uncertain whether he was allowed to prevail. She took one match easily, the next with more effort as he took her measure and began to respond. With the edge of her attention she saw Peskil had come over to watch with amusement. When she paused for a moment's rest, he jeered, "How fair is it to take on someone your own size, Saveze? I thought you said you wanted a challenge!"

Barbara glanced over at Tavit, curious to know how he would take the slight to his ability. He was gaping at her in surprise.

"You…you are Baroness Saveze? I've heard of you."

It was clear that whatever he'd heard had been somewhat embellished. "Indeed," she said dryly. "Have you heard enough about me to be willing to grant me a serious contest?"

The blades came up again, and this time he worked in earnest and managed a touch before she scored her win. His skills were still raw—like a green colt yet to turn promise into performance—but she saw willingness and respect. He was worth trying further. "As a rule," she said, "an armin should be more skilled than his employer. But for the sake of my own pride I'm happy to set that requirement aside. Perret suggested you were looking for a position."

"Yes, Mesnera."

He sounded wary. Had his last place been that bad? Or was she the source of his hesitation? On impulse she said, "I can't judge a man by the practice floor. I have an errand in the university district. Would you have time to accompany me?"

"Are you offering me employment?"

"Not yet. Only a chance at a trial."

He stood for a long moment in thought, but whatever his considerations were, at last he nodded and went to speak with Perret.

When he returned, strapping a borrowed blade about his waist, Barbara asked, "Can you ride?"

"Well enough," he said. "But I have no horse."

"Of course. That was foolish of me. Then as your first task, go hire us a fiacre."

Perret came up beside her when he'd gone out. "Will he do for you?"

"I don't know yet. I think I see why you thrust him in my path. He has the makings of an armin but he needs some seasoning in a post where there's little chance of disaster. And he's a bit too young and handsome to be set to guarding someone's daughters."

Perret snorted. "No, I thought he might do because you need someone you can train up in your own ways."

"I'll give him a trial. If he hasn't come back by the end of tomorrow you can assume he's off your hands. Except as a student, mind you. I hope you'll grant me that." Perret was choosy about students, but the man was already under his wing after a fashion. He nodded and she added, "If you would, send my horse on to Tiporsel House. And if Tavit isn't back here by sundown you can send his things there as well."

She wasn't ready to begin making serious inquiries after Chautovil, but there was groundwork to do. A question here and there. She could pretend no claims to a direct connection—their paths wouldn't have intersected—but perhaps she could invent a mutual friend to seek. That would give an excuse to ask after others in his circle. And the Red Oak tavern was the best place to begin. Some of the denizens must still remember her from her own student days—before those days were overshadowed by her duties to Margerit. As they approached the entrance, Tavit stepped out before her, not to block her path in any way but to demand her attention. "Mesnera, there is a question…"

Memories of her own years in service flooded back. The echo of how *Mesner, may I speak?* prefaced every conversation. Was that what she wanted? But that had been the baron's quirk—that and her own peculiar place in his household. She stepped back from the doorway and nodded briskly.

"Mesnera, am I to guard you as a maid or as a man?"

Barbara tilted her head to consider the question. That he asked it at all was perceptive. "What do you think?" she prompted.

He hesitated, no doubt considering whether his chance of employment hinged on his response. "If I'm to treat you as a sheltered well-born maiden, then this is a test to see how I would prevent you from misbehavior." She could sense the invisible curl to his lip that gave his opinion of that. "But if I'm to guard you as if you were a man, then I need to know what sorts of slights and familiarities I should allow that wouldn't be offered to a woman."

Yes, very perceptive. "For now, consider it your duty to guard the honor and dignity of the name of Saveze. I can deal with anything more personal."

It was an educational afternoon. The quest for her fictitious friend turned up the names of several of Chautovil's associates and one of the *dozzures* around whom their circle formed, but no indications that their politics were worse than the usual. The more familiar undercurrents of the court were a world apart from this crowd, but Barbara knew some of the key players and saw no cause for alarm. She would follow the path far enough to reassure Elisebet.

Tavit had done well enough. He hadn't yet mastered the trick of invisibility, but his instincts were sound on position and movement. And Marken was right in one thing: there was a difference in how she was treated simply from having an armin at her back, even here in a place where she was known and recognized. *The honor and dignity of Saveze*, she thought. *It's a tangible thing and perhaps I have been neglecting it.*

On their return, when he would have climbed up on the box with the driver, Barbara said, "Inside," and motioned him to the facing seat. "So," she said as the carriage lurched forward, "do I return you to Perret's or do we continue on to Tiporsel?"

He was silent long enough that she realized he hadn't understood it as a question for him rather than for herself. She gestured permission to answer. Hesitantly, he did: "You said you would give me a chance at a trial…"

Barbara nodded. "This is your chance: a two-week trial. If you suit, then the standard contract." She leaned out the window to confirm the direction to the driver. "It's not just me you need to satisfy though. Marken's likely to be a tougher nut to crack."

"Marken is…?"

"He's armin to—" Her tongue stumbled on how to explain. He would need to know how matters stood soon enough, but *to my mistress* sounded awkward and crude. "—to Maisetra Margerit Sovitre, who owns Tiporsel House." She leaned forward and said, with quiet emphasis, "Maisetra Sovitre's safety and good reputation mean more to me than my own life. So Marken's opinion will carry a great deal of weight with me."

"Yes, Mesnera, I understand," he stammered.

Likely he didn't, but that would come soon enough. They were careful enough to allow society the ignorance it preferred, but it was impossible to keep such secrets within the household. She softened her tone. "Marken can help you make a good start. I've worked with him since the old baron's time. He knows my habits."

* * *

Some time later she found Margerit, as expected, in the library and kissed her cheek in greeting.

"Not changed yet?" Margerit asked. "I heard you come in ages ago. What have you been up to?"

"Getting my new armin settled in," Barbara said, enjoying her surprise.

"At last!" Margerit laughed. "And when do I meet this paragon?"

"He's hardly a paragon, but I think he'll do. And for the rest, are you going visiting tomorrow? Perhaps I'll join you."

"I have lectures all through the morning."

"Of course, I'd forgotten. I've hardly seen you lately between your studies and this alchemy thing."

"It's not as bad as that," Margerit protested. "And the term is finished after next week, so we'll have all summer."

"Then decided? No summer lectures?" It would be the first time she'd skipped a term by choice.

"I'm tired of begging for crumbs. I'll get more use out of studying with Akezze all summer than an entire hall full of *dozzures*. And it means we'll be free to spend floodtide out in Chalanz if we want." She laughed. "Jeanne is already making plans for that."

Jeanne was always making plans. This year, Jeanne's plans also included accepting her invitation to spend the summer at Saveze. She had offered on a whim of the moment and been surprised when Jeanne had agreed. It would be a smaller, quieter party than she was used to, once the floodtide party broke up. "I should go change," Barbara said. "Do I remember correctly that we're dining in tonight?"

"And tomorrow with the Marzims, so don't go riding off all over the place tomorrow afternoon."

"I'll have you know I was hunting down secrets for the dowager princess."

Margerit looked intrigued at that, but then she frowned suddenly and said, "Speaking of secrets, do you know anything about this?" She rose and went over to the table by the windows. "I was trying to find a copy of Desanger that I remembered seeing somewhere in here and I ran across this on one of the upper shelves."

"I thought I'd hidden it better!" Barbara expected her to produce a paper-wrapped package, but what Margerit brought out was a wooden box. For a moment Barbara was equally confused, but then memory returned. "That woman…Chamering, that was her name. You remember from last autumn? The one who said she was my mother's sister. She left it here. I'd forgotten all about it."

"Oh. I'll have someone put it back, then."

"No, leave it for now." Perhaps it was time to see what sort of legacy she'd been left.

"And what was it you thought I'd found?" Margerit asked, looking curiously back to the top of the tall case.

"Oh, that," Barbara said, feeling sheepish. She moved the steps down farther and climbed up to extract the parcel from behind the volumes that hid it. "Eskamer found something out at Urmai that I thought you might be interested in. I meant to save it for your birthday." She held it up tantalizingly out of reach.

"No secrets, Barbara, you promised!"

"Not even for a birthday?" she teased. But she handed down the parcel and watched as Margerit picked through the knotted twine and carefully unwrapped the book.

She glanced at the title page and said in surprise, "Another copy of Gaudericus? How many do I need?"

Smiling, Barbara stepped down from the little ladder and leaned over her. "I could take it back. But you might want to look at the colophon first." She watched eagerly as Margerit turned to the back and worked her way through the ancient script.

Margerit's breath caught in a gasp. "Tanfrit? Tanfrit's own copy?"

"That he sent her, according to one of the inscriptions. It's covered with notes all through the pages. I don't know if they're hers or a later owner's. Do you like it?" But there was no need to ask.

* * *

The next morning Barbara found herself contemplating the letter-casket again in that quiet space after Margerit had left for the university and before the Pertineks were stirring. The first clamor of the household had stilled, and drifting up from the end of the garden she could hear the faint calls of the rivermen bringing deliveries to the private docks.

The box was one of those casually beautiful pieces of furniture she had been surrounded by all her life, joined so seamlessly and invisibly it might have been carved from a single block and cunningly inlaid with marquetry in a design of roses. A small keyhole under the edge of the lip provided the only access, but of course there was no key.

A tap on the door pulled her attention away as Tavit entered. "They said you wanted to speak to me?"

"Yes, I should have sent for you last night to go over today's schedule but I thought you might need the time to settle in." Recalling her own first evening in Margerit's household and how at sea she had felt, she added, "Perhaps I shouldn't have waited. Always best to begin as you mean to go on, I say. But never mind. I don't think I'll be going out today until evening, so—" She looked him over with a critical eye. "I suppose you don't have anything better to wear? No, Perret said you'd arrived with just your traveling clothes. Tell Ponivin I said to arrange for a suit. Not livery; I don't hold with that for armins. But he should be able to find you something presentable before tonight's dinner."

"Perhaps it would be better to wait until my trial is over?" Tavit asked uncertainly.

She guessed at his hesitation. "Don't worry that I'll take it out of your pay. I don't count coppers like that. When you've taken care of the clothing, have someone show you all over the house and grounds. I want you familiar with every corner of this place by the end of the day. When Marken gets back later he can tell you what you need to know for the evening. We'll only be a few doors down, dining with Mesner Pertinek's cousin, so you might even find time to go speak to their people in advance, though it's hardly necessary. They're family, after a fashion."

"But begin as I mean to go on?" There was no trace of a smile when he said it, but Barbara could hear the same faintly ironic tone as when he'd stopped her outside the tavern the day before.

She nodded. "I'm too used to being my own lookout. Don't worry about whether something's necessary; ask yourself if it's proper."

"Marken said—" He paused, looking as if he were translating it into acceptable terms. "Marken said I wasn't to let you do my job."

Marken had most likely said something pithier than that, but if he were already giving Tavit advice on how to handle her, that was a good sign. She nodded in dismissal.

When he'd left she turned back to the inlaid casket. The lock would have been difficult if she'd cared about keeping it intact. Some trace of sentimentality prevented her from simply wrenching the box open, but a little work with a penknife destroyed the latch sufficiently to open it.

The contents matched the clues she'd gained from shaking the box. Letters: some thick and folded together, some brief and lying flat. Her mother's name stared at her from the direction on the top sheet: Elisebet Arpik, Countess Turinz. The hand was one she knew as familiarly as she knew her own. A letter from the baron—from her father—to her mother. She glanced at the date. June of 1798, half a year after her birth and only months before the Arpiks' world would finally collapse. Her hand trembled and she folded the paper again. She leafed through more letters. Most had the same direction but older dates, and then halfway through the contents, the name changed. Elisebet Anzeld. And Marziel Lumbeirt without a title following. Had they been corresponding that far back? When her father had still been in training for a priest and her mother an unmarried girl?

The letters held only one side of the correspondence. Whatever her mother had written in return lay elsewhere. Or, more likely, had been destroyed. The baron had been meticulous about concealing the affair, with the exception of that one last testament left in trust as her legacy. Did she figure at all in these missives? She unfolded those last pages again.

My dearest Lissa,

Had they been so unguarded? The rumors that had circulated later about the baron's continued bachelorhood had never mentioned any name. Had they been so certain their correspondence would remain secret? Or had he ceased to care?

My dearest Lissa,

I will not pretend to understand your newfound loyalty. There is no need for it. No reason for it. And there will certainly be no reward for it. If Arpik could not stir a scrap of affection for you during all those years when you strove to be a dutiful wife, what do you expect now that he has the proof of your betrayal before him?

The proof of your betrayal. *That was me*, Barbara thought. *I was the proof.*

You paid your penance long before committing the sin. When I was willing to risk everything, you were all caution. What use is caution now? Through all those years, you feared what you might lose, when you had nothing. Now you have something worth fighting for: your child, if not your love for me. Let me take you to Saveze. Arpik cannot touch you there.

Barbara leafed through the remainder of the text. More pleas. Plans upon plans. The desperation of a man at wit's end. And nothing had come of it. That much she knew. Whatever Lissa's written answer had been, her true answer had been to follow Arpik into debtors' prison. She reached back in memory. The baron had never told her mother's story plainly; it had always been hints and allusions. But none of those hints fit with this letter. The story she knew—the story she had taken in with every breath—was that Lissa's family had abandoned her and Lissa had withdrawn in shame from all other contacts. She could swear that the baron had outright claimed that he knew nothing of her plight until the last, when she wrote to him from prison. The casket of letters gave the lie to that. Barbara might not have her mother's letters in return, but their existence whispered from between the pages.

The baron had lied. By implication, if not directly. Why should that be a surprise? She'd seen him at work in the court and in his business dealings. He'd lied to many people in his time. She'd known his story for a lie the moment she knew the secret of her birth and seen the proof of her true parentage. But she hadn't before given thought to just where that story had gone astray from truth. Or how badly. Could she trust any of it?

At a sudden thought, Barbara leafed back to the previous missive. This one was quite different in almost every way: a stiff, formal letter on a single sheet and one of the few not addressed to Lissa.

The twentieth of March in the year 1798. To Maistir and Maisetra Sovitre, on the Molindrez, Greetings from Marziel Lumbeirt, Baron Saveze

I feel deeply the honor that you do me in asking me to stand as godfather to your daughter. I will meet you at the church of Nes' Donna Muralis at the time and day you name when arrangements have been made for the other child. Believe me to be your servant in Christ,

Saveze

The other child. Her? That would explain why she had failed in all her searches for her baptismal record back before she'd learned of her true father. Our Lady By the Wall was a tiny church out on the unfashionable western edge of the city. It must have been near to where the Sovitres were living at the time. A picture began to come clear: a small, private ceremony that would invite no notice and thus no comment. The cover of Margerit's christening to explain his presence. A chance for the baron to lay some small claim on his daughter in the role of godfather. No doubt the two mothers had stood up for each other's child, eliminating the risk of other witnesses.

She returned the letters to the top of the stack and leafed down to the very first.

The first of October, in the year 1787, From Marziel Lumbeirt at Saveze to Maisetra Elisebet Anzeld, greetings etc.

Barbara glanced back at the date. No, that was well before Tarnzais, when he unexpectedly inherited the title. *At* Saveze, not *of* Saveze.

I have sent this message enclosed with a letter to the most reverend mother who oversees your studies in the hopes that she will consider it suitable for you to receive. As I have written to her, in my father's day it was the custom of the Barons Saveze to hold a festival in honor of Saint Orisul's feast day. My brother has granted me permission to host the festival this year. In gratitude for the great kindness your family showed me in allowing me to travel with you here to Saveze for my convalescence, I would like to invite you and your charming namesake to attend as my special guests.

It was light and impersonal. And yet she had preserved it. Had they meant anything to each other then? Had some spark been struck on that journey? Or had it grown gradually, nurtured by chance and opportunity? Lissa would have been just on the brink of her dancing season, spending her last year at the school. And the baron... He had been meant to be a priest. Had Lissa turned his head? Or had his vocation never been more than a bending to expectations? Each answer only brought more questions.

She took up the next page. This one was both discreet and daring. There was no date, no salutation. If not for its place in the sequence, there would have been no knowing what it meant.

I will arrange to deliver this into your hands secretly as you requested, though I cannot like to do so. To my vow of devotion you answered that men's words are like the blooming of a rose: soon withered and forgotten. Since you will not believe what is written in my heart's blood, I set out this pledge in mere ink. I have written to my mother declaring that I will not take vows this year. Whether I take them at all depends on you. If you will not have me, God may receive what remains. When your dancing year is complete, if you are still of the same mind, I will speak to your father. But I think it more likely that the salles of Rotenek will offer you greater temptations than my poor promise. More than this I cannot pledge, for I will do nothing to bring your name into disrepute. Neither will I bring blame on the good Sisters who have you in their keeping. There has been nothing improper between us but no one would believe that if I speak before the season is complete. If these words suffice, then I will remain in hope until we meet again.

What a mix of caution and passion! And on what was it based? There were a few clues in the letters. A journey together under the watchful eyes of her parents. A day in company at a festival with the nuns as *vizeino*. But from the allusions, this must have been written as summer was coming on and Lissa was at the end of her schooldays. It was unexceptional for those of the manor and village to attend services at Saint Orisul's if they chose. More than one romance had been fed on nothing more than smoldering looks and a word in passing under public eye. More than half a year? *And how long did it take to know my own heart?* Barbara thought. *One month at most.* But if Lissa and the baron had both formed the attachment at a time when no other vows bound them, where had it all gone wrong? She reached for another letter.

When Margerit came in, Barbara asked, "So soon?" then looked up to notice that lamps had replaced daylight and saw the reminder of the untouched tea tray on the table by the door. She had been only vaguely aware of the comings and goings that accompanied them.

Margerit came to lean closely over her shoulder and ask, "The casket?"

"Letters," Barbara confirmed. "From the baron."

"Oh." There was a world of wonder, curiosity and patience in the one word.

Barbara shuffled them back into a single pile and pressed her cheek against Margerit's hand where it lay on her shoulder. "Do you mind waiting?" she asked. "I don't...I'm not ready to—"

"Of course."

"No secrets," Barbara said quickly with a reassuring smile. "But I've barely started looking through them and…and I need time to think before I talk about it." She looked up. "In what I've read so far, your mother shows up rather often. I wouldn't keep that from you." She smiled at the eager interest in Margerit's face and closed the lid of the casket once again. "Is it time to dress for dinner already?"

At Margerit's nod, she rose.

* * *

An invitation to dine with Lord and Lady Marzim always meant a noisy and cheerful affair, as long as there were no guests from outside the family to cast a veil of formality over the proceedings. But that was rare, as the Pertineks' notion of family was generous and encompassing and tonight was no exception. Barbara recalled that it had been scant months into her first season in the title before she had been included within that circle, as if truly a cousin-in-law. And as Lady Marzim refused to banish politics to the men's after-dinner brandy, Barbara felt no surprise now when her host leaned across his dinner partner to ask, "Will you be attending the sessions next week?"

She laughed. "I'm not yet so bored with life that I'll be joining the graybeards in their debates. If I'm needed for a vote, someone will let me know."

"I would have thought you might have a special interest in Chormuin's bill."

Barbara cast about in memory. "I'd heard he was slipping something in right when everyone's eager to finish before Holy Week. I thought it was just a matter of regularizing how evidence is presented in the courts. I may have studied the law, but I'm not likely to be allowed to practice. What special interest could I have?"

"There's a new clause added. He proposes to exclude the duel. Hadn't you heard?"

"Outlaw dueling?" came a woman's voice from the far end of the table. "That would make half the young men in Rotenek felons!"

"Not duels of honor," Marzim explained. "Only judicial duels. Now what do you think of that, Saveze?"

Without even thinking, Barbara answered, "It's long overdue. Duels of honor are another matter. Just as a man has a right to defend his body against attack, even though he fails, so too he's obliged to protect his honor, even if lies prevail. But judicial duels should have no place in a civilized world."

Several heads near her turned in surprise. "And yet you challenged that Chazillen boy," another man said.

Barbara frowned and glanced over at Margerit, but she was turned away, chatting with her neighbor. She tried to find the right words. "To invoke the *duellum iudicialis* is either the act of a bully or a desperate man. I'd prefer to think that I was desperate. But if Estefen had accepted, would it have made him any more guilty because I was skilled with a blade? No, let judgments be based on truth. And if there isn't enough truth, then find more truth, but there's no truth in the point of a sword."

Lord Marzim had a look of satisfaction, as if a deal had been struck. "Then I will see you at the sessions?"

She smiled ruefully. "I suppose you might. My first sally onto the field of debate!"

* * *

Having made her decision, there was a great deal of research to do in the days that followed. The volumes of legal commentaries that she'd barely touched in the past two years gave forth the history of the matters under debate—the ordinary revisions as well as those concerning the duel. If she were to make her maiden speech, she didn't care to look a fool even in the smallest of details. And, too, attending the sessions was sure to mean a chance to encounter Elisebet with little remark from anyone. It would be good to finish up that question about Chautovil before then.

She gave Tavit a day's notice of her intentions and was surprised when he asked, "The Red Oak again, or perhaps Filip's or the Cavern?"

He grinned a little when she raised a brow quizzically. "Marken said that it might be good to be familiar with the university quarter."

It seemed that *Marken said* would become a regular part of her life. "The Cavern, I think. But since you have some time to spare tomorrow, go see where Dozzur Basille's students go after his lecture—the older ones that seem to know each other. Not the well-born ones; they wouldn't be interested in this sort of politics. And not the quiet, bookish ones; they wouldn't have time for it. Don't be too obvious; wear something ordinary. Your old clothes will do if you still have them." She watched him store the instructions carefully away. "Questions?"

"No, Mesnera."

He should have had questions, but let him find his own way. "When you have time, start learning your way around the palace. You've heard my plans? So start with the area around the Assembly Hall. Take one of my cards and show it to the page at the gate. He'll pass you along to the right people." And when he looked dubious: "The palace is just another grand house. They deal with this all the time."

"Yes, Mesnera."

Tavit was doing well enough so far. Marken's only comment after the first few days was, "He keeps himself to himself. I like that." But Marken's tentative approval showed in the hints and advice that left their traces in Tavit's work.

* * *

The Assembly Hall was rarely filled during debates of the sessions, certainly not in the way it had been for the succession council. Even attendance for the votes didn't come close, unless the matter stirred serious passions. Yet it was crowded enough to require a long glance to find an empty space among suitable company. Tavit leaned closely to ask, "Will you want me to remain, Mesnera? Or should I return later?"

It took a moment to recall that he hadn't been steeped in the rituals of the palace as she had. She nodded toward the benches along the far wall. "Over there. I don't imagine you'll find the speeches interesting, but I always found it a good opportunity to study people."

He hesitated before going to take his place and asked, "Mesnera? Who attends these sessions?"

She looked at him curiously. Did he have an interest in politics? "The titled lords, the bishops, the great lords of state, a few of Her Grace's ministers, the mayor of Rotenek and those of the other larger towns. The generals, though they usually fall within one of the other groups as well. But never all at once. I doubt one in five has an interest in the day-to-day matters. I certainly don't."

"Then a well-born man with property but no title—he wouldn't attend?"

"Not these. The common sessions, perhaps." Ah, now light dawned. "Your last employer," she asked. "Who was he?"

Reluctantly, he gave a name. The family name was familiar, but not the man. "No, I don't think you need fear meeting him here. Not unless there were some matter that touched directly on his lands or family." Now she was curious. Whatever that bad business had been, did it still follow him here? But he offered no further clues and she let the matter lie.

The morning's session was nothing to the point of why she had come but she wanted the lay of the land, as if she were still an armin scouting out a new venue for her charge. At the midday break, as the others spilled out into the Plaiz to find refreshment in the cafés, Barbara saw her chance for a quiet word with Princess Elisebet. In Aukust's day, Elisebet had often been his representative to the sessions. Perhaps she continued attending out of genuine interest, or perhaps only for the appearance of interest. *If I were her*, Barbara reflected, *I'd want to make it clear that my concerns in government went beyond the needs of the moment.* But Elisebet's strategies were rarely that long-sighted, so perhaps the interest was genuine.

Barbara's report was short and to the point but Elisebet's questions kept her long past the interval, when she could have made other use of the time. As she returned to her seat, resigning herself to a grumbling stomach, a footman intercepted her with the information that Her Grace wished a quiet word.

Annek was sitting at a small table back behind the dais, taking advantage of the time to deal with a stack of petitions that sat at her elbow. She paused with pen in hand as Barbara approached. "My cousin seemed to have a great interest in what you came to say," Annek began. "I was hoping you planned to share your opinions more openly."

"That was nothing to do with the debates," Barbara replied. "A personal matter." And then, because there was no reason to conceal it and every reason to avoid the appearance of doing so, she added, "I was conducting a bit of investigation for her. It seems there are rumors that Chustin's tutor is a secret republican."

"And is he?" Annek asked with an amused look.

"Not secret, no," Barbara said. "But neither is he a zealot. He seems harmless enough."

"I can't believe that was the only thing that brought you to the Assembly Hall today." Annek had no need to demand answers directly.

"It seems I have opinions on Mesner Chormuin's bill."

"Ah, I was hoping that was the case. May I ask in which direction those opinions lie?"

It took no special knowledge to guess where Annek stood. Her father's long reign had left a waiting tide of modern ideas. Though Aukust himself had been forward-looking, he'd lacked the energy to help see them through and Elisebet had always favored the conservatives.

"I support it," Barbara said quietly and without elaboration.

Annek nodded. "I'll see that you have a chance to be heard." She had no direct power to dictate the proceedings beyond the voice given by her own minor title-lands, but unlike Elisebet she had the knack of quietly guiding others to want the same things she desired.

The afternoon passed without that chance. No matter. Three days' debate was scheduled and halfway into the next morning's session Count Amituz, no doubt at Annek's prompting, brought his arguments around to the suggestion that it would be well to hear the opinions of those who had acted under the laws they proposed to abolish. As if by cue, Lord Marzim rose to say, "I believe Baroness Saveze would be worth hearing on this matter."

Barbara rose when recognized, her heart suddenly pounding. A moment's reflection on the last occasion she'd spoken formally in this chamber returned a sense of calm. She wasn't fighting for her own life or for Margerit's this time. The worst that could happen would be to stumble and look foolish. She sifted through the histories and arguments she'd assembled in the past days and found the place where her thoughts wove into the debate as it stood. She was acutely aware of how she stood out among the throng, both for her youth and her sex. But that had been the case too many times in her life to be daunting. She took a deep breath and began.

It was, at the last, harder to find a place to end than to begin. The words poured out in an easy stream, as if she were arguing philosophy with Margerit back home in the library. From the corner of her eye she saw nods, frowns, whispered exchanges, but she kept her eyes on Annek to focus and saw there only approval and gratitude. It felt as if she'd been speaking for hours, but when she looked at the clock as she sat down, a bare fifteen minutes had passed.

The remaining speeches that day gave no sign whether any heed had been taken of her remarks. But when the summaries came the next afternoon, Lord Chormuin included the best of her arguments among his own, with a look and a nod to acknowledge them, and in the end the vote went his way, not easily but solidly. It was only the beginning, of course. The clerks would spend months drafting up the proper language; then would come the private negotiations to change a word here, a clause there. The commons would have their chance at amending it. The final approval might not come for another year when the approaching close of the sessions once more brought pressure to bear. That, too, she remembered from her years shadowing the baron.

As she followed the others out into the Plaiz to wait while carriages were summoned and sorted out, she accepted a quiet word of congratulations from Lord Marzim and nods of acknowledgment from several others as they passed. But when the crowd had dispersed, the stout figure of Baron Mazuk approached her, demanding a word in a more querulous tone. From the corner of her eye she saw Tavit taking a watchful stance and looking around. *Softly*, she thought, *this is all part of the game.* She remembered it well from the old baron's time. Mazuk was clearly looking for a quarrel—why, she had yet to determine.

"I would have expected better from you, Saveze," he said, "but you seem to make a habit of neglecting responsibilities until it suits you. Your father certainly knew the value of challenge and response in keeping the law."

Was this only about her belated interest in the session debates? "My father," she answered quietly, "had the wherewithal to buy the steel to make his case. That alone made his arguments strangely persuasive. But it didn't always make them just. And I'm not my father."

"No, you aren't." He snorted. "Just? If you were accused, would you leave your fate in the hands of some *burfroi* magistrate?"

"When I was accused, I had far more confidence leaving my fate to the law than to the arena." Technically, she had been accuser, not accused, but it didn't change the argument. "If the evidence were clear and the law were fair and I knew he wouldn't act from fear or favor, then yes, even to an ordinary magistrate. We live in a modern world now. Leave the duels for ancient stories."

"And what else do you plan to do away with in the name of your modern world? Swearing on relics? The truth-finding mysteries?"

Neither of those had fallen under Chormuin's bill, but it was a fair question.

"The *mysteria veridica* are a more difficult matter," Barbara said. "They have a valuable place in the hands of a skilled and talented practitioner, but can every judge distinguish that from a charlatan?"

"Like that Sovitre woman?"

His question came so quickly on the heels of her own words that Barbara couldn't guess which of the two labels he'd meant. Was he merely being dismissive or openly insulting? She knew she'd bristled because she saw the reflection of it in Mazuk's armin. She gripped tightly to her rising temper. Into the heavy stillness that had fallen between them, she heard Tavit's voice at her back, speaking lightly as if an idle question for her ears alone. "Perhaps I've misunderstood, Mesnera. The bill, it was only to ban duels of law, not those of honor, yes?"

Barbara's eyes narrowed and she stared down the baron, while answering in the same casual tone, "You understood correctly."

Mazuk's face turned red and he glanced at his own armin who shook his head almost imperceptibly. Armins had their own code, as Barbara knew well, and they hated to shed each other's blood for mere spite or clumsy words. He would be bound to answer any insult raised against his employer, but he had more leeway if it were Mazuk who gave the insult, and that sign had told the baron he might have to defend his own ground. Mazuk cleared his throat. "Ah, yes, in the hands of a skilled practitioner like Her Grace's thaumaturgist, we can agree, I think, on the value."

"As you say," Barbara said icily and turned away before her own temper broke through. She felt, rather than saw, Tavit at her back as she spotted her carriage and headed for it briskly.

But as the door was opened and the step lowered for her she turned to him, saying, "Thank you, that was deftly done." And then, almost as an afterthought, "Remind me on Friday to take you to see LeFevre to have your contract drawn up."

* * *

It would have been wrong to characterize her first participation in the sessions as a triumph but neither had it been a disaster. Margerit teased later, "Do you plan to make a career of politics now?"

Barbara shook her head. "Not even if Annek and Christ himself begged me. There are few topics where the old men are likely to listen to my opinions." They were lying entwined just before sleep in that time when the day's thoughts were most easily shared.

"Have you read any more of the letters?" Margerit asked.

"A few more. It's slow going. It's so hard to make them fit into what I thought I knew. It's as if these people are strangers to me. But they are," she added. "I never knew my mother outside the stories the baron told. And those were few enough. And now? I still only see her reflected in his words. It's strange to think that these are the people closest to me."

Margerit moved against her softly.

"Except for you, of course," Barbara added quickly and bent to kiss her.

"But you do have relatives," Margerit pointed out. "There's your mother's sister. Do you see her in a new light now too?"

"I don't know. She doesn't figure much in the baron's letters. Only a mention here and there of 'your sister.'"

"She could tell you more herself. Would you consider—"

"Perhaps," Barbara said. "When I'm ready." She didn't mean to be quelling but she wasn't ready yet to ask those questions…or have them answered.

"And then there's Antuniet," Margerit said with an air of broaching a new subject.

"Yes. Antuniet."

"She is your cousin, after all. I thought I might—" Margerit hesitated. "I thought about inviting her to join us for floodtide, if you didn't mind. She hasn't anywhere else to go."

"Did Jeanne suggest it?"

"No. That is, I don't think so. You know, I'm not entirely sure. She has a way of slipping her plans into your own before you even notice! But there almost seems to be a coolness between them at the moment."

"That one's a strange friendship," Barbara said. "Yes, invite Antuniet if you wish. If she'll come."

CHAPTER TWENTY-ONE

Antuniet

The gates of Rotenek were but a few hours behind when Antuniet began to regret accepting Margerit's invitation. The work could wait. Little enough would get done over the summer that a few weeks of idleness would make no difference. And a floodtide invitation was not a gesture to be brushed aside lightly, whether inspired by friendship or patronage. But the journey out to Chalanz in one of two coaches stuffed full of Jeanne's friends was no pleasant holiday.

Jeanne still blew hot and cold: now attentive and solicitous, now chatting merrily about nothing. Just when she most seemed the Jeanne of those intimate lunches in the workshop, she would turn away with a jest. Sometimes Jeanne seemed to forget her very presence, but other times that mortifying scene with the dancer at Carnival came back and she was glad of the inattention. It was hard to believe that one woman could hold in her head the depths Antuniet knew were there and the empty insincerity now on display. And why did it bother her so much? Jeanne was Jeanne, as she had always been. The endless stream of empty gossip droned on.

What could have been a three-day journey with only a little care stretched into four when they reached Sain-Petir and found the river topping the bridge just enough to spook the horses. It was decided to go up to Pont Estan, where the crossing was safer. Their hostesses had gone ahead, setting out when the first signs of the rising Rotein were seen, not waiting for the official end of the season. With luck they had outpaced the waters and crossed before the bridge was flooded, though Antuniet couldn't imagine Barbara letting a bit of water stop her.

On the final day of the journey, she took refuge in the third coach with Akezze and the trio of musicians hired out from Rotenek for the dancing. It was that or go mad. Even the wagon with the luggage would have been an improvement. Jeanne's friend Tionez had a knack for finding the most tender spots on which to sharpen her tongue. It hardly mattered whether the wounds were intended or not. And Tio's friend Iaklin giggled at every supposed witticism. Why Iaklin Silpirt had come at all was a mystery, unless it were simply to make up the required numbers. Tionez must have dragged her along, for Jeanne had more sense than to bring such an innocent into this fold. No, Akezze was a far more congenial companion, for she spent most of the trip with her eyes closed and a handkerchief pressed closely to her mouth. Conversation was entirely out of the question.

The musicians ignored both of them and kept up a low murmur barely audible above the noise of the road. They were another of Jeanne's conceits: bringing only women to entertain at their May Day revels. Antuniet sometimes watched them sidelong and wondered whether Jeanne had enjoyed more than just their music. She jerked her thoughts away. Jeanne's amusements were none of her affair.

The travelers arrived at last late on that fourth day and instantly turned the gracious calm of Margerit's house into a cacophony of confusion, misplaced baggage, reorganized arrangements and giggling dashes in and out of rooms. One might think they were schoolroom girls rather than the grown matrons and widows who formed Jeanne's most intimate coterie. Hopefully Margerit's servants were sufficiently accustomed to their mistress's irregular life to be too scandalized by any lapses in discretion. It was clear that the women considered this trip to be a holiday from their ordinary caution. Antuniet had taken note, with wry amusement, of the moment when Akezze worked out what interest it was that most of the other women shared. No doubt they had considered the scholar to be of no more importance than the musicians and servants in moderating their behavior. Antuniet supposed that she, too, now fell in the category of those whose opinion didn't matter. Who was she likely to gossip with who wasn't already present?

Escaping the chaos, Antuniet retreated toward the back of the house and found herself in a flowered courtyard nestled between the two wings of the building. An ornate fountain played in the center of a tiled expanse. She sat on the rim of the pool and closed her eyes, drawing in the scent of the roses and heliotrope and letting the sound of the splashing water wash away the tension and weariness of the road. She should return to her room. If she hoped to take advantage of the luxury of a bath before dinner, it would be good to put her request in before too many others. Instead, she rose and followed the sound of birdsong through a columned pergola.

The path led out onto a terrace behind the house and then farther down through wilder gardens and shrubberies spilling out toward the river. It reminded her of Tiporsel House but in larger scale. One could lose herself on these paths. Indeed, she hadn't gone more than a few turns when she came face-to-face unexpectedly with Barbara. She, too, looked as if she were escaping the invasion. Recovering quickly, Antuniet curtseyed with her usual brief, "Baroness, your pardon," as she turned to find a less traveled path.

"Cousin," Barbara returned. And then, "Still always so formal."

It seemed an invitation to conversation. She could think of nothing to say but, "Still always so impersonal."

Silence hung between them. How did one begin? On impulse she added, "You know, it doesn't bother me anymore. Being addressed as Maisetra."

The corner of Barbara's mouth twitched, but she couldn't tell whether it was humor or distaste. "I've tried, but 'Maisetra Chazillen' never sits right in my mouth. Which leaves us in the awkward place we find ourselves." She seemed to contemplate a question and then inclined her head in invitation. Their steps fell together on the path. "It's easier for you and Margerit," Barbara continued. "You long since made each other free of your Christian names."

It was, perhaps, an invitation, but she couldn't be sure. And it was an invitation only Barbara could make now. "That happened…before." Before her fall and Barbara's rise. "I wouldn't want to presume—"

Barbara stopped in the middle of the path and turned toward her. "Someone once asked me whether it meant anything to me that you and I are each other's nearest living kin. I've been thinking about that recently. I find it means a great deal."

The moment stretched out between them, then as one they began, "Barb—"

"Antun—"

It might have called for laughter. Instead they turned and continued side by side down the path toward the river, but the tension had drained away.

It was Antuniet who broke the silence. "He never invited us here, you know, old Marziel. He couldn't avoid having us out to Saveze a few times, with Estefen being his heir-default. That's where I first remember seeing you. But I've never been to Chalanz before."

Barbara looked back at the house. It was barely visible now through the branches. "It's a dreadful waste. We barely spend a month out of the year here at most. It's a lovely place, but it isn't Saveze."

Her voice had a possessive edge that Antuniet both understood and envied. The house on Modul Street had been home, but never in that same deep-rooted way. The Chazillen lands had belonged to another branch of the tree: a place to summer if nothing else offered, but not to pin your heart to. And even those were lost to her now. "Do you begrudge spending so much of the year in town?"

"No." And then a laugh. "You know, it never occurred to me to think about it before. The baron…the court was his life's blood. And now I could hardly drag Margerit off to rusticate for most of the year. She needs Rotenek like a fish needs water." Her voice turned almost shy. "She *is* my home. Nothing else matters. Saveze will always be there. And they hardly need me to run the estate," she finished more briskly.

Antuniet thought, *In five minutes I've learned more about you than in the last twenty years.* She offered her own confidence. "I wish we could have been cousins long ago. How different it might all have been." They had come at last to the stone wall marking the end of the property and the edge of the river. The water flowed past quietly but the flotsam traced a path that gave hints of swift currents and roiling eddies. The air had turned cold. "These days the world seems all out of balance and I feel like that leaf." She pointed to a green mote, spinning in the shadows under the bank. It bobbed as if tugged by a hidden anchor, spun once more, then sank under the water. Antuniet shivered, and not only from the rising damp.

"Pertulif," Barbara said cryptically.

"What?"

"Oh, he has a poem about leaves in the wind that I used to quote. But we aren't leaves, you know. We make our own destiny."

Antuniet scanned the water farther downstream, but the leaf did not resurface.

* * *

There was an expected rhythm to a country floodtide retreat. No one rose much before noon except the eccentric and the very young. Then there would be long hours sitting and walking in the gardens, engaged in idle talk, followed by whatever entertainments had been planned for the evening, stretching late into the night. There wasn't a one of the guests who couldn't lay claim to the title of eccentric—except, perhaps, for Iaklin—but Antuniet found herself one of the few whose eccentricity extended to rising early and seeking the calm of the gardens before it could be shattered.

They saw very little of their hostesses the first few days. Margerit had duties to her family and a circle of old acquaintances that must be tended. Jeanne had taken charge of their program, arranging little games and amusements and setting in motion plans for their private ball. The timing of the river's rising had inspired her to name the first of May for the crowning celebrations of the week. She was collecting everyone's memories of the country customs of their youth to add to the plans, starting with rising at dawn to collect wildflowers and the first dew, all the way through a late-night bonfire on the terrace. Even Margerit joined in the planning with a will once her obligations had been completed. But when they brought out ribbons and armloads of rushes onto the terrace to make flower-gathering baskets, Antuniet slipped back into the house to find some more rational refuge.

It had taken three full days to discover the library, though it held pride of place just off the front hall. The door had been locked—perhaps to protect it from careless depredations—and Antuniet had passed it by several times before searching deliberately and requesting admittance from the housekeeper. She sought that refuge again now, finding the door already open and the curtains thrust back to let the afternoon light spill through.

The shelves held an odd assortment. Uncle Marziel hadn't been known for his bookishness but he'd understood the value of a good collection that went beyond long ranks of matching bound volumes. And, of course, Margerit had set her hand on it since then. But it wasn't the tidy cases of well-read tomes that drew her interest. Rather it was the high shelves: the odd corners stacked two-deep, the texts no one had thought to examine since they'd been placed there long years since. When was it that Marziel had bought the place? She pulled out a red-bound volume thick with tipped-in color plates. Some of the collection must have belonged to the previous owner, as she didn't recall that the baron had been interested in cataloging the insects of the Carpathians.

As she stood balanced on the rolling ladder, reaching back behind a set of German poets for a more interesting-looking volume that had fallen almost out of sight, a rustling sound behind her made her turn so quickly she had to grab for the rail to keep her balance.

"I'm sorry to startle you," Akezze said from the far corner of the room. "I hadn't realized I was being so quiet."

Antuniet descended with her prize. The other woman had chosen a chair beside the tall windows, and the glare through the panes had made her nearly invisible. Now, leaning forward, the light turned her red-gold hair into a halo. "So this is where you've been hiding," Antuniet said. "Did you, too, find the chirping birds in the garden a bit too loud?"

A smile and a nod acknowledged that they weren't speaking of the ones with feathers. "We all find our own refuge. I could almost think I'd stumbled on heaven here, except that I'd seen the library at Tiporsel first."

Antuniet settled opposite her and leafed through the thin volume. Nothing but a book of household receipts after all. She set it aside on a table. "What brought you along on this expedition? I'd meant to ask on the journey out but you were in such distress I thought it better to leave you alone."

She grimaced. "Thank you for that. I'm not looking forward to the rest of the journey to Saveze; I'd forgotten how much I hate traveling by coach. I'll be spending the summer there tutoring Maisetra Sovitre in logic and rhetoric."

"Ah, I had forgotten. So she's grown tired of crumbs? Good. I always thought she was too weak on the formalisms. You can only go so far on mere talent."

"Far enough," Akezze said. "Did you know they sent a copy of her analysis of the Mauriz *tutela* to Rome?"

"Now there's a terrifying thought."

Akezze shrugged. "Likely some clerk will file it and it'll never be seen again."

"I thought Margerit was trying to gather enough students to keep you in Rotenek in the fall." Antuniet asked, "Will she succeed?"

Another shrug. "There've been enough inquiries already to make it likely. She's planning a whole series of…I don't know whether to call them lectures or salons. A bit of both, I suppose. And not just from me. We've been discussing other women whose work should be more widely heard. I'm surprised she hasn't asked you already."

"She has. But—" No, she didn't care to rehearse those arguments yet with too many others. "It's a worthy project, though to hear her talk about it you'd think it was entirely selfish."

This time Akezze laughed. "To her, it is. But if she isn't careful she'll be a second Fortunatus, gathering an entire college around her by accident! And you…What brings you along to Chalanz? I hadn't taken you for one of de Cherdillac's set before this. Or did your cousin the baroness invite you?"

One of de Cherdillac's set. That was a delicate way to inquire. Before she could think how to answer, the sound of the door knocker out in the entry hall startled them both into silence. It was unlikely to be ordinary visitors. One of the conventions of floodtide was the suspension of casual visiting.

The footman's voice drifted in, piquing their curiosity. "Maisetra Iulien, are you expected?"

A young but not childish voice answered, "Oh, you know Cousin Margerit never cares for that! Is she at home?"

So it was one of the country cousins. Antuniet went to the door and peered out. The girl was still a few years short of being brought out. No longer a child but not yet a young woman. She had an animated heart-shaped face, spoiled by the petulant look that crossed it when the footman asked, "Are you here alone?" Evidently she was well enough known to the household that liberties were taken.

"No one cares where I go or who I go with. Is Cousin Margerit here or not?"

"I believe she is entertaining guests," the man replied with no success at giving the hint.

Antuniet took pity on him and stepped out, saying, "I think everyone's in the garden. I can take you back if you like." And to the waiting servant, "Perhaps a messenger might be sent to let the, ah—"

"The Fulpis," he supplied.

"—the Fulpis know where their daughter has wandered off to."

The girl Iulien was staring at her and Antuniet could tell she presented a puzzle. "This way," she invited, leading off down the hallway. "I don't believe we've met before. I'm Antuniet Chazillen. You might almost think of me as a distant relation of yours—Baroness Saveze is my cousin."

"How would that make you a relation?" Confusion was plain in her voice.

Had she put a foot wrong? She should have expected that the Fulpis had sheltered their daughters from the more scandalous parts of Margerit's life. "Never mind. It was a little joke." Perhaps thrusting her into the middle of Jeanne's friends would be a poor idea. "Wait here," she suggested as they came out into the fountain courtyard. "I'll go find Margerit and let her know you've come." She quietly extracted Margerit and followed her back to avoid being claimed for cutting ribbons and tying bows.

"Whatever are you doing here, Iuli?" Margerit greeted her cousin.

The girl's face settled into a mulish look. "I never had any chance to talk to you the other day. Papa never lets me talk at dinner except to answer questions. And then you all disappeared afterward to talk about Sofi's ball."

And if you have no more conversation than that, Antuniet thought, *then it's no wonder he forbids you to talk.*

Then Iuli's voice turned more coaxing and she threaded a hand through Margerit's arm. "I never had a chance to sing my new piece for you: the one I wrote you about. It's been ages since you were here and I barely saw you at all."

"Your turn will come soon enough," Margerit said. "I'll come visit at least once more before we go. And then you can sing and play the clavichord for me and we can have a cozy chat. Does anyone know you've run off?"

Antuniet cleared her throat softly. "I believe they do by now."

The girl turned on her. "You had no business telling tales to my parents."

"Iuli!" Margerit scolded. "That's enough! There's no call to be rude to Maisetra Chazillen. I was going to wait with you in the library until someone came for you but I won't reward this sort of behavior. I'm sending you back right now with Marken."

They had all come back out to the front hall. She gave terse instructions to fetch both the armin and a carriage. "And you stay right here until he comes for you."

They left her there, muttering after them, "I'm not a child!"

But when Antuniet glanced back before they turned the corner, the girl's face had fallen from disappointment to something near to heartbreak. "She worships you, I think," she said quietly.

Margerit sighed deeply. "She thinks she can wrap me around her finger. I wish she'd learn to take some heed. It isn't only that she came here when her father expressly forbade it; it's that she goes running off all the time without any thought for what might happen. I only hear of it through her letters, but I can fill in the rest."

"I should think you might have some sympathy for that sort of thing," Antuniet said. "I seem to recall you broke a good number of conventions."

"I sound like my Aunt Pertinek,.. don't I? But it's different for Iuli. She isn't an heiress, not enough of one to flout the rules. And I usually knew what the consequences could be. Iuli doesn't think about them at all. I sometimes wish I could take her in hand. My Uncle Fulpi doesn't know any other way than cold silences. It worked on me but never on her. But they would never allow that."

It was one of those consequences for breaking the rules, Antuniet knew. What passed for eccentricity in Rotenek would still be scandal here. Even such a little thing as an unmarried woman managing her own household. It was no doubt a tribute to the power of Margerit's fortune that the Fulpis still received her at all.

* * *

Antuniet fell into the snare of the May Day plans at last after dinner when one of the women exclaimed, "A divination! We must have a divination. I remember we always did the one with eggs to tell how many children we'd have."

"I rather doubt it would be enlightening," Mesnera Penilluk said. "At my age, I don't need a mystery to answer that one."

"Then what about a true-love charm?" Tionez suggested slyly. "Wouldn't you like to know who's secretly pining for you?"

"Yes, of course," Iaklin added, ever eager to support Tio's plans. "May Day should be a sweetheart divination. My cousins did one with twigs to spell out names, but I don't remember the verses."

Antuniet expected Jeanne to betray her but it was Margerit who said, "Antuniet knows one. Didn't you say your book-finding charm was based on a love divination?"

"Yes," she replied shortly.

If they'd begged or bullied she could have resisted, but Jeanne only came over to sit close and said softly, "I won't let them force you to it. I know you think this is all silly nonsense. I was hoping you might find something enjoyable in all my schemes, but it's not your fault that I've failed in that. I'll find something else to distract them."

That crumbled all her defenses. It was true. Jeanne had been doing her best, and all week she'd been as petulant and unwilling to be pleased as Margerit's cousin Iuli. It was such a little thing to ask, and truth to tell she longed for Jeanne to ask something of her, to include her. That carnival outing that had ended so badly—it had meant the world that Jeanne had invited her, though she never would have admitted it. "If Margerit can gather the paraphernalia," she began, "I could put something together. I've never done the original version, you know, but I remember it well enough."

And so the next day they gathered up parchment, wax and herbs, and in the parlor over luncheon she explained each person's part. "You need to draw up a billet like this on the parchment square." She showed them the signs and symbols to trace out. "In the center, put your initials or some other personal mark. We only need to be able to distinguish them, and, of course, you each need to write it out yourself. Now fold it like so—" She demonstrated with a blank square. "—then you fill it with a spoonful of this."

Maisetra Pertrez wrinkled her nose at it. "What's in it?" she asked.

"This and that. Moondust and sea salt and a bit of cobweb to bind it." The contents were nothing out of the ordinary really, but Antuniet fell into the response Nurse had always given. She creased the paper carefully. "Then when you're done, tuck the ends away like this and seal it closed with a drop of red wax. They all need to look identical."

"How does it work then?" Jeanne asked.

"We put them in a bowl and draw out one at a time, like drawing lots. We need to make a circle around a fire. You were planning for a bonfire already,

176 Heather Rose Jones

weren't you? There are some words to say, then I crack the seal and tip the contents into the flames. If the person's true love is present, the sparks will point them out."

Jeanne finished for her, "And then we look at the billet and find out who it was! But what if her true love isn't present?"

Antuniet shrugged. "When my old nurse did the divination, it was fairly rare for the signs to be clear. That made it more of a game. And her rule was you never used more than a third of the billets. She had some reason for that but I think it simply gets tedious when you get too many failures."

Jeanne passed out the supplies and sent Barbara off to find enough pens and ink. When Akezze would have risen and left the table, she urged, "No, you too. Everyone should join in."

"Mesnera de Cherdillac," Akezze said firmly, "I mean no slight to you or to our hostesses, but if I have been harboring secret unnatural passions, I would prefer that they remain secret even to myself." Without waiting for a reply, she rose, curtseyed briefly and left the parlor.

"It's only a silly game," Jeanne muttered to no one in particular.

"Let her be," Margerit said. "Remember that she began as a poor-scholar and she has more than her own reputation to take care for."

Tionez's friend Iaklin suddenly looked nervous as well, as if it had only now dawned on her what it would mean if the divination found a match for her. Tio made a game of flirtation but everyone knew she wasn't serious. *And nothing good can come from that*, Antuniet thought. Tio's reputation was already a source of gossip. Maisetra Silpirt would need to keep her eyes open if she didn't want to stumble badly. But there—she'd fallen back into the habit of measuring and judging the words and actions of other women. That had been one consolation of having fallen so far out of favor: that she was no longer required to care what others did, or what they thought of her in turn.

Having once capitulated, Antuniet found it easier to join in the festivities. It was floodtide, after all: a time set aside for silly games and amusements. And if Jeanne's plans were not in her style, she could at least refrain from spoiling them for the others by pointedly standing apart.

Despite Jeanne's best efforts, no one rose quite as early as dawn to greet the May, but they all made it out into the gardens while every leaf and petal was still glittering with moisture. As they gathered flowers into baskets, a great show was made of blotting up the last drops of dew to bathe faces that mostly would never see the freshness of youth again. It seemed almost a parody of the ritual. Oh, a handful of them, like Tio, were young enough for the game. But more of Jeanne's close circle were at least a decade past the trailing edge of youth: women like Helen Penilluk who had come to an understanding with an indifferent husband, or widows like Marianniz Pertrez who had given society its due and now claimed their lives as their own. Some she had been surprised to see in that circle. She wouldn't have guessed that Alenur Iskimmai was in any way dissatisfied in her marriage until seeing her wander through the garden hand in hand with Ailis Chaplen. What little lies had they told their husbands to be allowed this holiday? Or was the honor of an invitation from Baroness Saveze enough of an excuse? Jeanne's amours were an open secret and she'd made a sound guess about Barbara and Margerit even before Jeanne's hint last fall, but before this trip there wasn't a one of the others about whom she'd heard more than faint rumors. It all should have seemed sad, but floodtide gave license for so many things.

After the flower-picking there was a dainty feast spread on a cloth laid across the lawns and Jeanne led them in composing riddles and rhymes. Fatigued from that exertion, most of the ladies retired to take their rest before the rigors of the evening's dancing. Antuniet wandered back into the gardens feeling restless and at loose ends. This week had brought…no, not memories of the floodtide holidays of her youth. Those had never been this pleasant or this elaborate. Primarily, it brought the reminder of how far outside this sort of cozy circle she had always stood—would always stand. It was time to return to Rotenek and her work. That was where she belonged now. But the visit *had* been pleasant. She'd nearly forgotten what it was like to live in this world. And if it were only Jeanne and the more sensible of her friends…

When she finally returned to the house, Barbara was engaged like a commanding general with directing the preparations in the ballroom. Every surface was being decked with flowers.

"No point in doing things halfway," she said cheerfully at Antuniet's approach. "They'll only go to waste in the gardens when we leave."

Several screens had been set up to make the space smaller. There was no need for the vast expanse the room was designed to provide. In one corner, a small bower had been set up for the musicians rather than banishing them to the gallery overlooking the dance floor. Antuniet spent a while trying to find words to express how delightful it must be to be able to throw such preparations at so small a gathering, but she gave it up when all her attempts sounded envious and bitter. In the end she retreated to the library again, where the books wouldn't require her to make pleasant talk.

* * *

Antuniet looked in the mirror one last time before heading down to the ballroom. She had last worn the rose silk that night at the opera. Jeanne was right: her dressmaker had worked wonders. It almost succeeded in making her look presentable. She touched her dark hair, hanging in unaccustomed ringlets. When had she ever hovered over her reflection before going out? That was proof enough that she was making far too much fuss over the evening. One of the housemaids had helped her dress her hair and manage the finishing touches on the gown. That, too, she had lost the habit of expecting. And then there was no remaining excuse to stay in her bedroom.

She paused in the ballroom doorway to take in the effect of Barbara's work. It was hard to tell where the room ended and the gardens began. The musicians were warming up with a soft concerto while the guests sipped champagne and sorted themselves out for the opening quadrille. It had been quite some time since she had danced, longer still since she'd done so with pleasure. The quadrille… She would struggle to remember the figures now. Perhaps she would venture to the floor after the first few sets. A country dance should be safe.

She saw Jeanne descending upon her, exclaiming, "Toneke! I'm so glad you wore that gown. You should always wear rose; it's the color that makes you bloom." She laughed gaily at her own joke.

Does she think to fool anyone into believing I have more than the one? But she smiled and nodded, trying not to think too much on the last time she'd worn the dress.

"Do you have a partner yet for the opening set?"

Antuniet's tongue froze in her mouth. "I…I don't know if I—"

"Oh, pooh!" Jeanne said, taking her by the hand. "If I can lead then you can follow. We'll step on each other's toes together if need be."

The reassurance failed. Jeanne was an excellent dancer no matter which part she took. Yet with that look of encouragement in Jeanne's eyes, she longed to—

Tionez interrupted her thoughts with a peremptory demand. "Jeanne, you simply must convince Saveze that I'm right. Tradition requires that she open the ball with you. We can't throw out all the rules, even for floodtide."

Antuniet glanced over to where their hostesses stood. Margerit looked annoyed, Barbara impatient. Clearly this hadn't been their idea. And yet tradition did dictate that a ball be opened by the highest ranking pair. Jeanne sighed. "You're right, of course. Tio, perhaps you will partner Antuniet in my stead."

"I hadn't planned to dance the quadrille," Antuniet said quickly, catching an inexplicable look of triumph that Tionez threw her.

She moved down to the end of the room to sit with Akezze while the others formed up, but they were both dragged into the second set willy-nilly, for the guests were exactly sixteen in all. Antuniet wryly held a hand out to Akezze, apologizing, "If we don't join in then we'll spoil it for the rest of them. I promise you, even without knowing the dance you'll likely do better than I will. If we make the fourth couple, we'll stumble through somehow."

Having survived to the last reverence, they were reprieved for the next few sets, for the longways dances were more forgiving of numbers. Antuniet found herself enjoying the spectacle as the women skipped and turned through the flower-decked space. Barbara was a very precise and proficient dancer, Margerit a hesitant and careful one, but when the figures brought the two of them together they were transformed into something wondrous. Alenur was carelessly showy in a way that almost seemed accidental until you noticed that she never put a foot wrong. Tionez always seemed to be paying more attention to the other dancers than to her own steps. And Jeanne… Jeanne was a figure of matchless grace, moving through the figures with easy perfection while never showing effort. And somehow anyone she partnered partook of that same grace for a space of time. Antuniet found herself swaying in place as she watched.

She started a little when Barbara's voice came suddenly beside her. "Would you care to join the next set? I don't recall that you cared much for dancing, but Margerit thought…"

Ah, yes. The considerate hostess. "I think you'd find me a less graceful partner than the ones you've been enjoying."

"I've been told I'm extraordinarily forgiving," Barbara said with a smile. She raised a hand in offer with a slight formal bow.

On impulse, Antuniet took it. She was tired of always standing to the side. And Barbara left little to forgive: she had a talent for leading one's movements and turning a misstep into a charming ornament. Was that from her swordplay? Whatever the reason, her confidence was infectious. When the set ended and the musicians began the promenade to signal the next, Antuniet gathered up her courage and moved toward the small knot of women clustered around Jeanne. Floodtide gave license, after all. Before she could speak, Ailis pulled Jeanne out onto the floor into place at the head of another reel.

The small table with the punch bowl was close enough to make sufficient excuse for her movement. Antuniet continued on past the dancers and accepted a cup, nursing it as she watched the figures start again. It was too much to expect that Jeanne would have a moment's free time before the end of the ball. But having set foot on the floor twice, she found herself solicited for another of the round dances. The steps were coming back to her now. This was nothing like her own seasons had been, when every ball was an ordeal to be endured and another ordeal to come later at home when her mother would inquire after every partner's slightest look or word.

The musicians struck up a promenade for the waltz and once again there was a voice at her elbow. "I'm determined this time," Jeanne said quietly. "Will you?"

All the confidence of the last few dances drained, away but she held out her hand for Jeanne to take and let herself be led out into the center of the floor. There was a brief confusion while their arms found their places and then the music changed. Almost, she caught that glamour that Jeanne cast over her partners. Almost, she forgot to think about where her feet should be and gave herself up to the music. But there was the close heat of Jeanne's hand on her waist and a wistful longing in Jeanne's eyes that seemed to demand… And then her heart raced and her balance faltered and she found herself shaking free and backing away repeating, "I'm sorry. Jeanne, I'm sorry. I can't."

When she found her way to the edge of the room and gathered enough composure to look back, Antuniet could see Jeanne circling past the other couples in the arms of another partner. It didn't matter who; there would always be someone waiting.

The evening was warm enough that Jeanne's plan to hold the late supper on the terrace was proclaimed to be inspired. And while all were being fortified with cold roasts and pickles and honeyed fritters, a brazier was brought out and a small fire—hardly worthy of the name bonfire—was prepared for the divination. Antuniet stood beside it, running her fingers through the little folded billets in the basket while the others ranged themselves on benches gathered on all sides.

There should be grand and portentous words spoken to put them in the mood, Antuniet realized. Her book-finding charm had been stripped down to a few muttered essentials to avoid drawing too much attention, but she cast her mind back to how her old nurse would have them all hanging on her words, and intoned, "The mystery of love is a deep mystery. Only those who see all things know for whom we are fated. Tonight we petition the saints—Falinz and Nikul—to share with us a glimpse of what fortune holds for us. Five will be tested." She held up the first of the billets that came to hand. "If there is a message here for you, perhaps you will be granted that glimpse of true love."

She held the folded slip up high. Like the public mysteries, half the success came from making a good show that would catch the enthusiasm of the participants. This hardly counted as a mystery—more like an old wives' charm—but she had too much professional pride for half-measures. She spoke through the sing-song verse of the mystery, trying to recall the original words from before she had devised her own. The billet was held over the flames just long enough to soften the wax and then she pinched the sides so it would spring open and let the contents fall into the flames.

A shower of sparks flew up, but they winked out quickly. There was a collective "Oh!" of disappointment as Antuniet unfolded the parchment and held it sideways to catch the flickering light. "A.C." She looked up. "Maisetra Chaplen, I fear your true love waits for you somewhere outside the circle of this fire." There had always been a stock of answers for the disappointed to soften the blow. She dropped the parchment in the flames and reached into the basket again as it shriveled and blackened.

When the contents of the next billet were cast into the fire, a swirl of sparks and smoke rose up, twisted by an errant breeze, and hung over Barbara's head before winking out. There were cries of appreciation for the effect and Margerit called out, "If anyone's name but mine is on that billet, there may be blood spilled!" provoking gusts of laughter.

Antuniet flattened it out and held it so the bold looping "M" could clearly be seen. "I hardly know why you bothered," she said, dropping the note once more into the flames. "It doesn't take a divination to see that one."

The next was once more noncommittal and the woman whose initials were revealed seemed relieved at the results. At the fourth repetition the sparks flew sideways at Tionez and seemed to follow her hand as she batted them away. Antuniet unfolded the note and read, "T.P.?" in a mystified tone.

Tionez looked abashed for a moment and then held up her hand with a laugh, pointing out the gold wedding ring there. "Alas, it's true," she said ruefully. "I love my husband! You may now cast me out of the sisterhood!" Again, there were catcalls and laughter.

Antuniet reached into the bowl, intoning, "The saints will speak to us one last time tonight. Whose fate will be revealed?" This time the powdered herbs met the flames in a brilliant blaze as the breeze shifted once more and drove the sparks to dance before Jeanne's face.

An explosion of mocking laughter ran around the circle. Someone called out, "I suppose this means you won't be sleeping alone tonight!"

"Tell! Tell!" another cried. "Who's been holding out on you?"

There was a stone in the pit of Antuniet's stomach and she stood frozen, holding the unfolded billet out over the flames until she snatched back her burnt fingers with a cry. The parchment fell into the fire and shriveled into a cinder.

"Oh no! Who was it?"

"I didn't see," Antuniet said flatly. And when there were demands to open the remaining packets to tease out the answer, she dumped the remainder into the flames, saying, "The divination is at an end. The fates have spoken." A swarm of sparks rose up like angry bees, scattering randomly among the women.

There was more dancing after that. The musicians had already gone to bed in anticipation of an early morning start on their return to Rotenek, but Ermilint's high, clear voice sang out a chorus-dance that had been popular a generation ago and a circle formed around the remnants of the fire. Then another singer took up a popular song with a waltz tempo and several couples claimed the tiled space around the fountain.

Antuniet leaned against the columns of the pergola to watch, trying to still the turmoil within. Jeanne, of course, was dancing, held in Tionez's arms, heads together whispering. Barbara and Margerit were once again caught in their own private world, enjoying the freedom to join their bodies into one with no gossiping tongues to task them for their transgression. They continued swaying alone in the space after the song had finished.

"Jealous?" Jeanne's voice whispered in her ear.

A knife turned in her gut. "What?" *How did she…?*

"Are you jealous of them?" She waved a hand toward where the two swayed in close embrace. "I am. Oh, I don't mean personally. I gave up on Barbara the first time I saw the two of them together. But I'm jealous that they found each other. I'm jealous that Fortune smiled so brightly on them and left people like you and me in the shade."

Antuniet said tightly, "Fortune never owed me anything."

"But don't you ever dream what it could be like?" Jeanne's voice was almost wistful. "To have one person in this world whose first thought on waking is of you? Whose last memory at sleeping is your touch? Who rejoices at your happiness and mourns your sorrows?"

The knife turned again and sank deeper. She twisted away from Jeanne's side and fled blindly out into the darkness, down the path toward the river. She stumbled over a tree root and fell, tearing the skirts of her gown. After that, she slowed her flight until she came out into the moonlight and sat on the stone wall at the river's edge. At first she didn't recognize the sound as emanating from her own throat. It was a harsh animal bleating, welling up from deep within. She stuffed her fist into her mouth to stifle the noise, and bit down until the blood came, as if pain could drive out pain.

She heard the footsteps coming down the path after her and thought, *Go away. Please just go away.*

"Antuniet?" The voice came hesitantly. And then, "Oh God, Toneke, I'm sorry. What's wrong? I don't know what I said, but I'm sorry. I didn't mean to—"

"Didn't you?" Antuniet asked, gasping to force the words out. "Didn't you tell me once that that was the price of your friendship? That I had to put up with your teasing?"

"Teasing? But I...oh." She fell silent. And then, "Toneke, I didn't mean it that way. I didn't think that you..." The quality of the silence changed this time. Antuniet dreaded what would come next. "Toneke...that last billet. Was it yours?"

Denial was impossible. Confirmation was unthinkable.

Through the darkness she heard the faintest of sighs. "Oh, Toneke, that's no call for tears. Don't you see? I'd stopped daring to hope—"

"—that you'd succeed in making me your next conquest?" Antuniet turned away, not wanting to risk meeting her eyes even by the wan moonlight. "Oh yes, you're very skilled. I've watched you at work. How long did you expect it to take? How many parties and presents did you calculate it would cost?"

"Toneke—"

She was shouting now because it was the only way to get the words out. "I'm not some cheap actress whose company can be bought for the night with a ball gown or a cashmere shawl."

Silence again. "I never meant it that way. Toneke—"

"Don't call me that!" The mocking endearment echoed in her ears.

When Jeanne's voice came again through the dark, it was low and tightly controlled. "They say if a man is starving and can't get bread, he will eat the husks from the threshing floor just to fill the emptiness in his belly. Don't blame me for what I've done when I was hungry." And then there was silence again except for the soft patter of dancing slippers climbing the path in the dark.

It wasn't possible to stay there forever. Even on a summer night the cold from the river crept in. And eventually morning would come and she would need to face... No. It was time to return to Rotenek. She could leave in the coach with the musicians in just a few hours, before anyone else was awake. Jeanne would continue on to Saveze, and if their paths crossed again after the summer...well, she would be stronger by then.

Antuniet slipped into the house by a side door, though the other guests all seemed to have sought their own beds already. She found ink and paper and wrote an apologetic note to Margerit, leaving it propped on the dressing table in her room. There was little enough to pack; no need to bother anyone else with the matter. The ruined ball gown she left in a heap on the floor.

CHAPTER TWENTY-TWO

Margerit

The glorious weather they had enjoyed for floodtide had turned to wind and thunder. The summer storm would pass swiftly, but it matched the change in mood that had come over the company after May Day as the guests departed. Margerit watched Fonten House slip behind them through the rain-streaked windows of the coach and sat back on the cushions with a sigh. "I wish I knew why Jeanne changed her mind," she said. "She was so eager to spend the summer at Saveze. I would have enjoyed her company. Did she say anything to you?"

Barbara hesitated long enough to betray herself. "No, she didn't say anything," she said carefully. "I have a suspicion, but it isn't my secret to tell." She turned with a half-smile. "The last time Jeanne endured a summer in Rotenek was in pursuit of me."

Margerit cast her mind back over the past week. Jeanne had been her usual ebullient self, flirting with everyone and giving preference to none. "But...but who?" she wondered aloud. And then, "That divination—do you think there was some truth in it?"

"I don't know," Barbara said, shaking her head. "And I'd rather not guess for now."

They took the trip in easy stages for Akezze's sake, though she declared that if it were possible to travel night and day it would be worth the misery to be done with it. But Chalanz to Saveze was four days' travel at the best of times and they stretched it to six to allow more rest. The last day of their journey was marked by the sight of Saint Orisul's, glimpsed with increasing frequency at every turn of the road, its bright walls gleaming like a beacon set up against the mountainside.

Margerit couldn't see it now without the overlay of that first time, fleeing across the countryside to sanctuary. But today she and Barbara traveled two different journeys on this road. Barbara's heart lay several miles farther on where the manor of Saveze sat nestled on a slight prominence overlooking the river, opposite the village. You could see in its bones the fortress that had once guarded the pass beyond. Those bones had been fleshed with more peaceful stonework in centuries past. The baron had corrected a generation's neglect but had declined to remake the place in the modern fashion. It was left a bit of this, a bit of that: towers of gray stone, white-plastered walls and blue-green copper roofs splashed against the green fields.

A boy working in the fields spotted the coach and ran ahead, setting up a cry. By the time they passed through the village the horses were slowed to a walk to thread through the small crowd gathered to welcome their baroness home. There was always a feeling of possessiveness in their greetings. They had known Barbara as a child growing up here while the baron was off in Rotenek, though no one had suspected her heritage then or how she would one day return to claim Saveze as her own.

It embarrassed her, Margerit knew, but she bore with it all in good humor. The staff of the manor itself were more businesslike. For several days they had already been dealing with arriving wagons full of boxes and trunks. Margerit spent several hours hunting down her books and taking inventory to make certain all had arrived safely. She wondered again whether she should have brought Tanfrit's Gaudericus. She'd barely had time to glance at it yet, but she hadn't wanted to risk it in travel. The unpacking took hours, for she was shy about interrupting the servants to help her. She still felt like a stranger among these people. Only a handful of the staff from Rotenek had come with them. Saveze was very much Barbara's domain, not hers. Everyone was unfailingly polite and respectful, but they treated her as a guest, not part of the family.

When the last of the books had been found and directed to the library, Margerit requested a bath and settled in for the luxury of doing as little as possible for the first few days. Barbara's plans were less restful. At dawn the next morning, Margerit rolled over to find her up and dressed in riding clothes.

"Hush, go back to sleep," she said. "I'm just going out with Cheruk to begin riding the *markein*."

It was one of those rituals of the nobility that Margerit had been oblivious to before their first summer here together. Not quite a mystery, but more than a mere survey of the lands. They wouldn't trace the true boundaries, of course, up along the stony mountaintops. But there was a path that stood in for those bounds and the riding of it in easy stages was not to be put off. "Do you think anything's changed since last year?" she asked sleepily.

"I certainly hope so! Estefen had this place for scarce two years and I'm still repairing the damage. LeFevre gives me all the numbers and figures, but that's not the same as seeing it for myself."

Margerit allowed herself several days of indolence with nothing more strenuous than reading through the sheaf of papers that Iuli had pressed on her at the end of their final visit, but then it was time for her own summer ritual. Over morning tea she asked Akezze, "Are you recovered enough for a short drive? I'm going up to the convent today and I thought to introduce you."

Akezze agreed somewhat reluctantly, but when she was handed up into the little one-horse gig, she commented, "This shouldn't be so bad. It's only the closeness of the traveling coach that does me in. I didn't know that you drove."

"Not in Rotenek," Margerit answered as she twitched the reins to give the horse leave to start. "I wouldn't dare try to manage a team in the city. But I had to learn the first summer I was here. Marken doesn't drive," she said with a nod to where he perched precariously behind them. "Barbara says it isn't done to go about the countryside with a coachman and footmen and all. So if I had to learn, I preferred this to riding. I never have been entirely comfortable on a horse's back."

They left Marken with the gig at the livery stable at the foot of the hill and climbed up the path to Saint Orisul's. He took his responsibilities in a more relaxed fashion here in Saveze. Country rules were different, it seemed. The portress at the gate didn't need to ask their purpose but escorted them directly to Mother Teres's office.

"You've come early," the abbess greeted her.

"Yes, we left at floodtide this year since I won't be attending the summer term at the university. I brought you a gift," she said, holding out the sealed paper.

Mother Teres took it without examining it. It wasn't the donation itself, of course, only a letter confirming it. But Margerit insisted on delivering it personally. "I've brought you another gift as well, if you like," she continued, turning to Akezze. "This is Maisetra Mainus. She's come to tutor me this summer but she fears I won't give her enough work to earn her pay. So I thought, that is…I know most of the students go home for the summer, but perhaps she could offer some classes?"

"We don't generally allow outsiders to teach the secular students," Mother Teres interrupted. "But perhaps she will have something to offer our own teachers. What subjects do you know?"

Akezze nodded in greeting and rattled off a host of topics.

Mother Teres looked thoughtful. "Yes, perhaps. I'll speak to the others and see what might be useful. And you, my dear," she said to Margerit. "Will you be lending us your services as well? I still recall how helpful you were with the pilgrims' mysteries that winter you were here."

Margerit wondered how best to answer. "I made that offer to Sister Marzina last summer but it seems she had no need of me."

"Indeed?" Mother Teres said. "I see." She turned to her assistant who sat patiently by the door. "If you would, ask Marzina to come speak with me."

Margerit wished she'd found a way to pass over the matter. In the months that she and Barbara had found sanctuary here, she had worked side by side

186 Heather Rose Jones

with the nun in charge of helping those who came to the convent in search of help with a miracle. But a careless word—a glance that carried too much meaning—had betrayed their secret to Marzina and she had turned cold and disapproving. *I hadn't yet learned to be circumspect that spring,* Margerit remembered with regret. She doubted that Mother Teres was that much more accepting, but she had the welfare of the convent's coffers to consider. There was no point in offending their two closest patronesses.

Sister Marzina appeared and asked, "You wished to speak with me?" without a glance at the guests.

The abbess rose from behind her desk. "As you can see, Maisetra Sovitre has returned to Saveze for the summer. I've let her know that we would be honored if the Royal Thaumaturgist could find time to assist us while she's here. I'm sure you have only to send a message to the manor if the occasion should arise."

"As you wish," the nun said stiffly and bowed again. She left, still without greeting Margerit.

As they made their way down the path from the convent, Akezze asked curiously, "So is it only outside Rotenek that people dare to disapprove of you?"

"I'm certain that there's disapproval enough in Rotenek." She turned it to a joke. "After all, if it weren't for me there would be an eligible baroness on the marriage market." She added, "And if it weren't for Barbara, there would be an heiress as well."

"But how many people know that? I didn't."

Margerit had the grace to feel abashed. "I never meant it to be a secret from you, but how does one begin that conversation? Sister Marzina knows because I was indiscreet once, and she's convinced it makes an abomination of my gifts."

"And yet that doesn't seem to bother you."

Margerit turned more sober. "It bothers me, but what's to do? I wouldn't choose a different life. But it's true—my Uncle Fulpi finds me something of a disgrace to the family name and that's why my cousins aren't allowed to visit me, not even at my house in Chalanz."

"And yet disgrace can be overlooked for a price," Akezze said dryly.

"Does it bother you?" Margerit ventured, wondering if she'd get a truthful answer. Akezze couldn't afford to have scruples about an employer's morals.

But they had come to the livery stable and there was no chance for Akezze to give an answer to that.

The visit to Saint Orisul's had broken the sense of holiday and on returning to the manor, Akezze asked, "Shall we begin your studies? There's no point in waiting. The summer won't last forever and we have a great deal to get through."

"Where did you want to start?" Margerit asked. "You know I'm not very strong on the modern philosophers, but I've been told that Wolff and Mazzies would be useful for my work."

"We begin at the beginning," Akezze intoned. "Your knowledge is all bits and pieces. I can't build without a sound foundation."

"What? All the way back to Aristotle, then?" Margerit asked, half-joking, but not dismayed when Akezze nodded.

Those first few weeks flew by quickly, if tediously. There was some frustration at going through the baby steps again, but she was on sure ground. The classics had always been her favorites. The blithe confidence of the ancient authors that all the world could be distilled down into simple truths was restful if inadequate. When they moved on to the medieval commentaries, her flaws began to show. The tangled arguments of the Sophists had always seemed a pointless distraction. And as a guest at the university lectures she'd never had a chance to take part in the disputations that might pry sense from them.

"It's not just an academic game," insisted Akezze. "You'd be surprised how many mysteries rest on faulty propositions and mistaken definitions. It can be more important to know how to spot a flawed argument than to construct a sound one."

And that was what made Akezze's lectures more than dry exercises. They pulled out Bartolomeus's *Lives and Mysteries of the Saints* and worked their way through the logical structure of some of the older ceremonies. When, after covering Descartes, they paused in the course of philosophers to take in the grammarians, even more began to fall into place.

She had always been able to see the wrongness of a mystery in the movements and appearance of the *fluctus*. And working backward from that she had developed an instinct for finding the flaws in the language and structure that generated it. But Akezze showed her how to predict weak points in the mysteries from the *expositulum* alone. For devotional mysteries it might not matter. Their essence was between the heart of the worshipper and the ears of God and the saints. No one was going to quibble that Aquinas had erred in composing the text of his *gloriosa* when it had stood unchanged for six hundred years. But in functional mysteries precision and meaning mattered greatly, whether they were the minor everyday ones, like a prayer to soothe the fever of a sick child, or civic rituals like the *tutelas*. And for the great mysteries like those she worked on for Annek, there the structure and language must be built as strongly as a bridge or tower, with no ill-fitting stones or crumbling mortar.

The summer days filled quickly. With Akezze's guidance she spent more time over her books than if she'd stayed in Rotenek for the summer term. Barbara finished the survey of her lands and projects and now there was time to drive out, whether for purpose or pleasure. And the reading was augmented one afternoon when Barbara placed a beautiful inlaid box in her lap, saying, "I've finished them. I...I'm not sure what to think anymore. Read them."

She left and Margerit opened the casket to riffle through the collection of paper it contained: the baron's letters. She hung poised for long moments between curiosity and doubt, then took them up as water to a thirsty soul.

It was easy to see how Barbara had become lost in those missives for days at a time. Margerit set herself a rule to read them only in the morning hours when Barbara was out riding and before her lessons. The story unfolded like a romantic novel: that first formal invitation, hints of secret meetings and growing passion, brief notes slipped hand to hand during the closely scrutinized chaos of the season. There must have been an accomplice. A maid? Perhaps her own mother? No, Margerit recalled, her mother would have been back in Chalanz by then. Then came the crushing disappointment when the season came to a close and he was free to offer.

I spoke with your father last night at the club. It seems his ambitions climb higher than the chance to address his grandsons as "Mesner" and I am to be dismissed as a penniless fortune-hunter. I cannot find it in myself to fault his caution. This year I have set in train several ventures by which I hope to remedy that judgment. They will take some time to show promise. Will you stand faithful to me and have patience?

And she had, for quite some time. There was a series of brief encouraging notes, chronicling the rise of Marziel's fortunes, his hopes, a reassurance that rumors of his return to religious studies were false, a note of triumph that the uncertainty in France that frightened others was an opportunity for those who were bold enough to seize it. Then a more worried tone: a whisper that Maistir Anzeld had spoken with this suitor or that, and one name appearing too often.

I saw you at the Saluns' ball but you never found the chance to slip away. Would there be such hazard in dancing with me in everyone's sight? I know you are as skilled as any woman at dissembling, for I watched you with Arpik and no one could have guessed from the brightness of your eyes that you didn't mean to encourage him.

And then later: *I must see you. Today, tomorrow. I must hear from your own lips that you have refused Arpik's offer. All of society is abuzz with rumor.* And in the next brief scrawl: *What have they threatened that you could not refuse? You held true for so long. If there is no other way, my carriage stands waiting. We could go to Genoa; my business flourishes there. Can you find some way to escape from your father's house when all are abed? I dare not try to meet you by day for you are always in an armin's shadow.*

Whatever plans he had urged had come to naught. The next sheet was not a letter but a black-edged card. The salutation no longer addressed Maisetra Anzeld. The date was more than a year later and leapt from the page. Seventeen hundred and ninety-two. The battle of Tarnzais, when the flower of Alpennia was lost against the armies of France. *On Sunday, the 14th of October will be held a memorial mass for the soul of Mihail Lumbeirt.* Written on the back in stiffly formal words: *Count and Countess Turinz are invited to join us for a reception at Tiporsel House after the services.* And it was signed *Marziel Lumbeirt, Baron Saveze.*

Had he sent it in friendship or bitterness? Had she received it with regret? She couldn't have known that fate would have rewarded faithfulness so completely. What had driven her to accept the marriage? The baron had alluded to threats, but had she needed any greater threat than the passing years? She would have spent four years out in society by the time she capitulated. And had she attended the funeral and once more faced the man who had loved her so fiercely? Did she know already what a disaster her marriage would be?

One morning Barbara interrupted her in the midst of her reading, saying, "I thought we might drive up to Atefels today. Can you spare the time? I was sent the oddest message about a stranger roaming the hills and from the description I think it might be someone you know."

"Who?" Margerit asked curiously.

But there was a twinkle in Barbara's eye that said she meant to keep the surprise.

Atefels was the smallest of the five named villages in the lands of Saveze. It lay eastward along the road leading to the pass. There the valley widened enough for fields and gardens below the rocky hills that rose up behind them. The village thought of itself as the first line of defense against foreign invaders, though in truth the last foreign army it had seen was the French heading east after passing through all of Alpennia. But the residents took their duty seriously to cast a sharp eye on travelers coming down from the mountains, even as they lined their pockets with offers of food and clean beds to the weary.

They made quite a cavalcade pulling up to the inn with the light gig and Tavit for an outrider and Marken following behind. Margerit found herself smiling to watch both armins ever so diplomatically declining to leave their charge in another's hands at the faintest whiff of risk. The innkeeper came out to greet them, unsurprised at the invasion.

"Welcome! Welcome, Mesnera! Come, sit! Will you have beer or wine?"

Margerit tamped back her curiosity. There'd be no skipping the formalities of hospitality to his baroness. So it was only after food and drink had been served and all the concerns of the village had been asked after that Barbara inquired, "So what are these stories that have been drifting down the valley? Who can tell me about them?"

"Ah, for that you've come to the right place," the innkeeper said. "It was my own message that brought you. Some foreign woman wandering in the hills. Could barely understand one word in five but she seems to think she's a friend of yours, Mesnera. When she asked where she was and we told her that she'd stumbled into the Barony of Saveze, she claimed that she'd met you in Rotenek."

Margerit hid a smile behind her hand, now certain of who they were dealing with.

He continued, "In the morning she goes wandering up into the hills and comes back with a basket of rocks. Then she paints them. That is, she doesn't paint on the rocks but she paints pictures of the rocks, if you see what I mean. They all get tipped out back of my garden after that. If today goes as usual, she should be back soon."

They settled in to wait, enjoying a bottle of wine in the sunshine of the courtyard and watching the occasional traveling coach pass along the road. After an hour, a pair of dark specks making their way down the slope opposite resolved into a sturdy middle-aged woman in a dark walking dress followed by an older man hunched under the weight of a sack.

"Frances Collfield!" Margerit cried when she came close enough to hail. "I knew it must be you!"

The botanist stopped and blinked in surprise. "Whatever are you doing here?"

"That's what I should be asking you," Margerit countered. "I thought you'd gone back to England last fall after your lecture."

"Oh, I did, I did," Miss Collfield said, pulling her wits about her. "But now you see it's summer and I'm back collecting again. There's no time to lose, you know. I have to complete my survey of the *Lecanorae* this summer if I'm going to finish my manuscript in time. My brother's started collecting subscriptions for the publication, so I can't dillydally."

"But why didn't you tell us you were coming?" Barbara asked. "I could have made arrangements for you."

"Well, I never quite meant to come *here* exactly. I started out in Geneva at the beginning of the summer and simply followed my nose and this is where it brought me. I confess I'm not exactly sure where I am. The innkeeper kept mentioning your name, but I didn't realize…So this is your land? What a charming place."

Margerit had to laugh. "But now you're here."

In the days that followed, Miss Collfield declined an invitation to enjoy more than the occasional dinner as she worked her way down the valley, but those evenings brought a liveliness to the quiet of summer. *It's like those long sessions in the library at Tiporsel*, Margerit thought. *Back when that was the only place Barbara and I could meet as equals.* And now, one by one, more quick minds were being added to that charmed circle. The season in Rotenek was so bounded about by rules and rituals. There had to be some way to re-create this experience in large.

Akezze's schedule had added two days a week when she went up to Saint Orisul's to teach. And though Margerit would have driven her up in the gig or offered to have someone take her, Akezze preferred to walk, saying that there was no point in spending the summer in the country and then wasting the opportunity to savor it. But one day, more than a month after their arrival, she returned with a formally worded request from Sister Marzina that Maisetra Sovitre might lend her assistance with one of the pilgrim's mysteries if it were convenient. And so, at the next trip back to Saint Orisul's, they again left the carriage at the foot of the hill and Margerit climbed up alongside Akezze and presented herself at Sister Marzina's office.

Marzina laid out the purpose of the ceremony in a few brief sentences. *So we aren't to discuss why I wasn't sent for before*, Margerit thought, looking over the rough outline of the proposed text. "The child they hope will be granted a miracle—how old is he?"

"Not quite seven, I think," came the answer. "It's been two years since the fever that took his hearing. They thought he might recover and then they tried what could be found closer to home. Likely it took most of the last year to save the expenses of the journey, so we'll do our best for him in the name of Saint Orisul and Our Lady."

The outline—for it could hardly be called an *expositulum* yet—followed the usual pattern: praise and invocation of the chosen saints, a formal statement of the petition and the desired cure, then a blank where the petition became more specific with praise and thanks to close. "You haven't decided on the elaborations yet?"

Sister Marzina gestured to where a girl in a student's uniform stood quietly waiting. "I was hoping to use Maisetra Perneld's gifts there in some way. Valeir, make your curtsey to Princess Annek's thaumaturgist."

The girl stepped forward and bobbed a greeting. One of the secular students, by her dress, and old enough that she must be in her last year at school. Margerit had thought at first that she might be a novice in training to assist Marzina. "And what are your talents, Valeir?" she asked.

"I…" The girl glanced at Marzina. "I hear things. They say I hear angel voices."

"Voices?" She'd never heard of an *auditor* whose perceptions came that specifically.

"It's just an old country expression," Marzina said sourly. "She means the usual humming and ringing, from what she's described. But I thought that since our miracle involves sound, it could be useful to monitor the *sonitus* effects as well as your visions."

"Yes," Margerit agreed, returning to the outline and taking up a pen, with a brief glance for permission.

Whatever lay between her and Marzina, they'd fallen back into their old working partnership easily. "The miracle I asked when Iohennis Lutoz was struck dumb would be a useful starting point," Margerit suggested. "I didn't have time to plan that one, but here is the structure of the part that was answered." She sketched out a few notes. "We can celebrate the basic ceremony and add changes based on what the *fluctus* tells us." *Akezze would scold me. But it's easier to work by feel than to plan it entirely from the beginning.* "Valeir, your task will be to stand in for the deaf boy. The more clearly you hear the *fluctus*, the more effective the mystery is likely to be."

Working through the preparations took several days—several mornings, rather, for Margerit still kept afternoons for her own studies. The girl Valeir stood awkwardly by at first while they rehearsed and tuned the ceremony, answering only when questioned on what she heard. But when she gave up on words and hummed a sweet but tuneless phrase, Margerit exclaimed, "That's perfect! Sing what you're hearing while we work. Then I can match it more easily to my visions." The key, Margerit thought, was first to open the boy's ears to the divine music and then to allow it to flow through him, clearing away whatever blockage the fever had left.

When all was prepared and they gathered in the chapel for the celebration, only minor details strayed from the path they had mapped. The boy was restless—fidgeting and hiding in his mother's skirts—until Sister Marzina thought to add more movements to accompany the words he couldn't hear. And then it was necessary for Valeir to sing with the *fluctus* again to guide the progress of the petition and response.

But at last a look of wonder grew in the boy's face and he stilled, looking around first at the space over the altar where Margerit could see the wisps of color coalescing at the *concrescatio*, and then staring at Valeir as if she were indeed one of the angels in the stained glass windows, and at last at his mother as she cried his name over and over. The miracle was granted.

When they were back in Marzina's office, making the final notes and comments on the *expositulum*, Margerit asked Valeir, "Will you be studying with Sister Marzina all summer?" Her mind darted ahead to the possibilities for training a true *auditor*.

"Only for another two weeks," Valeir said. "I should have gone home already but Mama's been busy with my sister's confinement and didn't want me underfoot. I start my dancing season in the fall and there's so much to do."

"Then perhaps after you return to Rotenek we could speak about further studies," Margerit suggested. "It isn't as easy to find the teaching you'll need at the university as it would be here, but I can advise you."

She looked doubtful. "I don't think Papa…"

"Perneld, that was your family name, yes? I think I've met your mother a time or two. I could speak to her."

But Marzina interrupted, "Valeir, return to the students' hall. Your work is done here." When the girl had left, she turned to Margerit angrily. "Is this how it starts? Is this the path to corruption?"

"I don't know what you mean," Margerit replied stiffly, though in truth she suspected she did.

"First you encourage her to disregard her parents' wishes. Then you tempt her with worldly power from a talent that should belong to God, as your own should belong to God. And when she falls from grace—as she will—then you will be waiting, won't you?"

She made it sound so…so hateful. And she meant to. But was Marzina so wrong? *Yes, I want Valeir to defy her parents' expectations and seize the chance to use her talent for some greater purpose. And yes, if I must stand ready to catch her if she falls, I will.* But it was the other matter that she couldn't let pass. The ugly shadow that lay between them.

"Marzina, do you remember what you said that day we first met? You told me that when my mother came looking for a miracle to be granted a living child, you created the mystery using Mesnera Arpik's pregnancy as part of the structure. You said you knew that Barbara and I would share a destiny. How can you be so sure this wasn't the destiny we were meant for?"

For a moment Marzina hesitated, as if remembering that long-ago day, but then her face hardened again. "The Holy Virgin would not have granted your mother her miracle only to let sin and filth into the world."

Margerit's mouth trembled. But she had stood alone in Saint Mauriz's cathedral working a mystery out of thin air when her life depended on it. And she had dared to lecture Archbishop Fereir on his own ceremonies. She could defend herself to one mean-spirited nun. "No, the Holy Virgin would not have granted a miracle to bring sin into the world. And yet She answered my mother's plea. And in bringing me into the world, She brought me to Barbara. And there I have found the closest thing I have known to divine love. Perhaps you should think on that."

There was no purpose to staying after that. Marzina might send for her again if there were a puzzle in need of assistance, but she knew they would never return to anything resembling friendship.

* * *

On an afternoon when the summer storms were sweeping down the valley and all sensible people stayed indoors, Margerit came out of her studies to find Barbara dressed in riding clothes and with a brief apology on her lips. "I know we'd meant to go over the accounts to make sure they're ready for LeFevre's review, but I'm called away." She laughed lightly, but it sounded forced. "Another mysterious stranger passing through, sending me secret messages by name."

Margerit could hear the tension underneath. "Who is it now?" There was no glint of humor in Barbara's eye this time and she pleaded, "No secrets."

Barbara frowned and bit her lip. "There was no name on the note, but…" She took a folded paper from inside her waistcoat and handed it over.

Margerit skimmed through the opening lines. "Barbara, how are you meant to read this? 'To a true friend of the Atilliets' or 'to a friend of the true Atilliets'?"

"I don't think that was mere clumsiness. The writer chose that ambiguity carefully. Read the rest."

There was little enough to puzzle out: a meeting place, a suggestion of matters of importance to Alpennia, a caution for secrecy, and no signature but the letter K. That alone narrowed down the possibilities greatly: not an Alpennian name nor yet French or Italian. "Kreiser?" she asked.

Barbara hesitated, then nodded. "That would be my guess, but why to me? And what does he intend?"

Margerit suppressed her first impulse to beg her to stay home. "You'll only know if you meet with him. Be careful."

"You needn't tell me that. Don't wait dinner for me, I may be late."

Margerit wasn't concerned when Barbara hadn't returned by dinner, nor even when dusk fell and there was no commotion in the yard signaling her return. There was no need to worry. She had Tavit with her and these were her own lands and her own people. But night drew in and the possibilities spun through her imagination, chasing off sleep. Yet sleep must have come at last, for she woke again to a single candle lighting the darkness and the sound of Maitelen helping Barbara undress from clothes that had failed to keep out the driving rain. When they were alone together and the candle blown out, she chafed Barbara's limbs into warmth again as the story emerged.

"I've let myself be caught up in a dangerous game," Barbara began. "You know those little errands I've been doing for Princess Elisebet?"

Margerit nodded, then realizing the darkness hid her response, said, "Yes, that matter with Aukustin's tutor, I recall. Were there more?"

"More than I cared for," Barbara said. "This and that. It seemed harmless at the time. But now…" She paused with a deep sigh. "It seems that Kreiser's master has given up hope of arranging an alliance through Efriturik and has set his sights on Aukustin instead."

"What do you mean? Chustin isn't old enough to be making alliances."

"But he's old enough to be betrothed. Kreiser never said it in as many words, but he asked me to carry a letter to Elisebet, and I think it concerns a possible marriage to one of the emperor's daughters."

Margerit thought it over. "That doesn't make any sense. There's no certainty at all he would inherit. It seems an odd investment for such a powerful family."

"Not an investment, perhaps. They may view it more as ensuring Aukustin's future." Barbara shifted in the bed and Margerit imagined she could see her lean, expressive hands gesturing in the dark. "Efriturik's connections to Austria are seen as a liability, but for Aukustin a connection could be an asset. Powerful friends. A counter to the return of French power."

"But why would he think that you would help?" Margerit asked.

A long pause. "Elisebet has always mistaken my neutrality for support. She must have said something to him that led him to believe…"

"Then what will you do?"

"I'll burn the letter."

Margerit felt a shiver run through her. Barbara's arms closed tightly in response. "Will that be enough?"

"He'll receive no answer. Elisebet will receive no offer. Perhaps they'll let it be." But it didn't sound as if Barbara truly believed it.

"You need to tell her. Tell Annek. Take the letter to her, whatever it is."

A sigh. "I know. But what if Elisebet is innocent in this? I don't want to make more trouble between them. What if I—"

"Is it your choice to make?"

Another sigh. "I don't want to leave you for so long. I could be a month on the road—I don't even know where Annek is at the moment."

Margerit's heart sank. Despite her urging, she wanted there to be some other way. But she heard capitulation in Barbara's protests. "We can talk more in the morning," she said. "It's late. Sleep now."

But when she rose in the morning, she found Barbara already giving orders for the journey and setting the household in order for her absence. "Margerit, I've told Cheruk to come to you for any decisions he'd need me for. And if LeFevre comes before I return, you know more about the accounts than I do. In any case, if Kreiser tries to contact me here, you know nothing, only that I've left on an errand." She turned to call over her shoulder, "Tavit, go see if the horses are ready. And remind the groom to send someone later to fetch them back from the staging inn."

"You aren't taking the traveling coach?"

"And announce myself at every change of horses? No, I daren't even wear my usual riding clothes. I might as well send a trumpeter ahead of me crying, 'Here comes the eccentric Baroness Saveze!' I've asked Maitelen to find me a better disguise. Let's go see what she's turned up."

When Margerit descended the stairs again a short time later, it was in the company of a dapper young man in tall hat and riding breeches. She struggled not to laugh at the dismay on Tavit's face when he met them at the door.

"So, do you think I'll pass well enough for a man?" Barbara asked. "You'll need to do most of the talking, I'm afraid, but we'll go less noticed."

"Mesnera, I don't…" Words failed him.

"Oh, it'll serve well enough among strangers," Barbara assured him. "It has before. People see what they expect to see."

"Yes, Mesnera." He recovered himself quickly and amended, "Yes, Mesner," as he took the small traveling bag that Maitelen handed over and went to secure it to the saddle.

"I fear I've scandalized my armin," Barbara said grinning, and leaned down for a long farewell kiss.

Margerit held her tightly until their parting could no longer be delayed. "Be safe. Come home to me as soon as you may."

And then she was alone.

CHAPTER TWENTY-THREE

Jeanne

Jeanne stepped back and leaned against the workbench as Anna closed the furnace door and locked it in place with a clang. The fire added to the fierce summer heat and she felt sweat running down her face but didn't dare to pull a handkerchief out until she'd washed.

Antuniet looked over at her. "Tired?"

"Oh, no," Jeanne said. "Just enjoying the moment. I think this is the time I like best: when everything is in place and we've done all we can and there's nothing left to do but wait."

Anna laughed. "Nothing for you to do!" True enough. She'd be tending the furnace all through the heat of the afternoon, making sure the fire stayed intense and steady for the most important stage. Anna continued, "I prefer the preparations: mixing and measuring and setting everything out and ready."

"What about you, Antuniet? What's your favorite part?" Jeanne watched her closely, wondering what she would choose to reveal.

Antuniet pursed her lips in thought. "It would have to be when we tip the matrix out of the crucible and crack it open to see what we've made. Nothing else counts beyond that."

Jeanne stood idle for several more minutes as Anna started tidying up the room, then she stripped off her gloves and apron and called out into the front room for Marien to bring water to wash. The summer had been one long moment like this: a space to breathe and wait for possibility to ripen into hope.

All along the road back from Chalanz, she had rehearsed over in her mind what she would say. How she would explain. What she should apologize for first. But in the end, standing on Antuniet's threshold the day after her return, she had said only, "What do we work on today?" and walked in before there could be any protest. That first week had been tense, with all that was left unsaid echoing between them. She had long practice in wearing masks and Antuniet had refused to be the first to speak of it, and so they both pretended that nothing had changed as old habits returned. But though they still tiptoed around what lay unspoken, everything had changed.

"Do we need to prepare anything for tomorrow?" she asked Antuniet as she, too, washed the dust and grit from her arms and face.

"Tomorrow is nothing but picking the stones out of the matrix and cleaning them. I know how tedious you find that."

It was true, Jeanne thought. The endless tink-tinking of the tiny chisels drove her to distraction and the whole was entirely too much like workman's labor. "I could read to you while you work." That, too, had become a habit: mostly going over extracts from DeBoodt that Antuniet had translated, but sometimes she brought the Parisian gazettes and once—to Anna's poorly concealed delight—the latest novel. Antuniet had scoffed at that but let her choose what she would.

The work was more meticulous now, more subtle. They hadn't the range of roles to test many new recipes, but there were small improvements to be made, changes to develop the purity and brilliance of the stones. Antuniet had taken one brief, passing suggestion DeBoodt made for cibation: growing the stones as a pearl grows, layer on layer, refiring each cleaned and polished drop with fresh materials. The technique showed promise, but failures flaked and shattered like ill-tempered glass. Antuniet thought the temperatures were the key: too low and the layers failed to wed, too high and threads of slag were trapped beneath, destroying the purity of the stones.

The next morning the pale straw-gold of the gems emerged slowly from the embracing waste. Antuniet took the first to come free and tapped it gently then more sharply with a small jeweler's hammer. As one, they all let out a breath of relief when it stood firm and whole. "A good lot," Antuniet proclaimed, slipping the stone into the waiting pouch and taking up her chisels again.

The second crucible was nearly finished by the time it grew too hot to work. Jeanne paused in her reading to dab a handkerchief across her forehead before the sweat could run into her eyes. There was a reason why society fled Rotenek in the summer. Baking heat settled into the bones of the city. It was impossible to look one's best or even to appear vaguely presentable. She tucked the handkerchief away and would have continued, but Antuniet sat back and declared, "That's enough for now. It's well past luncheon. I don't think I could manage to eat a bite, but perhaps we could find something cool to drink and take it up to the riverbank and try to chase a breeze."

Jeanne had been thinking the same herself, but she'd let go of directing other people's lives for now. That was part of the summer's calm. She closed the green-bound book and handed it to Anna to be locked away. "Antuniet, do you have a blanket we could take to spread on the river wall? Marien will be scandalized if I sit on the bare stones in my good clothes." Today she'd left behind the plain gown she wore for the dirtier work. Standards were important, even in midsummer.

There was a zigzag path down from the street that paced the riverbank to the tie-ups at the water's edge, where rivermen waited for passengers. They found a spot on the low parapet halfway down where there was some shade and a hint of a breeze coming off the water. When Marien began ostentatiously shaking the blanket out over the rough-cut stones, a group of workmen moved over to make room for them with a touch to their caps. They made a rustic picnic of it there in the middle of the city, sharing a loaf from the bakery and passing back and forth a bottle of cider, bought from a tavern on the way, as if they were factory women.

Rotenek was not entirely devoid of Society, of course. They watched as a pleasure barge slowly worked its way past against the current, under the power of four sweating oarsmen. Jeanne raised a hand to the figures lounging against the cushions at the front. They called and gestured to her to join them but she waved them off and turned back to Antuniet as a snatch of song drifted out over the water. "I think this is the first holiday you've taken all summer. If this swelter holds, perhaps we could take a boat down past the docks and out to Urmai. There's a lovely public garden there and we could come back by the evening mail coach."

"You can't keep from planning something," Antuniet said, but her tone was teasing rather than impatient.

Had she come even that close to joking? *Step by step, day by day,* Jeanne thought. And then she smiled as an image came to her. *Layer by layer: neither too hot nor too cold.*

"Was I so amusing?" Antuniet asked.

"Not you. I was thinking…of how pleasant it is just to be here." *With you.* But it was too soon to say that. Layer by layer.

The heat settled in for two more days. Another ceration was out of the question. By the second afternoon they'd exhausted the preparations that could be done without fire and left Anna studying in the workshop to spend the entire afternoon walking slowly along the river from the Pont Ruip up to the old city walls and back. "Does it worry you," Jeanne asked, "to leave Anna alone like that?"

"She isn't alone; Mefro Feldin is there and Petro is usually in and out. And Anna knows not to unlock the door to strangers. There's nothing to worry about like there was last winter."

"You dismissed the men Margerit hired to keep watch."

A shrug. "There was no point in keeping them, really. Not once Kreiser was gone. Margerit was the one who wanted them here. And I…well, there was no point in keeping them tied down over the summer."

And yet their presence must have provided some reassurance. "What are your plans?" Jeanne asked, to change the subject. "To refine the techniques, yes, and then to perfect more of the formulas. But when will it be ready? What do you want to present?"

Antuniet looked around as if for eavesdroppers. Did she fear spies on her work? Or was it only her usual caution? But no one was taking the same leisurely pace they were. There was little chance of being overheard unwittingly.

"I think…by early October. When I've had time to apply our improvements to some of the more complex formulas after we have more help again. I want…" She fell silent for a while, as if she'd never put the matter into words before. "I want to give Her Grace something useful, something to make the land stronger. To bind loyalties, to increase wise decisions, to make our soldiers braver and our ministers more eloquent and persuasive. The properties are all there; it's just a matter of putting them to good use. It will be for her to choose how to use them, but I need to prove that I offer something real. Something of value."

"Something to pay your brother's debt?"

A sour and angry look fell across Antuniet's face. Jeanne wondered just what had lain between the siblings.

"No," Antuniet said at last. "That can't be paid. Something to remind the world that Estefen was not the only Chazillen. That one man should not blot out the honor of an entire line. Jeanne, there's nothing I can do of any worth in this world except this one thing. There's nothing else for me to live for."

"I don't believe that," Jeanne said softly. "And you shouldn't either." But there was no response and they walked on in silence.

The day had cooled to a more bearable temperature by the time Jeanne returned home. As Tomric relieved her of her bonnet and parasol, he said mysteriously, "You have a visitor."

Visitors, surely, she thought on entering the parlor, for the two men were dressed in similarly plain traveling clothes. Then with a glad cry and an embrace she recognized Barbara beneath the disguise. "Whatever are you doing here like this?" She stood back to encompass the outfit with a wave of her hand.

"An unexpected journey. I'd rather it not be known that I'm in town. If I went to Tiporsel House they'd make a fuss and there would be no concealing my presence. I'd rather slip in and out quietly. Besides which, I need some information that I hope you can provide."

"*Bien sûr!*" Jeanne said quickly. "And I hope you'll take some dinner. Will you need a place to sleep?"

Barbara shook her head. "We'll be on the road again before dark, but dinner would be lovely if you can scrape a meal together. Though I don't doubt Tavit might be glad of a chance to close his eyes for a bit while we talk business." She glanced over at the lean young man and he nodded in confirmation.

Tomric was set about making the arrangements, then Jeanne pulled Barbara down onto the settee and demanded, "Now what is this mysterious errand of yours? And in such outlandish clothes! What can I do for you?"

Barbara settled herself and leaned forward earnestly. "I'm serious about the secrecy. Promise me you won't tell anyone I've been in town."

"Well, there's no one to gossip with," Jeanne protested. "No one who's anyone is still here."

"Not even my cousin. And that goes for the servants as well." She laughed. "I had to let Tomric know who I was or he'd never have let me through the door!"

"Yes, of course, since you ask," Jeanne assured her. "As long as you tell me what this is all about." She saw no reason to deny the likelihood of speaking to Antuniet.

Barbara shook her head. "Maybe later—much later—when the matter's past. I'm still not certain what the end will be. Now, have you heard anything of where the court is spending its time at the moment? The two princesses in particular? I know Annek's always on the move during summer and I don't want to waste my time chasing a cold trail."

Jeanne thought back to the bits of gossip that were floating around. She might be nearly a hermit but she wasn't deaf. "Elisebet is off ensconced at Fallorek for the whole summer, as always. But the main court...they were at Suniz a week ago. Ah! Now I remember Charluz said she was off to take the waters at Akolbin because everyone would be there after the end of the month. And for her, 'everyone' would be the court. So you're racing about the countryside carrying secret messages?"

Again a shake of the head. "Don't tease me over it; my lips are sealed. I promise you'll hear the whole story when it's done. And I'm grateful for the hospitality. And the discretion." Barbara caught up her hand and kissed it chastely in thanks.

When the hasty early supper was set out in the breakfast room, Jeanne stayed behind, trying to pry out hints and clues. "When I first saw you I was going to ask if you were running away from a lovers' spat." She smiled to make it clear how unlikely she considered the possibility.

"Far from it," Barbara said. And then, in an uncharacteristically arch tone, "Though I might ask you the same thing."

The question startled her and her instinct was to dissemble. "I have no idea what you're talking about."

"No? I think you do. Is there anything I should know about you and my cousin?"

So. It scarcely took someone of Barbara's perceptiveness to ask, but the officious edge in her voice prompted a teasing evasion. "Not at the moment," she replied. "Though I have hopes of changing that."

Barbara's response was in the same bantering tone. "I almost think that I should ask whether your intentions are honorable." But there was a harder edge underneath.

Jeanne said evenly, "I'll repeat what you once said to me, *ma chère*: it's none of your affair. And don't think to play the *paterfamilias* and bully me. I don't recall that Antuniet has placed herself under your protection." She was gratified to see Barbara color slightly. "Never fear, I have only the best of intentions with regard to your cousin. You know well enough that I don't need to pursue the unwilling." The color deepened and she was able to move their talk on to less fragile matters.

And then, as quietly as she had appeared, Barbara was gone again before dusk could make an invitation to stay more appealing.

* * *

With the sweltering heat broken for a while, there were two more cycles of cibation before the topazes had achieved an acceptable size—those that had survived the ferment without cracking or losing their purity. "That will do for now," Antuniet concluded when the polished stones had been examined minutely under a glass. "We may simply need to accept that more than half won't survive the furnace."

Jeanne took one of the rejected gems and held it up to the window. A dark thread wound along one side like a worm in a crystal apple and the light flashed on cracks within the heart radiating from that flaw. "And what do you do with these?"

Antuniet took it from her and swept it into an empty crucible along with the other flawed stones. "It may be possible to redissolve the materials and use them again. I haven't experimented much with that yet. DeBoodt seems to think that some materials can be cycled through the twelve gates many times becoming purer and stronger each time. But some, he says, become fixed and can't be redeemed if the work goes awry." She set the crucible aside and gathered the perfect stones more carefully into a folded envelope marked with the date and process.

"And next?" Jeanne asked.

"Next I'd like to try the alternate method of multiplication that includes the marriage of the spirit of the new layer to the matter of the core," Antuniet mused, leafing through her notes, "but that requires pairing of each of the roles. I suppose we could use one of the simpler formulas, but it limits us badly. Better to find a fourth to assist us, especially if we could find a double for the *virgo* role."

Jeanne gave a short laugh. "Among my friends? Don't be absurd!" She regretted the jest immediately when she saw Antuniet turn pale. But to apologize would only make the matter worse.

"Maisetra?" Anna said tentatively. "Perhaps my sister…"

"Ah, yes," Antuniet said, happy to turn the conversation aside. "You have several, as I recall. Your younger sister?"

"I don't think she would have the patience to learn the lines. I thought perhaps Iudiz?"

"Would she be willing, do you think? Would your father approve? Or is one alchemist in the family enough?"

"I'll ask them," Anna said. And then she put a hand to her mouth to cover a laugh. "But we'd need to work quickly; she's getting married next month!"

Jeanne lingered a while after Anna left for the day, watching Antuniet sort through her notes and papers. The matter had been touched on and she could no longer contain the urge to know. "Antuniet? May I ask…" She hesitated, and Antuniet raised her head, sensing more than an idle question. "May I ask who…how…"

Understanding dawned. "How I lost my virtue?" Antuniet's voice was suddenly tired. She looked back down at her papers and for a moment Jeanne thought she wouldn't answer. Then she stiffened and looked up defiantly. "There was a man. In Heidelberg. A boy, really. It was a game to him: to try to seduce me. And then…I needed to leave the city quickly…in secret. He could get me out. It was the only coin I had to bargain with."

Jeanne gave a silent sigh of relief. She'd feared much worse. "And then—"

"And then it was over."

How deeply had it marked her? It was easy to forget how young she'd been when she fled Alpennia—how young and how sheltered. "Antuniet, did your mother talk—"

"My mother," Antuniet interrupted with a curl to her lip, "talked to me about the importance of making a good match. If she had any concern about what would happen in my marriage bed it was only that it produce children. But that doesn't mean I was completely ignorant."

"It can be pleasant, you know," Jeanne said softly. "Whether with a man or a woman."

"Oh, no doubt! Else why would so many pursue it so eagerly!" But then she looked abashed, as if recalling how pointed her words might seem.

"And now you see yourself as damaged goods."

"Aren't I? Isn't that why you considered me fair game?"

It was the same bitterness as that dreadful night, but worn thin and pale. And it was such a complicated question to answer. "No," Jeanne said simply. This was treacherous ground. "I knew my heart long before I knew your history. I knew it that night at New Year's when you came to me for help. When you woke screaming from your past terrors and I knew that I would give anything…*anything* to be able to stand between you and your shadows."

Antuniet was staring at her and the bitterness faded to something duller. "Then it *was* the ring. I'd wondered about that."

"The ring?" Jeanne asked, bewildered.

"The carnelian. I never meant you to wear it. I only wanted you to keep it safe for me. And then when I saw it on your hand and you—"

Ah, yes, that ring. But it hadn't been the ring that had brought her down here time and again all through last fall, though she hadn't yet put a name to what drew her. Jeanne reached out to touch Antuniet lightly on the wrist to stop the flood of words. "Antuniet, you are a ruby in the mud of this world. You are brave and brilliant and your passion blazes like the summer sun. Do you truly think that no one is capable of loving you unless compelled by sorcery?"

The silence was its own answer. Jeanne longed to wash away that silent misery with a flood of kisses, but it was too soon. A clumsy move would undo all her careful work. Patience was the key. And when patience was hard, she recalled that when they'd sat around the May Day fire, it had been Antuniet's billet that had sought her out, not the other way around. That was hope enough to wait on and they still had half the summer in front of them.

She had loved and lost before. This time would be different.

CHAPTER TWENTY-FOUR

Barbara

One benefit of the court's peripatetic habits was that two more strangers arriving at the posting inn late one evening were little remarked upon. The mineral springs had made Akolbin popular since ancient times, but few who came for the waters would stay at so unfashionable an establishment as the Cartwheel. Barbara was confident there was no chance she'd be recognized.

She and Tavit had been traveling long enough to have fallen into easy habits after one initial quarrel. Tavit had been scandalized to find her taking charge of the horses and haggling with the hostlers over hire fees and the quality of the nags foisted on them. Barbara had emphatically pointed out that her disguise placed her only half a step above the tale his own clothes told. "It would be odd enough to remark if I let you serve me in all things. And remark is what I don't want. You can deal with the innkeeper and order us a meal."

There had been far less argument about sharing a room, however awkward it made the arrangements. Even if separate rooms would not have caused even more remark, Tavit considered his duties to extend to adding his sleeping body as an extra bar across the door. Within the first few days, an elaborate dance to maintain privacy had become second nature. And so, on the morning after their arrival, Barbara had leisure to make herself presentable while Tavit went off to the manor that had the honor of hosting the princess and her entourage to deliver a brief message requesting an audience.

Two hours later, that message had procured discreet entrance under the shepherding of one of Annek's pages. Such a casual meeting would have been far harder to secure during the season in Rotenek, but Barbara relied on the more relaxed manners of summer and the knowledge that Annek's purpose in traveling was to make herself more approachable.

"And what mysterious errand brings you so far from home and in disguise?" Annek asked her, her expression wavering between amusement and concern.

Barbara laid both the sealed letter and the whole history before her, starting from Kreiser's unexpected visit and tracing back as early as Aukustin's peril during the hunt at Feniz to explain her part in it. Much of it Annek had already heard.

"It's one thing to help watch over Aukustin's safety," Barbara said in conclusion. "But this…this steps across the line to disloyalty. I want no part of it. So I came to you."

"Indeed," Annek said. After a long moment of contemplation, with her fingers tented before her mouth, she added, "Thank you."

Barbara expected to be dismissed, but she knew the waiting game of old and stood patiently, watching the edges of thoughts flit across Annek's face.

"And what do you think?" Annek said at last.

Barbara concealed the surprise she felt at being consulted. "I think that the dowager princess had no intent to make this connection. I have heard nothing in my dealings with her that suggested she was looking outside Alpennia for friends. The whole of her game has been to paint you and your son as foreigners. But if this alliance were offered to her? I don't know that she would have the wisdom to refuse."

"Wisdom? Do you think a foreign alliance would be an unwise choice for Alpennia?"

Barbara thought carefully. Was this a test or was she genuinely seeking advice? "Not a poor choice in general. At the New Year's court I overheard what you told Kreiser about your son's future. If Baron Razik is to be Alpennia's next prince he will need a local alliance, not a foreign one. Now Aukustin, if he were chosen instead? Then an outward tie could do much to strengthen our position as long as it were offered in good faith. But this? Aukustin doesn't stand high enough to attract an emperor's daughter on his own. This could only be a maneuver to ensure his success and thus to place him under obligations that would be difficult to resist."

Annek nodded. "That was my thought as well. But you observe the court so sharply that I was curious whether you had come to the same conclusion. I knew several of this man's goals—" She held up the sealed letter. "—but I will be glad to know the rest. Now tell me, Saveze," she asked in a different tone, "why bring me this news in disguise? One might almost think you, too, had some deeper game in mind."

"It occurred to me," Barbara said carefully, "that if it were your thought to see the charade through, it would be better if no one could tell Elisebet I had come here first."

"To see the charade through," Annek repeated. "You mean to set a trap for my cousin?"

"Not a trap, no. But perhaps a chance to clear herself of suspicion? From what I know of her and from what Kreiser told me, I don't think she expects this offer. Wouldn't it be well to know what her reaction would be?"

Annek picked up the packet of papers before her and turned it over in her hands. "It would help if we knew the details of his offer."

"I made no attempt to inspect them," Barbara said. "Maisetra Sovitre says there are mysteries that can reveal tampering. She examined them briefly before I left but could find no outward signs."

The packet was sealed and tied up with just the sort of archaic binding that might easily conceal the *apparatus* of a small mystery. Annek examined it carefully. "There are ways to reveal the contents that don't involve disturbing the seal." She set the letters aside. "Do you need to return to Saveze immediately?"

"I am at your command," Barbara reassured her, setting aside her impatience to be home. "I'm staying at the Cartwheel by the eastern edge of town."

"Then remain there. I'll have word for you in a few days."

Barbara fidgeted while Annek deliberated. It would be a hard decision for her. *A chance to clear herself*, she had said. But it was true that it was more in the way of a trap.

Two days later, when Annek sent for her again and charged her with the mission she thought would come, she asked one favor. "It galls me to let Elisebet think I would work against you. Would it disturb your plans if I counseled her against what I believe this message contains?"

There was a glint of amusement in Annek's hooded eyes. "Would you like to know what it contains?"

"Better I shouldn't know in my guise as courier. But it's easy enough to guess, and that guess is something she should be warned against. I—" Was it too presumptuous to say? "I would like to see you reconciled with your cousin. If there's anything I can do to help bring that about…"

Annek's eyes narrowed and Barbara thought she had indeed stepped too far across the line. "Saveze, if anyone could reconcile my cousin to me, my gratitude would have few limits. But I doubt that you are capable of that task."

"Then, if you prefer, let me do this for the sake of my own good name."

"Yes," Annek said slowly. "Yes, I think that would be exactly the flavor this needs. And then return and tell me what she says. I will be curious to know if she takes the advice of one she seems to trust above her closer confidants."

Elisebet might be harder to approach for a private audience, ensconced as she was at the Atilliet summer manor of Fallorek, but in recompense there was less need of secrecy. It took only a change of coat and unpinning her tawny hair to hang free to turn disguise into ordinary eccentricity.

Elisebet received her in the morning parlor, where they worked through the rituals of hospitality.

"I hope I find you in good health," Barbara offered, "and that Aukustin is the same." Her son was always a safe topic between them.

"His health has been indifferent of late. A touch of melancholy."

Barbara discounted that. Elisebet took Chustin's every frown and sniffle as a sign of impending disaster. "I believe that boys his age are often moody. There must be a great deal to entertain him here after the confines of the palace in Rotenek." *Where he's scarcely allowed to step out of doors without being surrounded by tutors and attendants.*

The pleasantries took some time to accomplish but at last Barbara ventured, "Several weeks ago in Saveze I was approached with a message." She reached inside her coat just enough to allow a glimpse of the sealed packet.

At once Elisebet was all attention. Barbara scanned her face for any sign of foreknowledge or anticipation but there was only sharp curiosity. With deliberate casualness, she continued, "I understand the rose garden here at Fallorek is a wonder to behold."

Elisebet blinked a moment at the change in topic, then answered, "Indeed. Perhaps you would care to walk with me before the noon sun drives off the perfume."

As they entered the low-hedged pathways, she waved her ladies back out of hearing before asking, "What is this, Saveze? I knew you must have some special purpose in coming."

Barbara pulled out the packet but kept it in hand until she'd said her piece. "That Austrian, Mesner Kreiser, came to me in secret and asked me to bring you this." It was easy enough to color her words with anger. "I cannot like this. I don't know what you may have told Kreiser about me, but he is badly mistaken if he thinks I will work against Her Grace. And you are badly mistaken if you think what he sends is an offer of friendship. Whatever this may contain—" She held up the sealed packet. "—its intent is to serve his master and not you or Aukustin."

Elisebet held out her hand imperiously. "And what would you know of matters of state?"

"Mesnera, I know that you have no business meddling in those matters of state on your own behalf," Barbara said, even as she handed the letter over. She moderated her tone from anger to urgency. "I spent years standing at my father's back when he was the second greatest power in Rotenek after Prince Aukust, God rest his soul. I think I know something of how the game is played. It's one matter for me to help watch over Aukustin—that falls under my service to your house—but this smells of intrigues I want no part of. If that message is what I suspect, I beg you to leave me out of it."

She flinched as Elisebet clutched at her arm in a mercurial change of mood from arrogance to desperation. "How can you abandon us now? You don't know what I face—what peril my son is in. Even here Aukustin isn't safe from that…that foreigner's malice."

This was more than her usual distrust. Barbara asked, "What happened?"

Elisebet looked around in the frightened, furtive way that came over her more and more. "Friedrich. He came here."

"Is that such a matter for concern?" Barbara asked when no immediate details followed. "He has as much right to spend his time at Fallorek as you."

"He came with a gift for Aukustin. A spirited horse, trained by his own hand, he said. What boy could resist? And then, after he'd left, we learned the truth. Trained by his own hand indeed! The beast was vicious, unmanageable. I was forced to have it destroyed. Even here we are not safe."

Barbara listened with barely concealed horror. *No wonder Chustin has fallen under a black mood! To be given such a gift and have it snatched away so brutally...* She dismissed instantly the thought that the accusation was true. But something had set the horse off. Her mind skipped back to the hunt at Feniz. *Someone's been playing tricks with horses before, someone close to him who wouldn't be questioned.* Who could it be? Might the same man have been behind both accidents? A servant who'd been corrupted? Or...

"Yes," Elisebet hissed, mistaking the thoughts behind her silence and frown. "You see what I have to fear? Can you blame me for seeking friends where I can find them?"

"Friends, yes. But Kreiser is no friend to you." She returned to her pleading tone. "Barely half a year ago he was courting Efriturik and making overtures to Annek on his master's behalf. If he is making the same offers now to you, never forget that you were second choice. If Her Grace smiled his way, you'd be left behind in a heartbeat. Think on that before you return him any answer that could be a weapon against you."

That hit home. But Elisebet slid her thumb under the edge of the packet and cracked the seal, then unfolded the letter and scanned it quickly. Barbara tried to read the contents in her expression. Whatever it held was neither startling enough nor pleasing enough to cause Elisebet to betray her thoughts. She folded it again and looked up. "I thank you for your service. You may go."

Barbara hesitated only a moment before bowing in acknowledgment and turning away.

What did I expect? That she would share her plans with me after all I'd said? There was relief, in truth, that there would be no tale to carry back to Annek. She had kept faith with all sides and that could be the end of it. And perhaps now there would be no further imperious demands or desperate pleas.

* * *

Annek listened to her scant report with interest but little concern, as if she'd already put the matter behind her. "And she said nothing else?"

"Only the matter of Efriturik's gift," Barbara said, thinking it would be old news, but Annek lifted one black eyebrow in question, and that story, too, came out. "It isn't only Princess Elisebet's fancies," Barbara added. "Someone is playing dangerous tricks around Aukustin and leaving a trail that leads to your son." It would be insulting to add her own certainty that Efriturik himself was innocent.

"I said once before that I valued your sharp eyes," Annek said. "Use them for me. Discover who's behind this mischief if you can. Oh, not this moment," she added with a dismissive wave of her hand. "I won't keep you from home any longer. If Efriturik must be present to be blamed, then there should be no danger for the rest of the summer. But when we all return to Rotenek, the chance may come again. Look for someone who would gain if both Elisebet's son and mine came to harm." She rose in dismissal, adding, "I feel some mark of gratitude is called for, seeing that you've ridden from one end of Alpennia to the other in my service. Is there anything you'd care to ask for?"

Barbara evaluated the nature of the offer and grinned as she found an answer that suited its size. "Could your thanks extend as far as a courier's commission? The posting inns are strangely hesitant to hire their best horses out to an ordinary traveler. I'd rather keep to my disguise for the journey back, and your name could save me from the worst of the boneshakers!"

If anything, a royal commission made them more invisible on the return journey than they had been when masquerading as common men. No one looked beyond that seal and Annek's looping signature and, as hoped, the mounts they were offered were as fine as those in the princess's own stables.

They took a more southerly route, crossing the Rotein by ferry at Falinz, then heading east along the road skirting the hills. On the second day after, Barbara found herself staring at a worn milestone where the road branched, trying to think why the eroded name of *Villa Rabani* should be familiar. Rapenfil. One of the baron's letters, scant years after he came into the title, when his star was rising and Arpik's was beginning to fall. She brought those pages to mind. Every word was still burned in her memory.

I saw you at Pergint's ball last night and could no longer keep my silence. You have been too long absent from society and there have been rumors I feared to believe. Do not assure me that you are happy; your eyes betray you. But can you tell me you are content?

His words had been tender then, without the frantic passion of the earlier letters, but soon turned hard again. *I read what you do not write. You tell me "be careful" and I hear "I am afraid." Never forget that I will stand your friend to the ends of the earth. Your concern for your family's good name is misplaced. Arpik can do little harm worse than they've already suffered by tying their hopes to his promises. Even those promises mean nothing if you give him no sons. But on that I'll say no more. I know well enough where that fault lies. Be careful. And, as always, burn these letters.*

But she hadn't. Had their correspondence truly remained secret all those years? Or had Arpik never cared for anything beyond her dowry? In the end, even her dowry had had its limits. *Is it true? The city is abuzz with word that your father's house was seized in payment of your husband's debts. I hadn't thought Arpik was gone so deep or that your father would be so foolish as to pledge his own property as collateral. Arpik will never recover now; the illusion is broken and his creditors will smell blood. They say your family has left Rotenek for Rapenfil. You would do well to follow them.*

But that wasn't the only place she had seen the village's name. It had been on the card her mother's sister had left for her, on the line below *Henirez Chamering*.

"Mesnera?" Tavit's voice broke into her reverie. "Do we change our route?"

"Yes," Barbara said in sudden decision. "I have a visit to make. An aunt. Cousins, perhaps." She smiled at him ruefully. "I only hope we find them at home."

Once again she changed her appearance from male disguise to more feminine eccentricity. Maisetra Chamering had seen her riding clothes before. This way there would be no need for awkward explanations and they were far enough from the court that secrecy was no longer urgent.

Finding the farm proved easier than she feared. The name of Chamering was well known in these parts. "Just continue on down the road through the village," a carter offered when she asked the direction. "On past the mill and then left after that up toward the old abbey."

It was the sort of direction that would be easy for a stranger to lose, but they followed the road he'd indicated. It was haying season and the fields they passed were strewn with cut rows drying in the sun. In the far distance precariously laden wagons dwarfed those filling them. The scent was sweet on the warm summer breeze, though a hint of coming rain explained the urgency Barbara could see in the fields.

When the farmstead came at last in view it reminded her of that of Margerit's cousins in Mintun. Not a neat and tidy house, but well-kept despite its chaos, with bright whitewashed walls and sturdy fences. In the yard, a boy was mending harness at the back of a wagon. He jumped to his feet at their approach and shouted, "Mama! Visitors!" to be answered by a babble of women's voices from the kitchen beyond.

The boy darted forward to catch their horses' bridles, staring in awe. At the horses, that is. Barbara noted with amusement that he paid almost no attention to their riders. The steeds that Annek's name could command stood out against the cart horses tied at the gate like peacocks among geese. "Is Maisetra Chamering at home?" she asked, gaining his attention at last.

"She's coming," the boy answered confidently. And then, as if to make good on his word, he once again shouted, "Mama!"

So he was a cousin, Barbara thought, just as Maisetra Chamering came bustling out the door, blinking in the light.

In Rotenek she had stood clearly out of place, but here it was different. Here she was mistress. She wiped her hands on her apron as she approached, eyeing the visitors critically but with an air of harried welcome. Barbara swept off her hat to let her long braid tumble free for easier recognition. "Forgive me, Maisetra," she said, "for the unannounced visit. I was passing near and hoped you might be able to spare me an hour or two. I owe you a morning call, after all." She made no mention of the harsh words she'd spoken the last time they met. There was an apology owed for that.

The woman's eyes widened but she made no other sign of surprise. "Mesnera Lumbeirt," she said with a little curtsey. "Your visit does us honor. I'm afraid you've caught me on a busy day. We've dinner to make and take out to the fields before I can see you properly entertained."

"Please," Barbara ventured, feeling suddenly awkward. "Would you do me the favor of calling me Barbara? If I may call you aunt?" It was a start on the apology. "I've never had anyone to call aunt before." The woman nodded and they both relaxed. "And I can scarcely expect you to drop everything and sit in the parlor with me, but perhaps I could find a corner of your kitchen out of the way and we can talk while you work."

She turned to Tavit to see if he wanted instruction. He gave an amused nod in the boy's direction and she caught his meaning. "And perhaps my cousin could help my armin with our horses? They've had a long road and longer yet to go."

"See you finish that harness before we need it!" her aunt called back by way of permission, as they went through the short passage into the bustling kitchen. "He'll be talking of nothing else for the next week. It isn't often he gets a chance to handle as fine a piece of horseflesh as those."

"I thought he had that look," Barbara said with a grin. "I was the same way at that age."

The other women in the kitchen looked up to stare as they entered and had to be scolded back to work. There were still glances and giggles—more, Barbara realized, aimed at her clothing than her person—until Maisetra Chamering said sharply, "Don't gawk like a goose. This is my niece, Baroness Saveze, come for a visit. Do you want her to think we've no manners?" The hands quickly returned to chopping and mixing but the eyes still followed her.

In the end, the kitchen corner went unused and Barbara stripped off her coat and rolled up her sleeves to join in, for it seemed the likeliest way to talk easily across the hubbub. "I've read the letters," she said with no preamble.

"Her letters?"

"His," Barbara said, "to her."

"Ah, I wondered. And so?"

"I'm sorry for…for the things I said the last time we met." Barbara groped for an explanation. "The story I'd heard was…different."

"Not so very different, I imagine."

"Not in essentials," Barbara agreed. "But…" She paused. "Perhaps you can tell me what you know."

Maisetra Chamering shook her head. "We weren't close, your mother and I. How could we be? She was ten years the elder and—" She hesitated before plunging on. "So much of it happened when I was too young to be told anything."

Barbara could tell there was more behind that. *We weren't close.* "She was ten years the elder and beautiful," she suggested.

Her aunt winced, but the remark seemed to free her from her reticence. "Lissa was the golden one. The beautiful one. She was the one sent to school at Saint Orisul's while I made do with a governess at home. And talented: she could sing and dance and make pretty speeches. Well, maybe I would have too if I'd been given the chance, but she was so far ahead. Our parents had decided she would make a brilliant match and I would be lifted on her tide. Maybe it wasn't fair that they staked everything on her dowry, but, you see, once she had married her nobleman, then he would see me well-launched in my turn. That was how it was supposed to work."

"Only she fell in love with Marziel Lumbeirt."

"Perhaps she did, I don't know." She turned away to check something in the ovens and run a critical eye over the progress of the work before returning. "He was only one of the names I heard. I remember there were arguments and shouting behind closed doors. But I was only a child; no one told me anything. I know there was a great scandal. And then in the end she married Arpik after all. And you know the rest. I didn't know about...about Lumbeirt and you. Not until that story drifted out this way a year ago."

That can't be all! You're the only one who can tell me... "So she married Arpik after all," she prompted. "And then...?"

Maisetra Chamering shrugged as she piled warm loaves into a basket and covered them with a cloth. "And then he swept her off to his estate after that first season and we didn't see her for years. But you have to remember, the wars had started and everything was in an uproar. At first we thought he kept her away from Rotenek out of caution. We expected at any time to hear she would be presenting him with an heir. It was only later we knew he simply wanted her out of the way. It wouldn't have suited him to have a wife close at hand questioning his comings and goings. And then Arpik's house of cards came tumbling down and took us with it. I should have been brought out that year," she added, without any discernable bitterness. "We moved back here. What else could we do? I never did have my season. I was the nearest thing to on the shelf when Chamering offered for me." She turned and said fiercely, as if to convince herself, "He's a good man. And he's never been anything but kind to me, despite never getting a penny from it. And when my parents died he saw them properly buried with a stone and everything when they would have had a pauper's grave else. And we have five fine sons."

Barbara could think of nothing to do but nod. Whatever Maisetra Chamering claimed, it must have stung. Her elder sister married to a Count and she with a man who barely rose to the level of a gentleman farmer.

"But I never had a daughter," she added wistfully. "Do you know? At the end, when I heard of Lissa's trouble and Chamering let me travel to Rotenek to see her, I asked if she would let me take you to raise as my own. All she gave me was that casket of letters. And then later, when we heard she had died of a fever in...in that place, there was no mention of you. I thought you must have died as well. I always regretted that I hadn't begged harder for you."

Barbara looked around at the fields and wagons and cast her mind back across the years. What would that world have been like? So quiet and ordinary. And despite all she had suffered through, in that world her feet would never have been set on the path that led to Margerit or to the barony. She reached out and touched her aunt's hand. "What's past is past. Regret nothing," she urged. "I wouldn't choose to have had any life but the one I've known."

The dinner was packed and loaded at last and her young cousin had completed the harness repairs despite distractions. In the time she'd spent inside talking, the horses had not merely been fed and watered but groomed as if for parade. He was hanging on Tavit's every word as they discussed the finer points of the beasts. Seeing no signs that her armin wanted rescue, she told the boy, "I'd like to ride in the wagon with your mother. Perhaps you'd be willing to bring my horse along?"

At an admonition from his mother—"Say thank you to the baroness, Brandel"—he was up in the saddle and it was clear that his skill was as deep as his interest.

"Brandel?" Barbara asked curiously as she settled next to her aunt on the wagon seat.

"We christened him Eskambrend," she replied somewhat ruefully, "but he's never quite grown into it."

"After the ancient hero? No wonder he looks ready to charge off after dragons!"

"No, after his grandfather." Maisetra Chamering sighed. "He'll need to settle down soon. There was time to indulge in fancies when he was younger, but he needs to find a trade now. I fear your visit will have him dreaming and restless for months on end. It isn't every day you meet your cousin the baroness."

"He's your youngest?"

She nodded. "The rest are out with their father taking in the hay. Perhaps I've kept him too close. He was a delicate child. He was sickly as a babe and we nearly lost him to a fever when he was five."

"He hardly looks delicate to me," Barbara countered, watching him play touch-and-go with Tavit.

"I suppose I'm too used to comparing him to his brothers!" She laughed. "But there were years when even going out to feed the chickens left him exhausted. I convinced his father to let him be schooled, more than just reading and ciphering. We thought he might go for the church. It's never a bad thing to have a priest in the family. Or at least a clerk. But you're right: all he ever wants to read are romances of ancient knights and bold musketeers and the adventures of noble duelists! I hope your man isn't encouraging him in that nonsense. We'll never hear the end of it and it will make Petro cross." And then she gave a little start. "Oh my! Petro. Whatever will he say? I should have sent word ahead."

"Did he know you came to visit me?" Barbara asked.

"Oh yes. He didn't approve but he didn't forbid it. He thought I was putting myself too forward. I didn't tell him…"

Barbara finished the thought silently. *Didn't tell him I'd sent you packing.* "I'm sorry for that," she said.

When they reached the mowers, no one gave her much mind while unpacking and laying out the food, but when all the workers had fallen to, she felt Maistir Chamering's eyes on her and touched her aunt's arm to draw her attention. He was a ruddy, weather-beaten man, his balding head gleaming in the summer heat. Only the quality of his waistcoat differentiated him from the men working under him.

Almost shyly, Maisetra Chamering went to bring him over, saying, "Petro, I would like you to meet my niece Barbara, Baroness Saveze."

"I was passing by," Barbara added, "and hoped you would forgive the visit with no notice."

His reply was little more than a grunt and then as if thinking better, a curt nod and, "Mesnera, you're welcome. Will you be staying long?" It was clear that he had some trepidation at the thought of entertaining her.

"Not even to the evening, I'm afraid," she replied. "My journey can't wait. But perhaps another time, when it's more convenient."

His reply was noncommittal.

They would have set up a chair for her but Barbara insisted on settling onto the spread blankets alongside her host and shared the meal she'd helped to prepare. For all his surliness, she could see that her aunt's description had not been mere protest. There was genuine affection and partnership between them. He took the time to point out her other cousins, their names passing by too briefly to stick in memory.

Barbara watched Brandel as he paraded his newfound friend before his taller and more imposing brothers, to Tavit's silent amusement. She could tell that the topic must have turned to the armin's profession, for there was much gesturing and playacting of swords and the occasional glance at her. Whatever stories Tavit was telling must have been the embroidered versions of what he'd heard, for they'd had no adventures together that resembled anything of the sort. And then the boys cut willow wands for an impromptu mock-duel and she laughed. "Brandel really does live for the old stories, doesn't he?"

"Useless fairy tales," Maistir Chamering said dismissively. "Time he left it all behind. I'm sorry I ever let him go for that nonsense. But his mother…"

A glance was exchanged between them. It was clearly an old argument and one she had won.

"It's time he learned there's no place in the real world for daring adventures and dashing swordsmen. The sooner the better."

Barbara laughed again. "You couldn't tell that by my life!"

"But he lives in our world, not yours."

And he seemed as out of place here as she would have been. A thought struck her—the other half of the apology—and before she could think better, she turned to her aunt and said, "I can't pay you back for everything you lost for my mother's sake, but I could do something for Brandel, if you permit."

"What?" Maistir Chamering jeered. "Turn him into a swordsman like that nancy-boy there?"

She bristled at the slight to Tavit but let it pass. If he were a man who could see no strength beyond pitching hay and loading sacks of grain, all the more reason to press the offer. "Armin's a fading profession," she said in an offhand voice, "though you wouldn't know it from the court. But that's all it is now, really: a bit of playacting to amuse the nobility. But there are other professions in Rotenek he might be better suited for than what he can find here. And a courtier's training isn't the worst place to start for any of them.

He's what? Thirteen or fourteen? That's not too late to start. Think about it. If you choose, send him to me in Rotenek at the beginning of the season and I'll take him into my household and do what I can for him."

She could see worry in her aunt's face warring with recognition of the opportunity. Plant the seed. Let them consider it on their own. A letter could confirm her offer and then they would see what would come.

And what will Margerit say? I shouldn't have offered without asking. Yet at the moment it seemed the right thing to do. Time enough to make it right with Margerit when she was home again. And that day couldn't come too soon. She glanced up at the angle of the sun, judging how far they could go before dusk. She was relieved when her hosts took up their rakes and forks again and she could make her farewells.

CHAPTER TWENTY-FIVE

Antuniet

Antuniet sat at the open window in her bedroom and settled the tray securely in her lap. She ran her fingers lightly over the stones nestled in the bunched cloth that kept them from sliding and rattling. Some were angular and sharp-edged, others smooth as river pebbles; a few were rough like hardened hoarfrost. They caught the rays of early morning sun that struggled past the neighboring buildings and glowed like drops of colorful dew. This was a luxury—an indulgence really—that she'd started allowing herself on rising, born out of the need to remind herself that her progress was real and not an illusion of her dreams. The ordinary stones were locked away in a chest in the workroom but these she kept closer: the purest, most perfect gems, the ones that had survived through the multiplication and cibation—that had succeeded in wedding spirit and matter to fix their inherent properties and become true elixir.

The use of the twinned roles had been both more successful and more difficult than she'd expected. Iudiz Monterrez had fulfilled the requirements of her part and been willing enough, but she'd lacked some essential knack that Anna brought. Or perhaps it had only been a lack of practice and skill. There had been enough time to prove the method but not to develop it further.

She laid her hand across the tray, touching as many as she could reach. Their power was like the hidden heat of a new-laid egg or the buzzing of a gnat so tiny its presence was more felt than heard. She'd grown more skilled at detecting the power in the ordinary stones too: the ones where the fixation hadn't taken, or where flaws in the heart fractured the influence into mere echoes. In those the emanation felt as light and subtle as the feel of the sun on her skin or the faintest stirring of a breeze on the hairs of her arm. Most of those stones she would destroy if they couldn't be pulverized for reprocessing. A few would have their use as carefully budgeted coin, paid to Monterrez for his work on polishing and setting the better stones.

She longed for a few luxuries—ones Margerit's stipend should not be asked to cover. It would be pleasant to have a new gown suitable for a visit to the palace, or for any invitations that might come her way. But selling gems would risk the attention of those who held monopolies on that market. There were all manner of accusations that could be made against her work that could mask simple greed. Until she had a greater sign of favor than Margerit's patronage, better to remain invisible. She sighed. In the old days Mesnera Chazillen had practiced alchemy without fear of consequences. But that Mesnera Chazillen wouldn't have contemplated turning the Great Art to vulgar trade. It was dangerous to start wanting things again.

She closed the lid of the tray and put it back in the bottom of the chest that held her clothes. It was time to go down and unbar the door. Mefro Feldin grew more sour than usual if she were kept waiting. She had keys, of course, but ordinary locks were only for the daytime hours and against ordinary thieves. At night it took iron bars to keep the darkness out. Those and the amulet under her pillow were what chased the nightmares away and let the sweet dreams of success take their place.

When Jeanne arrived just before noon, they left Anna copying out notes for the afternoon's process and walked up to the riverbank. It had become something between habit and ritual even when the heat wasn't so oppressive that the excursion was necessary for comfort. Antuniet nodded to familiar faces along the river wall and acknowledged their greetings in turn as they found their favorite place just in the shade of the wall halfway down the path to the water's edge. There was an air of change in the life of the city, anticipating the month ahead when the cream of society would begin returning. But for now Rotenek still belonged to those who had no other home. And to those who had chosen to stay.

Antuniet had never asked Jeanne outright why she'd chosen to return. At the beginning of the summer she'd been certain of the reason and had been furious—too furious to speak of it. But here they'd been, week in, week out, sitting on the stone wall, watching the Rotein flow past. Laboring in the sweat and dust of the workshop. Laughing at the joys and frustrations of the work. Had Jeanne truly stayed, turning her hand to whatever labor was set before her, only in the hope of a few nights of passion? *It can be pleasant*, she'd said, but it was hard to believe that pleasure was worth all this effort. What did Jeanne want?

What did she herself want? She barely knew. That night in May she'd recognized the truth in the fire's portent: that her heart had seen something beyond the wit and gaiety. Had seen something and longed for it with an ache that went beyond this cautious friendship. But she couldn't have said then what it was she longed for, only that she knew it was beyond her reach. And yet here was Jeanne, within reach, and still she wasn't sure.

Jeanne had changed since the spring. Antuniet found herself missing… oh, the little things. She was honest enough to admit that she'd enjoyed the courtship before she knew it for what it was. That way Jeanne had of talking in touches: on the hand, the shoulder, once on her cheek. The teasing that had brought her back from the precipice of the winter's despair. The myriad of ways the pet name *Toneke* had fallen from her lips. *Don't call me that!* she'd cried. And never once since that night had it been uttered. And now she found she wanted…wanted something impossible.

Do you consider it impossible that someone might love you? That question had haunted her. One voice echoed, *Yes, impossible.* Another whispered, *But what do you mean by love?* Flirtatious glances and jealous rages? The awkward fumbling of bodies in the dark? *To have one person in this world whose first thought on waking is of you? Whose last memory at sleeping is your touch? Who rejoices at your happiness and mourns your sorrows?* But Jeanne had been speaking of Margerit and Barbara then, not something that mere mortals could aspire to. Her throat tightened. It was dangerous to start wanting things.

"You're pensive today," Jeanne broke in.

Antuniet felt herself blushing, as if Jeanne could see her doubts and questions. "I was thinking that we can almost see the end of summer now."

"Yes."

Jeanne's voice held an air of wistful regret. And yet what had the last months held that could be regretted?

"We should go back. There are still things to be done before the alignment this afternoon." Antuniet stood and shook out her skirts as Marien silently folded the blanket they'd been sitting on.

After Antuniet closed the door behind them and hung the keys on the hook beside it, she called into the workroom, "Anna, are you finished with your notes yet?" There was no response. She poked her head in and saw Anna's dark braid-crowned head laid across her papers, the pen still in her hand and one cheek smeared with ink. "Anna?" she called sharply.

The girl jumped guiltily, knocking the inkwell over across the finished pages. "Oh, Maisetra! I'm sorry! I didn't mean to sleep." She began mopping at the spreading stain with her apron, heedless of its ruin.

"Are you well?" Antuniet asked in some concern.

"It's nothing," Anna replied, belying the claim with an enormous yawn.

"Nothing but…?" Antuniet prompted.

"It's only that I was up all night baking. Iudiz's wedding…it's only two days away. There's still so much to do. But I promise I won't fall asleep again."

Antuniet felt a rush of guilt. Of course. She'd known the wedding was coming soon but she'd given no thought to the demands on her apprentice's time. She surveyed the mess and made a quick calculation. "You shouldn't still be here on such an occasion. Go, go. And I don't want to see you for at least a week. The work here can wait, and a sister only gets married once. Or in your case, three times! Mesnera de Cherdillac and I can find something to work on until you come back."

"Thank you," Anna said fervently as she continued to mop at the ink.

"No, leave the mess," Antuniet said. "I'll have Mefro Feldin clean it up. Go and wash, then we can ask Mesnera de Cherdillac's maid to escort you home."

Feldin balked at the request, after Anna had been packed off and things were set to rights. "I was promised I wouldn't have to clean up in that room. I won't have anything to do with…with unnatural arts."

"It's not from the alchemy," Antuniet said tartly. "It's only spilled ink. It could have happened just as easily in the front room, so take care of it, if you please."

As Feldin went off to find water and a scrub brush, Jeanne asked, "Why do you put up with that? She should show you more respect. If she were in my household I'd have shown her the door long ago."

Antuniet shrugged. "But you see, she isn't in my household; she's in Margerit's. And she knows it."

"Then Margerit should dismiss her."

"For that, Margerit would need to be told. No, Feldin suits my needs. I'd rather an honest surliness than false cheer."

Jeanne laughed, but it seemed a touch brittle. "In that case, what must you think of me!"

"Is your cheer false?" Antuniet asked.

"Not with you," she said hurriedly.

Antuniet knew it for at least a small untruth.

Jeanne waved a hand out at the city at large. "But for them I put on my mask and play my little act on the stage."

"And what applause do you get for your performances?"

"Why, I'm paid in champagne and invitations, don't you know?" Jeanne said more lightly. "And a very good living it is."

"And yet you've traded champagne and invitations for tea and hard work," Antuniet said, feeling that she was advancing past a line from which there was no retreat.

Jeanne smiled, but said only, "So is today's work all wasted with Anna gone?"

Antuniet bit her lip in thought and rummaged through her handlist of recipes. "We can't do the enhancement I was planning, but we could still use the preparations for the beryl process and substitute the influence of the moon for that of Venus…"

Jeanne looked over her shoulder and traced a finger down the column with the symbols marking the roles and properties. "Oh yes, you should definitely do this one," she said with an edge of teasing. "*To make the bearer tranquil and not at odds with those nearby*. And then you could give it as a present to your housekeeper!"

"A worthy goal, but I don't think that would work." Antuniet pulled out the zodiacal watch and checked its dials against the notes in the list. "The firing would have to start at moonrise and that won't be until almost midnight."

"But why not?" Jeanne said with infectious enthusiasm. "It will be an adventure! When Marien comes back I'll send her on home and we can take turns tending the furnace, as long as you show me what to do. It'll be like keeping vigil before a festival: we can entertain each other with stories all night."

Antuniet eyed her skeptically, but she seemed in earnest. "Why not, then?" She spread out the working notes and started noting the changes for the new ceremony.

* * *

When the first streaks of dawn lit the edges of the closed window shutters, the heat from the furnace had finally become pleasant rather than oppressive. Antuniet poked in among the coals to spread them out and let the chamber begin cooling, then looked over to where Jeanne slumped asleep over the worktable, just as Anna had been the afternoon before. A lock of raven hair had come loose to hang across her face and it stirred in time with her breathing. Antuniet fought the urge to go over and brush it aside, fearing to wake her.

They had failed to take turns tending the process after all, spending the long hours sharing stories in the safe intimacy of the dark, lit only by the furnace glow and one small lamp, until she had turned back from one last shovel of coal to find that Jeanne had succumbed at last to the lateness of the hour. As the process moved into the final stages of the congelation, Antuniet had remained standing, leaning against the bench, to fight off the same temptation to sleep. She'd watched silently over the mystical transformation of earthly matter to something finer and more elevated.

A growling in her stomach brought her mind back to those earthly matters. A faint clatter in the street outside told her that others were stirring as well. She gathered a few coins and slipped quietly out the front door and across the street to where a heady smell wafted out from the bakery.

"You're up early," the baker said as she counted out the money.

"Up late," she answered briefly.

He set a loaf before her, radiating heat fresh from the oven in a pale echo of her working crucibles. "Man cannot live by bread alone," he intoned, "but it's certain he can't live without it!"

She'd heard the witticism dozens of times before, on each occasion proclaimed as if he'd only just invented it. This time there was another voice laid underneath—a voice that came back to her from that dark night in May down at the bottom of the gardens. The warm, sweet aroma filled her lungs and entered into deep, empty places within her. It was as if the world had turned sideways and everything was strange and new.

She hugged the loaf as she crossed back to slip quietly into the workroom. Scarcely knowing what she intended, she broke open the crust and held it close by Jeanne's face until she stirred and woke, stretching and rubbing her eyes in confusion.

Jeanne looked up at her where she stood frozen, still holding out the piece of broken bread. Jeanne's eyes widened as if she sensed the portent of the moment. "What…?"

Antuniet fumbled for the right words. "You said to me once, *if a man is hungry and can't get bread*—" She stopped. Should it be this difficult? "I didn't know. I didn't understand what it was that—having had it and lost it—" She heard her voice start to break and stumbled on. "All my life I've been starving and I never knew it. But I…I see no reason why either of us needs to go hungry."

Understanding dawned. "Toneke, are you sure?"

For the first time, Antuniet heard no echo of mockery in the endearment. Perhaps it had never been there at all. She only knew that she never wanted to hear that name on anyone else's lips. "I'm sure," she answered, though she was very far from certain.

Jeanne took the bit of bread still held out between them and broke off a small piece as she rose. Antuniet felt the warm touch of Jeanne's fingers on her lips as the morsel was slipped into her mouth. No bread had ever tasted like this, not even in those desperate days when it had been most scarce. She broke off a piece in turn and passed it to Jeanne, then waited awkwardly, hesitantly as she chewed and swallowed. Jeanne giggled suddenly and Antuniet felt herself flush.

"I'm sorry…I don't…"

Jeanne hushed her with a finger across Antuniet's lips. "Don't worry. This isn't like alchemy. There's no wrong ritual."

The fingers traced slowly across her cheek and then around the curve of her ear. She shivered at the touch. She couldn't have said whether it was from nervousness or pleasure. Now Jeanne's lips found hers and traced the path her fingers had taken. It was…strange. Like nothing she had felt before. Uncertainly, she raised a hand to touch Jeanne's cheek and tried to imitate her movements.

They stood together for longer than she could track, their hands not in embrace but in exploration. Gradually Antuniet felt herself relax as strangeness became more familiar and more intriguing. Her body began to shape itself against Jeanne's more closely. A yawn betrayed her.

Jeanne pulled away and traced a finger down her cheek one more time. "Toneke," she said, "we're both exhausted. That's never good the first time. Marien will be showing up with a fiacre sometime soon to fetch me, and your housekeeper will come knocking at any moment. Take the day to rest and think. Things may look different in the evening."

Antuniet shook her head. "I'm not so changeable as that." But she was suddenly grateful for the respite. Another yawn overtook her. It felt decidedly unattractive. "When will you come back?"

"Come to my house for dinner," Jeanne urged. "I'll send a carriage." With a twinkle in her eye, she added, "My bed is somewhat larger and more comfortable than yours, if you're still inclined."

"I'm not as changeable as that," Antuniet repeated.

* * *

It can be pleasant, Jeanne had said. Looking back now, that seemed an odd choice of words: so pale and thin. *It can be pleasant*. Antuniet searched for a more suitable word, but the one that came most to mind was *strange*. Strange to be lying here in someone else's bed. Strange to feel another body beside her, soft in the rhythms of sleep. And the things that Jeanne had done, had shown her… Pleasant, but strange.

Memories came drifting back to her as sleep began to nibble at the edges of her senses. The awkward moment when Jeanne's butler had let her in the door and she realized he must know—they all must know. Long looks across the dinner table as her attention wavered between the exquisite meal and Jeanne's always-entrancing conversation. Jeanne's face as she rose and held out her hand, asking, "Shall we go upstairs?" The brief panic when Jeanne had begun to pull the pins from her hair and she was thrown back into the lodge at Uhlenbad with all the antlered skulls staring. And without knowing why, Jeanne had stopped and waited for her to come back into herself again. The laughing, teasing way in which Jeanne had turned undressing into a game, and then the long, slow exploration within the covers. Strange, but pleasant.

At the May Day bonfire, the smoke oracle had seemed a cruel threat: that she would never know love except the kind Jeanne had to offer. She'd thought she knew what kind of love that was. Now she knew the oracle for a promise: that she *would* find love, because Jeanne was the only person who had ever looked deeply enough within her to find something worth loving. She'd never expected to understand what it was that drove men and women together in the throes of passion. Men and women—well, perhaps she still didn't understand that. In this moment, what she felt for Jeanne had nothing to do with male or female; it had only to do with Jeanne. She couldn't imagine lying beside anyone else in this way with the feeling that all the world had shifted into place. She couldn't imagine melting under anyone else's touch, or feeling so at peace that she could fall asleep in anyone else's arms.

She woke, confused, in the dark to the sound of her name and the feel of hands shaking her.

"Toneke, wake up, you're dreaming."

She sat, feeling her heart racing. "What?"

"You had an evil dream."

Antuniet reached for memory but the substance eluded her. "I'm sorry," she said. "Did I wake you?"

Jeanne muffled an odd laugh and traced the lines of her cheek. "You were screaming as if all the demons of hell were chasing you. Do you have nightmares like that every night?"

Antuniet shook her head and laid back wearily against the covers. "I don't think so. I used to. But not since…Oh!" she said suddenly. "I forgot my chrysolite amulet, the one against night phantasms. You remember I told you about it back in the spring? That I would know for certain whether the enhancement worked? It's under my pillow, back home."

"Then I'll need to serve as your charm against nightmares tonight," Jeanne said, wrapping Antuniet in her arms. "It worked before."

Antuniet made a confused noise. "Before?"

"That night at New Year's. When I knew I loved you. You had dreams that night too, and I held you all night to keep them away."

She sounded almost embarrassed, but Antuniet couldn't tell in the dark. "If you knew then, why didn't you say something?"

"What was there to say? What would you have thought of me? All there was for me was to be a moth to your candle. A stray dog hoping for scraps from your table." Antuniet felt Jeanne's finger tracing down the profile of her nose and brushing briefly against her lips. "And you do know…" Jeanne continued. "You understand…society tolerates my little amusements because I know the limits. It's one thing to dally with actresses or flirt with married women. It's another to seduce the daughters of the nobility. And I had no reason to think you were willing to be seduced."

"But I'm not…" Antuniet strained to follow the logic of Jeanne's explanation. "I'm not a daughter of the nobility, not anymore."

Jeanne's voice was rich with amusement. "I think that could be conveniently forgotten for the sake of a delicious scandal. Shall we be scandalous some more?"

It was quite some time before they slept again. But when they did, there were no further dreams.

* * *

It was well toward noon before Antuniet could pull herself away. "But there's the beryl to clean free and Mefro Feldin will wonder where I've gone." Though at least the door would only be locked and not barred. Feldin might think she'd only stepped out for an errand.

"Oh pooh!" Jeanne said dismissively. "What do you care what she thinks?"

But she sent Tomric down to the corner to hail a fiacre and gave no further protest. "I'll come join you when I've set a few things to rights here."

"With all this coming and going I'm surprised you haven't decided to keep your own carriage."

"Oh, *la* no!" Jeanne retorted. "It isn't even finding the space for a stable,; there would be the groom and a stableboy and a coachman. It would nearly double my staff and for what? The horse would forever be throwing a shoe or coming down foundered. Now here you are and I won't kiss you goodbye because I see you're already blushing and we'll hardly be a few hours apart."

The workshop looked just as she'd left it, even to the scattering of crumbs on the floor by the table. She must remember to sweep that up since Feldin would stand by the letter of her contract. It wouldn't do to have mice. As she was coming downstairs again after changing into her working gown, the housekeeper poked her head out of the back room that served as pantry and storage to say, "I wondered where you'd gone. Bed not slept in...didn't know if I should worry. Maisetra Sovitre said I was to tell the city guard if anything happened to you, but—"

"I had dinner with the Vicomtesse," Antuniet replied, hastily assembling a story both true and safe. "It grew late so I stayed the night. You needn't worry about my comings and goings in the future."

Feldin didn't even bother to shrug before turning away. She'd done as much as she felt her duty covered.

The late night's working was still sitting on top of the now-cold furnace where she'd put it the previous afternoon, just before the fiacre arrived. An eternity ago. She broke the seals and undid the clips, then dumped the contents of the crucible out onto the workbench and set to work. Tapping the mass gently on the bench a few times shook off the powdery material where the flux had been quenched and broke the remaining matrix up into smaller pieces. After setting aside the largest lump from the center, she took a small hammer and broke up the smaller chunks, checking to see if any stray eddies of the congelation had formed wayward stones. They would have no value except for reprocessing. Finally she began picking at the central mass, teasing out the clumps that held the promise of gems within. Her heart quickened as always when the rough black matrix at last revealed a glimpse of fire within.

The first stone emerged slowly under her chisel. In some places the slag flaked away easily; in others it was embedded in small crevices in the stone. And then disappointment as she followed that embedding deep into the heart of the gem and it broke in two under her chisel. She sighed and reached for the next promising lump. Three satisfying stones emerged at last, though only one with the purity and size to consider keeping. Antuniet found herself humming an old song under her breath as she worked. *To make the bearer pleasant,* indeed! Though on a day such as this she hardly needed a stone's influence to bring pleasant thoughts. She smoothed her thumb across the faces of the pale golden stone, feeling for any last traces of matrix and considered Jeanne's idea to make a present of it to Mefro Feldin. The thought made her uneasy, as if she would be playing a prank on the woman. No, an honest surliness was better.

As if summoned by the thought, Jeanne came through the door, though in truth she had never been far out of mind for the entire day. She crossed straight over to the workbench where Antuniet was sitting and kissed her softly on one cheek, then more hungrily on the lips. "Be careful, I'm filthy," Antuniet said. And in the back of her mind a voice whispered, *And Feldin could pass by the doorway at any moment.*

"Are you nearly finished?" Jeanne asked. "I wasn't sure when to tell cook to have dinner ready, and you'll need to wash and change. I suppose it's too late for our river walk. We'll have to make time for it tomorrow."

Antuniet held up the beryl crystal. "There's one, at least, worth keeping. A good night's work, I should think."

Jeanne repeated, "A good night's work, indeed," but she wasn't looking at the stone.

* * *

In the days that followed, the Great Work was not entirely abandoned, but Antuniet found herself in the workshop more from habit than purpose. *There's plenty of time. I can't do much until Anna returns*, she told herself. But that excuse slipped away the afternoon they returned from the river to find a message from Monterrez that her apprentice would be returning to work on the morrow. The idyll was broken.

For the first time in a week, Antuniet declined Jeanne's invitation to dinner, saying, "I need to get things in order for tomorrow. It wouldn't do to leave Anna sitting idle when she returns." It was like coming sleepily out of a long dream, as she gathered together her working notes and found the place in her lists where they had left off.

Jeanne hung over her pretending to pout. "So now I must share you with your other mistress." It was only playacting, Antuniet knew, but she took the time to reassure Jeanne more directly before returning to her notebooks.

The world had shifted and everything was off balance. That was the excuse Antuniet gave for the next morning's fumbling near-disasters. Anna was slow and clumsy and couldn't keep her attention on the distillation long enough to collect the correct fraction. Jeanne seemed constantly underfoot, always expecting—though never demanding—her attention until Antuniet said, "Perhaps you could be useful by fetching us both some luncheon from the cookshop. I don't see how we'll have time to go out if we mean to be ready for tomorrow's process."

Jeanne was taken aback for a moment and looked as if she might protest, then answered with a brief touch on the cheek and roused Marien to accompany her on the errand. As the door closed behind them, Antuniet turned to Anna saying briskly, "Now let's pour this mess back in the alembic and begin again."

Anna's breath caught in a muffled sob. "I'm sorry—" she began and then could say no more.

Antuniet stared helplessly at the tears tracing down Anna's cheeks. She had no practice in giving or receiving comfort, but somehow the girl's face found a home on her shoulder and Antuniet's arms moved awkwardly around her. "Don't worry. It's not so bad as all that. Nothing's ruined." But even as she spoke, she knew this storm had nothing to do with the morning's work. "How was the wedding?" she asked. "Is your sister well settled and happy?"

"Yes." But there was no joy in the word.

Antuniet held her out at arm's length. "But...?"

Anna sniffled and found a handkerchief. It gave her time to compose herself. "But...at a wedding...the women are always joking and teasing about who will be next. You know how they do. I'm sure it's the same at every wedding. But every time someone would start, she'd look at me and turn silent." Her voice struggled. "It was as if I were a ghost walking among the living."

Antuniet could see it in her mind: the sudden silences, the careful turning away, the intended kindness that wounded more deeply than cruelty. "Oh, Anna, what have I done?" she said.

"Not...not your fault," Anna managed.

"But it was," Antuniet countered. "And there's nothing I can do to wash away the guilt." She felt utterly helpless.

"I see him in my dreams sometimes," Anna whispered. "I come around a corner and I see him with his knife, standing there and staring at me."

Antuniet shivered and a surge of hatred ran through her. Was he still out there somewhere? She'd had no glimpse of any of her shadows since that dreadful day. Royal protection might keep them safe, but what of justice? Barbara might know. She seemed to make it her business to know things like that.

"I have dreams too," she said quietly. "Do you remember the chrysolite we made for me? It helps to keep them away." She hadn't remembered how effective it had been until that one night when the nightmares had returned. "That will be your next assignment, to make an amulet of your own. Now go wash your face. The Vicomtesse will be back soon and you'll want to be presentable."

The afternoon's work was more successful, bringing them to readiness for the next day's process by the time Anna's escort appeared to return her safely home. With the door closed behind them and Marien sent off to hire a carriage, Antuniet found herself swept into a close embrace. Between a succession of passionate kisses, Jeanne whispered, "I've been waiting all day to do this!"

Her own arms were encircling Jeanne's waist as the door was thrown open once more with Anna breathlessly explaining, "I forgot my copybook—oh!"

Antuniet looked up to see Anna's expression turning from surprise to comprehension to embarrassment. "P—pardon me!" she stammered, continuing quickly on into the workroom.

Jeanne giggled and Antuniet felt a mixture of anger and panic washing over her. "Go wait in the carriage," she told Jeanne. "I'll be out in a moment."

Anna emerged uncertainly from the workroom with the battered ledger clutched in her hands, but she looked down, away, anywhere except to meet Antuniet's eyes.

"Anna, what you saw..." Antuniet faltered. "The Vicomtesse de Cherdillac and I..." What was there to say? How did one begin? Anna was blushing bright scarlet. "Your father..."

"My father wouldn't understand," Anna said quickly, looking up at last. She swallowed visibly. "He wouldn't understand what it means to find someone who can love you." The words were barely a whisper and she looked away again and hurried out the door.

Antuniet let out her breath in a sigh of relief. The past week it had seemed so simple. No, it had never been simple. But the difficulties were only now parading through her imagination. How long before Feldin figured it all out?

How long before her life was common gossip all along the entire street? How long before she would hear whispers and coarse words behind her back as she passed? And Maistir Monterrez would hear eventually. And yet...and yet she wouldn't take back a minute of it.

Antuniet followed Anna out into the street and took a moment to still her shaking hands before she could lock the door behind her. She climbed into the seat beside Jeanne and sat silently as the carriage set forth.

"Toneke, what's wrong? What did she say?"

Antuniet shook her head silently. She couldn't bring herself to speak openly with Jeanne's maid sitting across from them, even knowing that Marien must know all her mistress's secrets. And then, when they were alone at last, with dinner served and Tomric shooed away until called, her fears had faded and there were better things to speak of.

But those first innocent days were past. Now when Jeanne brushed against her in the workroom, or touched her on the cheek as they took leave of each other in the street, she would freeze and check to think who might be watching before she leaned into the caress. And that night, the nightmares came back, overwhelming the power of her amulet to dispel them.

CHAPTER TWENTY-SIX

Margerit

"Well, that was quite a success." Bertrut sighed happily as she settled herself on the cushions.

Margerit moved over to make room in the carriage and it swayed on its springs as Uncle Charul stepped up to sit opposite. She was content for Bertrut to claim her share of the credit for Sofi's coming out. They had closed the summer, as had become custom, by gathering in Chalanz and entertaining their old acquaintances with a grand ball at Fonten House. This year it had been in honor of her cousin's entrance into society. Soon enough, it would be Iulien's turn as well, though as yet that was hard to imagine. Now Fonten House was closed up again, the ballroom swathed in covers after its brief moment of glory, and a few days' travel would see them in Rotenek.

Barbara had left before the ball and returned to the city ahead of them. For an ordinary soirée it would have been quite the coup to have a titled baroness in attendance, but Barbara hadn't wanted to outshine Sofi in importance and had pleaded the press of business as an acceptable excuse.

"What's that in your hand?" Bertrut asked as the coach gave a lurch, her question almost swallowed up in the sudden clatter of iron shoes on cobbles.

Margerit looked down. "It's only a copybook that Iulien gave me—a story, I think. She writes poetry too, you know, but you mustn't tell the Fulpis; I'm sworn to secrecy."

Iuli had been on her best behavior all summer to be allowed to attend Sofi's ball—only watching from the corner of the musicians' gallery, of course.

Margerit had slipped away to bring her cakes and punch before it was time for her to be sent home. They had sat talking on a corner of the stair long enough to be missed down below. Iuli had said she'd been writing something special to show her. But Margerit had forgotten and hadn't made time to visit Chaturik Square again. Iuli hadn't forgotten. She came knocking on the door at Fonten House amid the bustle of the morning's packing, willing to provoke yet another scolding for running off to deliver it into her hand. Margerit opened it and leafed through a few pages, but the jouncing of the coach made reading impossible. She tucked it under the cushion to keep it safe.

* * *

The household barely had a chance to settle into the rhythms of Tiporsel House, when the feast of Saint Mauriz hit like the crack of thunder that began a storm. The start of the season and the university term followed like wind and rain, and in that first week, Margerit was hard-pressed to do more than meet her most important obligations. On top of that, there were Akezze's lectures to promote. Jeanne had promised to assist her in that, but Jeanne never seemed to be at home to visitors. It wasn't until they found themselves at the same concert that Margerit could guess why.

"Barbara," she said quietly, touching her on the arm for attention while continuing to stare across the narrow *salle* to where the other two women were sitting together, their heads close in conversation. "Were you planning to let me in on the secret?" There was nothing one could have pointed to for certain, no unmistakable outward sign. But knowing Jeanne and knowing Antuniet…

"Ah," Barbara said, following her gaze. "So the pursuit was successful." Her voice held a slight tinge of disapproval, but Margerit couldn't sort out the cause.

"Was that what you guessed, back at the beginning of summer?"

"Guessed, yes. But there was nothing to tell yet, even when I visited Jeanne during my travels. Shall we go join them?"

Margerit thought that if her first suspicions had been uncertain, the proof was the guilty look in Antuniet's eyes as she rose and they all exchanged courtesies. And seeing that, she said nothing except the usual sorts of things one said on meeting old friends again at the beginning of the season. The start of the concerto gave them all a chance to compose themselves and by the interval before the singers began, Margerit had found her way to safe topics for conversation.

"How has the work progressed? I want to hear everything. Perhaps you could come for a little dinner on Thursday? My aunt and uncle will be off at the Marzims', so we needn't worry about boring them." She glanced over at Jeanne, implicitly including her in the invitation. "And Jeanne, I've been trying to get a word with you about my lectures. You had such clever ideas in the spring and I need your help to make it a success. Akezze has promised to stay through the end of the year at the least and I'm determined to set her up properly."

Whatever awkwardness there might have been was smoothed away by the time Margerit first ventured down to the workshop on Trez Cherfis to see the summer's bounty for herself. "And are you ready to present them to Her Grace?" she asked, running her fingers lightly over the stones displayed before her.

"Not yet," Antuniet answered. "I still need to apply the techniques we worked out over the summer to the recipes with the more complicated roles. I need someone for the male roles—do you suppose Baron Razik would still be available? I'd rather not try to fit in someone new."

"Yes, of course," Margerit said, making a note to pass word to Efriturik by the complex pathways that protocol demanded. No doubt they would soon settle again into the comfortable ways of working that had grown in the spring, but there was always that first awkwardness between the worlds of men and women and the worlds of the court and city. Uncle Charul could drop a word. They frequented the same club.

And there was mystery work to do. Not for Princess Annek on this occasion, though soon it would be time to begin rehearsing the new version of the All Saints *castellum*. No, this project came to her in her own drawing room on the heels of Amiz Waldimen, soon to be Amiz Luzien.

"So you've caught your beau," Margerit said as they settled together on the damask-covered settee. She abandoned all attempts to fit a face to the name Amiz had so proudly announced. "Who is he? I thought I remembered all the men who were buzzing around you last spring."

Amiz's eyes held their usual sparkle of humor and excitement, but there was something deeper now. "You know how we always hire a place up near Eskor for the summer because Mama was told the mountain air is good for her health. Well, this year Papa had some tedious business that kept him traveling back and forth to Rotenek, so we went to stay with Mama's cousins near Akolbin instead. Not in the town itself, of course. That's such a crush, especially when the court is stopping by. No, they have a very pretty little estate outside of town but close enough that Mama could drive in to take the waters every week. And of course there were dances when the court was there, besides the country balls that Mama's cousins were invited to." She barely paused for breath before plunging on. "Well, that was where I met him. He was one of the neighbors. I'm sure we must have met before when we were both children, but of course he would have been a rude little boy like all the rest."

And no doubt you were a silly little girl. But fresh eyes see deeper. "And you fell in love?" she asked. Margerit expected her to dismiss the question with a laugh. She'd always been so cynical about the place of love in the marriage market.

But Amiz blushed and looked down at the teacup cradled in her hands. "I...I think so. That is, I feel that I must be. What else could make me want to leave Rotenek?" She laughed uncertainly. "His family never takes a house in the city for the season. I'll become quite countrified! But the way he makes me feel…it won't matter. Mama says—well, Mama hadn't quite abandoned the dream that one of us would marry up. But I think Papa is pleased with my choice."

There was so much she didn't need to say. Margerit had heard it all in Amiz's dissections of other people's courtships. If Amiz had been the eldest daughter, then her looks and vivacity would have been worth investing with a larger portion to win a higher prize. And if she had caught the hand of a well-born man, then her less-favored sisters could have benefitted enough from the connection to make up for some loss of dowry. But she came third, and her sisters had needed their equal shares to make ordinarily respectable matches. Beauty might have secured the heart of some younger son of an aristocratic family, but most likely he would bring tastes in excess of her resources. Men married down more often for money than for beauty. "When is it to be?" she asked. "Will you be married here or in Akolbin?"

"Here," Amiz said, "and before the end of the year. Late in November, I think, but Mama wants to have the betrothal party as soon as may be and she wondered…that is, I wondered if you…?"

The question wasn't of the betrothal party itself, of course, but the formal mystery that would precede it: asking the blessing of God and the saints on the expected union. The Waldimens belonged to several mystery guilds and no doubt one of them would be the sponsor with its own established forms. "But perhaps you could devise something more…more personal?" Amiz asked. "Nothing too elaborate," she hastened to add. "We'll only be at Saint Churhis, not the cathedral."

Again, she heard all the parts that need not be said. For a brilliant match, only the cathedral would have done, but the parish church that covered Plaiz Nof would be sufficient to impress country cousins. And a personal ceremony designed by… Margerit tried not to feel that she would be paraded as a prize, though that was likely what Maisetra Waldimen intended. "Of course I'll do it," she said quickly, cutting through Amiz's embarrassed fumbling. "I'll come to call tomorrow and perhaps your mother can have someone from your guild there to answer questions? And then I can spend the afternoon at Saint Churhis to draw it up."

Something far simpler would have filled the need, but the next day Margerit took her sketchbook to the church to lay out a true mystery, noting the dedications of the side altars and questioning the sexton on the history of the building and its key features. She built the structure in her mind and jotted it down in rough notes, speaking aloud the key phrases that would call the attention of the saints and lay out the intent of the ceremony so that she could see how the *fluctus* would respond. Amiz would stand *there* and her mother *there*. Her fiancé and whoever he brought would be *there* by the triptych of the crucifixion. The guild had their own favored prayers and structures for the *markein* and *missio* and she made no changes there. But the heart of the petition was tailored to what she knew of Amiz's hopes and expectations for the marriage. Yet it was hard to stay within those lines and not weave in a thread of her own hopes for her friend.

At last she came out of her reverie and felt the cold of the stones beneath her feet and the unexpectedly close presence of Marken beside her. She came suddenly alert and turned to him, a question on her lips. With the barest nod of his head, he directed her attention toward the back of the church, where a man leaned with artful casualness against a pillar. For a moment she thought she must be mistaken, misled by a trick of the light.

"Mesner Kreiser? What are you doing here?" She chided herself for her bluntness. She never could learn diplomacy.

"Oh, satisfying idle curiosity for the most part," he replied, strolling a few steps closer, then perching on the armrest of a pew just far enough away not to provoke Marken's protective impulses. "I had business in the neighborhood and recognized the crest on your carriage outside. I confess I thought to find Saveze instead."

Not here in Saint Churbis, she had meant. *Here in Rotenek. In Alpennia at all.* But he knew that, so there was no point to clarifying.

"One might ask the same of you," he continued. "What a marvelous time of peace and prosperity for Alpennia when the royal thaumaturgist has little better to do than plan betrothal parties. Quite a waste of your talents, I should think."

Margerit didn't mind that he had divined the nature of the ceremony so easily from the fragments she'd spoken aloud, but she minded the eavesdropping. And she was frightened by the casual nature of his presence. "If you think that Princess Anna would disapprove, perhaps you should speak to her about it," she said boldly. "I'm sure she'd be interested to know you're here in Rotenek."

A smile twitched across his narrow, fox-like face. "Who do you think it was that invited me to return? You might tell your friend the baroness that I'm pleased with her efficiency in delivering my messages. Both of them." He straightened up and turned to go, but paused for one last question. "How is your little alchemist friend doing? That Chazillen woman? You might have saved us all some trouble if I'd known she had such friends at court."

Margerit didn't realize she'd been holding her breath until his silhouette disappeared through the doorway to the porch and she let it go. "Marken, do you know where Barbara is?"

"I think she had business with LeFevre this morning."

Her mind raced. Had it been a threat? Would he dare? Had Annek changed her mind about protecting Antuniet's work? It didn't matter at the moment. Antuniet needed to know he was back and be given whatever reassurance she needed. "Can you find someone to take a message to her? Tell her to meet us at Trez Cherfis." She began gathering together her notes and sketches. "Go! I'll be fine for the two minutes it will take. If anything happens I promise to scream."

"Yes, Maisetra," he said in a tone that assured her that if he thought there was any true risk, the answer would have been no.

* * *

Antuniet heard the news with little emotion beyond a shadow at the back of her eyes and a moment's pause with a hand on the doorway as if to keep herself from swaying. But then her eyes went wider and she said, "Anna," and turned quickly toward the workroom.

"There's no need to fear," Barbara assured her. She had arrived at the workshop hard on their heels, for a rider could negotiate the city streets more nimbly than a carriage. "I don't think he'd be foolish enough to bother you, but just to make certain, we can arrange for a watch again. And see that your apprentice goes by carriage between here and her father's house. Just until we're certain. But what could Kreiser hope for, in any event? We have enough copies of your book that he couldn't hope to prevent your success by theft again."

"He could create his own stones. And if he could lay hands on my notes—"

"You still have Princess Annek's protection," Margerit protested.

"Do I? When it was she who invited him back?"

Margerit saw Barbara shoot her a warning glance. She would have stepped carefully even without it. "There could be many reasons for that. Why should it have anything to do with you? But perhaps it's time to show the princess your work. He wouldn't dare make trouble if she gives you some official recognition—not when he hopes to…" She hesitated. "Not when he has other plans that need her assent."

"I can't," Antuniet protested. "They're not ready. The ruby process is still unreliable and I've only just worked out how to differentiate the fixations for chrysolite. The key is—"

"The key," Margerit interrupted gently, "is to show Her Grace that her interest in your work will be rewarded. It's enough, what you have. If you wait for perfection, you'll never be ready. Shall I ask for an audience in your name?"

Antuniet closed her eyes and took a long, slow breath. "Yes," she said at last.

The door to the inner workroom creaked and Anna's pale face looked out. Margerit could tell from her expression that there had been little in the conversation that had escaped her ears.

"Maisetra—" she began.

Antuniet said briskly, "You needn't pretend you weren't eavesdropping. Better that you should know everything and be safe this time." As if for the girl's benefit, she turned to Barbara and said, "I never did learn what happened to Kreiser's hirelings, the ones who broke in here." She didn't speak aloud the other things they'd done.

Barbara's answer was careful and precise. "I hear they met with misfortune. An accident on the river. The water is cold and swift in January."

Their eyes met and Antuniet gave the slightest of nods. *I never wondered,* Margerit thought. *Did she—?* She had seen Barbara kill a man before her eyes, but that had been in the heat of an attack. *No secrets…but I never thought to ask.* And she was uncertain whether she wanted to ask now.

It was dusk before they could return to Tiporsel House. Two guards had once more been installed, taking shifts out of a hastily improvised barracks in the workshop's basement, and Anna had been sent home in the carriage with strict instructions to hire a ride for all future trips. Antuniet had balked at the suggestion that the guards be augmented with more personal protection. "No, everything that needs protection is here in the building. I won't have an armin poking into my comings and goings." And then, as if that thought led naturally to the next, "Jeanne. She should be warned."

"Will you be seeing her this evening?" Margerit asked.

Antuniet's answer was prefaced by the briefest of glances to where the new guard stood idly by the door. "No, she's dining with the Estapezes. But we have that working tomorrow—"

"And it will be daylight," Barbara interjected. "And she won't be alone. Kreiser may be ruthless but he isn't a fool. He attacked you once because he thought you were nobody. The Vicomtesse de Cherdillac isn't a nobody. I agree, it's the work that needs protection."

It had been that last mention of Kreiser that reminded Margerit of the other thing he had said and she repeated it to Barbara as their carriage crossed the Pont Ruip.

"Both messages," Barbara repeated. "Oh, Margerit, I've been played like a puppet. He never thought I was in Elisebet's circle. The message was always for Annek: that he would find other ears to listen if she wouldn't." She pounded a fist against the cushions in frustration. "And I did his will as surely as if I'd been on his payroll."

Margerit thought it best not to point out that it hardly mattered. That Kreiser no doubt had other cards in hand if she'd refused his errand. What galled Barbara was how she'd been tricked—she who prided herself on knowing every game being played in Rotenek and all the players in each. But this was a larger board with empires in the balance.

* * *

The long gallery that served as an antechamber for the palace offices was only sparsely populated at the hour they arrived, and the morning's chill had not yet been driven out by the bustle of the day's business. As Jeanne fussed over the last details of Antuniet's appearance, Margerit though she was more nervous than all of them together.

"You shouldn't have worn the brown. It's the same dress you wore the last time you were here."

Antuniet submitted to the adjustments and smoothing touches with what Margerit could see was discomfort and finally grasped Jeanne's hands between her own, saying, "Let it be. If she remembers the dress then she'll know that I haven't wasted Margerit's investment on vanity." She continued her grasp long past any need. "It means so much that you could come with me. Both of you."

That, more than anything, told Margerit how much had changed over the summer. This was a new Antuniet who no longer struggled to hold herself apart and aloof from the world. Margerit held out the wooden case containing the careful selection of gems to be presented and Antuniet finally untangled her hands to receive it. Only a few had been set in rings in the short time available. The rest were nestled in folds of white velvet to show their color to advantage, though color was the least of their properties.

Margerit had hoped to accompany Antuniet into Annek's private office, to lend her own voice to the petition. But when the summons came, it was for Maisetra Chazillen alone. It was more cheering that the summons came in the form of Efriturik, playing the part of palace page to escort her within. Well, perhaps that would be better. He might not have the deep knowledge behind the work, but it was easy to guess that Annek had encouraged his participation to have an inside view.

She slipped a hand into the crook of Jeanne's elbow, saying, "They could be hours if Antuniet feels expansive and Her Grace has the patience for it. We'll keep warmer if we walk."

She had never found her way past being shy in Jeanne's presence. She wished that Jeanne would open the conversation about Antuniet. She would have begun with a risqué joke. The vicomtesse had a biting wit that often put her to the blush. Finally Margerit ventured, "I was worried when you didn't join us for the summer as you'd planned."

"Ah, yes. I should have apologized for that long ago," Jeanne replied with a distracted air.

"You had other things on your mind."

Jeanne paused in their aimless promenade and turned to her with a carelessly lopsided smile. "I was madly and desperately in love and hadn't a thought to spare for anyone else."

"I'm glad," Margerit said quietly as they returned to walking.

"Are you? I'm not sure that Barbara approves, but she always takes delight in ordering other people's lives. How do you stand it?"

Margerit tilted her head to consider the idea. She hadn't realized she wasn't the only one to fall under Barbara's overcautious impulses. "I've never been sorry to follow her advice. And I've usually regretted it when I didn't. Why doesn't she approve?"

Jeanne leaned closely, as if divulging particularly spicy gossip. "She thinks I have designs on Toneke's virtue."

Margerit burst out laughing, then covered her mouth hastily as a crowd of women at the end of the gallery turned to stare. But whatever new confidences might have been shaken loose were muffled as one of the women broke away to join them.

"Jeanne, have you heard? Tionez Perzin has presented her husband with a son. That is, she's been delivered of a son and will present the child to him once he returns from Paris. What a time to be away!"

"A son! She must be pleased about that." Jeanne's mood had shifted instantly to the smooth insincerity of the parlor and ballroom. "But Charluz, is she here in town? I thought she planned her lying-in for Iohen's place in the country."

"She did." Another of the women had joined them. Margerit recognized her from some of Jeanne's parties, but she fell more in Elisebet's circles and their paths hadn't crossed beyond that. "But the moment she was allowed to travel she packed up the babe and his nurse and came to town. If Iohen's parents hoped that motherhood would steady her, they've learned differently. She arrived just yesterday, I think."

Margerit barely listened to the flow of news and gossip: who had yet to return, what matches had been made over the summer, who had joined or left Princess Annek's service. It seemed the honor of waiting on her was a mixed blessing and most were glad that protocol gave some respite after a few years.

"And they say Elisebet has dismissed half her waiting women," came a whisper, more quietly than other news. "Who knows what it is this time. That's why Elin is here," the whisperer continued, with a nod to one of the younger women in the circle. "She's to be interviewed for a position and we're all here to congratulate her."

"If she's chosen or if she's dismissed?" Jeanne asked with mock naiveté. The others joined hesitantly in the mirth.

An hour passed. The prospective attendant was summoned and led off down a corridor toward Princess Elisebet's apartments. Another hour, filled by another stroll from one end of the gallery to the other, nodding at the other loiterers. And then the door they never stopped watching opened at last and Antuniet emerged. Efriturik bowed to her with a few words they couldn't hear then left her standing and looking around as they hurried over.

The case of gems was gone. *Annek accepted the gift,* Margerit thought, though nothing of the details could be read in Antuniet's face.

"Yes?" Jeanne asked eagerly, grasping Antuniet's hands and holding them to her heart.

"It seems I have a commission," Antuniet said in a dazed voice, as if the import had only now touched her. "Twelve gifts. To be completed for the New Year's court. With specific effects designed for the recipients." She blinked and seemed to come to herself. "I hardly know where to begin. She wants…well, I need to design them carefully. There are only so many stones one ring can hold. I may need to rethink the settings. And—"

"A commission?" Margerit repeated. "Does that mean an appointment or only the one project?" She didn't dare to ask the deeper question: what this would mean for her quest to redeem the Chazillen name. Annek was more cautious than to give that away at the start.

"For now, I think, the one—to let me prove myself. But it means official recognition." And as an afterthought, Antuniet added, "She wants me to move the work here to the palace grounds. Jeanne, I know I promised I'd make time to go with you to Maisetra Chaluk's tomorrow, but I have an appointment with Annek's *salle-chamberlain* and with an architect to see if there's a suitable space for what needs to be done. I don't know where to begin. Should I start the work at Trez Cherfis? I don't know how long it will take to arrange the new facilities."

Antuniet was still babbling distractedly when they came out into the Plaiz and the carriage was brought around. Jeanne took advantage of the privacy of the interior to stop the flow of words with a kiss. Margerit looked away in embarrassment as Jeanne whispered, "Never mind about tomorrow. We'll have plenty of time."

"A commission," Antuniet repeated in wonder. And then, more surely, "A commission. It's only a step, but a long one. I need to know more about the intended recipients: their strengths and weaknesses. How best to enhance the effects Annek desires. I think—" She seemed to make a decision. "I think it would be best to ask Barbara for help."

CHAPTER TWENTY-SEVEN

Jeanne

"Toneke, you haven't answered my question." It was understandable, Jeanne thought, but she was attending to the conversation even less than she was attending to dinner. "Will you be moving your lodgings to the palace as well?"

"What? Oh, no, I wasn't granted that mark of favor. And it may be a month before the new workshop at the palace is ready. I can't wait that long to begin trial pieces for the commission. Most of the work will still be down on Trez Cherfis for now." She toyed once more with the trout *à la genoise*, then let Tomric remove it with roasted lamb. The elaborate dinner had been meant to be a victory celebration. "Jeanne, would you mind if I went home tonight?"

Jeanne's heart fell, but she reached out to cover Antuniet's hand with her own. "Of course not, dearest. But—"

"I have that appointment with Maistir Marzik tomorrow about what space and facilities I'll need for the new workshop. I need to have lists and sketches ready."

It was so very much like the Antuniet she had fallen in love with. Jeanne lifted the hand to her lips and kissed it, first on the knuckles and then on the palm. She felt Antuniet shiver in delight and added another kiss, more slowly. "As much as I will miss your body lying beside mine tonight, your mind is already far away and better you should keep the two together. But do finish dinner first," she chided. "Or my cook will be in despair."

On the morrow, the news regarding Tionez provided distraction. Jeanne found her at home, as expected. Iaklin Silpirt was there before her, holding out a small squirming spaniel and exclaiming, "See what Tio gave me! She says it's to keep me company now that she'll be so busy."

Tionez rose, saying, "Jeanne! I've been hoping you would call! I have such news."

"So I understand," Jeanne said, and kissed her briskly on the cheek. "A son, I hear. And I'm delighted you recovered so quickly. I know you feared to be languishing in the country for half the season."

"Oh, that, yes. My mama-in-law thinks it's almost indecent that I found the birth so easy when I have so little interest in the result."

"But that's not true!" Iaklin protested, struggling to hold the dog quiet as it squirmed on her lap. "I'm sure you love the child dearly."

"Oh, I'm delighted to have given Iohen a son, but he's such an ugly, mewling, puking little thing. The baby, I mean," she added with a merry laugh. "Mama-in-law found me a wet-nurse: a country girl who dotes on him entirely. She keeps him quiet and content upstairs, and maybe in five or six years I'll see the boy again when he can bow prettily and say 'How d'you do, Mama.'"

Half of that was only to tease the disconcerted Iaklin. Jeanne perched on the settee next to her and resignedly accepted the offer to admire the spaniel more closely. It sat shivering in her lap and she absently fondled it in the soft spot behind the ears. Why was it that nervous women like Iaklin always ended up with nervous dogs?

"But you haven't heard my news!" Tio broke in. "I've been invited to attend on the princess."

Jeanne was startled, until she recalled the conversation in the gallery the day before. "Elisebet? Yes, I'd heard she suddenly had a large number of open positions. Whatever started it all?"

Tio shrugged. "Some to-do with poor Chustin on the road back to town. The next thing anyone knew, Mesnera Sain-Mazzi was giving notice to half the servants and dismissing six of Elisebet's waiting women."

"It's a great honor," Iaklin suggested. Jeanne could see something close to hero worship in the way she gazed at Tio. Pray God she was never too badly let down.

"More a badge of my dreary new respectability," Tio said with mock despair. "That's what motherhood brings me. At least she didn't ask us all to move into palace apartments; I can't imagine keeping a child in close quarters like that. I'll mostly be there half-days unless it's a special occasion, so I'll have time to keep up all my visiting."

"Perhaps the appointment is a compliment to your husband's work," Jeanne suggested. "Do you know what it was that happened on the road? I heard something about a horse—" She stopped herself, trying to remember which parts of Barbara's story she was supposed to have known.

"It was when they stopped at Iser—you know the place, barely half a day's travel left to go? Well, they were just leaving when Chustin became sick as a dog. They had to spend the night and didn't that cause a fuss! Elisebet went wild, saying that he'd been poisoned. I doubt it was more than a bellyache— and who wouldn't get them with her for a mother? He's so wrapped in apron strings he can scarcely move."

"And she gave her entire household notice over that?" Jeanne asked in wonder.

"It wasn't the whole household," Tio said with a dismissive wave. "Only some of those who were traveling with them: a few footmen and maids and a groom or two. And her waiting women, of course. That was the scandal."

Iaklin gave a shudder. "To think that someone so close to you might—"

"Don't be a ninny," Tio said scornfully. "Even Elisebet didn't accuse them of poisoning the boy. She was only angry that they hadn't kept closer watch over him. As if a boy of fifteen would need or want such a flock of hens around him. When my brother was that age he was forever getting into scrapes and it did him nothing but good. It isn't natural for a boy to be that much under his mother's thumb. If she wants something to fuss over, she should get a dog." She snapped her fingers and Iaklin's spaniel leapt down to obey the summons. One more habit she shared with her mistress, evidently.

The next day Antuniet was once again tied up in planning with the *salle-chamberlain* but this time Jeanne wouldn't be put off. "It's such an enormous space!" she marveled as they were led inside. The master of facilities had chosen part of the old summer kitchens as the most appropriate location. They'd stood empty since the building of the new kitchens five years back and the old bakehouse had now been earmarked for Antuniet's use, being already fitted to handle fire. Little had been done yet except the beginnings of clearing out the dirt and drifted leaves, but there were fresh chalk marks on the floor sketching out where the equipment would stand and where to build the new movable furnace with its clockwork bellows and the automated fuel feed that had Antuniet as giddy as a debutante with a new gown.

"It will mean less work in tending," she explained, gesturing in midair to where the equipment would go. "A bin with the coal there—" she indicated an upper corner of the room next to the great chalked circle "—and a screw to deliver it evenly to the fire. That will save Anna the tedium of tending to it, and with more time for preparations we may be able to do a firing every second day." She had passed over the question of where her other participants would find time in their schedules to spend one morning out of every two doing her bidding.

"And we'll need the room for the twinned cibation," Antuniet continued. "You'll see on Tuesday. Even with only three primary roles, once we have six people in the old workshop we'll scarcely have room to turn around."

While Antuniet reviewed the plans and drawings with Marzik, Jeanne wandered around poking at this and that and trying to envision the bustling crush Antuniet had described. The cozy solitude of the summer was gone entirely. Not that the alchemy itself wasn't fascinating, but...

"I think we're done for now," Antuniet said, touching her on the shoulder. "I don't have anything else planned before dinner."

There was a warmth in Antuniet's words that stirred an echoing heat within her. Jeanne covered Antuniet's fingers with her own and pressed them closely. "Alas, I do have something planned for us. We have an appointment with Mefro Dominique. You simply can't go around in the same old thing now that you're Annek's alchemist."

"Shh, don't say that! It isn't true; it's only the one commission so far."

Jeanne shrugged. "Now that you have hopes of becoming her appointed alchemist. It comes to the same thing. You need new clothes."

"I've been saving up to have something made. There's a dressmaker Anna knows who's very reasonable. I won't have time to do much tutoring now and I can't sell any more of the lesser stones; that would get me in trouble. I can't afford Dominique."

"You won't be paying for it, so don't give it a second thought."

"Jeanne, I don't want…" The discomfort was plain in Antuniet's voice.

"I know," Jeanne said reassuringly. She didn't want to have that argument all over again, however silly Toneke was being about it. "That's why the bill will be sent to your cousin."

"To Barbara?" Antuniet asked.

"Unless you have another cousin lurking somewhere. And before you ask, yes, I suggested it to her. But you have to grant that she has an interest in seeing you look presentable. The honor of Saveze and all that."

Antuniet might still have been dubious, but once they were ensconced in the modiste's shop, she fell under the musical spell of Mefro Dominique's Caribbean-accented French, tactfully suggesting which of the newest styles would suit the maisetra best. "The young girls are all wearing overgowns of tissue and lace, but I think that would not do for you. You are too tall to be ethereal. And I remember you do not like the lace. The sleeves *treillagé* would be very becoming, I think. And with nothing but a bit of ribbon *à chevrons* on the hem."

Jeanne did her best to keep her opinions to herself. Toneke was determined to choose always the plainest and simplest styles and that didn't suit her own notions at all. "That might do for everyday," she said, ignoring Antuniet's muffled snort, no doubt contemplating that "everyday" meant working clothes. "But we'll need something more elaborate for the end of the year." To Dominique she explained, "Something suitable for the New Year's court. Nothing outrageous though," she added, thinking of the fanciful costumes that many affected.

"No," Antuniet said firmly. "This one will do for the New Year and you may choose the fabric. For everyday balls and dinners—" She hesitated, then turned to the dressmaker. "Do you remember the last gown you made for me?"

"Yes, maisetra. The rose satin with the pleating?"

"Could you make that again? The gown was ruined in an accident and… and it was very special to me."

Mefro Dominique turned to the girl who stood silently at her elbow. "Celeste, go look and see what we have left of the rose." She shrugged apologetically. "My daughter knows the stock better than I do. Now for the other gown it should be velvet, I think. What do you think, Mesnera de Cherdillac? There is a dark wine color that I think might suit."

Jeanne scarcely attended to the discussion of fabrics, assenting to whatever the other two said. Had that been meant as a peace offering over the gift? Or was it simply that the rose gown had been so perfectly becoming? It was so hard to tease meaning out of Antuniet's words beyond the simple facts.

* * *

Antuniet's prediction about the crush in the workshop when they began the next layering process hadn't prepared Jeanne for the difference in mood, even from the previous spring's work with Efriturik. Then she had felt an intimate part of the process; now she seemed to be in the way. Anna and Margerit were busy sorting out the supplies and equipment, while Antuniet explained the process and roles to their new assistant. Efriturik had brought his friend Charlin Mainek to be the double for his own role, and the presence of two young men had altered the mood of the assembly. She could hear the counterpoint as Efriturik showed off his own growing understanding of the process.

"It's a bit like playacting," he was explaining, "except that we *become* the properties of the materials, and then when we—"

"Playacting may not be the best explanation," Antuniet interrupted, turning the instructions back to more practical matters. Charlin was listening bemusedly with an air of being introduced to his friend's odder relatives. He was properly behaved in every way, but Jeanne suspected that Efriturik had given him a stern lecture in advance, for Charlin was stiffly and punctiliously polite in all his dealings with Anna. Still, the air was changed in subtle ways.

Jeanne shook off her mood when the working itself began. She'd hoped to partner with Antuniet as they'd done during the summer experiments, but the roles had been rearranged for the current formula. Now Antuniet and Anna mirrored Mercury as the transforming principle and she was paired with Margerit as the Queen to stand opposite to the twinned Kings. There was more interaction between the roles as well, adding and mixing the *materiae* with the solvents, packing the crucibles precisely with the seed crystals nestled in the mineral nourishment, all accompanied by the spoken parts that still sounded to Jeanne like a mummer's play. But Antuniet was right. It wasn't entirely playacting. There was a palpable change when Efriturik stepped into his role. Gone was the careless young man of the spring workings who had seemed always half-reluctant, as if his thoughts were on more active pursuits. Now when he took up the flask of solvent and intoned his lines as he dripped it slowly into the crucible, one could see the image of the prince he might someday be. Charlin's twinned echo was just that: an echo, speaking the words and making the motions without that same essential presence. The complexity of the work made for an arduous day, and Jeanne wondered if young Mesner Mainek was regretting agreeing to what must have seemed like an idle game.

But Charlin, too, had hidden depths, it seemed, for when the crucibles were finally clamped, sealed and signed and positioned carefully in the furnace, he uttered a quickly muffled exclamation. After the closing of the furnace door, Antuniet asked him, "Are you sensitive, then? I hadn't realized Efriturik chose you for specific talents."

She likely hadn't meant it to sound dismissive, but he took no note. "A little, but I'd been told we weren't to be doing mysteries. What was that?"

Jeanne's attention drifted off when Margerit joined in the explanation, comparing her own experience of *visitatio* with the alchemical manifestations. Would there never be time for a quiet word in private? Finally, when the men had left and Anna was dividing her time between tending the furnace and tidying the workshop, Jeanne asked, "Toneke, will your new gown be ready by the day after tomorrow? You remember Margerit invited us to the opera."

"Oh yes," Margerit urged. "If you have time. It won't be a large party in our box. My aunt and uncle have another engagement and you know I never remember to invite people on my own. So only Barbara and some friends of hers. And the two of you if you can come."

It was too much to expect Antuniet to be eager, perhaps. Having consulted the chart where the various workings were planned, she said, "Yes, I think that would be possible. Anna will be setting up for the next process but I only need to go see to the progress at the palace. Yes, that would work. And dinner first?"

Jeanne thought the question had been for her, but Margerit answered, "That would be delightful. We'll expect you then."

Two nights later, the performance turned out to be forgettable: another of Fizeir's tedious histories. That was unfortunate. When Antuniet took the time from her work, how preferable if the music were worth it! But if she regretted coming, it didn't show. They strolled out arm in arm for visiting during the interval and stopped by to greet Helen Penilluk and then to visit the Nantozes in their box, though Jeanne found herself carrying the majority of the conversation. "Whatever made you go all stiff and silent?" Jeanne asked when they once again stood before the Sovitre box. "I thought you were old friends with Ainis Nantoz?"

"I was," Antuniet said.

Jeanne would have pursued the matter except that Tio came around the corner, accompanied both by Iaklin Silpirt and Elin...what was her name? Elin Luson. The one Elisebet had been interviewing for a post that day Toneke went to the palace.

"Jeanne! I hoped to see you here. Where have you been keeping yourself?" Tio chattered on, rehearsing all the more public gossip of the court. "And now we really must go," she concluded with barely a pause for breath. "Iaklin, you two go on, I'll come in a moment." She leaned closely with a laugh and Jeanne's hand was caught up and pressed to her bosom. "Darling, you've broken my heart!" she whispered with a sidelong look at Antuniet. And then she was gone.

Jeanne felt Antuniet go rigid at her side and step away from her as if burned. "Toneke, don't…"

But Antuniet had turned away and ducked quickly through the door and out of the public corridor. Jeanne followed, grateful that the others hadn't returned yet. "Toneke, please don't pay her any mind."

"You told Tionez about us?" Antuniet's voice was shaking and she couldn't tell whether it was anger or fear.

"Toneke, I never said a word. Tio doesn't need to get her feet wet to know which way the river's flowing! But she'll be as discreet as she needs to be. She isn't as foolish as she sometimes pretends. And she isn't really jealous, that's all for show." Jeanne took Antuniet's hands in hers and pulled her close, but she drew away with a look out over the expanse of the theater.

"Are you mad? We might as well be on the stage."

"Pooh! They'll see nothing at all improper," Jeanne said. "You'll attract more gossip by acting guilty than from any attention I pay you." But she let go as the door opened and the other guests returned. "Now come sit by me and let's hope the second act is better than the first."

It wasn't, and Jeanne found her comments becoming more waspish as it droned on.

As the curtain came down for the second interval, Antuniet asked, "Don't you care for it? We needn't stay if you don't."

Jeanne squeezed her hand where it lay between their chairs, hidden from sight. "I care for spending the time with you."

"We could do that somewhere else," Antuniet said softly. There was an invitation in her gaze.

Jeanne smiled in return. "Yes. Yes, we could." She turned to their hostess. "Margerit, I feel devastated, but Toneke has a touch of the headache and I need to see her home. Will you forgive us?"

Margerit looked over in concern. "I'm so sorry. Of course—" She paused, taking the two of them in, then continued, "Of course you must go. Tell my coachman I said to take you. He'll be back before the performance is finished. Try to get some rest." But the last was said with an impish smile.

* * *

It was like living three or four lives at once, Jeanne thought. Not that she was any stranger to that, but between the usual course of the season, the alchemical work and the sweet, fleeting hours alone with Antuniet, she felt stretched thin, and hungry for those worlds to touch more closely. To have Antuniet there beside her at the dinners and concerts and the other pleasures of everyday life. She wanted more than a lover, she wanted…she wasn't quite certain, but she was impatient with the scraps she had. Antuniet's everyday life was filled with other concerns and when they met in public she seemed tense and anxious. Today they worked once more with the full crowd and there would be no time for as much as a cup of tea together. And yet she wasn't immune to the excitement at the progress they were making.

Antuniet met her on the doorstep as she arrived at the workshop and Jeanne took her eager face between her hands for a warm kiss. "It will be all day before I can do that again."

Antuniet drew back with a frightened look. "Not here!" she said urgently. She looked up and down the street, then hurried inside.

Jeanne left Marien to pay off the driver and followed, but the entryway gave even less privacy than the street, with the cluster of guards hurriedly rising from their dice around the small table and a gaggle of voices spilling out from the inner workroom. "Then where?" she asked more sharply than she intended.

Antuniet took her hand and led her back along the corridor and up the narrow steps to the small chamber above. "Jeanne, please, I need to be careful," she said as the door closed behind them.

"Of the coalman with his cart and the baker's girl? Why should you care what their sort think of you? People will find it more strange if two such friends as we are show no affection to each other. That would cause more comment." It would be laughable if Toneke's expression weren't genuinely pained.

"I care if the coalman makes filthy jokes about what Anna does here all day. I care if the baker's girl calls me rude names in front of other customers. I care if word gets back to Maistir Monterrez and he believes it. And yes, I would care if Mefro Feldin gave notice and I had the trouble of replacing her." The pleading edge in her voice was painful. "Jeanne, you've surrounded yourself with your own creatures, like a warm carriage rug wrapped around you. But I could be out naked in the cold tomorrow. Everything I've built could crumble."

Had she been the butt of rude remarks from her neighbors? Jeanne found it hard to imagine, but this was a different world and one where the rules she lived by might fail. The fear in Antuniet's voice wormed its way into her own stomach. "Do you want to end it?" she asked.

"No!" Antuniet's desperation rang true. "I couldn't bear to go hungry again! Not now." Truer still was the feel of Antuniet's arms suddenly wrapped around her. "Jeanne, you're my bread and my life. But I need to be careful."

Jeanne felt her quivering like Iaklin's little spaniel and held her until the shaking calmed. "Toneke, I'm sorry. I'll try to behave, but it's so hard to be here beside you all day without touching you." She smoothed a wisp of Antuniet's hair away from her eyes. "I wish we were back in summer."

"No, you don't," Antuniet said, the tension fading from her voice. "Now that the season has started again there's a glow about you. Another month of summer and you would have been screaming with boredom. We need to go down, they'll be waiting."

"Not yet," Jeanne insisted. She once more took Toneke's face between her hands and drank deeply of her lips. "There," she said, drawing back at last. "Now it's been done properly."

* * *

There was little hope of Antuniet's company the evening of a working. Even when the congelation proper was finished in good time and the furnace could be left to complete the incubation and cooling without constant care, she was loath to leave it entirely unattended. But the next day, when the matter had been quenched and only the picking over and cleaning remained, there was a chance at least for a few hours of quiet companionship.

Jeanne let herself into the outer room and nodded to the man sitting guard there. "Toneke?" she called. "I've come to keep company with you." There was an answering greeting from inside the workshop as she let Marien take her coat and bonnet. "I haven't brought any working clothes," Jeanne said on entering the workroom. "I'm promised to Maisetra Chaplen later and I wouldn't have time to go home to change. But I was hoping you wouldn't mind me dropping by."

Antuniet rose from the workbench, holding her hands up in caution. "I'm absolutely filthy. Be careful."

"Not all of you," Jeanne said as she set a kiss on her fingertips, then pressed them against Antuniet's lips. Antuniet gave a brief glance at the corner where Anna was working, but her head was bent closely over her workbooks. "I'll just sit myself here," Jeanne continued, "and keep out of the way. What is Anna working on that you have to pick through the matrix on your own?"

"Planning for the next multiplication," Antuniet answered as she turned back to work. "I thought it was time to see how well she can manage the whole process. And for the simpler workings it's best if she can carry on if I need to be elsewhere. We'll be adding another layer to this set of stones." She indicated the crumbled lump of slag and dross before her. "With the two cibations and the additional fixation between them, I think more than half the stones in each batch will be usable."

Jeanne picked up one of the cleaned emeralds already laid out on a cloth. It seemed enormous, almost the size of a pea. "This isn't large enough?"

"That one, yes. It was the best of the lot. Of course, it will be cut down for setting. If the stones were perfectly pure and flawless they could be smaller. It's purity that gives them their strength."

A mischievous smile crossed Jeanne's lips and she leaned closely to whisper, "Purity always seemed more of a weakness to me."

Antuniet looked blankly at her until she realized it was a joke. "Even so, I don't know how I'm going to fit all the stones needed for each ring. Too small and the properties have no power, but two of the gifts call for at least eight different properties. It has to be something the recipient is willing to wear!"

The green stone lay darkly against her skin as Jeanne pressed it to her finger and imagined the rest. "Why a ring? Most of the gifts are for men, aren't they? Wouldn't it be better to set them in a watch-fob or even the head of a cane? Something with more space?"

Antuniet frowned a little in thought. "When the stone's properties are meant to aid the bearer, it works best to be in contact with the skin. For those that affect those around you, it's less important but the strength must be greater. A cane might be worth considering, but one doesn't carry it all the time. A ring is the surest method. The gifts for women could be more varied; a pendant would work just as well. But I'd prefer to make them all similar."

The morning passed too quickly, but Alis would be expecting her. Best not to disappoint. "Will you be free this evening?" she asked on rising at last.

"Free to be with you or free to go out?" Antuniet asked without looking up from the work.

"Either."

Now Antuniet met her gaze. Perhaps she had heard the thread of longing that couldn't be suppressed. "I can come after Anna goes home, but I don't have the time for primping and dressing if we're going out to dine. Did you have invitations?"

"Yes, but I could send my regrets," Jeanne offered.

"Don't stay home on my account. Tomorrow would be better. I'm free for any of your plans tomorrow." Antuniet smiled invitingly and all the impatience melted away.

"Tomorrow then. Dinner with the Penilluks before the concert. I promise you, you'll enjoy this one. A new German composer who can pull the heart right out of your breast."

"Do you ever tire of all the concerts and opera parties?" Antuniet asked.

"To be tired of music is to be tired of life," she intoned with a dramatic gesture. "What would you prefer?"

"Only promise me that you'll make time for Akezze's next lecture. I want to see how she's being received."

"Of course." Jeanne said goodbye with another finger-kiss and reminded herself to beg Helen Penilluk for space for another guest. There was never any predicting when Toneke could make time to join her, but Helen wouldn't mind the short notice.

* * *

The alchemy days were coming more closely on each other's heels now. Jeanne found she had misjudged: two days after dinner at the Penilluks's should have been another easy schedule, but Antuniet sent a note scribbled in haste that she would be working late to prepare for the next day's process. Jeanne crumpled the note with a frown. At least that process would be only the smaller group. What had it come to that three or four people now seemed intimate! But when she arrived at Trez Cherfis in the morning, it was only Anna there to greet her.

"Maisetra Chazillen was called away to the palace," she explained. "There were questions about the construction of the furnace and she didn't want to risk delaying the work."

Now that was too much. "She'll be at the new workshop?" Jeanne asked. She'd set her heart on Toneke's company, however shared.

"Yes, but she said we should continue without her. I know all the steps for this one."

But Jeanne's mind was decided. "Some other time. It won't ruin anything to delay for a day. Marien!" she called. "Has the driver left yet? We're going to the palace instead."

"Mesnera," Anna began, "I don't think—"

"Don't you worry," Jeanne assured her. "I'll tell Maisetra Chazillen it was all my fault. I'm not in the mood for alchemy today."

She found Antuniet deep in conversation with the *salle-chamberlain* in a room transformed by carpenters and masons. The bare abandoned bakehouse was gone and the lines of what it would become were clearly seen. "Toneke, you're working miracles in this place!" she called by way of greeting.

Antuniet looked up, startled. "Jeanne? What are you doing here? What's gone wrong?"

"Nothing at all," she said lightly, crossing the room to tuck her hand under Antuniet's arm and look around her shoulder at the plans laid out for discussion. "I wanted to see what you were doing."

"But Anna—"

"Now you aren't to blame Anna. She gave me your message and I ignored it."

Antuniet pulled away and looked over at the waiting chamberlain to say, "Will you excuse us for a moment?" He bowed and moved away to speak with the carpenters. "Jeanne, you didn't leave her alone, did you?"

"She's hardly alone. That guardsman is there and I think your housekeeper is about somewhere. She won't come to any harm because I left any more than she would before I arrived."

"Jeanne, I needed that process completed today. And Efriturik will be there any time now. It's completely unsuitable for Anna to be alone with him; what will her father say? I was depending on you."

"No, Toneke! This really is too much!" Jeanne protested, stung by the rebuke. "Do you expect me to play chaperone to your apprentice? Or to be ordered around like an apprentice myself? I share your work to be with you, but you weren't there."

Antuniet's face fell, as if that thought had never occurred to her. "Oh, Jeanne, I'm sorry. I was wrong to expect..." Her mouth twisted in distress. "Well, it can't be mended at the moment. Anna will have the sense to turn Efriturik away and we can make up the batch later. And since you're here, will you stay? I'd like your opinion on some of this."

She'd been expecting a quarrel. The apology should have mollified her, but instead, with the grievance washed away, there was left a bitter taste of guilt at her own thoughtlessness. She was used to fiery arguments and passionate reconciliations. This soft yielding confused her.

With a hesitation that spoke of the fears she was quelling, Antuniet laid an arm across Jeanne's shoulders to bring them together over the drawings. That was more apology even than the words.

Jeanne leaned into her. It was enough for now.

CHAPTER TWENTY-EIGHT

Barbara

It was a certainty, Barbara thought, that disasters and unexpected guests always sought out the busiest week in the year. Yesterday it had been a frantic message from Antuniet's apprentice asking if Margerit could come assist with the process. And though Margerit had previously begged off from alchemy this week to prepare for the All Saints *castellum*, away she'd gone. And now, here was Ponivin interrupting the dinner guests with the news that, "A young person is at the door who says he is Mesnera Lumbeirt's cousin."

It took her a moment to remember what he might be talking about. The invitation had been given so long ago and there had been no response. And to send him with no notice? What could his parents be thinking? Ponivin was still waiting for instructions. "I believe that would be Eskambrend Chamering," she confirmed. "Take him—" No, she couldn't just send him down to the kitchen as if he were an errand boy without some sort of welcome. "Take him to the drawing room. I'll be there in a moment." She rose, saying, "Margerit, forgive the interruption. I'll see him settled and be back as soon as I can."

Her memory of Brandel had been of a slight, dark-haired youth, full of quick energy. He was more subdued now, standing in the middle of the room next to a small valise and looking around in wonder. He pulled off his cap hastily when she entered the room and bowed stiffly. "Mesnera Baroness, I have come at your invitation."

The poor boy looked like a fish out of water. "It's Mesnera Lumbeirt, properly speaking," she said briskly. "But you'll learn all those things in good time. Let Ponivin take your bags and come here by the fire." And to the butler, "Could you ask Mefro Charsintek to prepare a room? The one at the end of the hall might do." It had an excellent view but was too small to be comfortable as a guest room. "Or whatever she thinks best."

Brandel was still staring at her in awe. Well, and no wonder, when the last time he'd seen her she was in men's riding clothes, not an evening gown. She reached out her hand to him. "Come, you must be freezing. I'm sorry not to be prepared for your arrival but we had no warning. Did the letter go astray? And did you travel all this way by yourself?"

He shook his head at the last question. "I had a ride with a drover who was bringing bullocks to town. He had me handle the wagon while he managed the cattle. I would have written but I didn't know the direction. And I knew that once I got to Rotenek someone could tell me where Baroness Saveze lived."

The implications of his little story sank in. "You haven't run away, have you?" She shook him by the shoulders. "Do your parents know where you are?" This was more serious than a lack of notice.

"No, Mesnera!" he stammered. "They know I've come. Papa said—" The explanation came as if by rote. "Papa said that I could come to Rotenek if I pleased, but I'd have to find my own way here. And so I did."

Barbara recalled Maistir Chamering's surly dismissal of his son's adventurous fancies. And her aunt's comment on his opinion of her own visit. *He didn't approve but he didn't forbid it.* Perhaps this was as far as his approval had gone: that Brandel could accept the invitation if he were bold enough to seize it with no assistance.

"Well, you're here now, and the first thing you'll do in the morning is write your mother to let her know you've arrived safely. Now here's my housekeeper, Mefro Charsintek. She'll show you to your room and get you all settled in. And if you're hungry—which I have no doubt—you can go down to ask for something from the kitchen, but don't be a bother because they're still sending up dinner. I need to return to my guests but I'll come see you when they've gone."

* * *

There was no time to see her cousin properly welcomed in the rush before All Saints. For the first few days and with a twinge of guilt, Barbara begged Bertrut to look after him. Bertrut was quickly relieved of that task by her husband, who had far more experience dealing with young men and who offered to take Brandel around the city and see to certain other necessities such as a proper wardrobe.

Barbara's attention was instead focused on the last rehearsals Margerit was conducting for the revised *castellum*. It had been too complex, she'd said. Too reliant on the skills of the principals, given the large number of those required. What might have worked smoothly as designed for the disbanded

Guild of Saint Atelpirt—filled with dedicated scholars—had weaknesses when celebrated by the Royal Guild of Saint Adelruid, whose celebrants were chosen by rank and seniority rather than ability. They had rewritten the text together. Her own part was to know the strengths and flaws of the nobles who must take the principal roles. Margerit's part was to tailor the mystery's cloth to those shapes without sacrificing the effectiveness of the petition. Even long past the time when changes could be made, she was fussing over a word here and a gesture there. "Margerit," Barbara said firmly at last, "there's no purpose to this. It's time to dress for the dinner."

Last year's celebration had set the tone for the new mystery, combining what had previously been an irregularly celebrated ambassadors' ball with a public Guild Dinner for the *castellum*. Given one likely guest, Barbara was unsurprised to see Jeanne attending alone, though Antuniet's company was unpredictable even at the best of times. Barbara would have preferred to avoid Kreiser's company herself, but there was a time to retreat and a time to engage. She maneuvered herself from one conversation to another until she came up beside him as if by chance.

"Are you enjoying our weather?" she asked idly. "I had the impression that last year you found Alpennian winters somewhat cold."

He turned, as if they were resuming an interrupted conversation. "No colder than the weather back home." He shrugged. "And my time is not my own; I go where the emperor sends me. His business takes no account of weather." An odd smile came over his face, as if at a secret joke. "Or you might say that his business takes a great deal of account of the weather."

Barbara took up the challenge as eagerly as if their words were blades. A feint, a thrust easily beat away, another parried. He gave no ground. A casual mention that some of the young attachés at the embassy were organizing a pheasant hunt for the two Atilliet boys. "They've grown quite fond of Friedrich—almost inseparable—and said he mentioned how he misses a chance to shoot. Perhaps you'd like to join us? But no, I recall you are old-fashioned and favor the sword over the gun."

No chance that Elisebet would give Aukustin leave for that! Barbara thought. *That's only for the illusion of even-handedness.* Riposte. "I'm surprised Baron Razik has time for hunting at the moment. I understand he's been assisting the princess's alchemist in an important project. He seems to have something of a talent for the art."

There. That one had slipped past and won a touch. She had promoted Antuniet beyond her current status, but even should Kreiser discover that, it would be little comfort to him. She curtseyed formally, indicating that it was time to move on. One didn't linger in long conversation at affairs of this sort.

The celebration began the next morning with no disasters or delays. Even without the *visitatio* of the truly sensitive, Barbara could feel the improved flow of the mystery. The revisions had helped, but even more would be the repetition that would slowly settle the ceremony into the bones of the celebrants. How long would it take for Margerit's *castellum* to feel as natural and inevitable as ancient mysteries like the Mauriz *tutela?* Though the Mauriz proved that even the inevitable could be changed. The Mystery of Saint Mauriz had been celebrated again this year with the new Lyon-based rite. Princess Annek had returned—though returned was hardly the right word—to the Lyon text for her own parts for reasons of politics and diplomacy, reassuring Margerit in private that it was not due to any loss of faith in her analysis.

Barbara brought her attention back to the ceremony as her branch of the guild laid the next course of their *turris,* then passed the focus on to the next branch in turn. Close familiarity with the text left her free to cast an eye over the guests who sat quietly in the farther parts of the nave. Margerit, as usual, was ensconced in a corner of the choir, where she could best observe the *fluctus* as the structure built.

It was the armin's instincts that would never entirely fade that drew her attention to a woman standing in the shadow of a column where the less exalted guests were watching. It wasn't her appearance that caught Barbara's eye, though she was clearly foreign. The style of her pelisse suggested Rome, perhaps, though the warm brown of her skin and the tightly curled black ringlets falling from beneath her fashionable turban spoke of origins much farther south. No, it was the intensity of her gaze that had arrested Barbara's glance. If she had been watching the space before the altar where the celebrants gathered, Barbara would have concluded that she saw the *phasmata* generated by the mystery. But she was staring at just that corner of the choir where Margerit sat with her sketchbook. And that called for further consideration. But when the towers had all been raised and bound together and the *missio* pronounced to conclude, Barbara looked back toward the column to find the foreign woman gone.

On the following morning, Barbara was finally able to turn her attention to the problem of Brandel. He had been drawn by dreams of adventure and the romance of taking up the sword. It had been nothing but truth when she'd told Maistir Chamering that the world of his fancies was fading, yet it was a useful lure to focus his mind on more serious matters. She'd promised her aunt he would have a gentleman's education and a courtier's training. Most boys his age would have been off to school for some years now but that wouldn't do. A private tutor would make up the deficiencies in whatever his village schooling had been, and then the usual terms at the university for polish. More if he had the aptitude.

"But why do I need a tutor, Cousin Barbara?" he asked as they set out. "I can read and write well enough and I know the histories. What does an armin need with geography or rhetoric?"

They had settled on "Cousin Barbara" once Bertrut had drilled him on the proper forms of address for both public and private. Barbara thought he almost regretted not being asked to call her "baroness" at every chance. Well, he'd learn soon enough how little that connection would serve him if he strayed outside his place. And for the moment, to set an example, she was paying more attention to convention herself, having chosen a dark coffee-colored walking dress for the expedition rather than her usual riding clothes.

They went on foot today for Brandel's closer experience of the city. Perhaps on their return she'd let him lead the way to see if he remembered how to get them home again. To answer his question she turned to Tavit with a conspiratorial smile. "Tavit, where is Metonfels located? What is the principal produce and industry of that region?"

Her armin rattled off the town's situation, the quality of the land and that it was known for the excellence of its wine but that the woolen mills now stood idle because cheaper cloth was to be had abroad.

"And why might you want to know that, Tavit?" she continued.

He returned her sly smile. "Because Lord Seuz has lands near Metonfels and his rents have fallen with the close of the mills. His wife's brother had been a major buyer but now trades in imports. Lord Seuz will be holding a banquet next month that will strain his resources, but the honor of Seuz must be upheld. And he cannot avoid inviting his wife's relatives. And there will be a great deal of excellent wine served."

Barbara watched Brandel digesting the connections threading through his answer and their relevance to an armin's duties. He frowned. "So Lord Seuz might get drunk at his own banquet and start a fight with his brother-in-law?"

"Perhaps, perhaps not," Barbara replied. "But if it should happen, I would expect my armin to have predicted it. So we are going to the university district to speak to a few people about finding you a tutor. But I thought we might stop by Perret's *salle* on our way." That was the sweetener.

Excitement leaped in his eyes. Tavit must have been telling tales again. "I'll be learning dueling from Mefroi Perret?"

She grabbed Brandel by the wrist and pulled him around to face her, halting in midstride. "If I ever hear you've been dueling, I'll pack you off to your father before the next dawn." She released him and resumed walking, waiting until he had scrambled to come even with her again before saying, "In all my time I've only fought one duel, and that was meant as murder, not as a test of honor. No one with any sense is eager for a duel. You will be learning the art of defense, and the sword is only the beginning of it. You should learn to shoot as well. But Perret can't be expected to waste time on raw beginners like you. If you're respectful and convince him you're willing to work hard, he may assign one of his students to teach you." It wasn't entirely true. If she requested it, Perret might be willing to provide the occasional lesson, but she didn't care to spend her credit with him to that end. And she was taking Brandel's measure: he was willing to go to great lengths for something he'd set his heart on—his presence in Rotenek was proof enough of that—but he might not value what was given freely.

When they had finished at the *salle*, they turned south. The Red Oak tavern had been the first place she'd turned when looking for gossip concerning Aukustin's tutor Chautovil and for the same reasons it was her first stop again today. It was the chosen haunt of many of the more serious and sober students and there was always news of positions sought and offered. As if the thought had summoned him, when they came through to the quieter inner room to find an empty table, Barbara spotted Chautovil himself, looking more like a student than a respectable tutor, with his carelessly-tied cravat and his over-long hair falling in untidy chaos. The man looked up in startlement from the corner when he saw her.

"Now here's a lucky chance," Barbara said as they approached. "You may know—" The second figure behind him came into view, explaining his half-guilty look. Barbara offered a slight curtsey, saying, "Mesner Atilliet, I hope you are enjoying the day. May I take the liberty of introducing my cousin Eskambrend Chamering? He's newly come to town. Brandel, this is Aukustin Atilliet, Princess Anna's half-brother. And Maistir Chautovil, his tutor. Might we join you, Maistir Chautovil? You might be able to help with my errand here today."

They had both risen at the greeting, but Chautovil remained standing, eyeing her uncertainly. "Baroness, might I have a private word with you?"

"Certainly." And when he looked back at Chustin with a slight frown of concern, she said, "Tavit?" and tilted her head in the boy's direction. Tavit nodded and shifted to put the table within the ambit of his watch. It was an excess of caution; there was no need for them even to leave the room. The far corner provided seclusion enough.

Chautovil made no preamble. "If you're one of the shadows Princess Elisebet has set to watch over her son, then you will do as you must. But you would do him a better service if you didn't mention that you met him here."

Did Chautovil know that she had once made inquiries about him at Elisebet's request? She'd been as discreet as she felt the matter warranted, but she'd taken no serious pains to be secret about it. "It's true there's been an occasion or two when the princess asked me to have an eye to Chustin's safety," she offered. "But I have no warrant to spy on him or report his activities."

The tutor relaxed visibly. "Forgive me for the question. The boy is so hedged about with restrictions. How can I prepare him for…for the life he may someday lead if he never knows more of Alpennia than the inside of the palace?"

Barbara nodded in sympathy. "It isn't an easy task you've been set."

They drifted back to join the boys at the table. Chustin was holding forth on the wonders he'd seen and Brandel, she noticed, was polite enough—or new enough to Rotenek himself—not to scoff at the thought that the arches and imposing bulk of the *chasintalle* constituted a wonder.

"I want to see the ships down at the wharves and the Strangers Market where they unload the cargos," Chustin said excitedly. "My tutor said we might go there next time." And then he seemed to remember his manners and asked Brandel about his own adventures.

Barbara gave the tavern keeper her requests, then turned back to Chautovil. "I find myself in need of a tutor for my cousin to fill in a few gaps that hadn't seemed important back in Rapenfil. Who would you recommend? You're still new enough from your own studies that you must know who's looking for positions."

He mentioned a name or three and they fell to quiet discussion of their merits. Brandel had overcome his initial awe to answer Chustin's questions with the tale of his travels to the city. That tale was met with naked envy, though only Chustin's sheltered life could make the drover's wagon into an adventure. The two boys were nearly of an age: both thin and dark, though Chustin was the taller. Watching them, Barbara's thoughts spun off in odd directions, until Chautovil rose to depart.

When they were left alone at the table, Barbara caught Brandel's attention and said quietly, "An armin must always know when to be discreet. Mention to no one that you saw Mesner Atilliet today."

"Why?" he asked guilelessly. "And why did you say he was Princess Anna's brother when everyone calls him her cousin?"

"That," she replied, "I set as a lesson for you: to find the answer to those questions without giving away secrets. And you may not simply ask Tavit. And the second test today," she added, "is to see whether you've been paying enough attention to lead us home." She was gratified to see that he looked daunted but made no protest. He'd soon learn to expect such tests. They were far milder than the ones she'd been set at a far younger age.

He found the way well enough by heading north until they came to the river. Only once did Tavit correct the path and that was for form's sake. The Summeril district held no hazards to compare with the warehouses along Rens Street and she was no stranger to these narrow alleys, but it was no place for a well-born lady's afternoon stroll and Tavit took seriously her advice to tailor his watch to her wardrobe.

* * *

The understanding she had found with Antuniet at the beginning of the summer had failed to blossom into anything deeper. The brittle formality was gone, but the distance remained. On Antuniet's side the only change was a willingness to co-opt her into the alchemical work when an extra body was needed and she could fulfill the role. On her own side...Barbara found she could only describe the change in an armin's terms: that Antuniet now stood within the circle of her watch. But they had no public friendship, no ties that did not travel through another person. Even their social encounters were largely mediated through Jeanne's efforts. And yet despite that—because of it—when Margerit brought home the message that Antuniet wished to consult with her, should it be convenient, Barbara cleared the next day of all other commitments.

When Antuniet arrived, Barbara was in the library taking a few moments to quiz Brandel on his studies. Rather than sending him about his business, it seemed right to make introductions. "Antuniet, you haven't yet met my cousin, Eskambrend Chamering. He's joined our little household for a time." At her look of surprise, "My mother's family. Until this summer I knew nothing about them and now suddenly I have an abundance of cousins. Brandel, this is another cousin of mine, Maisetra Chazillen. Her mother was a Lumbeirt."

"But Cousin Barbara," he began, "if she's your cousin, then why—"

"Brandel!" she cut him off sharply. "Discretion. And...?" Her voice trailed up in expectation.

"...and a test. Yes, Mesnera," he concluded, finally remembering his public manners. And with a little bow, "It is a pleasure to meet you, Maisetra Chazillen."

Antuniet watched him leave with an odd look. Envy? "You're gathering quite the *saliesin*," she observed, using the old-fashioned term for that extended network of kindred, clients and dependents that still left traces in households like that of the Pertineks. Did Antuniet feel left outside that structure?

Barbara grimaced. "It's been a bit strange to have a boy in the house. And he has everything to learn. How is the work proceeding?" It was the only topic she could think of that might have brought Antuniet here.

Her face fell a little and she shook her head absently. "I don't know...I can't...I don't think it can be done."

Barbara raised an eyebrow and waited for explanation.

"It's the size of the stones," Antuniet continued. "I can make the ones I need easily enough, but to gather the sets of properties—it's too large for the setting, even for the larger men's rings. And I've talked it over at length with Monterrez and we can't think of any other piece that would achieve the necessary contact."

"Is the size so important?" Barbara asked.

Antuniet stared at her as if she'd said something witless. "Too small and they're only colored glass. The structure of the crystals magnifies the properties. It's different for each type of stone, of course, but you never obtain the enhanced properties with anything smaller than a pea. Not unless they're more flawless than anything I've managed so far. A very large stone will work, even with natural flaws. The purity is part of it too. Perhaps a perfect stone could be small enough. Perhaps someday I'll be able to achieve that degree of perfection. But not in time for the gifts."

"You could go to Princess Annek," Barbara said. "Explain the problem. Perhaps the requirements could be changed."

"No!" Antuniet protested immediately. "This is the task I was set. I can't fail now."

"Sometimes life gives us more than one chance," Barbara suggested gently. "Must you stake it all on this one project?" She could understand, although not share, the fear and panic that washed over Antuniet's expression.

"I never had a right to hope for even one chance," she said. "How can I ask for a second?"

"Then we must solve the problem somehow. What are your thoughts?"

Antuniet drew out her notebook and opened it to the page where the recipients' names were written, followed by the lists of properties that had been requested. "I thought—" she began. "You helped me identify what paths to take for each man. Perhaps we could review them again and reduce the number of the stones. It's easier to enhance one property at a time, to grant pure virtues. But the natural stones are more mixed, and perhaps that could be used to our advantage. This one, for example." She traced a finger under the listing for Albori, the foreign minister. "To give him wisdom in making decisions; to make him eloquent and bold in persuading others; but then also to brighten his vision and strengthen his lungs. There's no overlap I can find for the medical purposes, but with your advice I had fixed on sapphire, carnelian and agate to increase wisdom, confidence and the power to persuade others. If boldness needn't be strengthened, then perhaps agate alone would work. It grants prudent speech and cautious judgment. The effect wouldn't be as strong for the size, but if I can reduce three to one, then a larger stone—the central one in the setting—would be possible. If I could bring each design down to three stones, I might succeed. But I need your knowledge of the court again. Where can we skimp? Which effects will work with the natural virtues of the recipients?" She looked up, not so much in hope but as a drowning man might at the distant sight of a ship.

Barbara bit her lip and thought through the problem Antuniet had described. "I see what you're thinking," she said. "And for Albori, that could work as you suggest. He has no lack of confidence, only a weak sense of what and when to push. Perhaps…" She leaned over the notebook and ran her eyes down the list. "This one. I think something can be done here as well." They set to work paring away at the layers of the project to find what might be possible.

At the end, the edge of panic had faded from Antuniet's manner. As they bade farewells, Barbara impulsively offered, "We haven't seen you outside the workshop for too long; you look tired. Could you find time on Friday for a dinner? There's a concert—some French alto and they say Fizeir has done some settings of Pertulif that I'm eager to hear. Are you fond of his verses? We're having some friends here beforehand."

Antuniet managed a wry smile. "I've refused one offer of dinner for that night already. I have so little time to spend on entertainments at the moment; I think Jeanne would be cross if I squandered it on anyone but her. But I'm hoping to join her for the concert. There's a late working that day and Anna can't stay to tend it. But if I can get free in time, I'll come."

"Antuniet, don't—" Barbara hesitated. What did she mean to say? *Don't pin your hopes of happiness on Jeanne. She's a butterfly and you're only this season's blossom.* But there was no ground between them where that could be spoken. Her cousin had never yet acknowledged aloud that she and Jeanne were more than friends. And the rules must be followed. "Don't fret about the New Year's gifts," she finished after an awkward pause. "We'll make it work somehow."

* * *

The concert looked to be a wild success and a dreadful crush. As Margerit went to find their seats, Barbara edged her way through the crowd to where Jeanne held court with her fan fluttering in one hand and a nearly empty glass of champagne in the other. "You look sparkling tonight," she said. "Did Antuniet come with you?" It would be good to hear how the changes they had discussed were working.

Jeanne's mouth twisted in a pout. "No. It was maybe yes, maybe no, it depends on how the working goes. But I can't sit at home waiting in hope that the furnace will cool in time. This is my last chance to hear La Rossignole sing from her *Romeo* before she returns to Paris." She fluttered her fan coyly. "You know I have such a weakness for the trouser roles."

It was a disappointment, but not a surprise, and Barbara re-entered the press to join Margerit again. The music was a varied program. Maistir Fizeir had been venturing into the realm of art songs and offered a setting of Pertulif's most popular poem, *The Song of the Mountain*. Like most of the composer's work, it was technically precise but unsatisfying to the soul. "Though," Barbara admitted under her breath to Margerit, "I may be too hard to please when it comes to that text. But how could he assign a verse on the majesty of the mountains to a coloratura?"

"You should commission your own setting," Margerit whispered back to her.

Now there was a thought. She cast her mind about but couldn't think of any composer she'd be willing to trust with the task. Fizeir was the best Rotenek had to offer at the moment. The performers moved on to a selection of operatic pieces and when the French alto came out costumed for *Romeo* and began her aria from the balcony scene, Barbara could see why Jeanne refused to miss the performance. She reached over to entwine her fingers with Margerit's and they shared a brief glance. Young love…but theirs had escaped tragedy.

At the phrase where the singer should spot Juliet emerging on the balcony, La Rossignole reached out invitingly to the women in the front row of chairs where Jeanne's coterie had ensconced themselves. At a laughing push from her companions, Jeanne allowed herself to be installed standing beside the harpsichord as the object of affection. She took it in good part, lending just enough response for the performer to play to without distracting from the song. And as the applause rose up to signal the end of the set, La Rossignole drew Jeanne forward by the hand to include her in the bows, bending over her fingers with a gallant kiss.

Barbara lost sight of them as the crowd rose and refreshments were circulated once more. A greeting here, a word there, a glass of punch to bring over to Margerit, who had been cornered by one of Mesnera Arulik's protégés hoping for goodness knows what. She looked up and saw Jeanne close by, arms entwined and heads together with the singer, still playing the part of her Juliet. And then, looking past them, framed in the doorway at the other side of the room, she saw Antuniet: just arrived and flushed with what must have been a hurried pace.

It was like that moment when one saw someone fall from a great height, or the drift of a boat toward a waterfall, rushing faster and faster to the precipice. She saw Antuniet spot Jeanne across the room; saw the delighted smile, the eager approach. Jeanne turned, following her gaze. La Rossignole turned with her, standing too closely for accident, a laugh on her lips. Antuniet stopped two steps away. Her face folded in on itself: not the crumpled fall that presaged tears, but a slow closing like the unblossoming of a flower.

"Toneke…" Jeanne began uncertainly.

La Rossignole looked between the two of them and had the wit to say, "Pardon me, I fear I am *de trop*," before disappearing.

Antuniet's voice held no emotion that could be read. "I knew you would grow tired of bread and water someday, but I hadn't thought it would come so soon."

"Toneke—" Jeanne began again, reaching for her.

Antuniet raised her hand. In denial? To ward off a blow? She continued in that quiet, closed voice. "Don't fear that I'll enact you tragedies or embarrass you before your friends." And then she turned and left by the same path she had come, neither hurried nor taking note of anyone in her path.

Jeanne watched her silently, one hand pressed against her mouth, until Antuniet had disappeared through the doorway. Then it was Jeanne's face that crumpled with tears. Barbara looked around hurriedly and drew her off into a corner that afforded some privacy. She saw Margerit catch her glance and shook her head slightly to warn her away. What a tangle. She pulled out a handkerchief and thrust it into Jeanne's hand. "If you want to avoid a scene, take yourself in hand," she instructed sternly and a little savagely, as Jeanne dabbed at her eyes. "Don't worry, you'll fall in love again soon enough. You always do."

Jeanne looked up and for the first time, Barbara wondered how deeply this cut. "You don't understand," she said tightly. "Antuniet…she isn't one of my little entertainments. You don't understand," she repeated, once more fighting for control. When she continued, her voice was quietly fierce. "I have loved— truly loved—only four women. One of them is dead. One never found the courage to say either yes or no. You were the third. And Antuniet—" Her voice broke anew.

Barbara was startled by the revelation. She'd always counted herself as one of the "little entertainments." Now a flood of memories streamed past in a different light. That summer—and how it ended. And later, the risks Jeanne had taken and the unexpected loyalty. It felt as if an apology were called for. "Jeanne," she offered. "Jeanne, you know that when we were together I wasn't free to give my heart."

Jeanne smiled wanly. "And yet, somehow, when you were free, your heart was already taken. No, you had a destiny, I could see that."

"But Jeanne…why?" She was near to exploding in sudden exasperation. "If Antuniet means that much to you, then…why?" She made a small gesture to encompass the preceding events.

"I don't know! I get restless and a…a madness comes over me. I need to be doing something, to be out and about. I need the crush of the crowds, the attention and the champagne. I can't sit home waiting for her to spare me a moment. Antuniet has no use for me; I need to be *useful*."

"It seems to me you need entirely too many things," Barbara retorted. "Have you thought about what Antuniet needs?" Jeanne's silence was hard to read. "You think yourself ill-used if you're left to attend a few parties unescorted. But where have you left her? She's trying to claw together a few scraps of pride and honor, working long nights to complete an impossible quest. You're willing to play at alchemy when it suits you, yet you abandon her if she hasn't the time to dance attendance on you. If you were a man I'd call you out."

There. That cut through the self-pity. Jeanne met her eyes and said hollowly, "If I were a man I would deserve that. But breach of promise requires that a promise be made. There's nothing I'm allowed to promise to her, or she to me. I learned that as a girl in my first season."

"Then what is your love worth? No, don't protest to me. I'm not the one who needs to hear it. Jeanne—" No, she couldn't bear to go on hurting her just now. Everything necessary had been said. She couldn't bear to see either of them hurt, that was the dilemma. "Gather your things. I'll send you home in my carriage."

CHAPTER TWENTY-NINE

Antuniet

Antuniet would have thought sleep impossible but habit drove her to her bed to toss and turn in misery, until a dream overtook her in spite of all precautions. There was in her hand a crystal, a perfect pure gem that drew the eyes of all about her. And while she held that stone, a crowd gathered around her and bowed to her and watched her with adoring, obedient eyes and she knew it was the power of the stone that drew them. And for fear that she would lose it, she swallowed it and felt the edges and corners sharp inside her belly. But then she was alone in the cold and dark with her mother's voice sounding, "It was an unsuitable friendship. I have put an end to it." The stone burned inside her and she would have cried out but for that voice, "Remember always: you are a Chazillen. Do not disgrace me." And so she turned her face itself to stone even as her belly burned and bled until she could bear no more. She screamed but no sound came. And all around her rang the sound of mocking laughter until she came awake with a gasp.

Anna had the day off; that was one small mercy. At least one more day before there would be any need to find explanations. Antuniet lifted the crucible out of the cold furnace and readied it on the bench, undoing the clamps and cracking off the seals. She had prepared the quenching liquor while tending the heat the evening before, so it was only a matter of drizzling it over the hardened matrix to begin the putrefaction. That much could be done without thought or decision. After that, habit took charge. Washing. Food. Checking the progress of the putrefaction. Hours passed. The matrix had grown softer. Draining the quench. Three rinses with twice-distilled water. Upending the crucible onto the work tray and tapping the matrix out. The tapping continued. The front door. She heard the watchman's footsteps in the corridor, then a gruff, "Mesnera," the click of the latch and his footsteps receding again.

Antuniet turned toward the doorway, steeling herself. Jeanne looked as though she had been haunted in her sleep as well. She glanced at the emptied crucible and said, "What do we work on today?"

Part of her had longed for that knock, that voice. Part of her had dreaded it. Did Jeanne think they could simply begin again? Was the summer to be repeated? Slow courtship, fleeting moments of joy, then weariness and betrayal and a return to the start? It would be wiser to send Jeanne away before her presence renewed the gnawing hunger. But she kept those thoughts inside, deep in her belly with the stone. If work were the excuse for coming, then work she would have. "The matrix needs to be broken up and the gems cleaned," she said, turning away from the tray and ostentatiously sorting through her notes from the day before. "The tools are there in the rack. You've seen it done. Sort out the green jaspers by size but take extra care with the red ones."

It took all her will not to look back. She pulled out the list of planned work. She hadn't meant to begin a new process today but distraction was needed. Something complex enough to fill the brittle stillness. Behind her a chair scraped across the stones and the tink-tink of chisel on stone began. She took out a clean sheet of paper and began copying out the recipe for chrysolite. If she could combine the enhancements to strengthen knowledge and to dispel fantasies and terrors it might be adapted to good use.

There were days when she became so lost in the work that hours passed without noticing. This was not one of those days. The click and tap of the tools could only be drowned out by the recited verses that enhanced the *materiae* as she measured and mixed. Hunger was only driven away by the other ache. The corner of the room where Jeanne worked was ever in her awareness, tugging at the edges of her vision. When the tapping stopped, the silence echoed with her heartbeat. She paused in beginning to clear away the jars of *materiae*. Chair legs scraped across the stones, tearing the silence. She felt, rather than saw, Jeanne standing at her side and looked up at last. "What do we have?" Her voice creaked a little from long disuse.

"I think this is all of them," Jeanne said. "It was hard to clean the small ones completely. Six green, none larger than a pea. Two are something of a muddy brown; you didn't say what you wanted done with them. Only one true red but it's the largest."

Antuniet picked up the crimson stone and held it against the light from the window to check the clarity. No fractures or bubbles. No hazy patches where the fibers were misaligned. It was warm between her fingers and she could feel herself bending to the power it carried: softening, yearning. Her own art betrayed her. She shook off the influence. "There you are," she said bitterly. "Red jasper to cure pains of the heart and ensure love returned. Pure, perfect, flawless…and utterly false."

"It isn't false," Jeanne countered with quiet intensity. "It was never false, but it's never pure. That's where the poets lie to us. We're all of us impure mixtures and flawed gems." She snatched the jasper away and held it up. "There are no pure feelings. How can there be honor without the pride in keeping it? What does love mean without the courage to follow it? Bravery without wisdom is folly. Loyalty can't be only a fishhook on a slender line; it must be a thousand tiny stitches binding one heart to the other."

With a sudden swift movement she took up one of the empty crucibles from the bench and started scooping minerals into it from the open jars. "There's love; that's true." Five large scoops of the first and the jasper thrust into the midst of it. "But there's vanity as well." A spoon from the second. "And jealousy." A dusting from a smaller jar. "There's memory of loss and dreams unrealized. There's fear." She stirred the powders roughly with one of the small chisels that still lay on the tray. Traces of the colors swirled through the mixture like eddies in the river. "And there's pain." With a sudden movement she jabbed the chisel's tip into her finger and watched the drops of blood well up and fall. "There's always pain. It doesn't matter that it's often by my own hand." Jeanne thrust the crucible toward her.

Antuniet took it by reflex and Jeanne wrapped cold hands around her own to keep them there. "This is my heart: it is what you see. I don't know if it will come through the fire. But it's yours, if you will have it." Her voice was rough and low. She turned away abruptly and strode out of the room. The clatter of the door latch punctuated her departure.

Antuniet realized her hands were shaking with the strength of her grip on the crucible and she set it down on the workbench as if it were fragile crystal. It hadn't been an apology—not even an explanation. Only a plea for one more try. Could she bear to go through this again? *I needed bread and you offer me a stone!*

The two crucibles sat side by side. She should dump out the jumbled mixture and retrieve the jasper. That, at least, was a good day's work. But still she hesitated. She put little weight on signs and portents. It would never survive the firing—there was no hope of that. She didn't know which powders had gone into the mix, but certainly not the recipe for jasper. She paused with her fingers gripping the rim of the crucible but the thought of tipping the contents into the rubbish was unbearable.

This is my heart.

She didn't care for signs and portents. She could discard the ruined mixture and decide later what to do about Jeanne. The firing meant nothing. Either she was willing to forgive or she wasn't. If the answer were yes, then it wouldn't matter if the crucible burned to slaggy ruin like so many before. If the answer were no, then not even a perfect diamond would change her mind.

It's yours, if you will have it.

She feared to rely on signs and portents. What if it failed in the firing? She couldn't bear either path—couldn't bear the thought of never again feeling Jeanne's touch, couldn't bear to have her heart torn out time after time. She needed an answer. And it seemed a coward's trick not to try.

She stared at the jars of *materiae* still ranged along the bench, trying to remember which ones Jeanne had used. The whitesand? Or had it been lime? Some of the hematite, certainly, but how much? What process would bring them all into solution? No, not complete solution, for the jasper must be accounted for. Ceration, then. Strong waters to soften the jasper's nature without destroying it. Then in the outer spheres the heat and flux needed to conjoin the minerals into the salamander's blood, bathing the seed-stone with nourishment. As she measured and poured, the verses of the twinned cibation came to her lips. There was no partner to take the echo, but in her mind she heard the words in Jeanne's voice. Not Mercury this time. No king to join in the mystic marriage, only the twinned queens. Even as she worked she wondered at herself, as if watching from afar. This was no longer the Great Art but a form of madness.

At last she clamped the lid on tightly, took note of the position of sun and stars and marked the seals as best she could determine. The furnace had been ready for some time. She grasped the crucible in the tongs and cracked the door just enough to slide it in. *This time—this one time—give me the sight to find the alignments.* The heat made her eyes water as she turned the vessel in place bit by bit, as she had so often seen Margerit do. Was that only the waves of heat or had she seen… She moved it again, trying to follow patterns she wasn't sure of. And then—just when she despaired of being given a sign—the iridescent *fluctus* dazzled her eyes in a blinding flare.

Not daring to breathe, she withdrew the tongs and closed the door. Eight hours should be enough. She fed another scoop of coal into the back of the furnace and busied herself with putting things away and cleaning.

Time dragged as slowly now as it had earlier. She only noticed dark had fallen when Mefro Feldin poked her head in at leaving for the day, saying, "Was there anything else you were wanting?"

Antuniet's stomach growled. An honest pain this time. "Is there anything for supper?"

"If you wanted supper, you should have sent me out before the cookshop closed," she replied sourly. "There's a bit of cold pie in the pantry. I thought you'd be going to dinner with your friend like you always do."

"Never mind, the pie will do."

She settled in to read after that, timing the adding of coals to every ten pages. Sleep tugged at her and she found herself reading the same page over again. More coals. The book nearly slipped from her hands and she set it aside. More coals.

Dawn streamed through the window and she stretched stiffly…then came upright in a panic. The furnace! How long had she slept? She ran her hands just above the top, then tapped the iron door with a moistened fingertip. Cold. She thought she remembered hearing the midnight bells the last time she tended it. That should have been long enough.

Antuniet pulled the crucible out onto the workbench and took a deep breath before unclamping the lid, prepared for what she would see. The matrix was crusted and lumpy but not the glassy char of complete failure. She waited impatiently through the quenching, then tipped the crucible over and tapped the work gently onto the tiled benchtop. It fell out in a lump, crumbling a bit at the part that had been the bottom. She took up the smallest hammer and chisel and began chipping away at the matrix.

Hours later, what sat revealed was an irregular rounded mass like a baroque pearl, just a little smaller than her thumb. In the main it was the color of blood but there were shadows of other hues inside. The light glinted from a thousand tiny flakes and flaws in the stone and a thread of slag ran deeply through one lobe like a hidden vein. It should have shattered, but in her fingers it felt warm, like a living thing. What might it have been if she'd taken more care? *It is what you see.* That was her answer. She thought briefly of running through the streets to Jeanne's house. Of bringing her the heart-stone to show like a child with a toy. A shyness held her back. It was a sign; it needed the proper setting.

The pale autumn sun was reaching toward noon when her brisk steps brought her to Zempol Street. Monterrez's shop stood shuttered and dark and for a moment she was struck by dismay, until she recalled the day. The law set limits to what business could be done on a Sunday, even in the Jewish district. It set limits on an apprentice's Sunday hours as well but she often ignored those. Antuniet circled the block to come to the front steps of the residence and rang the bell. Anna answered it and, on seeing her, asked anxiously, "Did you need me today? You should have sent word."

"No, it's your father I've come to see, if I may. I have a commission for him."

A few minutes later, Monterrez took the stone from her and examined it with his customary care. "Not your usual work," he observed with a hint of reproof.

"An experiment. I'd like it set."

He raised his loupe again and turned it this way and that. "I could get two, maybe three good stones from it. They could be polished but I think they would shatter with faceting. Look there: what catches the light are a hundred tiny flaws. But something could be done. What style of setting did you have in mind?"

"No, no cutting. Leave it just as it is. I'd like to wear it as a pendant. Here." She touched her breast just under the hollow of her throat. "On a ribbon, I think. I haven't enough for a chain; there's been no time for tutoring since summer."

Monterrez looked up in surprise and calculation. "This will not be on Maisetra Sovitre's account?"

"No, nor the princess's. It's a personal matter." She drew out her thin purse. "I don't think I can manage gold, but silver will do."

He compressed his lips in thought and put his hand over hers. "Maisetra, keep your money."

"But—"

"The day will come," he continued quietly, "when I will ask you to make a special jewel for my Anna. That will be the payment for this. Leave the rest to me. It's a stone of power—" He made it a statement, not a question. "—so I will leave the setting as open as may be. When would you like it finished?"

Tonight! Before dawn, she thought, but that was scarcely reasonable. Tuesday would be the next of Margerit's lectures. She and Jeanne had planned to attend. She could wear the stone to speak where her voice might fail. "In two days, if it can be done."

He looked skeptical, but nodded.

On her way home, she heard singing as she passed the small church that served her neighbors. An impulse drew her in. She was careless about attending Mass and made the trek to Saint Mauriz's when she did, but she needed a place to think where her mind wouldn't echo in empty spaces. There was space on the last bench. She let the rhythms of the service set her mind adrift.

She had felt how the stone blended the chaotic strands into a whole: the jasper at its core, a trace of sapphire at one edge where the heat must have been stronger, overlying red balas. A trace of cloudiness in one lobe suggesting a vein of moonstone. Only the jasper should have been strong enough for its influence to be felt. It was as if the crystal as a whole lent the focus for each of its parts. No, not as a whole. The different stones had twined and grown together but she could see where the edges met. If not a single larger crystal, then they must reflect and magnify each other in some way. Could that be done more deliberately? She thought of the layered cibations. What if each layer could lend a different property? They would need to be added carefully in order; the heat needed for ruby would destroy lesser stones and the flux for carnelian would ruin peridot entirely unless something like jacinth were interposed. Some pairs she guessed could not be wedded at all. But if each layer could build on the last in some way… And then if it were possible to polish it down to a lenticular cabochon, exposing all the layers at once… Was it possible? Monterrez might know. At least he would try. She could return to the original lists she'd drawn up with Barbara's help. No need to try to set eight stones, only one eight-layered gem. And all the seed stones were likely in her hands already. *Oh Jeanne, you've given me the key,* she breathed in wonder. *Not pure, and yet more powerful for it.*

When the service ended, her footsteps home were the lightest she'd known in years.

In the morning the experiments began. The melding of the alternations must be perfect before she risked the good gems. Antuniet laughed suddenly as she explained it all to Anna. "Or, if not perfect, at least proven. We need to know which stones can be married together, which can be layered even without joining completely. But once I have those formulas and the ordering worked out, the entire set of stones might be finished in three weeks. Soon we'll have both furnaces to use."

"But there's barely six weeks in all until the new year. Will it be enough?" Anna asked.

"It will need to be," Antuniet replied more soberly.

The next day, Maistir Monterrez came himself to escort Anna home and to deliver the pendant. Antuniet waited until they had left before examining it; it seemed too private a thing.

The stone had been unsuitable to set with bezel or prongs. Instead he had cast a branching of slender threads, like ivy wrapping around a tree trunk. The gold flowed through the hollows and flaws in the stone, filling without concealing. He had followed her idea of suspending it from a ribbon, not to save the cost—for the clasp that closed it behind her neck was surely worth the price of a thin chain—but to keep the eye drawn to the stone itself. When she dressed—the rose gown, it must be the rose gown tonight—she fastened the ribbon carefully and let the stone fall against her skin. She felt it pulse briefly like the blood in her veins and then it was as if it had always lain there.

Antuniet arrived at the *salle* early. Too early to worry when Jeanne was nowhere in sight and yet she did worry. What if she decided not to come? She edged her way to where Margerit was standing at one side of the room, deep in conversation with a stranger. The woman was elegantly dark, perhaps another one of the French émigrés who had found refuge in Rotenek during the war? But no—though they were speaking in French, she had an accent of Italy, not that of the far Antilles like Mefro Dominique's.

"Antuniet!" Margerit called on spotting her. "Come, you must meet Maisetra Talarico. She's come all the way from Rome to discuss mysteries with me."

Antuniet curtseyed. "*Buona sera, Signora*." But she returned immediately to French for Margerit's sake. "Do you know if Jeanne will be here? We had—" How much did she know?

Enough, it seemed. With a stricken look Margerit began, "I don't know, but you needn't—" And then looking past her shoulder, "Oh. Here she is."

Antuniet hardly needed the warning. The gem at her throat had warmed suddenly and she reached up to caress it without thinking.

"What an unusual jewel," the stranger exclaimed. "What is it?"

Antuniet turned, meeting Jeanne's anxious gaze. The moment stretched out in silence, as if everyone else in the chamber had faded and only they two remained. When she spoke at last to answer the question, it was Jeanne the answer was meant for. "It's a heart that was given into my keeping," she said.

Jeanne's eyes flicked to the pendant, then back to Antuniet's face. Her lips parted as if she would speak but no words came.

Antuniet released the gem and reached out to intertwine her fingers with Jeanne's. They would try again, and again, if necessary. Not from the beginning; there was no way through but forward.

"It came through the fire," she said. "Flawed, but whole. Perhaps we will too."

She could not remember later what the lectures covered. All she knew was that the speakers had been Akezze and two younger women from the Poor-Scholars whose depth of knowledge and teaching skill could not be satisfied by the opportunities that had come their way. The evening was filled with the constant awareness of Jeanne at her side. Jeanne's leg touching hers. Jeanne's eyes constantly seeking her own. Jeanne's heart beating in close time with her own. And later…she did not return home that night.

* * *

The initial experiments were more successful than she had dared hope. The principle was sound; only the specific formulas need be devised. Soon she would need to assemble the full array of assistants again. And there were roles that still needed filling. A second for the *virgo* role. Perhaps Margerit would know someone.

The men hired to guard against any tricks Kreiser might try had faded to near invisibility, except for occasional crowding in the back corridors and that constant intangible sense of male presence, for good or ill. But one morning Antuniet was made suddenly aware of Perteld's presence—or was it Paldek? She still had trouble sorting the two out. Whichever had answered, an argument at the front entry disturbed the calculations for weighing and measuring. Antuniet saw Anna flinch—then try to conceal it—and touched her arm for reassurance as she rose to see to the commotion.

"And I say you have no business with Maisetra Chazillen or I'd know about it."

He was facing down a furtive-looking man in a frieze coat and low slouched hat. Not a tradesman, nor in service that one could tell, but by his manner a messenger.

"What is it?" she asked sharply, giving no instruction to let the man past.

"You're Chazillen?" The messenger must have seen some disapproval on Perteld's face sufficient to amend it to, "You're Maisetra Chazillen?"

She nodded. His open approach argued against a threat. True danger would either come secretly or wearing a uniform. She hadn't entirely lost the fear that Kreiser would gain Annek's ear and turn the princess against her.

The messenger stepped back and spoke as if by rote. "My employer, Maistir Langal, has some information that could be to your advantage, should you care to speak with him."

Now that was unexpected. She hadn't spoken to the debt-monger since that time a year past when he had declined to finance her, for which she was still grateful. What would he want in exchange for this information? The message was surprising enough not to be ignored. "When might he be available? Shall I come to his office this afternoon?"

The man shook his head violently. "He says not to come openly. Can you be at Saint Mauriz's—the chapel of Saint Mihail—at the evening bells?"

Antuniet nodded with relief. That was public enough and unremarkable. But what could call for such subterfuge?

* * *

Saint Mihail's mysteries had become unfashionable in the last century so there was small chance of being disturbed or overheard. In the chill shadows of the small chapel Langal came quickly to the point. "Your Austrian friend has people poking around into the question of what debts or scandals may have attached themselves to you and—curiously enough—to Baron Razik. And because there was a question of debts, naturally he came to me."

A blade of fear twisted in her gut. The feeling had once been as familiar as the embrace of an old friend. She hadn't realized she'd ceased being afraid all the time until now, when it returned. Debt had been the wound through which Estefen's honor had bled out. And all the other disasters had flowed from that. She'd been so careful. Scandal, he'd said as well. She felt suddenly light-headed and hoped Langal couldn't see. That was her own wound. "I have no debts to anyone but friends," she answered, avoiding the other.

"Oh, he found no stain on you that I know of," Langal said. "Your friend Razik has been more careless though. Debts...well, nothing worse than any young man might accumulate if he didn't care to confess his vices to his mother. The occasional poor choice of companions. And it seems he has been somewhat careless in his correspondence. Some indiscreet letters to a lady, promising things he should not have offered...the man I spoke with revealed more than he learned, I fear. He seemed to think there might be other entanglements to be found and that was how your name came up. The baron has been spending a great deal of time in your company..."

Antuniet almost laughed at the thought, but the noise would have drawn attention. "I can't think of a place less likely for illicit amours than my workshop!" *Except my own.*

Langal shrugged. "I have—" He gave a self-deprecating cough. "—made the investment of securing the more material assets involved. But it might be good for the baron's friends to take measures to protect his good name."

"You have the letters?" Antuniet asked sharply.

He laughed. "I was referring to the debts. No, from what I know the letters are still in the lady's hands at the moment. Some connection of one of the young men at the Austrian embassy."

Antuniet's mind raced, trying to untangle what purpose Kreiser might have. Was he still trying to secure his interests with Annek? Or had his tenders toward Elisebet been more than a feint after all? This was Barbara's realm, not hers, and she had no power to protect her own reputation, much less Efriturik's. Barbara. With that thought the puzzle fell into a more recognizable shape. "What do you want in exchange for this information? As I recall, you offer nothing freely."

Langal made only a fleeting show of offended innocence. "I put you onto Monterrez for no return."

She couldn't contradict that without explaining the carnelian talisman. "That was one; I hardly expect two."

He made no further protest. "There is a...a business matter that I would like to discuss with your cousin the baroness. She is unlikely to...We did not part on good terms in our last encounter. You would do me a great favor if you could gain me a hearing with her."

Barbara might grant it simply for her asking; she didn't know whether she could presume on their seedling friendship that far. But the warning about Efriturik—that was good coin in trade. She'd seen the impulse in Barbara, half guardian, half bully, that had drawn her own fate willy-nilly into her cousin's ambit. She knew it had been cast over Efriturik as well. Barbara would jump at the chance to meddle in his problems. And she suspected that Langal knew that from the first. This wasn't a compliment to her own influence over her cousin, only to her value as a go-between. "I will arrange it," she answered confidently.

CHAPTER THIRTY

Margerit

A dinner party could not be arranged in only one or two days, Margerit concluded, and certainly not when she was anxious to impress. It was nearly a week after she was first introduced to Serafina Talarico before she felt able to provide her a proper welcome to Rotenek.

"I've been in your city for nearly a month now," Signora Talarico pointed out cheerfully over the *potage d'Evrevisses*. "I had meant to arrive in time for your patron's *tutela*, the one you wrote about so brilliantly."

"But you were there to see the All Saints *castellum*," Barbara noted from the far end of the table.

They were eight tonight, for her aunt and uncle had taken the excuse to dine with the Pertineks, thinking to leave the scholars to themselves. Antuniet and Jeanne had made the time to come. Akezze had struck up an acquaintance already and was helping Signora Talarico find more suitable lodgings. To fill out the numbers, Margerit had invited the two of her old guild-sisters from the Atelpirts that she still met socially: Ainis Nantoz and Iosifin Rezik.

"You noticed me there?" Signora Talarico asked in surprise.

It would be hard not to notice her, Margerit thought. Signora Talarico's striking looks turned heads every time she entered a room. It wasn't that unusual to see darker skins in the western edge of the city or around the wharves, but far less common in the concert halls and salons.

"I notice anyone who takes such a keen interest in Maisetra Sovitre," Barbara said. "I've been watching for you since then."

"You mustn't mind Barbara," Jeanne added with a laugh. "She used to be Margerit's armin and she never lets down her guard."

Signora Talarico looked confused but the arrival of the salmon intervened.

"So you must tell us your story!" Iosifin urged. "However did Margerit's work come into your hands?" It was what Margerit had longed to ask as well, though manners had restrained her.

"My husband," Signora Talarico began, "was an assistant librarian in Rome at the Vatican. He is still, I suppose. The appointment still stands; his stipend is still paid. They took on a great many assistants when the archives started arriving back from Paris after the wars and no one keeps much track of who comes and goes. I was working with him and when he disappeared I simply kept up his tasks and no one thought anything of it."

"Disappeared?" Antuniet asked sharply.

Signora Talarico threw up her hands in amused exasperation. "He does that from time to time: a manuscript to track down, a question regarding interpretation on which he must consult. Sometimes he returns; sometimes he simply sends a letter to tell me where he's settled. The last time, I waited in Palermo ten months before he summoned me to join him back in Rome. When he needs me, he finds me. Marrying me was cheaper than hiring a clerk, he says. So it happened that I was sorting out all manner of arriving documents— ones that weren't part of the main shipments—and that was how I found your sketches and notes. When I had read through your analysis five times I knew I must find the scholar who wrote it even if it took years. But fortunately it was not nearly so difficult. Most of the time was spent in concluding my affairs in Rome and arranging to travel. But to find someone with so much promise, so much insight…there is so much to learn." She sighed. "For that I would travel to the ends of the earth."

Margerit could feel herself blushing at the praise. Even in the brief conversations she'd had with Signora Talarico she had seen the woman's sharp mind. "I can only be grateful that you came all this way to teach me," she said.

"Teach you? Heavens no, *cara mia*, I'm here to be your pupil, not your teacher! Do you know how impossible it is for a woman to study thaumaturgy in Italy? If I were interested in literature or languages that would be one matter, but anything touching on theology? My husband promised to teach me, but it is always tomorrow or next year. Your papers…they spoke to me. I have seen wondrous visions and felt the touch of angels' wings, but I want to know how to use the skill. And so I have come to you."

The evening reminded Margerit of nothing so much as those glorious days before the guild was betrayed. Throughout dinner the air was filled with the names of ancient authors and quotations known by heart. By the time the meringues and jellies were served, she had ventured once to address her visitor as Serafina, though it seemed too soon for such familiarity. Even Antuniet and Ainis had regained something of their old camaraderie. "I wish every day could be like this!" she sighed aloud.

"Would that it could be so," Akezze replied rather dryly.

"What I think she means," Antuniet added, "is that conversation may fill the soul but not the belly."

"Though I have more than enough work for the moment," Akezze hastened to add. "Thanks to your help. Who will be the next speaker for your *salon d'academie*?"

Margerit made a dismissive gesture at so grand a name for her little project, then said on impulse, "Perhaps Signora Talarico would favor us?" She explained how the lectures had started and grown.

"And when will we see your English botanist again?" Jeanne asked.

"Maisetra Collfield promised to visit next fall and bring me a copy of her book. It should be published in the summer, she thinks. By then I hope to have found a better home for the events. The *Salle-Chapil* is in such demand during the high season and it's really too large now that the novelty has cooled."

"A pity you didn't keep the guildhall," Iosifin said and immediately seemed to regret it, as a brief chill settled over the room.

"No, that was impossible," Barbara said. "And you were lucky to find a buyer for it. But why not ask at the university? The lecture halls aren't used in the evening as a general rule. See if they'd let you hire the Chasintalle."

"Now what did I tell you back at floodtide," Akezze said with a laugh, turning to Antuniet. "A second Fortunatus!" At Serafina's befuddled look she explained, "Do you know the story of how Rotenek University was founded? Fortunatus the mystic—you're familiar with his writings? He wasn't able to travel to Paris or Bologna to study but he corresponded with scholars across Europe and one by one teachers came to him, either to embrace his theories or to try to refute them. And once they came, they sought out other students for their keep. And those students attracted other teachers. They began with lectures out in the Plaiz Vezek where the old marketplace was, but then Prince Chonratus built the Chasintalle, with its lecture hall and dormitories and it grew from there."

Margerit covered her embarrassment at the comparison to Fortunatus by countering, "I'll inquire at the university, but I don't know that it would be suitable. I want to encourage the young women to come—the ones who aren't as bold as we were—and they may not be allowed to travel south of the river in the evening."

"The young women of good families, you mean," Akezze added. "Many of those who would benefit most already live there."

"Speaking of young women," Antuniet said, "I'll be needing a few more assistants once we start the final work. Margerit, I don't suppose you could find me someone to twin Anna for the *virgo* role? Anna doesn't think her younger sister has the steadiness to learn the parts."

At first Margerit's thoughts flicked to Iosifin and Ainis, but when a woman had reached the advanced age of thirty unmarried, it was no longer safe to assume that she was therefore untouched. And it was a question that would be unthinkable to ask directly. But then, with her mind on girls with missed opportunities, she offered, "Perhaps Valeir Perneld. She's only in her first dancing season, so she should have the time. I met her at Saint Orisul's this summer. She has some sensitivity to *fluctus*, if that would be helpful. She thinks her parents wouldn't allow her to take classes, but this would be different. And you're planning to do the new cibations at the palace workshop, yes? Then there should be no objection. I'll ask if Her Grace would be willing to make the invitation; that would be impossible to refuse."

"Margerit, you'll become a politician yet!" Jeanne teased. "Now could we adjourn to the drawing room? I recall that you keep a very fine port and since we've banished the men, we can be comfortably scandalous together."

The evening couldn't last forever, though it continued long past the time when Margerit heard her aunt and uncle return.

After the guests were gone and they had retired upstairs, Margerit asked, "Barbara, what was it you were discussing so seriously with Antuniet? You had your heads together in the corner for half an hour."

Barbara grimaced. "Do you recall Langal? The man who was pursuing Arpik's debts?"

Margerit nodded. It was awkward for Barbara to discuss the man she had once thought her father: Arpik or Count Turinz or sometimes "my mother's husband." Arpik's debts had set the whole course of Barbara's life in motion, and Langal's efforts to collect on them had been at once subtle and brutal. He'd hoped to goad Barbara into uncovering her true parentage while there was still time to link Arpik's notes to Saveze's wealth. He'd failed in that but the marks remained, both on her mind and body. Barbara rubbed absently at the scar on her temple that lay half-concealed under a wave of her tawny hair as she continued, "It seems he has some business to discuss with me. And as an earnest of good faith he passed on a warning about some mischief that Efriturik became tangled in."

"But what is that to you?" Margerit asked. "You aren't Efriturik's armin. It's not your responsibility to chase around pulling him out of scrapes."

"It's not that type of scrape. But why wouldn't it be my responsibility? He could be our next prince. Don't we all have the duty to have a care for his reputation? Especially in the face of foreign meddling? Yes, it seems Kreiser is tangled in this too. I doubt the goal was to bring him down. More likely to set a hook in him. But I'd find a way to thwart Kreiser for no other reason than satisfaction. The man irritates me."

"Be careful," Margerit warned, but she said no more than that. Barbara was cautious enough, except when honor drove her. And if it were a matter of honor, no warning would make a difference.

* * *

Margerit had seen the palace workshop before but it had seemed cold and hollow while the construction was in progress. This evening it felt inhabited and alive, from the gleaming tile on the benchtops to the shelves crowded with bottles and apothecary jars. And in the center of the room stood the engineers' masterpiece: the great revolving furnace, with its wheels and gears standing ready to align the work to the fraction of a degree. The floor tiles radiated from it in a compass rose but that was just for show, as were the chased zodiacal designs on the gears. "Antuniet," she breathed, "it's beautiful!"

Antuniet looked up briefly from where she was sifting powders. "That wasn't my choice, but I'm not paying the workmen's fees, so they can dress it up however they like, as long as it works. Anna, could you check the copper? I'm not sure we have enough of the triple-distilled for tomorrow."

Margerit traded her coat for a pinafore and tied a scarf around her hair. "But it's still beautiful. Doesn't that speak to how much Her Grace values your work?" She knew Antuniet still had sleepless nights worrying the gift would be found wanting.

The answer was one of Antuniet's self-effacing shrugs. "It could all be nothing more than a show for others. Why else go to all this length before I've proven myself? But the equipment functions; that's what matters. We ran a simple process yesterday to test the alignment and it's as precise as even your *visitatio* could make it."

And tomorrow they would begin the first of the layered *cibations*. Antuniet had chosen to perform that work here, leaving the workshop on Trez Cherfis for testing the marriage of the layers. Margerit looked back toward the door. "I thought Jeanne was close behind me. Should I—" But the sound of several voices through the thick oak answered her as it swung open.

"But Jeanne, I scarcely see you anymore! Elin and I have the evening off and we were all going over to Ermilint's to play cards."

And not just Tio and Elin, but Iaklin as well, Margerit saw. How annoying. Antuniet muttered in disgust, "Tionez!" barely low enough to go unheard.

"Antuniet," Tio demanded. "Let Jeanne come with us just this once! You're too selfish with her time."

She was answered with Antuniet's familiar cool, half-mocking stare. "Mesnera Perzin, I assure you that the vicomtesse always does exactly as she pleases and needs no permission from me."

Margerit would have thought that they'd quarreled again but for Antuniet's gesture: a brief movement of her hand to caress the scarlet pendant that now always hung at her throat. And she almost missed Jeanne's response: the barest touch of her fingertips to her lips. She might only have been covering a cough. The coolness had been for Tionez, not for Jeanne. As if nothing out of the ordinary had passed, Jeanne said, "Not tonight, Tio. There's no time for anything but alchemy this week. But we're promised to Verneke Albori's ball. You're invited, I assume?"

Margerit moved to draw away the uninvited visitors. "Have you seen the lovely tile work they've done over here? Mesnera Perzin, are you enjoying your new position? I confess I've always thought Princess Elisebet to be something of a dragon!"

Tionez saw through the ploy but there was little she could do, so she laughed and answered, "Not her, it's Sain-Mazzi who's the dragon. I wouldn't cross her if I valued my head. And I think poor Chustin is terrified of her." She idly picked up a dark green bottle that was standing on the bench to show to Iaklin. Antuniet moved swiftly to remove it from her grasp.

"Don't touch that unless you care to have your pretty skin stripped off like a butchered rabbit." She replaced it farther from the edge. "And I don't know why it should be 'poor Chustin.' There's little enough in his life to pity."

"No? Elisebet is so terrified he'll come to harm that she barely lets him set foot outside her apartments." She lowered her voice conspiratorially. "His tutor's been taking him out into the city when his mother's not around. I helped them sneak out last week to go up the river past the Port Ausiz to see the horse fair. Not that Elisebet has forbidden it directly, of course. No one would dare act against her orders if that were the case. But the way they cosset him! He's mad for stories of foreign lands. The greatest treat he can imagine would be to go down to the wharves and see all the barges and the sailors at the Nikuleplaiz. And she thinks he can be fobbed off with picture books!"

Margerit had been gently herding the three visitors toward the doors, which Marken helpfully opened as they approached. "It's been so lovely that you could stop by and see the new workshop. Maybe next time you can start a new fashion for grinding ores." And in the pause it took for Tionez's face to twist in distaste, she and her friends found themselves standing on the other side with the door politely closed in their faces.

Margerit leaned against it for a moment as if anticipating a renewed assault. "That was one thing we weren't bothered with at Trez Cherfis," she said to the room at large. "Do you think we'll become the latest curiosity?" But no answer was expected or needed and they set to work.

* * *

Days later, Margerit struggled to shake off a haze of fury as she strode through the front door at Tiporsel, only vaguely noticing the footman's scramble to open it before her. As she struggled with her gloves, a clatter of footsteps heralded Brandel's descent to the foyer.

"Oh!" he said in disappointment. "I thought it was Cousin Barbara."

Margerit bit back a sharp reply. Her mood wasn't his fault. She still wasn't accustomed to the noise and chaos a boy his age brought into the house. Not that she and Barbara hadn't produced chaos on their own a time or two. "I don't think she means to be home before dinner." The gloves dropped onto the side table, followed by her bonnet. Dealing with the faculty masters had not only been unproductive but had made her late. She crossed to the parlor and poked her head in, feeling guilty until she saw Aunt Bertrut entertaining her guest. "Signora Talarico? I'm so sorry I wasn't here when you arrived." She crossed the room and gave her aunt a brief embrace. "Thank you for playing hostess for me. We'll be in the library for the rest of the afternoon, I think."

Her guest waited patiently as Margerit cleared the small library table and spread out the *expositulum* for the All Saints mystery—not the one they had celebrated just recently but the original, fuller ceremony that the Guild of Saint Atelpirt had developed. Her movements must have betrayed the lingering anger, for Serafina observed, "I think it did not go well at the university?"

"No." Margerit looked up and dropped all pretense. "They said—" She searched in memory for the precise words to give proper force. "They said that Rotenek University had stood for seven hundred years without the disgrace of allowing a woman to lecture in the Chasintalle and they were disinclined to break with that tradition." She sighed. "I'll find another place. LeFevre—my property manager—he's been keeping an eye open."

"But have they forgotten their history?" Serafina asked. "I thought that the famous Tanfrit had been named a *doctora* at Rotenek."

"I didn't know that," Margerit said. Her curiosity was stirred. "Where did you hear that story?"

"I don't recall; some old correspondence? I read so many things. Perhaps it's as much a myth as Pope Joan. Your university should know, I would think. Now show me what you've done here. When I saw the celebration at the cathedral I could see the...what did you call it? The *fluctus*? But I couldn't tell how the ceremony called it forth."

They worked through the towers and walls of the *castellum* and then began the comparison to the revised ceremony. Serafina was quick to follow the logic and question a detail here, a phrasing there. But when she called for paper and began to sketch out a design of her own, Margerit hesitated. "I'd prefer to wait until Barbara can join us." She reached for an explanation when Serafina looked doubtful. "The mysteries...we always work on them together. She has an instinct for the larger questions. Not about how the ceremonies work but about how to use them in the world. And it's always been a special time between us; I wouldn't feel right to exclude her."

Serafina sat back and cocked her head curiously, setting the long ringlets of her hair to swaying. "Tell me. The *accademicas* of Rotenek—are many of them lovers of women?"

Margerit was too startled for words and could only gape at her.

"Perhaps I must beg your pardon. Is this something that isn't spoken of? I only thought...You were so open at the dinner. You and your baroness, and the alchemist and her friend, but not, I think, the other two. But you must tell me if I have gone beyond what is proper."

It would be bad enough if she becomes known for saying scandalous things, Margerit thought, *but worse if it sets other tongues to wagging*. As delicately as she could, she explained, "If a woman is granted the reputation of an Eccentric, society does not question too closely the details of her life. But it would be another matter to have vulgar accusations attached to her name openly. That becomes a matter of honor. And matters of honor are still sometimes settled with swords." She searched Signora Talarico's face to see if she had properly understood.

A thoughtful expression replaced the curiosity. "I see. It is quite the other way around in Rome. Everyone's vices are discussed openly in the marketplace

278   Heather Rose Jones

but practiced in private. I had a lover once who was the most notorious sapphist in the city, but she would never say so much as *buongiorno* to me if we met on the street and I could never be seen to enter her palazzo. Though perhaps that was only me," she added wistfully.

"But I thought you were married!" Margerit blurted without thought.

Serafina laughed. "What has that to do with the matter? I must amuse myself somehow when my husband's away! But I see I will need to change the manner of my discretion. I promise I will try not to embarrass you or say anything that would require your baroness to challenge me to a duel!"

Margerit returned to arranging the papers to cover her confusion. She was accustomed to such matters being understood without being acknowledged. Was it truly so obvious to a stranger that she and Barbara were lovers? Or was it only if that stranger were a sister in spirit? Signora Talarico would be granted some license as a foreigner, and a more than ordinarily exotic one at that. But if she meant to remain in Rotenek for long, she was correct that she'd need to learn to hold her tongue.

Margerit ventured one piece of advice. "You might do well to become better acquainted with the Vicomtesse de Cherdillac—Antuniet's friend. She knows better than the rest of us how to play that game safely. Now would you like me to have a copy made for you of any of the *expositula*? You may come here to study them if you please, but between my own classes and helping with Antuniet's work, I don't keep to the usual social hours." And the matter seemed settled between them after that.

* * *

The stones for the presentation were being worked at the palace, but there were still more firings than could be done in one furnace: seed stones to be grown, further experiments to refine the layered cibations like today's work. Those could still be fit into the cramped quarters at Trez Cherfis. Even without the full crew for the twinned processes, the old workshop felt so crowded now. It was several minutes before Margerit sorted through the crowd of attendants in the front room to realize that only Anna, Jeanne and Efriturik were there. "Where's Antuniet? Will she be back soon?"

"I thought perhaps she'd been out early to see you," Jeanne said. "Anna found no one here when she arrived but the housekeeper."

"And does she know anything more?" Margerit asked.

Efriturik shrugged. "She said nothing to me or to Maisetra Monterrez."

Margerit leaned out into the hallway, calling, "Mefro Feldin!" toward the back of the house, where sounds of bustle could be heard.

The housekeeper put in her appearance after a delay just short of insolence, saying, "What did you want, Maisetra?"

"Maisetra Chazillen. Do you know where she's gone?"

The housekeeper shrugged. "It isn't my business to keep track of her comings and goings." And then, just as she was on the point of leaving, she fished a folded message out of her apron pocket. "I suppose this might say."

"Why didn't you give that to me at the start!" Anna cried in frustration.

Feldin looked her up and down. "You didn't ask," she snapped. "And I don't take orders from the likes of you."

"Feldin!" Margerit said sharply.

She turned, only slightly abashed. "Begging your pardon, Maisetra Sovitre, if you'll excuse me, I have work to do."

"What a sour old thing!" Jeanne said as she broke the seal on the folded note. "Why do you allow her such insolence? I wonder that you've kept her on this long."

"It isn't the easiest thing to find someone willing to do for an alchemist," Margerit said with a sigh. "Not in this neighborhood. She was the best I could find and Antuniet seems to rub along with her well enough."

Jeanne scanned the brief lines of the message. "Well, there's an end to the work we planned today. She's off to Iser. Something about a barge and a shipment and a dispute. She says she expects to be back in time for the working tomorrow afternoon."

"To Iser!" Efriturik exclaimed. "Half a day's travel each way. Surely she could have sent someone else."

"Could we do the experiment without her?" Margerit asked. "Anna, you've taken charge before. You could direct us."

Anna shook her head. "Not this one. Maisetra Chazillen didn't have specific plans. She meant to use your *visio* to adjust the fusion of amethyst over garnet. It's tricky because the crystals are such different shapes. We could do a different formula, I suppose, but I can't think of any that we need."

Jeanne had been frowning over Antuniet's note again, but now a faint grin crept across her face. "I have the very thing. Anna, could you fetch DeBoodt? You can read his codes, can't you? And those handlists we drew up over the summer. There's a process that Antuniet and I did once, just the two of us. Surely we could work through it with what we have."

Anna brought the book up from the basement lock-room and Jeanne went hunting through the notes until she found her goal. "Here it is!" she said in triumph, reading out the rubric. "*An enhancement of beryl to make the bearer tranquil and well-mannered and not always at odds with those around him.*" She looked up at the others with a mischievous smile. "Do you suppose we know anyone who would benefit from the effects of such a stone?"

Efriturik was the first to catch her meaning and frowned. "Better than a waste of time, but if you and Chazillen worked it together, then you will have no need of me. Send word when there's real work to do again."

After he left, Anna ran her finger over the list of *materiae*. "I suppose... we could do it easily enough. Everything we need is here in the shop. And the roles...With the three of us we could even add this elaboration to the enhancement: *To turn discord into friendship.*"

They set to with an air of children playing in the absence of their governess, or apprentices given their first solo project. But as the work progressed from measuring powders to the diagrams and spoken parts of the enhancement, seriousness returned. The process took most of the morning, for there had been nothing prepared in advance. And then a few hours delay to begin the firing to wait for the best conjunction to come into alignment. With the crucible finally in the furnace, Jeanne said, "Anna and I can tend it for the remaining time. And if she gives me instructions, I can do the quenching in the morning without troubling the two of you. My first transformation!"

At the end, a shadow of doubt crossed Margerit's thoughts. Had they done right to craft such an amulet on their own? But Anna had said nothing against it once they were begun and she would know best what Antuniet's opinion would be.

CHAPTER THIRTY-ONE

Jeanne

"That will do nicely. Thank you, Marien," Jeanne said as the last curl was pinned in place. "And for the gown, I think the green with the rouleaux at the hem. What do you think, Toneke?" she asked without turning her head. "I shall be the leaf and you the rose tonight." She gazed into her dressing table mirror, watching as Antuniet slipped on the thin cotton chemise and then stood waiting for Marien to have time to assist with the corset. Too frank an admiring stare still put her ill at ease but that was no reason not to enjoy the sight.

Jeanne smiled as those long limbs disappeared under the froth of white cambric. Antuniet was no longer so painfully thin as she had been half a year ago. Dressing, too, had become one of their rituals. It had seemed only sensible for Antuniet to begin keeping her best gowns here at the house, where they could be properly cared for. She never went out in the evening without coming here first, so there was no reason to forego Marien's help. Undressing…they could manage that by themselves.

Jeanne turned from the mirror and reached out to catch Antuniet's fingers. Nothing more; not until they were in private together later. "You're quiet tonight. I hope you don't regret agreeing to come. I know you have little use for balls, but if you aspire to be the royal alchemist you can't avoid them entirely. What's worrying you?"

"Not that." It was no denial. She fingered the scarlet pendant at her throat, sparking a familiar shiver. "Jeanne…do you ever feel…compelled?"

That called for more tangible reassurance. Jeanne pulled Antuniet's hand to her lips, heedless of the witness. "Only by your radiant beauty."

Antuniet flinched as she always did at compliments. "I'm serious," she said, as she pulled away. "I can feel that the stone has power. Does it have power over you?"

Did it matter? "You know I loved you long before this," she said, stroking the gem with a fingertip. She watched Antuniet blush in turn, as if some more hidden place had been touched. "What is it that worries you?"

"That stone that you made for Mefro Feldin. I know you all meant well by it, but I wish you hadn't."

Jeanne released Antuniet's hand and stood to let Marien drape the gown over her head. "Why not? I should think you would appreciate the change. Even I could see the effects."

"It worked well enough," Antuniet said ruefully. "Oh Jeanne, I…I think it was wrong. Not wrong to influence her so, but to do it without her knowledge. To lie to her. You said it was a good luck charm."

"You haven't the same qualms about the rings you're making for Annek." Jeanne could hear a peevish tone in her voice and hastened to amend it. "I'm sorry. Of course I should have asked."

"The rings are different. Those who receive them will know what is intended. And I know I've used amulets before for my own benefit. But those had only a passing influence on those around me. Jeanne, I can't deny I wish Feldin were more pleasant, but she has the right to her own thoughts."

"I'd grant her the right to her thoughts more gladly if she kept them more to herself!" Did she deserve even so mild a rebuke? "Don't blame the others; it was entirely my idea. So did you tell her?"

Antuniet shook her head. "How could I? I told her it had been a mistake—a misunderstanding. That it had been a different stone I'd meant to give her. I offered her one of the layered stones: carbuncle sheathed in fluorspar. It should be harmless enough. It gives a blue light when heated long enough and the only enhancement was to increase the sensitivity so that even the warmth of a hand will set it off. It was enough to convince her it had power. But she thought I'd accused her of theft and I had much to do to soothe her sensibilities."

It was not the best foot on which to start the evening. Antuniet had agreed to the invitation to the Alboris' ball only because her schedule allowed it and she knew the usefulness of being seen in society. But Jeanne knew there would be little enough to entertain her. The balls held in the Grand Salle were the backbone of the season. Not public balls; nothing so gauche. Each had its different host and flavor. Each was held nominally in honor of some son or daughter standing on the brink of adulthood, though the true purpose was simply the business of society. Each had its own list of guests: old and young, established and fresh, from high to…well, to the middle, at least. And always that flower of Rotenek's best families, without whom no affair could be considered successful. The balls flowed gently into each other like the renewed conversation of old friends. Maisetra Albori's guest list leaned toward the artistic set and the old middle-class families that had produced her daughter's school friends. For once, Jeanne hadn't needed to hint for an invitation for Antuniet. Verneke had known her long enough that such things needn't be said.

They arrived in the midst of the crush and their hostess passed them off apologetically to Count Chanturi, who had been making his own bows just before and who offered an arm to each of them for the slow promenade through the new arrivals to the rooms beyond.

"Rikerd, you must know Maisetra Chazillen, I'm sure," Jeanne said, though it was impossible that they hadn't met years ago.

"I'm quite familiar with the Chazillens of old." There was an odd note in his voice. "And I've been hearing a great deal about you lately. The alchemy, of course." He turned back. "Far more than I've been hearing of you, Jeanne. No parties, no pleasure drives or other schemes, no new flirtations. What have you been up to?"

She gave him a sharp look, but accepted his pretense of ignorance. "Why, alchemy, of course! I have a new pastime, you see."

He gave Antuniet another speculative look, saying, "You always did have the knack for turning dross into gold." But before Antuniet could do more than stare, he laughed apologetically. "Forgive me, Maisetra Chazillen! One might think I meant to slight you by that! It's only my feeble wit seeking a target. Perhaps I should take it elsewhere and leave you to better company." He released them at the door of the ballroom with a nod to both and a promise to claim a dance if they would allow.

They made their way at last to the edge of the dance floor where the press of the crowd was greatest. After some searching, Jeanne spotted Tio by the punchbowl. But for all her pouting at being neglected it was scarcely ten minutes before she exclaimed, "Oh! There's Alenur!" and darted off across the length of the *salle*. Well, there was no value in what one had, only what one desired. Mesnera Arulik provided a space of entertainment, amusing them with *bon mots* from her most recent salon. "You really should have come," she chided them both, though Jeanne could tell it was aimed more at her.

"Count Chanturi was right, you know," Antuniet said as they worked their way slowly through the crowd.

"Hmm?"

"You haven't been planning entertainments. I always loved hearing you talk about them, even if I would have been bored to tears to attend. I hope you haven't given that up for me." Antuniet paused where a delicate windowed bay jutted out, enclosing an indoor garden. "Let me sit here for a bit while you find some hapless hostess to draw into your schemes. Come find me when you want a spot of quiet, or when it's time to go in for supper."

"Are you sure you aren't sorry you came?" At a shake of Antuniet's head, Jeanne reached out and touched the heart-stone pendant, then pressed her finger to her lips. "You are always with me." It was hard to accept that the merry crowds that were her lifeblood sent Antuniet fleeing into corners, but they were coming to a truce.

With that permission, Jeanne looked across the room and saw Maisetra Saltez watching the dancing from a cluster of other mothers and *vizeinos*. There was someone who'd be glad of her hand in things. Last year's skating party had been a wild success. She made her way idly around the edge of the dance floor, nodding as she passed acquaintances, pausing to exchange a word with friends, until she came as if by chance to her goal.

"Mari Saltez, how lovely to see you again. I hear that charming son of yours has his commission at last. Will he be able to visit you before the end of the year or is he trapped in some dreary camp, drilling recruits?"

Maisetra Saltez turned with a little start. "Vicomtesse! I didn't see you. No, we won't be seeing him for months, I fear." She glanced back at the dancers nervously.

Jeanne followed her gaze. Well, that was enough to make a mother anxious. Chazerin was dancing in the arms of Perrez Chalfin. And the glances and shy blushes that passed between them suggested it might grow to more than a passing entertainment. Quite a prize if she could bring him to the gate. "Such a lovely dancer," she murmured. "Do you know the family well?"

"A little," came the answer. "My husband was at school with his uncle many years ago. He died at the very end of the war, you know—the uncle. But young Perrez remembered he'd said some very kind things and procured an introduction on the strength of it."

On such slender threads were alliances woven. Likely the uncle had done little more than mention a name, but Chazerin's blossoming radiance was reason enough to stretch the truth. And what match couldn't use assistance? "Your little skating party was quite the rage last year. What are you planning to surpass it, now that Chazerin is fully out?"

"Nothing more than the usual." Her answer almost sounded as if meant to be quelling. But she was distracted, that was all.

"Oh, but it's so dull with always the usual. And it's really very easy to change this and that and be more memorable. If you wanted a few hints—"

"Vicomtesse de Cherdillac," the woman said with audible hesitation, "you needn't trouble yourself."

"It would be little enough trouble. I must keep my hand in, you know."

"Mesnera, please. I do not think your plans would do my daughter credit. I bid you good evening," the woman said and turned away.

Jeanne stared at her departing back with her lips parted just short of a gape. She had still found no suitable reply when Count Chanturi came up behind her to whisper, "I do believe that was a cut."

"It must have been. But whatever could have brought that on, Rikerd? I can't think of anything I've done to slight her."

"Can't you guess?" Chanturi asked. "There are some rather vulgar rumors floating about the city. About you and…"

An icy finger touched her heart but she brushed it away with a wave of her fan. "Oh, pooh! There are always rumors. And if you are any friend of mine you know better than to repeat them. No one cares about rumors."

His expression remained serious. "No one cares when you amuse yourself with actresses, you mean. But it's said that you've taken up with a young woman of good family—I do not name names. Someone they have known all their lives and received in their own drawing rooms."

"The hypocrites!" Caution was lost in a sudden flood of anger. "None of them have received her at all since her return except for my sake!"

"Ah ah ah," he tutted. "A little less heat if you mean to maintain denial. That is exactly what has given the gossip wings." He took her by the hand and led her toward the edge of the dance floor to appear as if they were waiting for the music to change.

Chazerin Saltez was still circling through the figures, entranced by her admirer. "She'll never win him," Jeanne said sharply to purge the remnants of her bile. "He may dance with pretty young girls, but when he marries it will be to a hard-headed woman who can manage his affairs."

The outburst failed to renew her balance. No one else had changed toward her, had they? She thought back on whom she had seen across the past month. It had been all her closest circles. She hadn't arranged any entertainments since Margerit's floodtide party in May, except for helping with the lectures, but that hardly counted. But the invitations still came: the dinners, the opera parties. She searched her memory for any coolness, any subtle slights. "Maisetra Saltez is a nobody."

"And if a nobody dares to snub you…"

This was what Toneke had feared. She dared a glance toward the far end of the room, where Antuniet was sitting on a bench by the windows, talking to someone beside her. No, Toneke mustn't hear about this. Not now, when the work was all-important. She gave a forced laugh to shake off the mood. "Well, I suppose I'll need to find other amusements than organizing parties."

"I had a thought about that," Chanturi said. His voice turned more serious than his expression. "There's a musician I know, a young woman I've taken on as a protégée."

Jeanne looked at him crossly. "You may believe the rumors far enough to know I'm not interested in an introduction to your pretty little protégée. Not even as a misdirection."

"Nothing like that!" he said with a smile. "I've seen what you've done with Sovitre's lectures. She made them possible but you made them fashionable. If you find time weighing on your hands, you might turn your talents to launching the career of my young friend. She's been so unwomanly as to take up the violin—scarcely a parlor instrument! And none of the chamber consorts will have anything to do with her, of course. She needs to be launched in the proper setting. You might take up the challenge."

Even before he'd finished speaking, Jeanne found her mind measuring the likely reception, selecting a venue and thinking of other performers who might set off such a talent. "A challenge indeed." He'd succeeded in distracting her and for that she was grateful.

The last strains of the cotillion had faded away and the musicians had struck up a promenade introducing the next set. Chanturi lifted her hand to his lips, saying, "And now, my dear, if you haven't forgotten how, would you favor me with a dance? I make it a rule always to dance with the most enchanting woman in the *salle*."

"Flatterer!" she teased, allowing herself to be led out to the forming set.

* * *

The workings were more complex now with half the stones completed and only a few layers left to add on those remaining. The roles had strained their limits today, even with the addition of the Perneld girl and with Barbara pulled in for symmetry. But the salamander had been roused and bled, the lion had devoured the sun and the king and queen wed under the sign of the pavonade and now two sets of stones were safely aligned in the furnace. They had been beautiful: one with a ruby core glowing under layers of sapphire and beryl, the other shimmering with a hoarfrost of emerald. She had learned enough of the symbols to tell that tonight's ferment would cover them over with pure crystal. The next process would cloak the bright colors with lesser material that could not withstand the forces that had created the gemstone cores: sard, onyx, jargoon. Then at last the cutting and polishing would reveal the brilliant hearts again. How that could be done was a mystery, but it was the ordinary mechanical mystery of Monterrez's craft. Four identical stones were made in each batch in expectation that half would fail in the finishing. Those remaining would be destroyed. It seemed a great waste but Antuniet thought it too much a risk to keep them. The layered gems were too closely aligned. Twin might call to twin with unknown effect. Only one must be left to do its work.

Anna and Valeir Perneld had been sent home already and the men were rousting the armins from their eternal game of cards in the alcove by the door. Jeanne didn't hear the sound of the knock and looked over only when she heard Elin's frightened voice exclaiming, "Oh! Forgive me. I didn't mean to disturb—"

"It makes no mind," Efriturik could be heard to assure her. "We've finished. You're here to see Mesnera de Cherdillac?"

This was no social call—one look from Elin to Iaklin made that clear. Jeanne hurried over to where they still hung back in the doorway. "What's to do?"

Elin glanced doubtfully at the men but Iaklin blurted out, "Have you seen Tio today? Has she come by?"

"Tio?" Jeanne said. "Good heavens no! Why would she have come here? I haven't seen her since the Alboris' ball. Shouldn't she have been attending on Princess Elisebet today?"

"No, the princess is away from town until tomorrow. Tio came by this morning and then said she was going visiting, but I just thought...I hoped..." Elin's voice faltered and Jeanne wanted to shake her.

Iaklin once again filled the gap. "Aukustin's gone missing."

That brought all ears in the room to attention except for Antuniet, who pointedly continued setting the jars of minerals in order. Efriturik was the first to speak. "Missing? Or is this just another of his mother's freaks? No, Mesnera—" to Elin "—you needn't look at me like that. I know what lies your mistress tells of me. But is there true reason for concern or are you only frightened for your position?"

Barbara followed on quickly with, "Have you sent for his mother?"

Elin quaked visibly. "No. She'll know soon enough when she returns, but we need to find him before she hears he was gone. If Mesnera Sain-Mazzi hadn't gone with her, we wouldn't even have that reprieve."

"And what have you done?" Efriturik's questions came hard on each other's heels. "Where have you looked? Where might he have gone?"

Jeanne could see that hysterics were near. She took Elin and Iaklin each by an arm and led them a few steps away from the others. "From the beginning."

It came out in a confused counterpoint. Chustin had taken to his room after breakfast, saying he was feeling poorly and didn't want to be disturbed. No one had questioned it until well past dinner and then he was nowhere to be found. One of the gardeners said he thought he'd seen the boy leaving with his tutor, but Maistir Chautovil had left town for a few days as well. "And then I remembered something Tio had said and sent for Maisetra Silpirt—" Elin started, with Iaklin continuing, "—and I thought of that masquerade of Tio's at Carnival."

Yes, that dashing young man she'd played at impersonating.

Margerit chimed in on the tale. "Aukustin was mad to see the ships down at the wharves. And I remember Tio telling us she'd helped him sneak out at least once."

There was a long moment of silence broken only by the low crackle of the furnace and the steady click of the clockwork drive. "She wouldn't!" Efriturik said in disbelief.

"She would," Jeanne countered with a sinking heart. It was exactly the sort of foolish trick that would appeal to her.

Iaklin wailed, "She'll be ruined! She can't keep this one secret, not now."

Barbara said what they all feared to think. "Ruined? She'll be lucky if she isn't dead, or worse. They only need to stray a few streets away from the Nikuleplaiz and the Strangers Market to fall into more trouble than she could imagine. If they haven't returned by now..."

"Or been pressed." It was Margerit's armin. Jeanne had rarely heard him offer more than a few words at a time. When all eyes turned to him, he continued, "The barges need extra hands for the stretch down to Iser. It happens all the time. A few likely lads get lured on board, then offered a place on the poles as the only way to earn their way home. If they were down at the wharves showing an interest in the ships, that's where I'd put my money."

"No," Efriturik said, still doubting. "Perhaps no one would recognize my cousin, but all Mesnera Perzin need do is tell them who he is. It makes no sense."

"It makes no sense to a man," Jeanne said briskly. "But if Tio's discovered after all this, it isn't only her good name that's ruined. There's her husband's career, and no doubt the position of anyone thought to have helped her." She looked pointedly at Elin. "She might easily think her only hope is to bluff it through."

While they'd been debating, Barbara had begun to take action, sending her armin for the carriages and barking orders at the rest of them like a tyrannical housekeeper to the underservants. Only Efriturik bristled at the treatment. "Have a care, Saveze! You aren't the only person in Rotenek capable of saving a reputation!"

And what is the story behind that? Jeanne wondered. *What has she done to step on his toes?*

Barbara stiffened in turn but her response was more mild. "What part do you prefer to take?"

He was taken aback, as if expecting a duel of wills. The edge of challenge in his voice retreated. "You know the wharves. Do you truly think they've been tricked on board and taken?"

Jeanne could see hope and truth warring in Barbara's face. "An even chance, I think. Better than even if nothing worse happened."

Efriturik nodded. "Then I'm for Iser. Charlin?"

His friend nodded grimly. "The moon will be up soon. Iser is closer by the coach road than the river. With a few swift changes of horses we should beat any barge that left after noon. And with that and luck we could bring them back before dawn." All the ways the plan might fail were left unsaid.

"I'll cover the Nikuleplaiz and the docks," Barbara countered. "If there's news to be found, I'll follow it."

Jeanne lingered until the last of the rescuers had scattered to their tasks. The room echoed hollowly as Antuniet made the final adjustments to the furnace mechanism. She had ignored it all. "Toneke?" Jeanne said at last. "Would you come home with me tonight?" Antuniet looked up and hesitated, as if calculating the next day's tasks against the moment's desires. It was hard: to lay this need before her after the weeks of setting her desires aside. "I'll lie awake fretting all night," Jeanne offered. "It would be easier if you were there."

"Of course," Antuniet said, as if there were no question.

But there had been a question. And when they were rolled in each other's arms later, skin pressed to skin, Antuniet's lips sought to erase that doubt with fervent hunger. Jeanne longed to respond as the attention deserved but at last she said, "Toneke, just hold me tonight." She could feel Antuniet stiffen beside her. "No, no, there's nothing wrong. I'm worried, that's all."

"Tio!" Antuniet made it an oath. "What has she ever done to deserve your concern?"

Jeanne rolled the question around in her mind. "She reminds me of myself when I was young."

Another rude noise cut through the dark. "You were never that selfish or heedless."

"Oh, but I was. You didn't know me then; you wouldn't have been out of the nursery yet." Jeanne winced at the reminder of the years that stood between them. There was so much of her life that Antuniet didn't know. "I was so unhappy. And I'd found that virtue paid me no return, so I tried other roads. Tio at least has the grace to know that she has no right to be unhappy. So she walks along the parapet of a bridge, hoping and fearing that she'll fall into the flood to be swept away."

There was silence for a time, then Antuniet said, "I nearly threw myself from a bridge once, but I never expected all the world to dive in after me."

Jeanne turned and buried her face in the angle of Antuniet's neck. "And yet for your sake, I would have drained the river dry. You needn't be jealous of her."

They slept at last. It was still full dark when the distant thud of the knocker broke the night.

Fearing as much as hoping, Jeanne struggled into her chemise and dressing gown while Marien came in with a lamp. "Stay here," she whispered to Antuniet when she would have risen as well. "I don't know who it is and there's no need to add that fuel to the rumors about us." She bit her lip, recalling that she hadn't meant to worry Antuniet about the gossip.

Tomric was before her to the door. She hadn't thought to warn him, but he'd had sense enough not to keep the unexpected visitors waiting on the stoop. Jeanne hurried down the last few steps and rushed to throw her arms around the slight figure wrapped in an oversized greatcoat. "Tio! You're safe!"

She was answered by a muffled sobbing against her shoulder. Jeanne looked past to the second figure in the doorway. "Mesner Mainek, what of—"

"The other wanderer is safe too," he said. "Efriturik took Aukustin to the palace. Vicomtesse…see to it that your friend is known to have been in Rotenek yesterday and this night. In Rotenek and in your company."

Jeanne's mind leaped past his words to their meaning. "So Efriturik is to take the blame?"

A nod. "I'll leave you now and take the news to Saveze. Say as little as you can manage until the smoke has cleared and we can see what fires still need to be quenched."

"Thank you," she said to his departing back.

With the door closed again, she gave Tionez a shake. "Enough tears. We have work to do if you mean to keep your reputation from tatters. Marien, could you go ask Maisetra Chazillen to come down? And Tomric, some tea in the breakfast room, if you can."

There was at least an hour before dawn and she intended to have a plan by then.

CHAPTER THIRTY-TWO

Barbara

Looking back, Barbara was grateful that the threatening storm had waited until after their late-night adventure to begin in earnest. Snow had started falling in the afternoon and by the next morning lay heavily on the cobbled streets and drifted against house walls. Though it continued to fall, Brandel returned from his early-morning expedition across to the stables with the news that there was no reason their ride need be postponed.

She smiled at the enthusiasm of youth. "I'll hold to my promise," she told him, "but not so far as we'd planned. Just out the Port Ausiz to the fairgrounds. That will be far enough for the horses to settle down and sufficient space for your lessons."

Even that shortened plan seemed doomed when a liveried messenger appeared just as the household was dispersing to the day's plans. He presented a crisp note sealed with a simple but unmistakable "AA." So. No need to guess what it was about.

Barbara looked up from the unfolded paper to Brandel's disappointed face. "My promise must be postponed, I fear. Or—" She looked to where Tavit stood waiting. "I don't suppose you'd be willing to cede your place to Brandel this once? We're only going to the palace so it would all be kicking your heels in the galleries in any event."

Tavit bowed slightly. "As you wish, Mesnera." It was only the dignity of rank that called for attendance there at all.

"Go change your coat, Brandel. Quickly. The good one."

She calculated her appearance. With the streets in unknown state it still made sense to ride rather than to bring out the carriage, but perhaps a proper habit rather than breeches. She could only guess what Annek's mood might be.

The ride over was a litany of instruction, until Brandel seemed petrified at the responsibilities of his post. Good. Mistakes were harder to correct than overformality. She left him waiting in the long gallery with strict orders to speak to no one unless addressed and to assume that anyone who did so was a *mesner* unless told otherwise.

She was ushered into the small, dark-paneled parlor: the one Annek used for private business, though that meant nothing in itself. After the briefest glance of acknowledgment, Annek continued reviewing the papers handed to her one by one by the dark-suited secretary who stood at her side. Barbara composed her mind to read nothing into the wait. She had learned that game from the old baron. There had been times when he had kept her standing for an hour until he deigned to give instructions. From what she knew of Annek, this was no game of wills, only the tedious ordering of a busy schedule. But she had no doubt of its effectiveness on those less accustomed to patience. The secretary was sent away at last, confirming that this was to be private business.

Annek sat back, folding her hands on the table before her. "You have been busy of late, Saveze," she said.

Barbara nodded. No need to give an answer until there was a question.

A pause, as if to see what she would offer up. And then, "What do you know of this business with Aukustin?"

She had her evasions rehearsed. "I know the gossip that sped about the city yesterday." She chose her truths carefully. Efriturik had stood by his story and she would follow his lead as she was able. "It's said that your son thought it would be good sport to show his cousin around the wharves at the Nikuleplaiz and that they ended by mischance going downriver for a space and didn't return until well after midnight."

"You *know* this," Annek said, daring her to overreach.

"I have heard it said," Barbara offered.

"And I would guess you know it for a lie," Annek said. "You know as well as I that my son was on the palace grounds all that day. If alchemy has taught him how to be here in Rotenek and on a barge to Iser at the same time, that's a great mystery indeed. My cousin chooses to believe the story for her own reasons. I'm more interested to know why it was put about at all. If my son's name is to be dragged in the mud once more, I would know the purpose."

"Have you asked your son?"

"I have," she said. "And now I'm asking you."

The pause that followed was longer than Annek's patience. She snapped out, "My father, of blessed memory, once said a thing in your presence. Perhaps you remember? The truth, unstintingly."

Now the resemblance to the old baron was stronger. In his time, that tone of voice would have brought her to one knee in instant obedience but she had the dignity of Saveze to uphold now. So she only curtseyed deeply. "Your son is protecting the reputation of a lady," she began.

Now that startled her. "A lady?"

"One of Elisebet's waiting women who helped the boy slip out. She meant no harm by it, but she had no sense either. Mesner Atilliet took the blame on himself because that would be believed and no one would question further."

Annek raised a brow at that, for clearly *she* had questioned it. "The lady's name?"

There could be no holding back. "Perzin. Tionez Perzin."

The name seemed to mean nothing to her.

"Her husband is with the embassy to Paris."

"I see. Perhaps I should recall him to keep a closer eye on his wife." But it had the tone of sour humor rather than decision. Annek sighed and frowned. "Efriturik has put me in a difficult place. If the story stands, I must be seen to disapprove." She sighed again. "He may keep his secret chivalry."

Barbara thought the interview might be at an end, but just when she expected a dismissal, Annek asked, "What of that other matter of Efriturik's?"

"Your Grace?" She received that look again that warned her not to pretend to ignorance. This time there was no other reputation to protect. "Some information came into my hands regarding a…a friendship that might be misconstrued: some letters to a lady—"

"Another lady?"

"A different one. I believe she's the sister of one of the Austrian attachés." She gave what other details were necessary to satisfy Annek's command and concluded, "I arranged for the letters to be returned to their author."

"Baroness Saveze," the princess said at last, "in the future, I would ask that you consult with me before you take such measures to defend the name of Atilliet. I forgive the past for your good intentions but you take too much on yourself. Perhaps you could trust that my judgment might be as good as yours." The steel of the message belied the delicacy of her words. "I know your history, Saveze. You could be a useful tool, or turn in my hand and cut me. Don't give me reason to blunt your edge."

Now Barbara did sink to one knee to beg forgiveness. "It was never my intent to set my will against yours."

"Get up, get up," she said impatiently. "Don't turn this into a tragic drama. I might have expected women to cause trouble for my son, but I hadn't expected it to take quite this form. Perhaps it isn't too soon to think about a bride for him: some girl strong-willed enough to take him in hand, with an impeccable Alpennian pedigree and not too many ambitious relatives." Annek eyed her speculatively. "I don't suppose you have any plans to marry."

There was a perilous question! Barbara was caught off guard and knew she shouldn't have been. An unmarried woman who would bring one of the oldest and most respected titles in the land to the match? Did she say no and give the impression she was available? But she could hardly imply there was a suitor in the wings without being asked to produce one. "I think perhaps Efriturik would prefer a bride younger than himself," she ventured.

"He will take the bride I choose for him," Annek said sharply. "And it will be someone I can trust at his side on the throne: a woman with sense, not some pretty face. My stepmother was pretty enough in her day, and see where that's brought us. Alpennia would be the better if my father had chosen someone with brains instead."

It was a mark of her mood that she called Elisebet stepmother and not cousin. Barbara waited patiently until Annek shook her head and waved a hand, as if to dismiss the path of her thoughts. "Now tell me: this project of Maisetra Chazillen's—do you think it will succeed?"

The change of subject once more caught her off guard. "I've seen the work. It has succeeded already, and little enough remains to be completed. She will succeed."

"I'll be curious to see what comes of her art when it's had time to work." She frowned again, more thoughtfully this time. "I know what your cousin wants, but it can't be done. I will not reverse my father's judgment against the Chazillens. That would lead to his every act being questioned. What sort of woman is this Antuniet?"

That was a dangerously unbounded question. "I've had little enough opportunity to know her. My father…There was bad blood between the families, you know. You'd do better to ask your thaumaturgist."

"Maisetra Sovitre might give me a less guarded answer but I think you are the better judge of character. Tell me plainly: if I fail to offer what she wants, what will she do?" Annek stared at her intently with the eagle gaze inherited from her father.

What would *Antuniet do?* "A year past…I don't know. But she has ties now that would make it difficult for her to leave Rotenek, I think."

It seemed to be answer enough for the moment but Barbara's heart sank. Antuniet had staked all her hopes on this chance. She thought of pleading on her cousin's behalf but it was a poor time to ask for favors. And then the audience was truly at an end.

* * *

Christmastide had crept upon them unawares, with only the Advent services to mark its approach. Somehow Antuniet's project had infected the entire household at Tiporsel, even at several removes. All attention was focused ahead to the New Year's court.

In past years, Margerit had known the dull disappointment of her Uncle Fulpi's refusal of her invitation. She had been particularly hoping for her cousins to visit, Barbara knew. It should be a time for family, but instead it was when Margerit most felt the gulf that had grown within hers. Barbara had briefly considered reaching out to the Chamerings but it would be too great a journey for them. And they were strangers still; this was not a time to add complications to the household.

Yet Tiporsel's bench in the cathedral was well-filled for the season's services and mysteries and Barbara felt something close to familial pride when glancing past Margerit down the row of worshippers. The Pertineks, of course, that first and most essential addition. Brandel, who was every day becoming more woven into their lives.

What she felt when her eyes lighted on Antuniet was more complex. The invitation to join them here had been accepted immediately and without comment but always there was a distance, a holding back. With Antuniet came Jeanne, slipping easily into any gathering, as always. And now the most recent addition: Maisetra Talarico, still too much a stranger in Rotenek to have found a regular home for her worship. It was not a family like other houses, but more of one than she had known before in her life. What was it Antuniet had called it? Her *saliesin*. Yes, that fit.

Next came the frantic lull between the mysteries of the Nativity and the spectacle of the court at the year's turning. Antuniet's work was all in other hands to finish and Barbara found herself idle, when she most longed for distraction. That distraction came in the memory of an unfinished debt. She hadn't meant to let weeks pass before she returned to the question of Langal's purpose. It was time to close that book.

The last time she had approached Langal's house, she had been following one of his shadows up the narrow lane in back meant for servants and deliveries. This time she came in state in the carriage adorned with her crest, and an armin to precede her and rap on the door, demanding entrance. And if any passersby took note and speculated on the state of her finances because of the visit, she was content for them to draw mistaken conclusions. For all that the house stood in a respectable part of town—a neighborhood where money could buy the chance to rub elbows with good birth—the interior was as different from its neighbors as a cart horse from a thoroughbred. Langal had no wife that she could recall hearing of and evidently no need or desire to impress his clients favorably with comfort and beauty. Not squalor—far from it—but more a tradesman's office than a home.

Barbara could see enough hesitation when she entered Langal's presence to guess that he wasn't accustomed to rising in respect for his guests, no matter what their station. But rise he did, nor did he offer even a pretense of suggesting that Tavit wait in another room. Barbara made a show of inspecting the available chair before settling into it. Their encounter would be rife with playacting; they both knew it and she thought perhaps Langal was enjoying it. His message about Efriturik's difficulties might have bought him a hearing, but that was all. She still remembered vividly that night on the bridge with his men: the attack, her wound and what had come after.

"You have business to discuss with me," she began bluntly. "But I can't imagine what it might be. All that was concluded three years ago when I came of age and you lost any claim over me for Arpik's debts."

He sat as well and settled his beetle-browed face into what was meant to be an inviting expression. "No, I freely confess you owe me nothing now. Not even this meeting. As it happens, it was to offer you something that I asked you here."

It was easy enough to show no curiosity. Barbara waited for Langal to explain, looking idly about the room. Her first impression had been somewhat mistaken. There were a few touches of comfort and luxury here: a portrait by Helez of someone other than its present owner, an ornately inlaid clock standing tall in the corner. They had the air of being a pawnshop's contents rather than the furnishings of a stately home. She continued to wait. He would come to the point in his own time.

He began at last, "I should like to discuss an entirely different matter involving Mesner Arpik: the Turinz title-lands."

"I should think you'd have sold them long since," Barbara said, not bothering to conceal her surprise. "I have no claim on them and no interest in them either. They must be quite a burden on you. I imagine that managing property is a different matter from collecting mortgages."

"It isn't quite that simple," he said, steepling his fingers dramatically. "There are encumbrances."

She shrugged. "My right is extinguished and there are no other heirs that I've been able to find. You hold the mortgage; no one but you has any claim to it now."

"No claim to the land, that's true. But they *are* title-lands and the title lies unclaimed. No buyer would be willing to risk being tied up in court for years."

Barbara searched her memory of her studies in law. Her first concern for Arpik's affairs—before she even knew his name and rank—had been to guess what Langal's purpose had been in pursuing her. Back then the matter had seemed straightforward: her debt-ridden father had sold her to the baron and then died. She'd had no resources to pay the debt, being property herself. It was not until her majority freed her of any legal tie to Arpik, for good or ill, that she'd learned Langal's real goal: to prod her into uncovering her true parentage so he could gain access to the Saveze fortune. She'd given no thought at all to Arpik's title as Count Turinz. Once the matter of the debt had become moot she'd washed her hands of the rest. "Surely the title extinguishes at some point," she said.

Langal nodded. "Next June will be twenty years since Arpik's death. Twenty years for the heir-default to make a claim if there is no will. Ten more for another heir within seven degrees to step forward and make a claim. No buyer with any sense would touch the property until that term is complete. As you say, the lands are a drain on my resources and a vacant estate brings no profit."

Not entirely vacant, Barbara thought. There would be tenants, of course. And given what she knew of Arpik, they might have prospered more in neglect than under his presence. But the collecting of rents and fees was another matter and there was no telling what had happened to the manor itself.

He continued, "I don't care to wait another ten years for a chance of profit. I would be willing to let the property go for a pittance to anyone willing to redeem it."

For the first time, Barbara could see where he was leading. The thought was ridiculous. "What is that to me? I'm no kin to Arpik—I have Marziel Lumbeirt's deed on that—and I care nothing for the Turinz legacy."

Langal stared at her as if she'd lost her wits. "The law doesn't care about blood. It didn't matter for the debt and it doesn't matter for the title. Arpik never disclaimed you. You were his wife's child. That makes you his heir-default whether you will or no."

She laughed. "And why should I care? A disgraced title and a ruined, neglected estate? Do you think I would be tempted by the thought of being Countess Turinz when I'm already Baroness Saveze? You waste my time." She stood.

He might have thought it a bargaining ploy. When he rose after her his voice carried a tone of urgency, even desperation. "A title should not be so carelessly cast aside. You will have heirs someday, I presume. A second son might thank you for giving my offer more consideration."

That made her pause. The fate of the Lumbeirt line was not a topic she enjoyed contemplating. She was the last, unless… Well, there was no point dwelling on that. To marry and get heirs—it would risk what she held most dear. Dearer even than Saveze itself. Margerit might protest that they could find a way to make it work, but she knew better. Even the most pliant of husbands would find such a position untenable. And yet Langal's point held true. The future was uncertain; who could say what use she might someday find for the despised name of Turinz?

She turned and seated herself once more. "So, Maistir Langal. It seems you have wares you find difficult to sell to anyone but me, and I have no strong desire or use for them. Exactly what sort of pittance did you have in mind?"

* * *

It was the expectation more than the outcome that made the New Year's ceremonies the pinnacle of the season. If the business of the day itself failed to provide sufficient entertainment, it was supplied by the endless speculations concerning what had failed to occur. Last year, Efriturik's installation as Baron Razik had supplied the first. This year, he contributed to the second by his absence. There was no need for speculation; Princess Annek had made clear that it was the price of her official displeasure for the escapade on the river. Whatever price it had cost Efriturik had bought one thing: no one had questioned the story. A much chastened Tio still had her place in Elisebet's retinue. Aukustin, too, was absent but that caused little enough talk. He wasn't yet of an age where his presence would be expected, and his mother's excuse that he was feeling poorly was given no credit at all.

Barbara filled the time before the presentations began by strolling down the long galleries arm in arm with Margerit. Half the crowd was doing the same and the other half was standing at the sides watching them. She had favored a gown in the same braided military style that had turned heads the year before, but Margerit had foregone her silken scholar's robe for a more conventional dress in pale blue trimmed with white lace. Antuniet looked stunning in a garnet velvet as brilliant as the gem at her throat, with the sleeves tucked and pinched into a latticework and the hem drawn up at one side in a swag to show the dark gold slip beneath. Barbara was too honest ever to have thought her cousin pretty, but one couldn't deny that today she drew the eye. The deep color turned her stiffness and height into majesty. And someone had taken her hair in hand, for a cascade of carefully-arranged curls replaced its usual severely-pinned control.

"You look magnificent," Barbara offered, as they joined her where a trick of the doors and passages left a quiet pool among the streams of guests.

"Thanks to your gift," she replied, looking grateful for the distraction.

"Is it? I'd thought the other gown—"

Antuniet twisted her mouth in a rueful smile. "I may be a two-dress dowd but I know better than to begin the New Year wearing a gown that's been seen before. I was saving this one."

"You needn't have," Margerit protested. "Only say the word—"

Antuniet's face closed a little. "You have been very generous to me but I prefer to avoid obligations that I'm not in a position to repay."

Ah yes, Proud Antuniet! But it was a pride Barbara could understand and respect. She touched Margerit's hand where it caught the crook of her elbow. "Let it be for tonight," Barbara said. To smooth over the moment, she asked Antuniet, "Has Jeanne abandoned you?"

"She flits here and there." A shrug, but of amusement, not annoyance. "I send her off to give me some quiet, and then in time she returns. I'm not in a mood to hear the chatter of her friends until this is over." She waved a hand toward the Assembly Room.

And how would she feel when it was over? Barbara had debated with herself whether to reveal the thoughts Annek had shared. Was it better for Antuniet to know the likely limits of royal gratitude, or to enjoy one more hour of hope? And who was to say Annek hadn't had a change of heart? Better to hold her tongue.

"And here the butterfly returns!" Margerit laughed. "We'll leave you to your quiet for now."

Not all their encounters were as pleasant. Baron Mazuk took the trouble to set himself in their path and Barbara tensed, still recalling their words after the debates in the spring. His expression fell short of belligerent by very little and it was impossible to forget that the night was traditionally used to find an excuse to settle grievances. Margerit felt her tension and slipped her hand free. With the same reflex that might once have driven her to touch a sword hilt, Barbara briefly glanced toward the end of the hall where the armins watched. Tavit met her eye and came alert, though she gave him no other sign. Nothing would happen here in the crowd. At his shoulder she saw Brandel lean forward with a question and be quickly hushed. He'd been granted leave to attend for his education but the first lesson was to hold his tongue and watch. Mazuk stepped forward with a brief formal bow of greeting. Nothing to do but see it through, whatever his purpose might be.

"Baron Mazuk," she returned. "I hope the season finds you well."

"Well enough, well enough. Maisetra," he added with a nod to Margerit.

Barbara relaxed the slightest amount. So she wouldn't be expected to take offense in that direction.

"I hear you're claiming a second title, Saveze." His opening was blunt but that could be excused as simply his way. "You waited long enough to take up that responsibility."

His comment echoed something he'd said in the spring after the sessions. *Is this what his true grudge was back then?*

Barbara threaded her way between confirmation and denial, since neither would answer. "That rumor has traveled quickly. It's not for me to claim, but it's true that I've petitioned Her Grace to settle the Turinz question. It leaves complications hanging about my life that I'd prefer to leave behind. By law, it seems I'm still the heir-default, but I'm sure Princess Annek would entertain other claims should they come to light."

And were there other claims? She ran through an inventory of Mazuk's connections. Was this a personal matter to him? No, not a matter of descent, one of geography. His title-lands lay cheek-by-jowl with Turinz. Had he been hoping to add to them? Or was it more complicated than that?

He harrumphed in reply. "It just seems a touch…greedy to me, considering what you started from."

Now he was trying for provocation. Barbara tried to deflect him with humor; this wasn't a night when she cared for distractions. "If I were greedy, it wouldn't be for Turinz. There's little enough value in it."

"Still, it isn't everyone who has a chance to inherit two titles," Mazuk said slyly. "Why stop at two? Perhaps your mother arranged an even greater legacy. Just how many fathers might you produce?"

The thrust fell so wide of the mark that she could only laugh, to his bewildered surprise. Had he expected her to react to the intent of the insult regardless of the substance? "Recall that the entire basis of my title is in being Lumbeirt's bastard and so the daughter of an adulteress. If you mean to provoke me to a challenge, you'll need to find another glove to drop." He tried to protest but she continued, "We've had our differences over law, but there's no need for this. If the vacancy in Turinz has caused problems for you, we can discuss it when I know whether the matter is mine to address. Or if you want to test my skills with a blade, I'd be delighted to have you join me at Perret's *salle* for a friendly bout or two. But there's nothing we need to settle tonight."

He seemed baffled, but relieved, as if he'd expected a different response. Perhaps she should look more closely into how matters stood in Turinz sooner rather than later.

They moved on. After another half an hour of empty pleasantries, the encounter with Kreiser was less tense. He was all politeness and smiles, answering Margerit's wariness with charm and adding, "I think perhaps I have underestimated you, Saveze."

"How so?" Barbara asked. If this were to be more verbal fencing, let him take the lead.

"I took a great deal of trouble to set certain things in motion. And after turning my attention away for a moment, I find you have brought them all to naught. Like smoke in the wind." He waved a hand, as if dispersing the very thought.

Barbara answered his vagueness with the faintest suggestion of a bow. Let him make of that what he would.

He glanced down toward the other end of the gallery. "I fear I've underestimated your cousin the alchemist as well. That's a harder loss to take. If I'd known…I thought the treasure I was pursuing lay within the covers of a book, not inside her head. She's gone beyond all her teachers. I should have suggested to the emperor that he offer her a position in Vienna, but too late for that now."

"She wouldn't have taken it," Barbara replied. "But if you like, I'll pass along your compliment."

"Will you be returning home to Vienna then?" Margerit asked.

He considered her, as if looking for guile in the question. "Yes, in the spring, though perhaps not for the reason you think. Perhaps someday you will visit me there." Barbara felt the return of his attention. "You've been keeping quite a close watch over me. You might do well to expand your interests. There are more people than my emperor who have concerns in Alpennia."

Barbara debated asking, to see if he would reveal more, but Kreiser bowed again and moved on.

And then it was time for the processions and receptions. Barbara parted from Margerit for their different roles in the pageantry: vestiges of the pomp of an older time that seemed more and more out of place.

It seemed an eternity before the name of Chazillen was called and Barbara watched Antuniet make the slow, stately approach through the center of the crowd, carrying an ebony box before her as if it were a holy relic. Annek had seen the rings already, of course. Yesterday they had been presented and examined, Antuniet's claims verified by those who could judge their worth. Now the box was received and opened. A nod, a smile, words too low for the watching crowd to hear. And then the voice of the majordomo ringing through the hall: "In recognition of the services that Antuniet Chazillen has performed for Alpennia, We appoint her as alchemist to Our court, with use and command of the facilities We have caused to be built for her, and she is granted a suitable pension as a sign of Our favor."

Polite applause covered the long moment that Antuniet remained unmoving. Then slowly she rose, curtseyed and turned. They all would take her stunned expression for surprise and pleasure. Barbara knew it for deep disappointment and slipped around the edges of the crowd toward the back of the hall. Most of the watchers had already turned their attention to the next presentation but there were a few eager well-wishers following after Antuniet. Jeanne was there before her, accepting the congratulations and fending off the most pressing.

Barbara claimed the privilege of pushing through and leading Antuniet out the doors at the end of the hall and into the empty corridor beyond. Awkwardly, she gave Antuniet a brief embrace and whispered, "I'm sorry."

"Don't!" she said tightly.

Barbara stepped back and gave her a moment to regain control as Jeanne joined them, asking, "Would you prefer to leave now?"

Antuniet shook her head. "I can't. There's still the supper to see through." Yes, when the formalities were done, there would be a more private celebration for those honored today. And it must be treated as an honor whatever she felt. The rings were to be distributed then, alongside other gifts. There would be no begging off.

Antuniet raised her chin and schooled her face to stillness. "It was always such a small hope." Her voice tightened and she shook her head again. "It's done."

CHAPTER THIRTY-THREE

Antuniet

There was a usefulness, Antuniet thought, to having a reputation for stiffness and reserve. What had been promised as an informal supper looked likely to drone on for hours. Out in the side chambers off the galleries people would be satisfying themselves with lighter fare. Jeanne would be there, no doubt missing her company. But Jeanne always found something to entertain herself.

For a time, the need to make polite conversation distracted her from her disappointment. Eventually she took refuge in silence. Disappointment! Such a tame word. There had always been so little reason to hope, but hope had been all that sustained her in the dark days. Roasted duck and a paté of oysters replaced the veal roulade before her. She'd always thought that failure—if it came—would come from within: a failure of her art or of her skill. It had never occurred to her that she might triumph in the Great Work and yet fall short of the prize.

Where is all your pride now? Where is your vow? Why did you even think— It was the same voice that haunted her nightmares: cutting, accusing... Her mother's voice.

This time she had an answer. *No, Mother. I didn't fail. I did my best. Everything I set my hand to succeeded. There is nothing more I could have done. To change Annek's heart was never within my power.*

And for the first time, she believed it. The voices stilled. It was like the opening of doors and the sun blazing into dark spaces. She had done the best she could have done and would accept what came after. This was her life now: no way out but forward. Perhaps failure was as liberating as success would have been.

As the final course was removed, Antuniet looked around the room. There were perhaps four dozen guests in all, those who had received some special mark of favor during the court. There were minor gifts too, it being the season for gifts. She received from Annek's hand a fan with ivory sticks and a painted scene of the triumph of Athena. Afterward, she tapped it restlessly against her knee, below the table, where it couldn't be seen. She'd never learned the art of the fan; perhaps Jeanne would teach her.

The rings were distributed with great ceremony and explanations of their properties. Antuniet watched intently as each one was slipped onto its recipient's finger by Annek herself. It was too much to expect that the virtues of the rings would be apparent at once. They were designed to be more subtle than that. Any visible effects could be ascribed to the simple power of the ceremony itself.

Princess Annek's words were carefully couched in diplomatic praise. No need to tell Lord Ehing that he was known for needless fears when one could say that his talisman would aid in discerning the true importance of matters. Mesner Albori's gift was described as adding to his eloquent persuasiveness. No need to dwell on how it was also meant to sustain his health so he could continue in his duties.

There Antuniet thought she could see her art at work. By the time the last of the rings had been distributed, Albori's habitual wheezing seemed to have quieted somewhat. She saw him glancing constantly at the stone. Once he looked in her direction with an air of wonder. Antuniet suddenly had visions of being besieged for charms against fever and gout.

When the pastries had been consumed, the guests were released at last. Strains of music and laughter from the assembly hall showed that the dancing was well begun. The thought of pushing through that crush in search of Jeanne was daunting, so she found the narrow stair to the upper galleries and climbed for a good vantage. No one went there unless seeking privacy; it was a quiet place from which to watch.

She leaned on the rail and looked down across the crowd. The figures of the dancers swirled beneath her gaze like eddies on the river. There, at the side, the nodding feathers on Jeanne's turban were a beacon above the sea of heads. She stood in animated conversation with Count Chanturi and a slender young woman in a pale blue gown. How she sparkled in such a gathering!

Antuniet had almost forgotten what it was to see Jeanne in company. Their own time together was quieter. Even the moments of passion seemed filled with intensity rather than laughter. She had never been able to play the games of flirtation and light gaiety that Jeanne so enjoyed. It always felt false. Yet she couldn't help but envy the animation that lit Jeanne's face now as she leaned toward the young woman and said something that made them both laugh. Antuniet absently stroked the pendant at her breast. She no longer had doubts. Not in that way. But at what cost? By what right should she expect Jeanne to give up this life she so enjoyed? She could do her best; but if her best were not enough? As she watched, a tightness rose in her throat. Perhaps it was time to accept that as well. She turned away from the rail to find the stair down to the floor.

Jeanne turned at her approach and crossed the space in a few quick strides to join her. "Have they released you at last?"

"Yes," she said, looking past to where Chanturi and the girl still stood in conversation. Jeanne turned her head to follow her gaze. "She's very pretty," Antuniet offered in as even a tone as she could manage.

"Mmm," Jeanne answered, as if she didn't trust herself to say more.

The words Antuniet meant to use congealed in her throat. How did one… "*Non in solo pane*," she said at last.

A curious glance. "Not by bread alone?"

"Jeanne," she blurted, before she could lose courage, "I can be your bread and water, but I can't be your cake and champagne. It isn't fair of me to ask you to give up champagne. I would…understand if sometimes you wanted more."

Jeanne's mouth parted in surprise. "Toneke, that's a generous offer. Are you certain?"

"No, I'm not certain!" The words burned on her tongue and she kept her eyes on the floor for fear of not being able to get them all out. "I'm terrified. I'm terrified I might lose you to someone more charming, more beautiful than I could ever be. But I'm also terrified that I'll lose you by holding you too tightly. I don't make you laugh the way she did. I can't flirt and I can't dance. And the parties you enjoy so much only leave me tired and lonely. I can see where it will end. What you feel for me will shrivel up into regret and obligation."

She felt the touch of a kidskin glove under her chin and Jeanne's fingers warm through it, drawing her face up so that she couldn't avoid her eyes. "Toneke, no one can see the future, but have more faith in me than that." Jeanne's eyes searched hers, looking for that faith. "Do you trust me?"

"I trust you," Antuniet said, "but I want you to be happy."

"I *am* happy. I am more happy than I deserve to be. And it wasn't what you thought." She nodded out across the floor toward the blue-gowned girl. "Iustin's nothing but a musician Chanturi wants me to help launch. He thinks I should turn my talents to a better use than opera parties." With a lightness that Antuniet saw through, she added, "It seems my days planning opera parties may have come to an end. I have finally succeeded in moving beyond mere eccentricity to outright scandal. I'm finding it strangely liberating."

Antuniet felt Jeanne's fingers entwine in her own and her hand was raised up to be kissed, there in the grand assembly room before everyone. "And now I would like to take advantage of my newfound freedom. I refuse to believe that you can't dance. Will you dance with me now?"

The waltz had been playing for some time when they joined the dancers. There was space only for a dozen turns across the floor—barely time for a few whispers to begin before the music faded and they were left gazing into each other's eyes. Suddenly, Jeanne pulled her by the hand out past the curious watchers into the gallery beyond until they came to a niche by the stairs where a measure of privacy could be achieved. Jeanne took both her hands and held them up against her breast. "Toneke…Antuniet, come live with me."

"What?" she said, too startled to be more articulate.

"Live with me," Jeanne repeated earnestly. "Share my house. Let me see your face across the breakfast table every morning. Let me give you this certainty: that whatever may happen out here—" she waved her hand to encompass the assembly beyond "—I will never come home to anyone but you."

"Are you certain?" Antuniet could see all the difficulties. The workshop on Trez Cherfis was nothing to take comfort in, but it had been her refuge for over a year. Almost a home. To be instead a guest in another's house, even in Jeanne's… And if there had been gossip before, what would they bring on themselves now?

"I have never been more certain of anything in my life."

* * *

It wasn't as simple to leave Trez Cherfis as it had been to arrive. When Monterrez had first hired the building for her, she had brought little more than the clothes on her back and the worn satchel containing her one treasure. Now there was all the remaining equipment and supplies to deliver to the palace grounds. Even having taken her best gowns to Jeanne's house long since, she would need to borrow a valise for the rest of her wardrobe. And there was the staff. The two men who had shared the duties of guard took the news in good part, but Mefro Feldin bristled when told that her services were no longer required.

"But it's not as if I could keep you on," Antuniet said, attempting to soften the dismissal. "Mesnera de Cherdillac has her own housekeeper." No need to mention that even if the post were vacant and had Feldin not succeeded in offending everyone, she was far from being suitable for a vicomtesse's household.

"So this place isn't good enough for you now you have a royal appointment?" Feldin said acidly, as if even the veneer of deference had peeled away. "You may turn your back on what you've done here, but I won't forget. It's a hard time of year to be looking for a position."

The hint of threat was unmistakable, but Antuniet wanted only to be done with the matter. "I'll ask Maisetra Sovitre to give you two months' wages to see you through. And a character, if you need one." Though what sort of character it would be she didn't care to promise. And whatever it was that Margerit offered her, it failed to induce her to remain until the place was emptied.

Antuniet paused in the doorway to look back at the bare rooms before locking the door for the last time. So much had happened within these walls.

The final task had been to clear out the little charms and mysteries she had laid on all the windows and doors—more comfort than protection in these last months. She pulled the door shut and removed the key. Behind her, Jeanne sat waiting in the hired fiacre. "Shall we go home?" she asked as Antuniet climbed inside.

It was a dizzy, disorienting feeling to come home to a place one had known as a stranger. Antuniet had expected…she wasn't sure what she had expected. Not this. Not the ease of slipping on a well-tailored glove. Tomric greeted her at the door with the same distant affection he showed to Jeanne. Marien bustled into the room after her to set her few things to rights. The maid laid out her dinner clothes with a vague but unmistakable hint that she was grateful her mistress was settling down at last. Did Jeanne know how lucky she was to be surrounded by such loyalty? Of course she did. No doubt her present security was the product of long years of careful attention.

Antuniet wandered aimlessly around the room, running her fingers over the polished mahogany of the dresser, peeking out between the curtains at the view of the yard behind. This room was the match to Jeanne's bedroom, connecting through the small dressing room. Who had used it last? She knew that Jeanne had never installed any of her passing flirtations in this house. The furnishings followed the fashion of the previous generation and had a hint of a masculine air. She tried to remember what she'd heard of Jeanne's marriage. Had they lived together here? Or had she only inherited the house after his death? It didn't matter. Evidently the room was to be hers now. She was still staring out the window when she heard Jeanne's footsteps behind her and felt her arms encircle her waist.

"Do you like it? I don't know that you'll get much use of the bed but I wanted you to have your own room. I didn't make any changes yet. I wanted you to make it over for yourself."

It was the purest luxury: to lean back into those arms and breathe in the scent of spice and roses that always followed Jeanne. Yes, it could be home perhaps, in time.

They made love that night, not with the hungry fervor of their earliest encounters, but in a long, slow exploration, as if time no longer had any meaning.

There was so much and yet so little to do. When it came to the work itself, Antuniet felt at a loss, like a runner who has finished his race and stares blankly around. She moved from task to task, idly organizing the notes and lists that had accumulated during the last few months and trying to remember the projects she had set aside for the commission. The furnace in the palace workshop had sat cold for two weeks now while the old quarters on Trez Cherfis were cleared out. Anna was still unpacking the crates and baskets to combine the contents of the two buildings.

"Have you found the double alembic yet?" Antuniet asked, seeing the last of the glass vessels set carefully into their stands.

"No, Maisetra," she answered. "And not the brass-bound box you asked me to watch for either."

Antuniet frowned and began circling the room, reviewing the contents of every shelf and cupboard. The alembic might simply have been broken and discarded in the confusion of the move, but the other was more worrisome. The small box had little real value. The stones it held had no special enhancements but they were her first experiments in the layered cibation. No doubt they would turn up eventually. She thought she'd last seen them in the upper chamber on Trez Cherfis; perhaps they'd been packed with her personal things by mistake. She was crouching to poke through odds and ends thrust into a cubbyhole that was meant to store kindling, when the door opened and Anna's hurried, "Welcome, Mesnera!" claimed her attention.

"I fear you've caught us still in disarray," she said, climbing to her feet as Princess Annek entered with the usual crowd of attendants. In truth, the greater part of the chaos had been tamed but the room held neither a presentable tidiness nor the forgivable clutter of work underway. "Is there something I can do for you?"

"I was curious to see what you plan next," Annek said as she looked about the room.

"Whatever you command, of course," Antuniet said. "Anna, fetch a seat for Her Grace if she wishes."

"We don't mean to stay." A wave of the hand cut short Anna's scramble. "I was only curious to know how matters stand. In time, I have a few ideas to discuss with you. But for now, I think perhaps I should like to see where your own vision takes you." She hesitated; one might almost think she was embarrassed. "You have a remarkable talent. I am sorry I was not able to reward you as you desired."

She seemed sincere enough, though it was also true that nothing had prevented her but her own choice. Antuniet nodded in acknowledgment but moved to a new topic. "Will Baron Razik continue to assist with the work?" They had seen nothing of Efriturik since before the New Year's court.

Annek's response began stiffly. "It's time for my son to move on to other responsibilities. I think perhaps I shall allow him to take up a commission." But then her voice warmed. "He's grown steadier under your watch. I confess I lent him in answer to Maisetra Sovitre's request as much to keep him busy and out of trouble as to have another set of eyes on your work."

Well, there was no surprise in that.

"It's changed him for the better. I hadn't thought to have that to thank you for. I've been thinking…" But whatever her thought had been, she chose not to complete it.

"He's no scholar," Antuniet said bluntly. "But he has a flair for the work and I could always rely on him." It was true and she'd miss his presence. At the first, she'd thought him no different from the usual run of young noblemen, and she had little patience for that sort. But he'd become part of the close-knit crew that had brought their ship to harbor at last. "I think you can give me little credit if he's matured," she said. "Young men are best when given an occupation they value. A cavalry commission will suit him better than alchemy, I suspect."

"Perhaps," Annek agreed. But Antuniet felt the weight of her measuring gaze until at last she signaled to her retinue and they wheeled and left like a flock of pigeons.

"We'll need to find another assistant or two," Antuniet told Anna after the princess had left. Margerit had been a rock of support but she had her own studies to take up again. And Jeanne—no doubt Jeanne would come any time she asked, but the workshop no longer need be their meeting place. Better to leave Jeanne free for her own pursuits. And there was no need to lean on those few ties now. A royal alchemist would find it far easier to hire assistants and even to find new apprentices than a penniless exile could have hoped for. And with Annek's open patronage, there was no fear that her studies would be taken for anything darker.

* * *

With the press of the work drawn back and the seal of royal approval, Antuniet found her evenings more and more turned outward. If the rumor of scandal had reduced the claims on Jeanne's time from the more staid of the matrons, it caused no diminution in invitations from old friends. And there were still those who could forgive much for a chance at the ties Jeanne could provide. "Any tool for the job," Jeanne said cheerfully when Antuniet questioned her about an invitation from the Marzulins. "I scarcely knew who they were either, but they fit my requirements. It wouldn't do to try to launch Chanturi's violinist at the *Salle-Chapil* under someone like the Penilluks or the Aruliks. No one would pay much attention to the music; it would just be another party. I need a hostess who would be too flattered by the offer to question the choice."

"Flattered indeed." Antuniet cast her eyes over the ornate invitation. "I don't know whether to be grateful or insulted that she's invited me."

"Be flattered for yourself," Jeanne said. "For I never even mentioned your name. It was Maisetra Marzulin who asked if she might aspire to the company of Princess Annek's alchemist on the thread of our friendship. I've shamelessly allowed her to use my name in the invitations. Tio has promised to come as well."

That might have set her mind against going if it hadn't meant so much to Jeanne. The concert was to be a small affair, no more than fifty guests, perhaps. The sponsor Jeanne had chosen to approach was a man of middle years who had made his fortune in canal-building and was now setting about the business of seeing that his children would climb a few steps higher in Rotenek society than he had. Of course, it had been his wife whom Jeanne had approached, and she had taken some coaxing, for she was badly daunted by the list of names that were proposed. Antuniet had listened to Jeanne's tales of the struggle day by day over breakfast.

308 Heather Rose Jones

"I don't know why she thought they were buying that enormous house out past the north gate if it were only to entertain shopkeepers," Jeanne had complained. "Though I suppose Maistir Marzulin bought it just to show he could. But their place is exactly the size for what I have in mind. Something intimate to set Iustin off at the start. Rumor will whet the appetite. Soon people will be clamoring to hear her play simply to hold it over their friends who haven't."

Antuniet looked around as they entered the half-filled room. Not so large as the ballroom at Margerit's place in Chalanz, but enough that Rotenek standards would consider it vulgar for a townhouse. Much of the crowd might be thought vulgar as well, but that was all part of Jeanne's plan. Her complex logic had reminded Antuniet why she'd hated her mother's attempts to teach her how to plan entertainments. Baits and lures, flattery and envy, pride and curiosity. But this was Jeanne's artistry: to bring people together for a purpose beyond them all and convince each one he had the best of it.

The *burfroi* crowd had been carefully seeded with more elevated guests—ones with enough reason for their presence to be unremarkable, and lending enough cachet to cast a mantle of success over it all. There was Count Chanturi, of course, over by the pianoforte, speaking with his protégée and with Ion-Pazit, the composer who would accompany her himself. And Chanturi had drawn in Felzin and one of the Salun brothers. Emill Chaluk was well known as a great admirer of Ion-Pazit's work, and with her one could include her two nephews without seeming too forward. Chaluk was holding forth to them on the intricacies of the composer's rhythms, to the rapt entertainment of a small crowd. And as promised, Jeanne had delivered the younger set as well. Tio, Elin and Iaklin had accepted, which Maisetra Marzulin had unaccountably considered a great coup, giving rise to outrageous rumors that Princess Elisebet herself might make an unheralded appearance. The rest were nobody Antuniet expected to know.

When the music finally began, Antuniet could see why Jeanne had chosen such a setting. Ion-Pazit's work was...daring might be the kindest word. A traditionalist might say he broke rules, but it was clear that he merely considered rules to be beneath him. Jeanne whispered that he'd agreed to let the Mazzies girl perform this work only because the other violinists capable of the part refused to touch it, and those who were willing to put up with his temper he considered to be idiots.

Iustin Mazzies addressed the piece with the focus and tenacity of a striking hawk, though there were parts where Antuniet thought the better image might be a terrier on a rat. The two seemed not so much to be playing in concert as to be locked in combat over the soul of the music. The least one might say was that the unrelenting intensity of the piece left no one unmoved.

With the final chord, there was a moment of stunned silence, as if the audience were uncertain what it had heard. A few quick glances passed among the crowd, gauging whether they were meant to approve of it. Then a sprinkling of applause began, gaining ground as the uncertain ones feared to be left behind. That was Jeanne's genius as well. A more sophisticated crowd might be less willing to be led against their own taste. Antuniet hadn't cared much for the music, but the artistry—of all types—that she could admire.

There was still the reception to be endured afterward, with Antuniet keeping close to Jeanne's side to avoid being drawn into other conversations. And that meant attending on their hostess as she accepted the congratulations of the guests. Tio and her set seemed determined to make their curtsey and leave early.

"It was so kind of you to come," Maisetra Marzulin repeated to each. "I hope you enjoyed the concert. We had hoped perhaps you might be joined…" Her voice trailed off. The rumored hope of Elisebet's presence was too presumptuous to voice.

Elin began, "It wasn't possible. Not under the circumstances—"

Tio hushed her but added more pleasantly, "I wouldn't have missed the concert. Jeanne has quite an eye for talented young women."

When Maisetra Marzulin laughed politely and moved on, Jeanne lowered her voice to ask, "What was that about? No, not your comment. The other matter."

Tio glanced back at her companions. Her voice, too, came in a whisper. "It's Chustin. Princess Elisebet is in quite a state from worry over him." Antuniet felt Tio's glare as she added, "And don't tell me she's making too much of sniffles. The boy's ill. Has been since Christmas. He sleeps sixteen hours in the day and suffers from evil dreams. She's had four or five doctors to see him and taken him to her favorite thaumaturgist as well but they only shake their heads."

Well, perhaps there was something in it this time. Certainly Tio wasn't feigning concern and she didn't seem given to mad fancies. The news sobered the remainder of their evening. Yet, all in all, the affair seemed a success. And by the time they reached home, Jeanne was planning the next setting for Iustin's conquest of Rotenek's concert halls.

CHAPTER THIRTY-FOUR

Margerit

"Have you ever considered adding music to your mysteries?" Serafina asked.

The thin winter sun had faded enough that Margerit had risen to light the lamps and ring for someone to tend to the fire. She paused for a moment to wonder why it seemed such an outlandish idea. "We never have. It isn't traditional in Alpennian ceremonies." Saying that, she realized how thin an excuse it seemed.

Barbara seemed less taken aback. "I saw one once in Genoa that included hymns, but of course I have no idea whether they added to the effectiveness."

"I've always wondered about that," Serafina continued. "In Rome there's such a separation between mysteries and the sacraments proper. Music belongs to the Mass, for the most part. But I experienced a mystery with music once in Palermo that—" Her eyes went misty for a moment and she hugged herself tightly. "I can't explain. I would give anything to feel that again."

It was the long, quiet season between the New Year and the beginning of the Lenten term. Margerit had plunged into working through the Mauriz notes alongside Serafina—not student, but not quite teacher. More a renewal of those exciting days during her early studies when she and Barbara would explore the whole universe of philosophy and argue out from first principles to last conclusions together. Barbara had taken up the return to their close studies enthusiastically.

"Perhaps," Margerit said slowly, "the difference is in how rare *auditors* are in comparison with *vidators*."

Serafina shook her head. "You forget how rare it is to sense the *fluctus* reliably at all. Don't argue from your own case. If we were discussing market-charms I might agree. But the formal mysteries have either been set for centuries or are built up out of parts of those, like what you described of your new Mauriz. I could accept that a new mystery like that one might exclude hymns and music because its sources did, but not that it was a deliberate and considered omission. If words are the building blocks of powerful mysteries, why shouldn't music—which stirs our hearts so strongly—add its part? You said yourself that you sometimes see the *fluctus* as currents of music."

"Have you ever seen it happen?" Margerit asked.

"Only that once. I see things—wondrous things, and I feel…" She laughed. "I haven't the words. That's why I came to you! I know something is happening, but I don't know what or why—or how to bring it about."

A knock on the door interrupted them. "That will be someone to build up the fire," Margerit said, and called out an invitation.

Instead of the expected maid, Brandel poked his head in. "Pardon me, Cousin Barbara, Maisetras, but there's an urgent message come from the palace. I told him I'd fetch you." Barbara began to rise but he said, "No, it's for Maisetra Sovitre. I think she's asked to come. The man is waiting."

It wasn't unusual for Annek to send for her unexpectedly, but never with such urgency. The only project she was working on at the moment was a review of the Royal Guild's Easter mysteries, and surely there was no rush to finish that.

Afternoon had faded to dusk by the time the carriage turned through the gates of the palace grounds, crunching on the crusted snow piled in the shadow of the walls. And after that, there was an hour to wait in the chilly gallery. At last she was escorted in to find the office deserted except for the woman behind the writing table.

Princess Annek looked far more worried than Margerit had seen her before and barely acknowledged her salutation except to say, "I thank you for coming so quickly." She gestured to a chair opposite her. After Margerit obeyed, there was a long silence, as if the princess weren't certain how to begin. "Do you have any experience with *mysteria veridica*? With truth mysteries?" Annek asked at last.

"No," Margerit said in surprise. "Not really; I've never studied them. I thought…that is, I know they're used in the courts on occasion. Barbara told me something about that—that they weren't part of Lord Chormuin's bill. But I thought they were rare."

"Yes, like any of the lesser mysteries, there's the problem of finding a reliable practitioner. The magistrates sometimes call in a priest to administer them, whether they have any skill or not. They're more use in frightening people into confessing than to distinguish between truth and lies. I may have need of a means to distinguish just that. Or to prove the innocence of someone wrongly accused. Do you think you could devise a truth mystery that would make the judgment evident to all?"

"I don't know, Your Grace. I don't think it's possible, unless..." She considered carefully. "I would need to study the existing forms. Isn't the judgment usually returned in a vision? That makes it difficult. But it might be possible to tie it to a tangible sign." She thought back to that first time she had been so blessed, when the cherries bloomed for her on Saint Chertrut's day. "Yes, a physical sign so all can see the result. When would you need me to be ready?"

"That is uncertain," Annek said. "Perhaps it won't be necessary at all. Tell me, how well do you know Maisetra Chazillen?"

And what does Antuniet have to do with this? she wondered. But perhaps there was no connection. "Well enough. We've worked side by side for the past year," she said. "And before that—" She hesitated, but Annek knew the whole story well. "Before that we worked together in the Guild of Saint Atelpirt."

Princess Annek tapped a finger softly against her lips while she considered. "Do you know any reason why Maisetra Chazillen might have a grudge against my cousin Elisebet or her son?"

"No," she said quickly. Too quickly, perhaps. "I don't think that Antuniet cares for politics at all. She had no part in her brother's plot against you. She never openly supported any side in the succession. I think the only cause she cares for is the Chazillen name."

"Yes," Annek said slowly. "And if that were the matter, then why—" She shook her head. "There has been talk. Your friend has opened herself to suspicions and accusations. I do not speak only of the alchemy."

Now it was "your friend" and not "my alchemist." Margerit felt a chill. The indifference of society had its limits. "Your Grace?" she ventured hesitantly. "Might I ask...It would be easier to devise the mystery you want if I knew what sort of truth I'm seeking."

"You have heard that Aukustin has not been well."

Margerit frowned. "I heard something of that, but nobody gave it much credence. Princess Elisebet is always concerned over something."

"It seems this was more serious," Annek continued. "Aukustin has been ill since before the New Year's court. Badly ill. Doctors have been no avail. Princess Elisebet consulted a thaumaturgist but evidently the man was perplexed, until he thought to examine Aukustin's chambers. Whatever he saw there, he had them take the bed apart. And hidden in the mattresses were a number of curious stones."

At that word, Margerit felt a shiver. "Many people use amulets and talismans. Could they have been meant for his protection?"

Annek shook her head. "I know only a little of the matter, and that only through my spies. But the thaumaturgist said at least some of the stones were clearly of ill intent. And now I expect that Elisebet is recalling that my son has been hard at work all this autumn creating powerful talismanic gems. She's ever eager to blame him for any accident that befalls Aukustin, and that affair with the ships was ill-timed. But it seems to me that were Elisebet's prejudice set aside, it would be more natural for suspicion for this particular affair to fall on my new alchemist. So I ask you again, do you know of any reason why Antuniet Chazillen would seek to do harm to Aukustin?"

"No!" Margerit's emphatic answer came from her heart, not her head. Did Annek think to turn suspicion away from Efriturik by offering Antuniet in his place? "I can't imagine any reason why she would have an interest in him at all."

"Very well," Annek said, though she seemed far from convinced. "But you can see why I might have need of a means for establishing the truth beyond any doubt. Whether my son or my alchemist, someone will come to be blamed in time. I don't know if it will be a matter for the courts…There's nothing yet of accusation, only rumor. Before that changes, see what you can do. And keep this matter as quiet as may be." But as Margerit was departing, she added, "You have leave to tell Baroness Saveze. Tell her I'd like to see her keen edge brought to bear on it."

It would have been exhilarating to be set onto a new type of mystery, if not for the cloud of peril hanging over it. Barbara received the news with a frown of concern, but when she heard the message from Princess Annek, a fierce interest leapt in her eyes.

"What does she mean by that?" Margerit asked.

Barbara grinned. "It means she's unleashed me to look for the true villain."

"Do you think that this is Kreiser again, meddling in Efriturik's affairs?" The thought was new, sparked by Barbara's words.

"Perhaps, but it's hard to see how it could benefit him, unless his goal is simply to bring down both Alpennian heirs at once. Either the stones were meant to be found and the plot is aimed at Efriturik, or they were meant to stay hidden and Chustin was the target. But could the one who put them there know which it would be?"

Yes, it was exciting to have a new challenge. Too exciting, should she be unsuccessful.

Serafina took the news of the change in focus for their studies with curiosity. "But that's what it means to be a royal thaumaturgist," Margerit explained, leaving the details silent. "I'm set to odd little projects all the time." To deflect her curiosity, Margerit told her of the installment ceremony for Baron Razik.

"I've heard of mysteries used for determining guilt," Serafina said, "but I never studied them before. I think Kant considers the problem, but he seems to think that truth means such different things in philosophy and in the courts of law that there is no point in pursuing them by the same means. I do recall that he dismisses the possibility that a *veriloquium* could be used to answer philosophical questions. They answer only what is understood in the mind of the one questioned."

"Kant," Barbara said, noting down the name. "Margerit, you're more familiar with the modern philosophers. What do we have of his?" She crossed to the shelves and searched until she pulled out a thick black-bound volume. "*Judgment*?" she asked.

Serafina shook her head. "No, I think it was his *Reason*, but he won't have any practical advice on mysteries. He was a Lutheran you know."

"Who else?" Margerit asked. "Barbara, when you studied law, did it cover this topic?"

Barbara paused her pen. "There's a long section in the *Statuta Antiqua* that discusses the circumstances of their use, but not the rituals themselves. I remember there was that brief section in *Fortunatus*, but only from a theoretical point of view and nothing at all as detailed as you'd find today. I rather suspect the topic is too…I suppose I would say too practical for him. I'll read through the *Statuta* to see if they mention any names or cases and perhaps LeFevre would have ideas. It wouldn't fall at all within his legal interests but he likes to read through records of old cases and may remember mentions of times when *veriloquia* were used."

"And what about Prince Filip?" Margerit asked with a sudden thought. The other two stared at her. "I remember from my history books. There was that scandal over his cousin's parentage during his reign and I think they used some type of *mysterium veridicum* to sort it out. I don't think the chronicles mention any details beyond that, but the archives—"

Barbara nodded sharply. "Yes, that should fall within the records that still survive. I don't know whether those years would be in the palace archives or held at the cathedral but—" A slow smile crept across her face. "I think perhaps I shall set Brandel on it. He needs to be reminded that adventure can be found in books other than romances."

It was the old excitement again. That sense of a small band hunting down the secrets of the ages. Urgency gave it an uncomfortable edge. Margerit knew she could be as discreet as the grave and the story would still find its way out through others. Annek might have good cause to keep the matter quiet while it was resolved and Elisebet's people were strangely silent as well, but too many people would know some small fragment, people who had no such qualms.

Whispers soon grew into rumors that sorcery had a hand in Aukustin's malady. Margerit found it easy to laugh off the gossip the first time it came to her in the corridors of the opera house. Everyone knew how Elisebet jumped at shadows where her son was concerned. It was harder to dismiss the strained looks on the faces of Elisebet's ladies when they were seen about town. And yet no names were named, no accusations made. Perhaps even Elisebet realized there would be no turning back once that was done. Proof would be needed, proof of a sort that could stand under law.

Sorcery, the rumors said; nothing more specific. But sorcery was a slippery charge, more often used from malice than conviction. Margerit watched Antuniet carefully as *l'affaire Augustin* was discussed before her, but she gave no sign that she considered it anything to do with her.

By the end of a week, their research had outgrown the library tables. Margerit briefly considered commanding an office at the palace for the work, but that seemed too public. Here there was no close scrutiny from outsiders.

"Aunt Bertrut?" she began one morning. "I'm going to need to take over one of the other rooms. I need more space for our books and papers. I thought perhaps the dining room? Or perhaps the front parlor? I could bring in some trestles but then you'd need to entertain visitors somewhere else and I'd hate to ask you to use the upstairs sitting room."

"It's your house, dear," Bertrut replied mildly. "How long do you think it will take?"

"I don't know," Margerit said with a frown. "Perhaps a week? Maybe two?"

"We have the Faikrimeks invited for dinner on Wednesday."

"Then it must be the parlor, I'm afraid. Do you mind dreadfully? I wish I had some proper place to do my work. What I want is a home the size of Fonten House but here in Rotenek!"

Aunt Bertrut took her at her word. "You could take a house out past the north gate, I suppose. There are always estates on offer there. But everyone would stare if you gave up a place on the Vezenaf to move to the edge of town! We'll rub along the best we can for now."

Barbara had obtained the *expositula* for the truth-mysteries used in the Rotenek courts and together they picked them to pieces, teasing out the formulas and structures that lay beneath. Serafina was mostly silent the first few days, taking the notes from their discussions and listening intently.

"Did you have any thoughts?" Margerit asked, after watching her puzzle through the diagrams.

"More questions than thoughts," she admitted. "I'd rather watch you work. I want to see how you go about developing the ceremonies. I want to see the paths you follow in your analysis and how you map them. When I read the notes you'd taken on the Mauriz *tutela* it was like nothing I'd seen before, and I've reviewed a great many treatises on the structure of mysteries at the Vatican."

Margerit wished she could invite Antuniet into their circle but suspicion cast a shadow over everything. Better to keep the matter close for now.

By the sixth day they had begun building the parts together again. Brandel had contributed his mite, though the chronicles he had tracked down only confirmed that once, years ago, someone had built a *veriloquium* whose judgment was visible to all.

When she had real hope of success, though not finished in the details, Margerit brought her report to the palace.

Annek listened closely and cast a quick eye over the outlines of the ceremony. "And this…this *lux veritatis* will work as you say?" she asked. "The answering judgment will be apparent to all present?"

"It should be," Margerit said. "Baroness Saveze could see it plainly in the changes to the quality of the light and she has no special sensitivity at all. I thought it best to use the flame as a signal, as it fits best with the language of scripture. The only concern is with how the saints interpret the question of truth."

"*Quid est veritas?* What is truth? Isn't that what Pilate asked Our Lord? Even the saints have been known to bend the truth in service to greater truth. But I think if the need comes, we can set questions that can be answered clearly."

"Will we need it at all?" Margerit ventured to ask. "I've heard that Aukustin is nearly recovered."

Annek's lips thinned as if she would not answer. But then she said, "I don't know. My cousin seems unlikely to let this pass. Eventually Efriturik will need to return to Rotenek. Then we shall see."

Has he been kept away deliberately? Margerit wondered. But that might make sense. If Elisebet planned to make an accusation, she would need to wait for his return to lay the charge officially. Would she dare? Even as she asked herself the question, Margerit knew the answer. Elisebet had been slipping further from sense where Aukustin was concerned. If she truly believed that Efriturik had meant to harm the boy, she would have no qualms about accusing him, even though it tore the land apart.

Barbara, she knew, would have her own news to take to the palace. In moments between their study sessions, she'd been busy about the town with her own sources of information: the boy's tutor, Jeanne's friends among Elisebet's ladies. But none had been forthcoming with more than expressions of vague concern. The dowager princess's household had closed ranks waiting for her to act.

"There's little I can do on that question," Barbara told her in a private moment, "unless I know the nature of the amulets. And the date when Aukustin's malady first started. Now there's a problem! How do I tease out the real illness from Elisebet's fancies? I can't go to Elisebet herself unless the matter becomes public. I've been half expecting her to send for me as she has in the past."

As Margerit worked to put the final touches on the *veriloquium*, Barbara cast her net wider. "I'm not saying I've written Kreiser out of the question entirely," she said. "But Elisebet has been right in one thing: there have been some very strange accidents around Aukustin for more than a year. Every time—the true accidents, not the ones Elisebet imagined—he should have been safe among friends and members of the court. At least one of the hands behind this is someone close." She was pacing back and forth as she spoke. "That's why Kreiser doesn't fit this time. The first incident I know was at that hunt a year ago at Feniz. Kreiser would have been newly arrived then. No time to get a man in place within Elisebet's household."

"Unless there was one already," Margerit suggested. "Would the ambassador have planted men within the court?"

Barbara paused to consider the question. "Undoubtedly. I can't rule that out. But I don't think—" She hesitated. "I don't think Kreiser works so closely with him. The ambassador has been in Rotenek for ten years. Kreiser has the feel of a new man, a hungry man. He came here on Antuniet's track for a specific purpose, though he seems to have stayed on other orders. He's looking to make his mark in some way. But the one he wants to impress is the Emperor Franz, not some minor diplomat in Alpennia. And he—" Barbara frowned in concentration. "I can't explain. That last time we met him at the New Year's court, it was like crossing blades at the fencing *salle*. You learn things about a man that way—things he doesn't mean to tell you. This doesn't *feel* like his work."

Barbara's eyes went far away in thought once more. But if those thoughts produced any concrete plan, she was not yet ready to share it.

CHAPTER THIRTY-FIVE

Jeanne

Jeanne hesitated in front of Tio's door before raising her hand to the knocker. If it were only that Tio had grown stiff and silent in public, the tension in Princess Elisebet's household would be explanation enough. That, too, could explain Tio's absence from their usual haunts. But it had become clear the night before at Maisetra Pertrez's affair that Tio was very specifically not speaking to *her*. What other explanation could there possibly be for Tio's sudden interest in Chara's new carriage when she approached? Everyone was all secrets and silences these days but from her it was too much to leave unanswered. If they were no longer to be friends, Tio would need to say so in her presence. Jeanne rapped sharply upon the door.

"Is Mesnera Perzin at home?" she asked. It was a bit early for proper visiting. She had chosen the time deliberately to have a chance at finding her alone. The footman who answered gave her entrance with no comment, so he'd had no specific instructions to refuse her. Not chancing that it had been an oversight, she presumed further on familiarity and said, "No need to trouble yourself announcing me. I know where she'll be this time of day."

Sure enough, Tio was in her dressing room, contemplating a choice of shawls. But when she turned in startlement her face suffused with guilt, not pleasure.

"Oh! Jeanne! I hadn't expected you."

"And when have we ever cared about that?" Jeanne said, giving her a quick peck on the cheek and settling onto the velvet chaise. That would make her more difficult to dislodge. "Now tell me all the news. It's been ages since we had time to chat."

Tio twisted the delicate cashmere in her hands until Jeanne was surprised it didn't rip asunder. "I wish I could. Jeanne, I…" Jeanne waited, refusing to smooth the path. Abruptly, Tio exclaimed, "I think I hear the baby crying."

"Don't be silly," Jeanne said. "You hear no such thing and if you did, the nurse would be far more use than you would. Let's not mince words; we've known each other too long and too well for that. I won't ask anything about the goings-on at the palace, if that's your concern, but talk to me about something. Whatever you please. What have I done to offend you?"

Tio looked ready to cry and finally sat on the edge of the chaise next to her. "It's not…It's not you. You know I trust you. But I don't know…I can't… She's always there beside you. And everyone's been whispering about you. Oh Jeanne, I don't know what I can say. I don't know what to do."

She, Jeanne thought. "This is about Antuniet?" The question came out more stiffly than she had intended. Tio had been jealous for the last year but this came from more than jealousy.

Tio shook her head but not, it seemed, in denial. "I can't talk about it. Sain-Mazzi would kill me." She sounded genuinely afraid. "She doesn't trust anyone; she spies on us all. She'll know you've been here. Jeanne, please, just leave me alone. Everyone will know soon enough." She looked toward the window, as if expecting someone to appear momentarily. "Then it will all be over."

Over. What would be over? And what did it have to do with Antuniet? But Tio refused to say more and it seemed cruel to add to her distress. Jeanne gave her a brief hug and stood. "You needn't think you've driven me away entirely. I wish you would trust me."

Tio's cryptic fears infected her. What could Antuniet possibly have to do with the currents running through Elisebet's household? No one was telling the half of what they knew or even what they guessed. There was no use to ask Barbara anything; she'd tried already to no avail. And her other sources of gossip cut too broadly across palace allegiances for the topic to be safe, for what everyone did know was that it concerned rivalry between Atilliets. Toneke had fixed herself to Annek's star to be sure, but so had many with ambitions in Rotenek. That alone shouldn't draw her into the affair.

Impulsively she rapped on the roof of the fiacre to signal the driver to stop. "I've changed my mind," she told him. "Take me around to the north side of the palace, the gate by the gardens." Antuniet wasn't expecting her but there were no firings planned these days, no work that couldn't be disturbed.

The most convenient route to the new workshop went nowhere near the main gates off the Plaiz. So only the unsettled mood of the day presaged the uproar drifting out from the palace proper. It came first in the form of footsteps, just a few, more rushed and more frequent than would be typical on that part of the grounds. Then two of the palace guards crossed past the windows that gave out toward the garden, heading on a path that led to the gate. Even Antuniet found that unusual enough to comment.

"Was there something happening when you came in?" she asked.

Worry pooled in the pit of Jeanne's stomach. "I don't know. Everyone's on edge today for no good reason. I went to see Tio this morning and she—" A heavy tread stopped in the corridor outside the door. "Let me," she said when Antuniet would have gone to open it. Why this dread?

More guards. The one standing in the doorway bowed politely to acknowledge her and asked, "Is Maisetra Chazillen within?"

"Yes," Antuniet said, coming up behind her. "What's wrong?"

"Her Grace has suggested that it might be better for you to return home, if that's convenient. I've come to see you to the gates."

"It's not convenient," Antuniet said sharply. "And if I'm to be interrupted in the middle of my work, I'd prefer to know why."

Whatever it is, Jeanne thought. *This is what Tio meant. That we'd know soon enough.* "Give us a moment to set things in order," she asked the man. "And perhaps you could send someone to arrange for a carriage? We hadn't expected to be leaving so soon."

He signaled to a second man still waiting in the hallway. Unlike everyone else in the city, he seemed willing to answer questions. "It's nothing to do with you, Maisetra," he said to Antuniet. "I'm surprised you haven't heard already. The Dowager Princess Elisebet has accused Baron Razik of using sorcery to attack her son. She arranged to lay the charge when he rode through the palace gates at noon. We've been asked to keep the grounds clear. In case of trouble between the two sides."

"Sorcery?" Antuniet said in amazement. "But that's absurd. Baron Razik hasn't the slightest interest in—"

Jeanne thought the realization must have struck them both at the same time. Sorcery covered a great many charges when stretched: any dabbling in matters outside the purely physical, save those that fell under the church. Sorcery was rarely invoked unless there were harm done. Yet there was one such field in which Efriturik had been thoroughly involved: alchemy. And if that were what lay beneath…

Jeanne caught Antuniet's eye and tried to give a warning. "Yes, of course, we understand," she said to the guard. "Anna, have you finished there? Get your things and we'll be on our way."

They took the long way home, looping down south of the river to deliver Anna home. The carriage ride was silent until they were alone again. "What can it mean?" Antuniet asked. "Has Elisebet entirely lost her senses?"

"Not entirely," Jeanne said slowly. "Something has been wrong with Chustin. Oh, I doubt Efriturik had any more to do with it this time than any other. But Elisebet has been determined to make bad blood between them. And Toneke, we must be careful." She told her of the visit to Tio and the warning. "I don't know what that means. Whether Tio was afraid that I'd let things slip to you and through you to him, or whether it's been whispered that you might be accused as well. That's why I came to see you, not even knowing what I should worry about."

She saw the old haunted look cast a veil over Antuniet's eyes and reached out to clutch her hand tightly. "Don't be afraid. You've done nothing wrong."

"When has that saved me before?" she said grimly. "And we have done wrong—what they would count as wrong." Antuniet stared out the carriage window. "We should have been more careful. We've set ourselves outside the walls and now the wolves have come. What if I'm to be sacrificed for Efriturik's sake?"

"There's no reason even to think that," Jeanne said. "It's not you that Elisebet hates."

But that night Toneke woke screaming again as she hadn't for months, and Jeanne could do nothing but hold her.

* * *

The accusation might not have broken the peace except that it came in the week of Carnival. Even so, there were fewer than a dozen open quarrels in the streets, and only two of those settled honor with the point of swords. Like all sensible people, Jeanne kept close to home despite the holiday.

Then, with the somber arrival of Lent, it seemed that all was still again. The law would take its measures in due time. Elisebet might lay a charge in anger, but the arguments would take longer to build. After two days of quiet, Antuniet ventured to return to her work and Jeanne finally found the uncertainty unbearable. Surely Barbara's tongue would be looser now.

She took the brief trip to Tiporsel and asked if Baroness Saveze were at home. Maisetra Pertinek met her with a cheerful countenance that left Jeanne wondering whether her quest had been in vain. Had Barbara's household been left entirely untouched by the unrest in the city?

"They're none of them here at the moment, Vicomtesse," the woman said. "But I expect them soon. They've all gone off to the cathedral for experiments. Would you like to take a cup of tea while you wait?"

Jeanne nodded absently, then smiled to make the acceptance more gracious. "Yes, if it's no trouble."

"Oh, not at all. I'm at home this morning," she said, "and only waiting to see if anyone calls. I'm afraid I'm entertaining in the breakfast parlor at the moment. Margerit has taken over the other for her project and there's papers everywhere." She shrugged, though her voice held pride, not impatience.

They made idle conversation; it was a skill like any other, to prattle on when one would prefer to scream. Jeanne was torn between wishing that another visitor would arrive to distract them and recalling that most of Maisetra Pertinek's intimates bored her to tears. But at last, with a noise of chatter out in the entryway, the scholars returned. Jeanne made her excuses and went to meet them.

Margerit's greeting was not guilty, perhaps, but sheepish. "I was wondering when we might see you. Let's go into the parlor. We can be more private there."

Jeanne looked around at the clutter of books and papers as they entered. This could only have to do with palace matters. She should have guessed from Bertrut's hint but the woman's unconcern had been misleading. Even before the door could be closed behind them, she demanded, "How long have you known? Why didn't you warn me?"

The dark Italian woman—what was her name? Talarico. She asked softly, "Should I leave?"

Barbara shook her head. "You might as well hear the whole story too. After the accusation came out, I'm sure you've guessed." She gestured to the maid who waited out in the hallway. "Lutild, could you bring us some tea and cakes? And then see that we aren't disturbed."

Jeanne waited impatiently, her mind racing over the possibilities. What had they been working on? And how did it relate to Elisebet's accusation? Margerit laid out the matter in a few quick sentences, concluding, "So we have the mystery ready and have only to wait until the specifics of the trial are set."

The details of the *veriloquium* had faded in importance to the other topic. "Stones? Amulets?" Jeanne repeated. This was worse than she'd feared. "But if they make that accusation against Efriturik, how is it that Antuniet's name hasn't been mentioned yet?"

Margerit said, "Annek thinks she may be drawn in, but—"

"It hardly matters," Barbara cut in. "Any plot they devise to trap Efriturik will touch her as well. But once he's cleared, what need would they have to pursue it?"

"And all this?" Jeanne gestured to the diagrams and notes.

It was Maisetra Talarico who provided the answer, having followed the story closely. "Your princess cannot be seen to show favor. But neither can she risk having her heir dragged through a public trial." No one bothered to correct her on the subtleties of Alpennian succession. "There must be a public vindication. One that cannot be questioned, but just as much one where the outcome is certain."

"And one that doesn't depend only on the proof of her own thaumaturgist," Margerit added. "Elisebet would never accept the proof of the *veridicum* mystery if it came by my word alone."

"And best," Barbara added, "to be able to demonstrate the true villain at the same time."

"But who?" Jeanne asked in bewilderment.

"That I have yet to determine," Barbara said.

Jeanne realized in relief that no one there had the slightest suspicion that Antuniet might indeed be guilty.

Barbara continued, "When last I tried, no one in Elisebet's household would speak to me. But that was before the charge was laid. I'll try again. Chautovil is a possibility. I've had good relations with him. Whoever placed the amulets must have access to Aukustin's chambers."

"But that could be most of the servants," Jeanne said. "No one would question them."

"Any, but not likely more than one. A plot such as this couldn't be kept secret with more. And not over the time it's been in process." Barbara recounted the whole series of accidents. "Always the goal has been to lay the blame, if not on Efriturik, at least in his vicinity. A servant, yes, but also someone else outside who pulls the strings. Someone who wants to harm both sons of Atilliet."

"Revolutionaries?" Maisetra Talarico asked.

The thought was startling. "I doubt it," Barbara said. "Too subtle for their sort."

"I wish I could see the amulets in question," Margerit said. "It might be possible to weave them into the truth-mystery. Or they may even bear traces of the person who placed them, if they truly are more than simple stones."

"Or even simply give clues to their origin by their nature," Barbara added. "But that would be hard to manage. No doubt Elisebet has them locked up securely somewhere until she will produce them as evidence."

"Perhaps," Jeanne said slowly. "But if we could at least get sight of them…" One strong possibility grew in her mind. "Tio," she said.

She could tell that Barbara instantly took up her thought. "Would she do it?"

Jeanne's voice turned grim. "After what Efriturik did to keep her secret? She will do it or forever be under a debt of honor."

It wasn't a matter to be managed lightly or quickly. When the demand was laid before her, Tio shrank and wriggled like a fish on a hook. It would be difficult, she protested. Very difficult.

"Not impossible." Jeanne seized on the omission.

"Not impossible," Tio agreed. "The princess keeps some of them in a locked jewelry case in her room. Her thaumaturgist has the rest. But I can't take you there! And if I were caught trying to remove it…Unless—" All eyes fixed on her. "Next Tuesday Elisebet and Sain-Mazzi will both be away from the palace all morning. I might be able to borrow the case for an hour."

"If you can borrow it, why not simply take it?" Talarico asked.

"It wouldn't do any good. They'd still have the others."

"Bring them to us at Antuniet's workshop," Margerit suggested. "That's close enough to Elisebet's apartments to get them back quickly."

"I can't be seen going there!" Tio exclaimed.

"You've managed disguises before," Jeanne said sternly. "Think of something."

"If I'm found out, I'll lose my post, or worse." It was a last gasp of protest.

"I didn't know your position meant that much to you," Jeanne said. "More than my friendship and your honor."

Tio shook her head miserably. "I'm afraid."

"Of whom?" Barbara asked sharply.

But Tio didn't answer.

* * *

The silence in the workshop was as thick as fog. At first Barbara had paced back and forth restlessly, until Jeanne thought her nerves would snap. "Would you be still!" she hissed at last. Barbara paused in surprise, then sat sheepishly. Margerit fidgeted. Only Antuniet appeared cool, bent over her reading, until one noticed that the pages never turned. Within that silence, the distant sound of soft slippers on the tiled corridor floor sounded like the ticking of a clock.

All eyes turned as Tio slipped inside, her face pale as glass.

"I have it," she said. But there had been no need to say so, given the way she clutched something close against her breast, hidden beneath her cloak. She set the small box down on the table beside Antuniet, who closed her book and moved it aside.

"It's locked," Barbara said in dismay. "Do you have the key?"

Tio shook her head in mute unhappiness.

Antuniet nudged the small hanging padlock with a finger. "It doesn't matter. I can deal with that." She rummaged on a shelf and came back with the stub of a candle and a feather. "I've had a bit of experience lately with Saint Leonhard's lock charms." She lit the candle and whispered a few words over it as she worked with wax and the feather until the lock snicked open. She stepped back. "I shouldn't touch them," she said. "In case I need to swear to it. Tio?"

Tio reached out with trembling hands and lifted the lid. They all crowded closely, peering at the contents as if they held the secrets of the ages. Barbara was the most practical and brought a lamp over.

Some of the stones seemed nothing but river pebbles. Others were carved with strange symbols like ancient seals. One was coiled like a marble snake and another seemed a bright blue beetle.

"Well, it's no wonder they sent him sleep with bad dreams," Antuniet said. "Onyx and jacinth, and there an eagle-stone. Whoever put this together knew something of what he was about. I don't see anything that would cause real harm and much of it is mere trash." She pointed at the beetle, careful not to touch it. "A scarab from an Egyptian tomb: nothing but glazed clay. No properties at all unless someone's laid a charm on it. Ammonites are said to give prophetic dreams; that might have added to his distress, but I suspect it was included just for looks. These were meant to be found. Can you shift things around to show the rest?"

Tio picked the box up and shook the contents gently. Margerit gasped suddenly. "Mother of God! It's one of yours!" She looked up across at Antuniet as if for one moment she doubted. Tio dropped the box on the table with a clatter that made them all jump.

"Give me that lamp," Antuniet asked Barbara and held it up as she craned her head over the box. "Yes, it's one of mine," she said flatly. "More than one." She moved to catch the angles of the light and pointed in one corner. "I see four of the layered stones."

"But you destroyed the extras," Jeanne protested. "I saw you do it!"

"Of the enhanced stones. The ones from the New Year's gift, yes. But there was a box of my first experiments. It disappeared and I couldn't find it after the move. And that one—" She pointed at a particularly brilliant stone. "I know every gem that came out of my workshop as I'd know my own children. That is the one I gave to Mefro Feldin."

"So," Barbara said.

Jeanne could see her eyes harden and didn't care to know what plans she was making.

"But Chustin was ill before New Year's," Margerit protested. "Before you dismissed her."

Antuniet looked into the distance as if calculating back. "I don't know when the stones went missing. I gave Feldin that one in early December. Had they planned this already and using my creations was lucky chance? Or was the entire plot born out of Feldin's theft? If they wanted to tie the matter directly to Efriturik, then the ordinary stones wouldn't be enough. They'd need some of mine."

Jeanne felt a sudden dread. "The gem we made for her—the one to make her more agreeable—might it have made her more easily persuaded?"

Antuniet shrugged as if that part didn't matter. "Unlikely. It shouldn't have continued its influence after I exchanged it, but—" She paused, remembering. "Jeanne, when I asked her about that stone, she said I was accusing her of theft. Perhaps she thought she might as well make the accusation true."

Just as bad, Jeanne thought.

"That gives us our first good clue," Barbara said. "Find Feldin and we can learn whom she passed them on to. Tio, best you take them back now before anyone has a chance to miss them."

Tio nodded in relief and locked the box again. With a furtive glance up and down the corridor, she slipped out.

When the others had gone, Antuniet began pacing the room urgently. "Jeanne, what shall I do? What shall I do?"

Jeanne said, "We'll go home and we'll wait for Barbara to find your housekeeper."

"But Jeanne, they have *proof*." Her voice was anguished now. "No one will believe I had no part in it. I must go. Leave Rotenek. Oh, Jeanne, will you come with me? We'll need money; do you have enough?"

"Toneke, you don't need to run away this time. I won't let anything happen to you."

"Jeanne, don't you understand? Once they call it sorcery, Annek won't protect me. And we've already become a scandal. You said so yourself. When they come for me you may not be safe." And with another thought, "Oh God! Anna!"

Jeanne wanted to slap her as if she were a hysterical kitchen maid. "Antuniet, have faith."

"Have faith in whom? In a princess whose gratitude extends only to her own interests? In the law that took everything from me once before? Who should I have faith in?"

"Have faith in Barbara. If anyone can solve this puzzle, she can. Have faith in Margerit. And in Annek, who set her to devise a truth mystery to prove your innocence before ever this came out. Have faith in God and the saints that they will bring the light of truth to bear on everyone."

"God cares nothing for me," Antuniet said flatly.

Jeanne took Antuniet by the arms and shook her gently. "You don't mean that. And if all else fails, have faith in me! I will die before I let any harm come to you."

"Oh, Jeanne, you can't promise that. You have no power."

"Perhaps not, but I have friends."

CHAPTER THIRTY-SIX

Barbara

Barbara had never thought that tracking down the Feldin woman would be simple. It came as no surprise that she had disappeared. Her room had already been relet to another, and the landlady knew only that she'd paid and packed her things. Antuniet could recall little that might be of help. "To be honest, I tried to have little to do with her. It suited the both of us." Her voice was tired as she responded to the insistent questions. "What's the use?" There was something of the same bleak darkness in her eyes that Barbara recalled from that morning on the bridge a year past. No frenzy this time, only a tired bleaching of all hope.

"The use?" Barbara said. "Have you given up so quickly?"

"Every morsel I've ever won only made the next loss deeper," Antuniet replied flatly. "There's a poison in my fate. It will taint everyone around me. Jeanne refuses to let me go and now I'll have that on my conscience as well. But why do *you* persist? No one would blame you if you washed your hands of me. You can scarcely expect me to believe it's family loyalty."

That was so far from true that Barbara didn't know where to begin. A year past it had been simpler: against both their wills, Antuniet had fallen within the scope of her watch. Back then her interest had been proprietary. But now their lives were woven together too tightly to be so casually parted. What she felt for Antuniet she couldn't say easily, but that didn't matter.

She leaned forward. "Even if you and I were nothing but strangers to each other, I would do this. For Jeanne's sake. For Margerit's sake. Even for

Efriturik's sake, because the easiest way to clear his name is to clear yours. Doubt if you will that I would chase halfway across Alpennia for your sake alone, and yet I would."

And seeing the broken-winged bird that Antuniet had become, caused a hot anger to begin welling up. Feldin—and whoever else might have set all this in motion—would regret the day their paths crossed hers.

In the end there was no need to go as far as halfway across Alpennia. Tavit turned up the final clue. They'd tracked down the men who'd stood guard over the place on Trez Cherfis and one recalled that Feldin had mentioned going to stay with a married daughter back home. "Though where home was I couldn't say," he added.

"In Pemenz surely?" Tavit suggested. And as they rode back to Tiporsel, he elaborated, "She'd been in Rotenek long enough for most of it to wash away, but she still called a duck a dab and softened her *p*'s. I couldn't say which village, but I'd bet it would be within half a day of Luzpont."

"That's right," Barbara said. "You're from Pemenz yourself, aren't you?"

Margerit acquiesced to her hurried travel plans with no protest. "Is it far? Will you need the traveling coach?"

"Best, I think, to go on horseback," Barbara answered and Margerit directed Maitelen in the packing of a scanty saddlebag. "The roads are uncertain if another storm comes through. Time enough to worry about carriages if I'm able to bring her back. Easier to pass unnoticed that way as well," Barbara added. There were some tasks where the public trappings of a title made things more difficult. But, then, she'd never had the luxury of going completely unnoticed in her work.

Brandel proved an unexpected challenge to the smooth departure. "But, Cousin Barbara, why can't I come with you? Tavit said—"

"Tavit does not make the plans," Barbara said quellingly.

Brandel seemed to accept the refusal, but in the early morning when they were to set off, he appeared silently in the hall wearing riding clothes. Barbara had no doubt that there was a bag packed somewhere close but out of sight. She shot Tavit a warning glance as they sorted out their gear in the foyer with the horses waiting outside. If he'd been encouraging the boy, they might have to have words. "No," she repeated firmly.

"But why?" Brandel insisted. "You said I should see more of the world."

Why indeed? "Because I have a duty to you and to your mother and I think this trip might go beyond that duty. There are things I have no business exposing you to at your age."

Tavit wisely held his tongue until the horses had turned out through the gate onto the Vezenaf. "Do you truly expect this errand to be dangerous?"

"Not to us," Barbara said shortly.

* * *

It was a very different journey than the one they'd taken together in the summer. No need now to play disguise to the hilt. If the eccentric Baroness Saveze chose to make a winter journey on horseback, that was her own affair, and news of her presence was unlikely to outrun them and come to the ears of those she sought. She could command lodging and good horses in her own name this time, but now the urgency was greater than a mere desire to return home promptly. If everything went well, they might be back in Rotenek in no more than a week, but there was no predicting what might pass in their absence. The weather was brisk but the roads good, finding that balance between mud and ice. Thank God for that.

"Where do your own people live?" Barbara asked as they approached the edge of Luzpont. "Would it make sense to enlist their help?" She saw Tavit's face pale beneath the shadowing brim of his hat and knew the question had been a misstep.

He shook his head vehemently. "No, they'd be no help." But there was no elaboration.

More caution and less openness were called for now, but it was a good wager that Feldin hadn't been convinced to quit Rotenek merely for the asking, and that inducement might leave traces.

Now Barbara held her tongue and kept her name quiet in the common room of the inn and Tavit let his accent broaden to coax gossip from the locals, though he kept the heavy scarf wrapped loosely about his head as if to muffle any personal recognition.

"I'd a mind to look up my cousin while we're on the road if I had time," he shared over a pint of ale. "Name's Feldin. Though no doubt she's had enough of cousins come out of the bushes since her good fortune. I thought her daughter still lived around here, but I could have mistaken the town."

They tried the same line in Sain-Pol again. It wasn't until Fillen that a nibble appeared.

"You're right at that," an hostler replied to his bait. "For I never heard she had cousins around here. Her daughter still lives down by the mill but she's not living there. Took the old Palfrit cottage off the north road, so you may be right about good fortune."

There was no point in dawdling now. If Feldin caught word that strangers in town were asking after her… Barbara made a quick decision and turned to the hostler. "No time to leave our path that far, I'm afraid. We're behind in our journey as it is. I saw a hack-chaise in the yard. Is it spoken for already or might we hire it? I hadn't expected the roads to be this good in January but that way we might make Suniz by dark." The fabrication rolled easily off her tongue. And the name of Saveze might secure the carriage without the tell-tale eyes of a postillion. It was unlikely Feldin would consent to go with them easily.

The next step would be the riskiest. Would she be alone? There might not be nephews and a son-in-law to deal with, but perhaps a hired man? Swords would be of no use in coercion unless one were willing to use them.

Tavit had less experience skulking in shadows than she did and she saw few enough shadows in the farmyard as they approached. A direct approach seemed best. The carriage was left behind a stand of willows along the edge of a narrow track that disappeared quickly into a snowy field.

The cottage was small and snug. The sort that might figure in the dreams of a villager exiled to the city. A bit of yard. No doubt when winter was past she'd be acquiring chickens and perhaps even a cow. A woman used to labor who now had a bit of money could live very comfortably here if her past weren't pursuing her. A thin thread of smoke rose from the chimney, and they watched from the edge of the trees until confident that she was alone.

"Ready?" Barbara asked Tavit. He nodded.

They crossed the yard swiftly, parting to cover front and back doors. Tavit called out the sort of hail a neighbor might use on approach. They'd weighed the risks of complete surprise against even that much warning. A sudden invasion would be more likely to provoke screams. When Barbara heard the sound of the door opening and a suspicious greeting, she slipped through the back door and latched it behind her. Tavit had driven the woman back in and done the same. Barbara pulled off her hat and shook her hair loose for better recognition. She was on edge for the possibility that they would need to muffle shouts but Feldin was wide-eyed in recognition and just awed enough for silence.

Tavit pushed her down none too gently into a chair and held her there.

"What do you want?" she asked in a mixture of outrage and fear.

"I am quite certain that you know why we're here," Barbara said, leaving the woman's imagination to work on her a few moments yet.

She shook her head, either in denial or refusal.

"You left Rotenek very suddenly," Barbara began.

Feldin thought she saw a chance to bluff it out. "There wasn't any work. I told Maisetra Chazillen it was a bad time to be let go. What was I to do but come back home?"

"No work? And yet I hadn't realized the savings from a housekeeper's wages could set you up this comfortably," Barbara said, looking around pointedly.

The place showed none of the indifference she'd displayed in Antuniet's workshop. Sparsely furnished, but with good and comfortable things, and curtains at the window that showed the sign of a dexterous hand. No doubt the daughter had set her up to begin with. Feldin remained mute, finding no explanation that would serve.

"Let us be blunt," Barbara continued. "Before you left the city, you stole something from my cousin. And that theft has made a great deal of trouble for her. You stole some of her work."

"She gave it to me!" Feldin protested. "A gift for luck, she said—that fancy friend of hers. I'm no thief." Curious, how her mind had altered the circumstances to eliminate the exchange.

"I don't mean the gift," Barbara corrected her. "But the other stones."

"That was no theft!" she protested again. "They were trash, to be discarded she said. I heard her myself. It's my right to keep the castoffs of the household. Or will you hunt me down as well for the heels of stale bread and the dust from the bottom of the coal sack? You've come a long distance to pursue me over rubbish."

Again, her mind and tongue had twisted the truth into something that left her innocent, but at least she didn't deny taking the stones. How would Margerit's truth-mystery interpret such a statement? As an ordinary charge of theft, the matter might be absurd, but these weren't ordinary circumstances.

"But you didn't take those pretty trinkets just to hang about your neck, did you?" Barbara said, giving just the slightest emphasis to the words *hang* and *neck*. "Someone else was very interested in those stones." It was a fraction better than a stab in the dark, but Barbara knew she must tread carefully not to give her ignorance away. A shadow of guilt crossed Feldin's eyes and Barbara probed again. "Someone came to you in secret asking questions." Again the flinch. "You felt no special loyalty to Maisetra Chazillen. Why should you? She didn't even pay your wages. And it was quite a comedown having to work for an alchemist. You were owed something extra for that, weren't you?" She probed step by step, watching Feldin's reactions. "Just some samples of the work, they said. Isn't that right? And you knew which ones wouldn't be missed immediately." She knew she was inching closer to the truth. "You might have guessed what plans they had for those stones, but it was nothing to do with you."

Feldin nodded eagerly, as if seeing a clear path out. "Who am I to question my betters? He said they'd be grateful. Important people, he said. They'd see I got what I was due."

"But they aren't here, and I am." Barbara pulled the woman closer until their faces were mere inches apart. Feldin's breath stank of garlic and fear. "Do you know who I am?"

"B...B...Baroness Saveze," she stuttered as she turned pale.

"No," Barbara said softly. "I'm Lumbeirt's duelist. I've killed two men with my own hands and sent a third to the executioner's sword. Those who hurt people under my protection have a habit of disappearing. I tracked you down and I can promise you, there is no place on earth that I cannot find you if I choose. If you care to live, you will return with me to Rotenek and cast yourself on Princess Annek's mercy. Give yourself up as a witness and cleave to the truth. Do that and I will forget you ever crossed me."

But Feldin's body sagged in her hands before she was finished speaking, and whatever answer the woman meant to give was delayed until she could regain consciousness.

Barbara looked up and saw Tavit staring at her. She released her grip on Feldin's garments and found her hands shaking in the rage she'd allowed to show. "Let's be quick about it. Go get the carriage so we don't need to carry her so far."

He nodded briefly and headed for the door.

* * *

They changed horses at every post station to make time. Barbara didn't dare to risk leaving Feldin unbound, but there was no need to prolong the woman's discomfort. And she dreaded learning what might have transpired in Rotenek in their absence.

When the city came in sight Feldin began a ceaseless moaning. "They'll kill me. They'll kill me for sure." Though she wouldn't say exactly who she believed "they" were.

Barbara closed her ears to the plaint until it was needful to use a gag to keep her from attracting attention on the crowded streets. Feldin's fears were strong enough to drive one change in plans. Despite invoking Princess Annek's name, Barbara had always meant to hand her over to the city magistrates. But without knowing where and how high the trail would lead, would that be safe? Annek might be seen as having too great an interest in the matter for impartiality, but she would have the greatest interest in keeping Feldin alive.

The interminable hours together in the carriage had brought one further profit: a detailed description of the man who bought the stones. Of middling height, thin, with hair that fell straight and somewhat overlong to the edge of his collar. Pale blue eyes—that was unusual enough to note—and a slightly hitched way of walking, as if an injured leg had never entirely healed. That last plucked chords in Barbara's memory. A groom at the hunt at Feniz, swearing, *Mesnera, I saw to the girths myself!* No, not him, the other groom. The one who had stood ready with a second horse in case Aukustin had need. A groom made sense. The matter with the other horse—the gift from Efriturik—it would have been easiest for a groom to meddle there as well.

She cast her mind back. The illness outside Iser. More difficult perhaps, but in the confusion of travel there would be opportunities. The amulets in Chustin's bed though. That would have been more difficult. He would have no business there. And there was no question that his orders must have come from elsewhere. A groom might have personal grudges but they wouldn't take this elaborate a form.

But threaten as Barbara might, Feldin could recall no one who resembled Kreiser, no fox-faced man, no foreigner. Barbara felt oddly relieved. There were actions she still couldn't forgive him for, but she had come to respect him as an adversary. It would have been disappointing to find her instincts so mistaken.

With Feldin safely transferred to the palace guards, Barbara ventured, in all the dirt of travel, to beg a moment with Princess Annek to give her report. "And you're certain of all this?" Annek asked, after hearing the story and all the conjectures that followed.

"I'm certain as far as it goes," Barbara said. "I don't doubt the woman would lie if she thought it served her purpose, but what use would lying be now? She might be guilty of theft but I see no reason to think she knew the purpose the stones would be used for. And whoever directed this will believe that she's betrayed them as best she can, so there will be no mercy expected from that side."

"And this groom," Annek said with a frown. "Do you think he's still a danger?"

Barbara gave it some thought and said hesitantly, "Not for the moment. I'm certain Princess Elisebet keeps a close eye on her son these days; I doubt he's allowed outside her apartments. We could move to secure the man with more deliberation safely enough."

Annek gestured to cut off that thought. "Leave him to me."

But Barbara ventured, "There might still be a chance to erase the charges. If Elisebet still has any trust in me...Let me go to her and tell her some small part of what I've learned: that I've traced the stones and that Efriturik is cleared. There's still time to settle this without the humiliation of a trial—still time for a reconciliation."

"You have too much faith in my cousin's good sense," Annek said. "That would have taken a miracle, and it's gone too far for reconciliation. The matter is in our hands now and has become far more delicate."

"Your Grace?"

"My cousin, it seems, caught wind of my preparations. She arranged to have the case taken up by the magistrate who most disapproves of veridical mysteries. Even had the archbishop himself performed the rite, he would have refused it, and he says he would give no credit at all to a secular thaumaturgist. He seemed curiously eager to judge a case of sorcery. It's a pity, because Elisebet puts great store in signs and portents. If we'd been able to work the mystery before her, I think even she might have been convinced."

Was all Margerit's work for nothing? "But with the Feldin woman as witness?" Barbara asked. "Surely we can still set out the truth."

"That won't be necessary. I would have preferred not to intervene, but I cannot risk it. Efriturik has claimed the right of his birth and appealed his case to the royal court. I have set a judge of my own choosing to hear it. He will accept the *veriloquium*. By that much I can distance myself. It won't satisfy Elisebet or her party, but it will satisfy the law and the rest of Alpennia. Truth will have its day. If you favor lost causes, go to the Dowager Princess and try your best. It would save us all a great deal of trouble. But I wouldn't wager a *teneir* on your success."

When they emerged from the palace, Barbara eyed the thin afternoon sun. She would need to hurry. She didn't care to put off the errand for another day, but Elisebet couldn't be approached still in traveling clothes.

The doors of Tiporsel and Margerit's welcoming embrace almost made her change her mind but to strengthen her resolve she followed a kiss with, "One more errand today and then I'm done. Send Maitelen up to me and some hot water if you can manage it quickly." She turned to Tavit where he stood waiting for instruction. "No need for you, at least, to be dragged out again today. Tell Brandel to attend me, then go and get some rest."

"And when will you rest?" Margerit asked.

"When it's over—but God knows when that will be. Come up with me and tell me everything that's happened while I was gone that Princess Annek didn't see fit to mention."

* * *

Weariness dragged at her feet as she entered the palace corridors for the second time that day. There had been no chance for a return message from her request for audience but she was shown into Elisebet's sitting room with little delay. Elisebet sent her ladies away at Barbara's entrance, except for Mesnera Sain-Mazzi, who stood behind her chair rigidly at attention as if she filled an armin's duties. It was easy to see why Tio and the others called her a dragon. Barbara shook off her weariness and marshaled her thoughts for the best arguments she could make.

"Mesnera Atilliet," she began, "you have trusted me in the past when you had concerns for Aukustin's welfare. Whenever you've asked, I've stood ready to guard the sons of Atilliet. Trust me now, I beg you." It was stretching the truth perhaps, but it played to Elisebet's sympathies. "When I heard of the evil attack on your son, my one thought was to hunt down the one responsible and bring him to your justice."

"We know who is responsible," Sain-Mazzi said, stepping toward Elisebet and laying a hand protectively on her shoulder. "He already stands accused."

Barbara answered as if it had been Elisebet herself who spoke. "Accused is not proof and I went hunting for proof. In finding it, the trail was not at all what it seemed at first." There would be no point in directly challenging their accusation. No counter to the thrust, but a beating away. She poured out the tale, stripped of all specifics. How she'd learned who had supplied the stones and tracked the thief down. That the amulets had been supplied to... Here she faltered. What excuse could she give not to name the man? She passed over that. "I have yet to trace that person further, but I could find no connection at all to Baron Razik. I know why you suspect him, but in this he must be considered innocent. It would be a blessing for all Alpennia if you withdrew the charges."

"The charges will stand," Elisebet said imperiously, "and I will see justice done by whatever means it takes. Annek thinks to thwart me but even the royal court must answer my challenge. I know who my true friends are—the ones who stand beside me. Though they've become few indeed these days." She placed her hand over Sain-Mazzi's where it lay on her shoulder and the older woman gave a triumphant stare. "If you are a friend, as you claim, take up my challenge."

In a heartbeat Barbara knew what she meant. "No," she said firmly.

"Challenge him in my name!" Elisebet demanded. "Make him defend his claim of innocence with his own body. The *duellum iudicialis* has yet to be outlawed entirely. Challenge him in my name or I must consider you among my enemies."

"No. And three times no," Barbara said, shaking her head. "Least of all, you know my stand against judicial duels. How could I hold my head up in council if I made a challenge now? Second, I don't believe his guilt. It would be an offense against God if I took up my sword in the name of a lie. And last of all, he bears no obligation to accept the challenge and he'd be a fool to do so when the law will vindicate him on its own. Let someone else take up your useless quest; I will not."

"You have made your choice," Elisebet said coldly. "And I will not forgive you or those who stand with you. Razik may be able to shelter under his mother's skirts, but others cannot."

What have I done? Barbara thought in sudden panic.

But there had been no other choice, no other path. It had always been likely that Antuniet's name would be brought into the matter.

Barbara curtseyed stiffly, as if dismissed. "By your leave," she said. "Doubt it if you will; I have Aukustin's welfare in my heart."

* * *

A soft voice, urgent in her ear, woke Barbara, with the sun streaming high through the windows where the curtains had been drawn open. "I'm sorry, dearest, I wish I could let you sleep," Margerit said.

"What hour is it?"

"Just past noon."

"Dear God," Barbara said, throwing an arm across her eyes to cut the light. "I don't know whether to call that late or early anymore. What is it?"

"We only just heard; I thought you'd want to know. Elisebet's groom: he's dead."

That banished the last traces of sleep. "Dead?"

"An accident, so they say. With a carriage. It happened this morning but no one thought it of any importance. Tavit was out earlier and heard something on the street that caught his ear. He's confirmed it as best he could."

Barbara had vaulted from the bed and was reaching for clothing before Margerit even finished speaking. "No accident could be that convenient."

But how? Who had even known he'd been identified? Feldin had never known the man's name or even his employment. Annek knew everything but she had the most to lose from the man's death. "But no one knew!" Barbara said aloud.

"You told Elisebet…" Margerit ventured.

"Only that Feldin had passed the stones to someone else. She couldn't have any idea of the man's identity. Certainly not that it was one of her own servants. I'm not sure I even said it was a man."

"Perhaps she knew already?"

Barbara shook her head vehemently. "If there's one thing I'm certain of in all this, it's Elisebet's concern for Aukustin. She never would have tolerated someone under the slightest suspicion—" She paused.

There had been someone else in that room. She saw again the way Elisebet had reached for that hand in comfort. *I know who my true friends are—the ones who stand beside me.*

Who stood to gain from the rift between the Atilliets? From the division in Elisebet's own house? In an instant all the fragments fell into place like a mosaic pavement forming one face. "Sain-Mazzi!" she said, as if it were an oath.

"What?" Margerit asked.

"Mesnera Sain-Mazzi. She was there. She heard. She's always been there: dismissing Elisebet's other ladies after the poisoning at the inn; allowing no rivals except silly young women like Tio and Elin. She means to control Elisebet by leaving her no one else to turn to. And through her, to control Aukustin."

"But why?" Margerit protested. "What has she to gain?"

"What has anyone to gain? Power? Influence? They all play these games with people's lives. What does it matter in the end? But she's to blame, I would swear to it."

"You can swear all you like," Margerit reminded her, "but it's an oath that won't carry any weight unless you can prove it."

CHAPTER THIRTY-SEVEN

Antuniet

They came with no warning, as she'd always known they would.

Jeanne had been begging her not to leave the house, but only work could damp down the fear. And so they found her at the workshop and there was no need to invade the peace of Jeanne's home. There were two in uniforms, aside from the palace guard for escort, and one in the dark robes of the city magistrates. The fourth was a clerkish sort, who intoned with no preamble, "In the name of the Dowager Princess Elisebet Atilliet, I raise a charge against Antuniet Chazillen of sorcery and conspiracy in an assault against Mesner Aukustin Atilliet." As he continued reading the details of the charges, her mind grew numb and her eyes fixed on the absurd green buttons studding his chest. They clashed with the otherwise drab stuff of the waistcoat. An affectation? An attempt at fashion? Or perhaps his tailor had chosen whatever was to hand? Silence drew her mind back. They were all staring at her, as if expecting some response.

"Is my apprentice to be charged as well?" she asked sharply. Anna was pressed into a corner, trying to remain invisible.

"There are no additional names mentioned in the charges," the clerk said.

"Then if you will permit me—" She crossed over to where Anna stood, daring any of them to stop her, and whispered quickly, "Go. Take the news to de Cherdillac. You know the direction? Take this." She reached back to unclasp the pendant from her neck. She felt naked without it. "Give it to her for safekeeping. Take my reticule; there's money to pay the fiacre. Then go home and don't return here unless I tell you myself."

"But Maisetra—" she protested.

"Go."

When they led Antuniet out, she locked the doors behind her as if it were the end of an ordinary day and placed the key in the hands of the guard. He took it with a sheepish expression; his face was familiar, though she couldn't have put a name to it.

So it had come to this at last. Sorcery. She could almost laugh. There was nothing but science in what she did, despite the odd trappings used to invoke the greater powers. Sorcery, but not treason. No, of course not. Although it was everywhere implied. And conspiracy. There could be no conspiracy without conspirators and without one conspired against. And who could that be except Aukustin Atilliet? Conspiracy against an Atilliet should be treason, but treason was a charge that could only be heard in the royal court. And they wouldn't risk letting her slip through their fingers the way Efriturik had.

It was well on toward evening before she had visitors in her little cell. For hours she had wavered between expecting them to all come in a cloud as they always did and expecting no one at all. But in the end it was only Barbara, with her armin left outside when the guards insisted the rules allowed only one visitor each day. One visitor and ten minutes. Barbara looked worn and tired and fumbled through an unaccustomed apology.

"This is my fault, I'm afraid."

Antuniet felt a laugh burbling up in her throat and suppressed it only because hysteria would waste precious time. "Your fault? Of all the people entangled in this, you are the last person who bears any blame. How could it possibly be your fault?"

"When I returned yesterday, I went to Elisebet—with Annek's consent— to tell her that we'd traced the stones and could prove Efriturik's innocence."

A tiny flutter of hope sprang up in Antuniet's breast, but it was not echoed in Barbara's grim face.

"It was foolish, perhaps, to think she might back down now, but I hoped at least to plant some doubt. To ease the way for her to save face. But justice means nothing to her now. She's set on vengeance. She still wants to pursue Efriturik, even with his case in the royal court. She will claim that it's favoritism and not truth that saves him. She demanded that I be her champion and challenge him in the *duellum iudicialis*. And when I refused, she took her revenge by charging you as well."

Antuniet stood and began pacing. "Don't flatter yourself so much, cousin. She would have come to this in any event. She needs blood, and if she can't get his, she'll have mine, because mine is the only blood that makes sense given the charges. What does it matter that I mean nothing to her? Pride must be satisfied. But you say you traced the stones past Feldin?"

Barbara hesitated for too long. Did she fear listeners? Well, no doubt they were there. "You needn't mention names. Can you get testimony? Will it clear me?"

"The man is dead," Barbara said. "Feldin worked at the bidding of a man in Elisebet's household. I knew him from her description. He died this morning and it was no accident. I didn't think…I never named him or described him when I spoke with Elisebet, but—" She dropped her voice so low that Antuniet had to stop and lean closely to hear. "—Sain-Mazzi was there. No one could have known who the traitor was except the one who gave him orders. It was her; I'm sure of it. From that moment, he was a dead man. I might as well have done the deed myself."

Sain-Mazzi. Yes, that might almost make sense. "And Feldin?" she asked anxiously. Was it all slipping away?

"Safe, for now. She's held at the palace. We can be sure of her testimony for Efriturik. That will still be given under the *veriloquium*, but you're to be tried by the city magistrate. He bears no obligation to admit testimony from another court and he's already refused the use of truth mysteries. There's no telling if Feldin will give him the same tale."

The fear curled in its familiar home in her belly. "Then I'm condemned."

"No!" Barbara protested.

"Feldin doesn't matter," Antuniet said. "They have all the evidence they need for sorcery. When the stones are presented in court, the work of my own hands will condemn me. And Feldin? Even if she tells the truth, no one will believe her. They'll say she lied out of fear of you or from loyalty to Annek. And all the light of Margerit's pretty little mystery won't penetrate the walls of that courtroom."

"If we could get your case transferred to Annek's court—"

"But you can't. They've avoided all charges that would be heard there. Efriturik has the right of birth to appeal, but I don't. I lost that with everything else when Estefen was executed. I have nothing except the law and the evidence. And the evidence will betray me."

Surely Barbara had considered all these things as well? Antuniet had failed so utterly. Instead of redeeming the name of Chazillen, she had brought this additional stain to it. She ceased her pacing and sank to the hard wooden bench.

Barbara sat close beside her. "Antuniet, I won't abandon you, even if all hope is gone."

"And isn't it already?"

"If there's no other way, I will stand your advocate."

Antuniet caught the meaning behind her words. "But you told Elisebet—"

"I wouldn't betray my principles for Elisebet, but I would for you."

For the first time since the whole matter had begun, Antuniet felt tears start in her eyes. She dashed them away with the cuff of her sleeve and turned her face away. "But why?" And when there was no answer, "I don't know that I would be strong enough to forbid you. Thank you."

"There's a better way," Barbara said, "though I don't know if you would take it. If Annek agrees…But I don't want to raise your hopes…"

* * *

After Barbara was gone, the hours ticked by, measured by the regular faint *tonk tonk* of a drip somewhere out of sight. A gutter pipe, from the metallic echo. No windows gave any clue to the sun's passage but the chill of evening quieted the sound. Then she was glad for the lack of windows. Powerful friends could do that much at least: an interior cell where the cold could be kept off with blankets. Good food and plentiful, when it came. It could have been far worse. Higher friends could do more, of course. Efriturik had spent no time inside these walls. He'd been released on oath as soon as the charge was laid. If truth could not be held as constant, even less could justice. There had never been any possibility that a son of Atilliet would suffer worse than humiliation and count that bad enough.

What were the penalties for sorcery in the ordinary courts? Her imagination had never shied away from picking at wounds. Gone were the days when such a case would have been handed over to the church—not unless there were blasphemy involved as well. It was such an elusive charge, sorcery. So easy to believe; so hard to prove. And so rarely brought against anyone with standing. What penalty would Elisebet have sought had Efriturik not escaped her grasp by claiming privilege? It didn't matter, except to guess what she herself might face. And even so, would Elisebet have been mad enough to demand the ultimate penalty? It wasn't right or just to have one law for princes and another for such as her. And yet, justice be damned, if she had the same right to appeal her case to Annek, she would, so long as honor remained.

She slept in fits and starts with no dreams that she could recall. The nightmares that had preyed on her while waiting were satisfied with her waking fears now.

In the morning, Jeanne came. She hadn't slept well either; that much was clear. Even paint and powder couldn't conceal that she'd been weeping. She wept again now, held close while Antuniet found herself playing the awkward role of comforter. Jeanne's voice came muffled, "I meant to be strong for you."

"Hush, hush," Antuniet found herself saying. "You needn't be afraid. Barbara has all manner of ideas in train. Do you know? She even offered to bloody her sword in my name."

"She would do that?" Jeanne asked in surprise.

"Well, I'm not as shocked as I should be," Antuniet said in an attempt at humor. "For all her grand speeches about justice and law, I know she has few qualms about settling matters in dark alleys. I suppose I should be glad I'm under her protection. There was a time when I would have been on the other end of her blade. Though God knows why she's taken me in. I've brought no honor to her house or lineage." She was babbling and she knew it.

Jeanne wasn't fooled. "I couldn't bear to lose you. I couldn't go through that again."

But the time had ticked past and the guards were at the door. "Something will be arranged, I'm sure of it," she said to Jeanne through the bars. She'd meant the words more for Jeanne's sake than her own, but in the light of day she felt half convinced by them.

That day when she'd returned to Rotenek, near penniless and alone with nothing but DeBoodt's book and her vow, she never would have believed that her brightest gems would come in human form. Jeanne, Anna, Margerit, Barbara—all tried by fire and enhanced through the long, slow layering of work side by side. Was there need for any other talismans than these?

The hours stretched out empty after that, without even expectation to fill them. Counted only by the drip, drip, dripping echoing hollowly. Another meal. A second blanket offered—what luxury! She thought back on the little room in Heidelberg that sometimes had given up its coal to feed the workshop furnace. Would she still have left, knowing it would come to this, if Kreiser hadn't pursued her? Knowing she could die here with her oath left unfulfilled and the name of Chazillen even more a curse? Yes, even so. Not to have tried—that would be the true shame.

* * *

Another night of fits and starts. She woke once, thinking she felt Jeanne's touch and reached for the spot at her breast where the jewel should hang. Later she woke to screaming—not hers this time—echoing down the corridors from some other cell. Another dawn. How long did the wheels of law take to grind? She realized she had no idea. A fortnight, at least, between when Efriturik was charged and when the magistrate had been named. But now Elisebet had her magistrate chosen. Surely it would be swifter for her?

Barbara was the next day's visitor, bringing news. Efriturik had been cleared: Feldin's testimony, Margerit's *veriloquium*, the brisk efficiency of the royal court, all joined in harness. There was nothing else to tell for now.

* * *

The dripping that measured her days stopped. She didn't notice until one long afternoon passed in deafening silence. Perhaps the last of the ice had melted on the roof somewhere overhead. She'd stopped counting the days. Each was much alike except for the identity of the one visitor she was allowed. Most often Jeanne, sometimes Barbara. Once Margerit came and could find nothing to say, spending her brief minutes in mute witness. It was enough to know she was not forgotten. She could have asked any of them what day it was, but what did it matter? All would pass in time.

Her mind filled with the absurd injustice of fate. To have come so far, to have learned so much and to have triumphed in her chosen art, only to fall victim to petty palace jealousies and superstition. To know the truth and have no way to prove it. And the most bitter irony of all: to have the work of her own hands brought out in evidence, pointing its finger at her in accusation, like the telltale beam of a watchman's lantern, with no way to turn it on the genuine traitor.

That was what Margerit's mystery had been meant to do: to use the light of divine judgment to point to the truth. To point the light... Her thoughts caught for a moment, recalling the box of stones that Tio had risked so much to show them. What else had it contained beyond the amulet she'd given Feldin—the one with that child's trick of the blue light? There had been ammonite and scarab, far more prominent in memory than effective in use; onyx engraved with a goat's head and jacinth. What else? What else?

She closed her eyes and tried to bring the box's contents to memory. Had there been a moonstone or crystal spar? She remembered a flat square crystal, but it might have been quartz. In a pinch, any lens would do. There had been a handful of polished spheres and cabochons. Surely one would have the right properties.

A plan took shape, born out of hope and nourished by desperation. Would they be there in the room when she came to trial—every person needed for the resolution? She couldn't imagine Elisebet leaving such a thing to chance. But would Sain-Mazzi come as well? Surely she would. She must be watching over Elisebet ever more closely now. Was there a way to ensure it? What did she have a right to demand as defendant? Barbara might know. She rehearsed speeches in her mind, playing out as many scenes as she could imagine. But the plan she kept to herself, not wanting to tease the others with what might be a vain hope.

* * *

Another meal, another sleep. *Let it just be over.* Yet when they came for her at midday, her only thought was, *So soon?* She was led out, not through the yard toward the *salle-iust*, but to a bright and comfortable room that must belong to the warden. Jeanne was there and Barbara as well. Such luxury for a visit! The guards closed the door behind her, remaining outside, and she was bewildered until she saw the other figures in the room.

"Your Grace," she said, sinking to a curtsey on unsteady legs. "Mesner Atilliet." This was no time to presume on familiarity. "How may I serve you?" She couldn't keep the edge of irony from her voice.

"It weighs greatly on me," Annek began, "that you should be in peril in place of my son. And you have strong advocates who have urged me to find a way through. But we have a conundrum." She paused with pursed lips in a way that should have been maddening. "How can we best see that justice is served and not merely the law? It is a delicate matter. If it were a lesser offense, I would have a freer hand—and if I had not expended so much goodwill for my son's sake. My cousin will hold me to the letter of things, and there are those who support her whom I don't care to cross needlessly. Yet we still have several possible paths." She held a packet of papers in her hand.

Antuniet wondered at first if any of them were a pardon. But no, that would break the letter of the law that Elisebet would insist on. For a moment, a flutter of wild hope stirred, but that was dashed by Annek's next words.

"I cannot go back on my word in the matter of my father's judgment on the Chazillens now, not in the midst of this trial. It would be seen as too self-serving. But there has always been another option. When the line of Chazillen was disenrolled, those of the name who were not condemned were free to petition *trans-familia*, as your cousin Sepestien did. Baroness Saveze has asked me to allow you to take the Lumbeirt name in respect of your mother and I have agreed. Become Antuniet Lumbeirt and take again the status of your birth. Then we can resolve the charges against you." She lifted the document in her hand and held it out.

For a moment Antuniet stood silent. What was it she had told herself? That regardless of the injustice, if she were offered the same escape Efriturik had taken she would seize it? And here it was: adopted into the Lumbeirts, once again to be addressed as *Mesnera*, free to claim the privilege of royal justice and only one small price to pay. To no longer be a Chazillen. If the offer had been made on the day of her brother's execution she would have rejected it as an insult. Barbara was staring at her in anxious trepidation. Now she saw it for an act of love, though at little cost to Barbara herself.

She thought of her desperate plans for the trial, of the trick with the stones. That might fail; this was sure. And yet…she'd told herself that she would take this escape if it left honor intact. And since the day Estefen died, honor had driven her to one purpose and one purpose alone. Everything else had been stripped away from her: dignity, pride, chastity. Only the name remained. And if she could not redeem it, at least she would continue bearing it.

"Do you have an answer?" Annek asked with a hint of impatience.

"My cousin makes a generous offer," she said slowly, not daring to look at Jeanne for fear of what she'd see there. "I would not insult the baroness by comparing the house of Lumbeirt to a mess of pottage, but I will not trade my birthright for it. I have sworn to bring honor to the name of Chazillen. I cannot do that by trading it away, even to save my life."

She ventured a look toward the others at last. Barbara looked grave, but she nodded as if she understood. Jeanne was biting her lip to keep it from trembling.

"A fair answer," Annek said, nodding slowly as if in approval. She, too, looked over at Barbara. "You predicted correctly, though I wouldn't have credited it. But it was gracious of you to offer."

She set the sealed paper back on the table and took up a second document that had lain underneath it. "There is another possibility, though now I wonder whether you will hear it." She tapped the new papers against one hand, as if even now debating some decision. "It was a thought that came to me even before this matter. I expected to have more time to consider, but fate has forced my hand. I find you a formidable young woman. You have resources and dedication that Alpennia would be much poorer for losing. And despite the matter with your brother, no one can deny the deep roots the Chazillens have in this land. I told you once before that I was surprised and grateful for the influence you've had on my son. Someday, if he is prince, he will need the support of a strong woman. I wonder, since you will not change your name for Lumbeirt, would you consider changing it for Atilliet?"

Her meaning sank in only gradually. When it did, Antuniet's hand flew up to cover her mouth. Not—as they must believe—to muffle a gasp or sob, but

344   Heather Rose Jones

to stifle an undignified giggle. *Oh Mother!* she thought. *Could I drag you out of hell for just two minutes now, I'd show you this and then throw you back again!*

Through all those long years when nothing she had ever accomplished had weighed in the balance of that one failure... No, it would have been absurd to imagine it might come someday to this. Surely this hadn't been Efriturik's idea!

She glanced over at him. There was nothing of the eager lover about him, more the apprehension of a man facing a strange dog of uncertain temper. If it weren't for her predicament, there could not have been a woman in all of Alpennia less tempted by such an offer, or more certain of her unsuitability for the role. And she *was* tempted, just for one fleeting moment.

The moment fled entirely.

"Your Grace, it is a great honor you do me. But as I have said, I cannot fulfill what I owe to my family name by leaving it behind. More than that, with all respect to Mesner Atilliet, I think we should not suit."

Jeanne came unfrozen at last and rushed to her side to whisper urgently, "Toneke, don't think to refuse him for my sake. I'd rather see you alive and safe."

Antuniet shook her head ever so slightly and touched Jeanne's cheek. "It's nothing to do with you. I'm sorry."

"Well," Annek said as she rose, setting the rest of the witnesses into disarray, "you make it very difficult to help you, but I will look for other means to try." She called out to those waiting behind the door and it opened with suspicious promptness. "We've finished here."

Had it been the right thing to do?

Lying on the hard pallet that night, Antuniet played over both offers in her mind. Was it nothing but stubborn pride to have refused? To trust the slender thread of her own cleverness against a generous certainty? No, surely there were some things worth standing one's ground for. To give in now, after all these years? Wouldn't that be an acknowledgment that none of it had ever been worth the struggle? She could accept the thought of living all her life as Maisetra Chazillen, but not as Mesnera anything else.

* * *

She'd thought there would be no more warning for the final act than there had been for any other scene in this play, but Jeanne came one day with a change of clothing: the brown woolen walking gown that had been her first, most practical gift. And she brought a word of promise: tomorrow. They kissed passionately at parting, not caring who might see, in case all should fail and there would never be another chance.

The courtroom was packed, both floor and gallery. That was no surprise. Rotenek must have its show and she would do her best to give a good performance. She'd thought of several parts to play but in the end her own self seemed easiest: proud, haughty, cold and always in command. She gazed steadfastly out over the crowd as if she were, indeed, a princess, but that was to mask a desperate search among the faces. Of her friends she had no doubt. There was Jeanne, dry-eyed but pale. Beside her, Barbara in her braided coat, wearing her sword in case it came, at the last, to that. But there, apart to one side, where the prosecutor would stand: Elisebet, all somber in black and veils, playing the royal widow as she often did in public. At her back stood several ladies. Was it? Yes, Sain-Mazzi was among them. The stage was set; let the play begin.

It took no playacting to settle her face into impatience with the long speeches at the start. The forms must be followed. Now they began to lay out the charges: Aukustin's illness, the search for answers. One would not expect Elisebet or her courtiers to take the stand. That place was supplied by Escamund, the thaumaturgist who had found the talismans. That was a gamble when the charge was sorcery, but he was a man of sober and upstanding reputation. Now the stones themselves were produced: the small mahogany box that she had seen before and another bound in brass that held the rest.

Feldin was brought forth to testify to the origin of the alchemical gems. What reassurances had they offered her? Did she know she faced the one who had ordered the death of her contact? Here she was free to lie about the theft as she had not been in the royal court, but there was no need. She was asked only to identify the stones. Yes, Feldin said, she had kept house for the alchemist. Yes, she recognized the magical gems that lay before her. One couldn't miss them, she said, pointing out the brightly layered stones, their mottled beauty standing out like peacocks in a henhouse. She would know them anywhere. No mention of the gift or of the theft or anything of her own part in providing them.

So, that was how it would be. Antuniet let go of any regret in what she planned. And then the moment came when all eyes turned to her and the magistrate asked if she had aught to say in her defense.

"I do," she said loudly, stepping forward from the box where she had sat throughout the morning. "Let me examine these amulets that are said to be my work. Would you take the word of an ignorant old woman regarding the esoteric arts? I will know the work of my own hands."

A murmur passed through the courtroom. Had they expected her to deny all? She made a show of picking through the boxes. "This? Trash," she said, setting several aside. "And this?" She held up the carved onyx cameo. "Beautiful work, but not mine." There was more to her method than mere performance. She passed over several possibilities: too irregular in shape, too flawed. But there! Perfect. A flawless crystal lens encircled by a frame of golden serpents. No doubt it had been chosen for the imagery. She palmed it and returned to the ebony box. "Now this?" She let the pride show in her voice as she lifted the layered stone reverently. "This is part of my greatest work," she said. "Do you know the properties of this stone?" As if commanding a lecture hall, she left no pause for answer. "This stone cannot abide the touch of evil. It knows; it remembers. And it will speak."

A gasp and then a silence in the room as if they expected a voice to sound. She had been holding the gem carefully in her fingertips so as not to release its light. Now she palmed it, warming it to life and holding the crystal lens before it. She would need a little time to gauge the focal distances but even a gross effect would suffice.

"Tell me, *O Lapis Loquax*, who first touched you with ill intent?" She turned slowly, holding it up and manipulating the lens as she came to face Feldin. From the corner of her eye she could see Elisebet's rapt attention and Sain-Mazzi's sudden concern. With the slightest final movement of her fingers, the azure light shone blindingly in Feldin's eyes and the woman shrieked and fell to her knees.

"Mercy! Mercy!" she cried. "I swear, I meant no harm to you!"

"What is your crime?" Antuniet intoned, like an oracle of doom.

Feldin turned toward the magistrate and held her arms up in appeal. "I'm a thief. I stole the stones from her."

"And I forgive you," Antuniet said, turning away and twisting the lens sideways to unfocus the beam. "But how did my jewels come to be in Mesner Atilliet's chamber?"

Feldin whimpered in fear. Surely she knew the man was dead, but not what her own danger was. "I sold them to a stranger. I didn't know who he was or what he planned for them. I swear."

An excited murmur was rising in the crowd and the magistrate took the time to restore order. Did he believe her trick? He'd refused to allow Margerit's *lux veritatis*. She had the right to speak but would he consider this to go beyond what was permitted? Before she lost the crowd's attention, Antuniet turned to gaze at the stones in her hand as if listening.

"My amulet has more to tell," she announced. "It cries out in anguish at being used against a son of Atilliet. *O Lapis Loquax*, tell me whose hand placed you in Aukustin's bed?" Again she turned slowly, focusing the lens up on the rafters, where the light would not be seen until she found her target. The blue beam splashed across Sain-Mazzi's face. She threw a hand up before her eyes. A natural reflex but it drew attention.

Elisebet was staring at Sain-Mazzi, her mouth an "O" of disbelief growing slowly to horror. "No, not you," the princess whispered.

So quickly her devotion could turn to suspicion where Aukustin was concerned. Sain-Mazzi had cultivated Elisebet's fears too well. If the stones had power to harm, then surely they had power to speak and accuse.

"It's nothing but a stupid trick," Sain-Mazzi protested, holding her hand still before her eyes to avoid the blinding glare.

But Elisebet stepped away, protesting, "Tell me it isn't true."

"Be still," Sain-Mazzi hissed. "He was never in any danger! I gave you the tools you needed and you've blundered them all away."

"You viper! I trusted you and you struck at my very heart! At my son!" Elisebet's cries rose up in escalating vituperation, until she half swooned into the arms of those nearby.

Antuniet felt Sain-Mazzi's eyes on her, glaring impotent fury. She left it unanswered.

"The stone has spoken," she intoned and loosed it from her fingers to douse the light.

She turned back to the magistrate. "That is my testimony and the testimony of my hands. I leave judgment in yours."

A masterful performance, she thought. But how to extricate them all from the tangle now? And only the charge of conspiracy had been answered. There was still the matter of sorcery and her little charade had only strengthened that charge.

The magistrate called for silence again, a harder task this time. He invited Princess Elisebet back into his chambers to calm and compose herself.

When he emerged, he said, "The princess has considered this new evidence and withdraws the charge against Maisetra Chazillen, that she did bring harm to Aukustin Atilliet through sorcerous means."

Antuniet closed her eyes briefly and let out her breath. It had been a great gamble. Her reputation as a scientific alchemist would take long to recover, but she would have that time. She was still in a daze, waiting for some official release, when Jeanne took her by the hand and led her through the crowds, with Barbara and her armin elbowing a path through to the waiting carriage.

It wasn't until she was safe inside with the steps drawn up and the doors closed that Antuniet looked down at her hand where she still clenched the telltale stone, its warm glow again seeping between her fingers but with no direction now. "I…" she began. "I want…" And then she began weeping uncontrollably in relief.

* * *

They all let her be that first day back in Jeanne's house. She drifted from room to room, marveling at the ordinariness of the birdsong in the back garden at dawn and the softness of the carpet underfoot, the way the steam rose from her cup as Jeanne silently poured the tea. It would take more than one day to believe in this again but there would be today and tomorrow and the next and the next.

The next morning Barbara brought the outside world to her in the form of two pieces of gossip.

"They say that Princess Annek and Dowager Princess Elisebet were seen entering the cathedral side by side yesterday and together asked for a Mass to be said in thanks for Aukustin's recovery. And—" She paused to make sure her listeners noted the importance. "—this morning Efriturik and Aukustin were seen riding together out past the Port Ausiz. That's quite a change in the weather, though I'm sure it was carefully calculated."

"And that's your doing, Toneke," Jeanne said, taking her hand, as she did now at every excuse.

Antuniet began to shake her head.

"No, don't deny it," Jeanne insisted. "Perhaps it was for your own ends, but the wall is broken now. With Sain-Mazzi gone…" Indeed, the dowager princess's chief waiting woman had found foreign travel to be suddenly attractive, even with snow still deep on the highest passes.

There was a second visitor just as luncheon was to be set: a messenger from the palace with word that Maisetra Chazillen was wanted at the palace workshop to discuss the future of her work.

Antuniet turned to Jeanne at his departure and said, "Well, no doubt she's having second thoughts about the advisability of a royal alchemist." She waited for the old familiar terror to uncoil in her gut but she felt nothing. Not a numbness, but at least an absence of fear. Her belly contented itself with protesting the postponed meal. "I may need to find some other way to earn my keep. I suppose I could return to tutoring, though it's unlikely to pay for ball gowns."

Jeanne forbore contradicting her. "Whatever comes, we'll face it together. Hurry and change; best not to keep Her Grace waiting."

The workshop stood almost as she'd left it that day—how many weeks ago? The furnace gleaming, the jars of *materiae* set out in neat, orderly rows. Had Anna come ahead of them to tidy up? But no, she rose to greet them in a soft russet walking dress, not her working clothes. Antuniet allowed strict order to lapse for a moment when Anna ran to throw her arms around her, saying, "I wanted to come see you, but they wouldn't let me. I knew you'd be all right."

"Then you had more faith in me than I did," Antuniet said, returning a quick embrace before restoring dignity. "And who said you should be here? I thought I told you not to come until I sent word?"

"She did," Anna said, nodding toward the door.

Antuniet turned to Jeanne in confusion. Surely she hadn't known. But it was Annek who stood there in the doorway behind them, attended by a cloud of ladies and secretaries in more state than seemed necessary for the occasion.

"You have shamed me," Annek said with no other preamble. "I should have found a way to see you cleared. Instead, it is you who have cleared the shadow cast over my house. I have said it would take a miracle to reconcile my cousin to me. Alchemy, it seems, can work miracles as well as any mystery can. My cousin may never thank you, but I do. This shame, at least, can be removed and I will bear the consequence."

She signaled to the secretary standing behind her and he brought forward a document hung with ribbons and seals. He began to read. "Be it known that Antuniet Chazillen is enrolled among the nobility of Alpennia. This enrollment shall apply solely to Antuniet's person and to the heirs of her body. And to preserve the Chazillen name, those heirs will keep her name and status regardless of whatever husband she may take." The legal phrases continued rolling from his tongue but Antuniet's ears no longer heard them.

"You see," Annek said as she passed the document over, "I restore the Chazillens through you alone. That saves my father's word and my own honor.

There should be land with an enrollment and that, I fear, I cannot offer. But all the rest is restored."

Antuniet stared at the parchment in her hand. Only after the crowd of attendants had swept out of the room in Annek's wake did she realize she'd said no word of thanks, nor even curtseyed.

It was done. She'd won. Estefen's crime was washed away. No, not washed away; rather, it was finally buried with him. From this day on, whatever honor the family name might carry was in her hands alone. But family meant more now than a name inscribed on parchment.

She looked up to see Jeanne and Anna gazing at her expectantly.

"Well?" Jeanne said.

Antuniet blurted out the first absurd thing that came to mind. "I'm hungry; we never did have luncheon. Shall we all go off to Café Chatuerd? Today, nothing but cake will do!"

Bella Books, Inc.

Women. Books. Even Better Together.

P.O. Box 10543
Tallahassee, FL 32302

Phone: 800-729-4992
www.bellabooks.com